FROSTED TORMENT

MARKED MORTALS SAGA

E. L. VALENTINE

ISBN: 979-8-9904793-7-1

EBook: 979-8-9904793-0-2

Printed in the United States of America

FROSTED TORMENT

BOOK ONE

MARKED MORTALS SAGA

E. L. VALENTINE

V P

BOOKS

TRIGGER AND CONTENT WARNINGS

Reader discretion is advised. Recommended for ages eighteen and older. Please check your triggers before proceeding. This list is by no means the entire list or an extensive list.

The following are: Mentioned, Suggested, On Page, Off Page, Implied, Threatening, Talking of, Attempted:

Suicide, Self-Harm, Panic Attacks, Drug Use, Alcohol Use, Smoking, Grief, Trauma, Abandonment, Sex, Course Language and Profanity, Death, Car Wreck, Fire, Burning People, Bones, Torture, Gore, Blood, Weapons, Guns, Decapitation, Torture, Stabbing, Murder, Emotional Abuse, Verbal Abuse, Graphic Violence, Battle, Hostage Situation, Magic, Religion, Occult, Demons, hell, Fallen Angels, Animal/Human/Supernatural Death.

Please protect yourselves and your loved ones.

You matter! If you need help, there is hope. Call the National Suicide Prevention Lifeline: 800-273-8255

988 LIFELINE

Website: suicidepreventionlifeline.org

For the anxiety ridden author who struggles daily to combat imposter syndrome and still rises to make the dream a reality.

To my love: the most important person, whom without unending love, encouragement, support, and who took care of ALL THE THINGS so this book could come into fruition, I love you.

It is by going down into the abyss
    that we recover the treasures of life.

Where you stumble,
    there lies your treasure.

The very cave you are afraid to enter
    turns out to be the source of
    what you are looking for.
    The damned thing in the cave
    that was so dreaded
    has become the center.

You find the jewel,
    and it draws you off.

In loving the spiritual,
    you cannot despise the earthly.

— JOSEPH CAMPBELL (1904-1987)

FROSTED TORMENT

BOOK ONE

CHAPTER 1

I clung to the toilet, feeling the urgency of another wave of last night's drinks making a violent reappearance. Some of it splattered into my hair. I pushed my soiled hair from my face, then leaned back against the cold bathtub and closed my eyes. I tried to shut out the consequences of my actions.

"Happy birthday, Noa," I whispered to myself, feeling a wave of bitterness.

How did I end up celebrating amidst such self-induced misery?

A low voice echoed next to me and whined, "You did this to yourself."

"No kidding, Dos. Now hush," I gritted through clenched teeth.

I couldn't recall the guy's name. But a local rugby player, my latest mistake, stayed passed out on the living room floor, oblivious. The last thing I needed was for him to think I was as unhinged as the town gossip suggested.

People often called me disturbed when they overheard me

conversing with invisible entities. My three best friends were the only ones who knew I could communicate with spirits and accepted my gift. Though I had no plans to see the random guy from the bar again, I preferred him not to spread rumors about my supposed instability. Not an ideal reputation to have for a bookstore manager in the heart of this small college town.

Ever since kindergarten, I've had two constant companions that only I could hear and somewhat see on occasion. I didn't know their origins when they first appeared, but their sudden presence terrified me.

Over time, their frequent visits had not dulled the shock of their arrival. They came and went on their own terms, easier to explain away as, imaginary friends in childhood.

"He meant no harm, doll," Uno's singsong voice crooned in my ear.

Her form flickered in and out of sight as she puffed on the shadow of a cigarette holder. She blew a kiss at her reflection in the mirror and winked.

"Please, not now, guys." I exhaled. Feeling exhaustion seep into my bones, I kneaded my throbbing temples.

Dos's shadowy shoulders slumped, reflecting his regret. "Happy birthday, anyway," he murmured.

I glanced at the faint outlines of what used to be human, now hovering in the doorway. "I won't feel guilty today. Now leave," I insisted with a dismissive wave of my hand.

Certain there was nothing left to expel, I lay on the cool floor, letting it caress my face. I sought a moment of solace amidst the chaos that surrounded me. My phone vibrated across the tiles, and I shoved it away, ignoring the same call as I had done for the past three days.

As I pressed my forehead onto the floor, a stinging sensation pierced through my upper lip. I rubbed it to work out the pain as another one shot up into my nose. Tears poured from my eyes. It was odd since I hadn't felt that way since my surgery years ago.

My cleft lip felt like it was being torn apart. Then another excruciating jolt, resembling a punch to my jaw, spread across my face, and my legs couldn't propel me to the sink fast enough. My fists came down on the counter as my knees buckled under the pain, but I caught myself on the edge of the sink.

"Motherfucker!" My voice bled through the paper-thin walls of my apartment.

My neighbor banged on the wall. "You're always so f-ing loud, Noa."

I returned the favor somewhat harder as I turned on the faucet. "Deal with it!"

Her rattled voice trailed off, and I shook my head while splashing icy water across my face, certain the entire building had heard the exchange. Water dripped down my shirt as I traced the snake-tongued scar, while a tingle played across my lips. The kind that came after sitting on my foot too long. It spread outward into my hairline, then stopped.

I blew out a puff of air waiting for another assault, but nothing else followed, so I pulled my hair into a ponytail and then peeked into the living room. The gift to myself from the previous night spread himself naked across the blanket on the floor. Still asleep, he rolled onto his back, pulling a sheet across his muscular thighs, and I caught a glimpse between his legs.

That was the reason I had let him stay. His exquisitely carved chest remained on display like a museum statue, and his muscular arms called for me to let him hold me once more. As much as I craved mounting him again for one last euphoric ride, I couldn't recall his personality or voice; not a risk I wanted to take and get turned off. That was not a birthday gift I desired.

Besides, a headache brewed at the base of my skull, so finding pain meds fast before a migraine set in was now my priority. As I dug through my bathroom drawer, I found a pill organizer that contained more colors than a crayon box. One compartment with an 'E' sat in the middle, and I raised my hands to the sky in praise.

It went down smooth with a gulp of whiskey straight from the bottle I'd left sitting on the edge of the bathtub. Hair of the dog and all. As I wiped my mouth with the back of my hand, I peeled off my shirt and dabbed my neck and chest dry of the remaining water, then turned to check my lip in the mirror one more time.

No tears or blood, but my hands shook and my anxiety meds caught my eye, where they remained unopened on the counter for months.

"Don't do it," Dos warned. "The pills won't help."

"You're still here?" My tone came out harsher than intended.

I didn't know if he was right, but I heeded his advice since he always cautioned against the bottle. If only he could tell me what I did need. I didn't listen to lingering spirits, often doubting those who refused to move on, but I trusted Dos.

And honestly, I felt better after quitting them anyway. Weed soothed my nerves far better than any prescription, so I wrung out my hands, needing to find my vape.

As I turned around, dancing prisms of orange and purple swept through my apartment as afternoon sunlight streamed in.

I turned and smiled at the rainbow edges dancing along the patio door. Beyond, snow-covered mountains and frosted grass gleamed.

A frigid gust of Montana's December air burst through the cracked door, soothing me. I reveled in it as I stepped forward, bracing my arms in the doorway. The chill kissed my skin, and my bones vibrated against winter's caress.

I fought to hold my ground as my nipples peaked into icy tips. If the piercing wind could reach my heart, it would kill the pain dwelling beneath. Though my bravery lasted only seconds before my hands slipped and I tumbled over the nameless man, catching myself on the couch.

My rash decision now bore instant regret, as it often did. Rugby guy ran with my old college crew, so not a total stranger, I told myself, grasping at straws. Caramel skin glowing in the sunlight, full lips slightly parted, and long lashes rested on olive cheeks. Despite being no match for Lex Sazerac and his captivating gray eyes, I couldn't help but let my eyes linger on the current erection in front of me.

Lex only had eyes for impossibly beautiful women. They graced fashion spreads, did cocaine in the morning, and partied all night. Except he never touched any of it and treated his body as if it were a temple.

He stood by his rule not to date his sister's friends either. Despite only being two years older than me, being his sister's best friend became my greatest obstacle. So, I settled for cheap thrills with random guys.

"Hey," I said, nudging Mr. Rugby with my foot a couple of times, and he let out a soft moan. "You've gotta go. I have plans."

He grabbed himself over the sheet, then stretched with a grin when he saw my bare chest. "I have one more birthday gift for you, Noa."

Gross. Definitely a mistake.

"I appreciate the offer," I said, sucking air through my teeth. "But it's not happening."

I yanked on my favorite worn hoodie draped over the arm of the couch, covering my naked skin. My eyes scoured under the couch for my vape until I spotted it tucked against the wall. Meanwhile, Mr. Rugby stomped into the bathroom like a sullen child, the chiseled curves of his ass flexing as he walked.

He griped from the other room as I exhaled a puff of sweet blueberry vapor, leaving a sugary taste on my tongue. The scent never failed to make me smile.

Needing music, I stood to put on a record. But I noticed the old shoebox where I kept mementos and news clippings about the fire that destroyed my childhood home, scattered across the floor. I didn't remember taking it out.

I shook my head and replaced each treasure with caution. The cops never found the arsonists who burned my family home, with my mom inside. But they weren't looking for any either.

They ruled her death a suicide. They claimed the fire began in her bedroom, where she locked herself in with bottles of alcohol and pills. Erratic at times, yes, but not an alcoholic. Anger resurfaced at their ignorance, or was it incompetence?

As I reorganized the scraps of my past, I noticed an old bracelet my mother had gifted me. It hid under some faded photographs of my Gran Sasha, whom I had never met. My mom said the jewelry was a family heirloom. She warned me to never lose it, but it looked like a rusty, beaten-up junkyard relic.

I tried scrubbing away the tarnish once, to no avail. It wasn't a great accessory, much like myself. Something unwanted, like a discarded fixture in my disappointing life. Even so, I didn't want to lose this link to my mom, so I slid it onto my wrist, vowing to do better.

Mr. Rugby emerged from the bathroom, as if entitled to more from me. I turned to see him yank his jeans up off the floor and pull them on without zipping them. The sharp V of muscle above his hip dipped south, and I fidgeted with my shorts.

The sight stirred a hunger inside me. But I wouldn't gratify his undeserved satisfaction. As he grabbed the doorknob and glanced back, I offered a wave before he pulled it shut, applying unnecessary force.

Another long, soothing drag of vape entered my lungs, and I closed my eyes, remembering my purpose. Find the ones who killed my mother and kill them. One crime scene photo showed two figures of light that weren't reflections of the flames, despite the police claiming it was a camera glitch. I called bullshit then and now.

I knew better, with Uno and Dos whispering truths in my ear, but it didn't matter how much I begged for a different answer. The police closed the case. With no family left, I moved to my godparents' farm. By sixteen, my life was a dull, anxious routine, with an endless supply of anxiety meds.

As the new girl in a small town, shoving and teasing about my scarred face became everyone's new favorite game. With my deep onyx eyes, some even called me a demon. I did my best to ignore it and kept to myself.

My free time was spent searching for answers about my mom and the fire, only to hit one dead end after another. The spirits had no useful info. Either I didn't ask the right questions, or they didn't want to get involved.

I let out an exhausted groan and set the shoebox of my past on the counter next to my vape, then decided to put on a vintage Tom Petty album. My body melted into the thrifted orange corduroy couch serving as my bed. Despite a couple of cigarette burns and cat scratches along the side, its soft embrace was worth it.

I found peace wrapped in the lemon-colored goose-down comforter trimmed in tiny white pom-poms that Ivy forced into my hands before we went out last night. Though something darker would have suited my soul, I couldn't shred her gift even if it wasn't my exact taste.

A sudden knock interrupted my brief moment of self-care, jolting me upright. I glanced around, confirming Mr. Rugby hadn't left anything behind. I rushed to check my calendar for a tarot reading I might've forgotten about, but no client was scheduled today.

And no way any of them knew my home address. Worry lines creased my forehead. What if one of them had finally decided to follow me home because they didn't like what I'd told them? And now, with hardly anyone around, they decided to make their move?

"Get lost," I snapped, then tilted my head back, squeezing my eyes shut.

Ivy's sing-song voice called out to me. "Come on, Noa. My hands are full!"

My eyes shot open, and I leaped up, combing my hair and gagging at my breath. With no time to brush, I swished the gunk away with mouthwash, then ran over to stop my record player. When I flung open my apartment door, the knob hit the wall so hard that it left a dent.

"Why didn't you text me that you were coming early?" I asked, rubbing the dent and inspecting the damage.

Nothing I couldn't plaster and re-paint before I moved out. As I stood upright, Ivy breezed into my apartment with Barbie-hued lips that brought more color than my new comforter. Her hair transformed from its usual blonde curls to a deep lavender hue.

A beautiful contrast to my drab apartment. I didn't even have artwork on my walls. Perfect teeth flashed across her thin face; then she leaned in and placed a soft kiss on my cheek.

"I did," she acknowledged with knitted brows. "You didn't answer, but here I am. And I brought your favorites."

She handed me a large double mocha peppermint latte and a blueberry muffin. Dusted with sugar crystals from my favorite bakery, I breathed in the scent of the warm muffin and moaned in gratitude. The savory aroma filled my messy apartment.

As Ivy glanced around the cluttered space, I popped open the refrigerator and poured one shot of peppermint schnapps into my coffee cup. Taking a quick sip after a bite of the muffin, my eyes rolled back in sheer delight.

She wrinkled her nose, disapproving of my drink of choice. "Alcohol doesn't look good on you. It doesn't smell good either." Her concern was evident in her tone.

"It's my birthday," I argued as I chewed another bite. "What are you doing here so early?"

Her eyes narrowed as she considered my question. "Who else is going to bring you breakfast and gossip with you about Jude?"

I swallowed a mouthful of muffin. "Who is Jude?"

"The guy you took home from the bar." Ivy shook her head. "Seriously, Noa? You're not in college anymore. You're a full-fledged adult and need to act like it."

I set the muffin aside and walked past her into the living room as I headed to the couch. "What is that supposed to mean?" I inquired, a note of defensiveness in my voice.

She grabbed my arm, stopping me in my tracks, and turned me to face her. With my hands in hers, she looked deep into my eyes.

"You're better than how you're living," she huffed. "You deserve better."

I paused for a moment as her expression softened. "I don't, Ives. Not yet."

She brushed my dark hair out of my eyes and smiled. "You do. Let me help you, please."

"No," I replied, my tone unyielding.

Her need to do more than I wanted made me uncomfortable, and I decided laundry was a better distraction. I stepped away and kicked the dirty sheets toward a small closet to the left of the kitchen. After loading my washer and pushing start, I looked back at Ivy, who now sat with her arms crossed.

The thorns of her personality threatened to prick me where I stood. I sat down next to her, trying to ignore the sudden tension between us.

"I've saved up enough money," I said. "I wanted to tell you after the party, but now is as good a time as any."

She leaned back, rubbing her forehead with the back of her palm, contemplating the news. "You're ready to leave?"

My eyes met hers, and I smiled, placing my hand on her thigh. "Yes, but come with me, Ivy. I don't want to do this without you."

Her mouth twisted in disappointment, and she stood up to shut the patio door. "Texas is too hot and not something I want to get used to."

When she turned to face me, I could see the reluctance in her eyes, but I knew deep down she was considering my proposal. I waited in tense silence, studying the way the curls framed her face. Her vividly painted lips narrowed in thought. After what felt like an eternity, her expression turned to skepticism.

"I can't," she said, waving her hands at me. "And you're going to get sick if you keep leaving the door open like that."

I nodded, then let out a quiet breath, not wanting to push the issue. "I'm hot-natured, and I let Dust Bunny in to get warm last night."

She paced back and forth, worry covering her face. "You're not acclimated to Texas weather anymore. Besides, who will take care of that rabbit?"

I stood grateful for how much she cared about me, but nothing would stop me from searching for my mom's killers. Stepping in front of her path, her balance wavered, and I pulled her close.

My eyes pleaded with her as I said, "I'm coming back, and I hope you will look after Dust Bunny while I'm gone."

Her mouth gaped open as though she couldn't fathom the idea. "I don't exactly pet-sit, Noa."

She dropped her hands to her side, and I grabbed my new comforter as a distraction. Throwing it over my shoulders like a cape, I twirled around the living room. Anything to ease the seriousness that our conversation had become.

"You worry too much, Ivy. Dropping by once or twice a week is all Dust Bunny needs." I laughed and kept spinning until she broke.

Her shoulders finally relaxed as she grinned under suspicious eyes.

Then she pulled me onto the couch into a hug. "I can't believe you're leaving me."

"Won't be for long, but I know my mom's killers are still out there, and now I can try to do something about it. Like, really try."

"You think so?" Ivy asked.

I sat upright and pointed to my chest. "This full-fledged adult knows so."

Ivy didn't understand my need to figure out the truth behind my mom's murder after all these years, and it was murder. If I couldn't prove it, I didn't know how my state of mind would be in the end, but I had to try. And maybe, just maybe, I could find a way to move on from the pain and the guilt that had consumed me for so long.

Ivy looked up at me, and I bit the inside of my cheek as her gaze lingered too long. She flung her hair back with a look of exasperation, then placed a hand on my calf.

"Enough of the serious. Have you heard from Jack and Claire?" she asked, shifting the topic.

"Multiple times," I replied, twisting a loose thread on the comforter while my mind wandered. "They've been calling, but I don't answer."

"And when was the last time you talked to them?" Ivy's curiosity spread across her face.

Eyes squeezed shut, I cracked one open to meet her gaze. "Too long. Disrespectfully too long. I'm a horrible person for ignoring my godparents, aren't I?"

"I wouldn't say—"

Ivy began, but I cut her off with a sharp, "Then don't."

A laugh bubbled up from deep within me, startling us both. As it reached my lips, the washing machine thumped with a force that drew our attention to the sound. Ivy jumped up with such speed that I nearly toppled off the couch.

"Why, Ivy Sazerac, I had no idea you knew anything about unbalanced washing machines!" I teased.

She rolled her eyes and straightened, extending a hand to signal for me to stay put. "And Noa Drake, you'd be surprised at what I know," she declared.

Ivy moved clothes around inside the machine with unexpected ease. Then, with a satisfying click, she closed the lid and turned back to face me. Then, a series of quick, loud knocks rattled the door. She walked over to check the peephole, and her shoulders slumped with a resigned sigh.

CHAPTER 2

A tall man with a fiery, crimson ponytail beamed. His head poked above a mountain of clothes spilling over his arms, and I let out an elated squeal, much to Ivy's amusement.

"Joss! You actually made it," I exclaimed.

"Just your friendly neighborhood delivery service," he chuckled.

Next to him, a jewelry satchel sat on top of a makeup case that stood as tall as his hip. I rushed over to relieve him, shoving my comforter into Ivy's hands. Jossy unloaded everything on top of the blanket, including matching lace undergarments, which Ivy then dumped onto the couch. Jossy's impeccably tailored navy suit clung to him with a flawless fit as I leaped up to embrace him.

I straightened his crisp jacket when my feet touched the ground again. "Lawyer things look good on you, but you should've told me you were coming."

He planted a gentle kiss on my forehead. "And ruin the surprise? Happy birthday, Noa."

"Let's get started," Ivy announced, clicking open her extensive makeup kit.

My hands grew clammy as Ivy held up potential outfits against my frame. As she deliberated over eyeshadow hues to best accentuate my features, I batted them away, uncertainty gnawing at me.

"Wait a minute," I stammered. "It's too early for all this. You guys got here way too soon."

"Thank goodness!" Ivy scrutinized me with pursed lips before recoiling from my scent. "First things first, you desperately need a shower."

I rolled my eyes. "One, that's rude. And two, Jossy just got here. I want to catch up."

Ivy cradled my face in her hands, caressing my cheek with her thumb. "One, social media keeps you disturbingly informed, but I won't hold that against you, since you're my best friend." She stepped back, placing her hands on her hips. Shaking her head in disapproval, she added, "Two, I need hours to work my magic on you, so go shower, please."

"She won't let this go, Noa," Jossy urged. "Lex is meeting us at the party too, and I'll hang out while you get dressed."

"Lex too?" I tipped my head down to conceal my elated grin.

Ivy lined up lipstick shades, a knowing look in her eyes. "Jossy twisted his arm."

My eyes flew open wide. "Why would you do that?"

"Because he's your friend," Jossy maintained.

We had been friendly in freshman year, but now Lex was a vague acquaintance. "You shouldn't have done that."

Ivy gave my shoulder a playful nudge. "Who cares? Besides, it's not only your twenty-fifth birthday, but it's also—"

"Ugh, please no reminders," I groaned.

I flung myself over the side of the couch before collapsing onto the clothes, except Ivy wasn't having it. She grabbed my ankles and dragged me to the floor.

"It's New Year's Eve, Noa! We're celebrating whether you like it or not."

"I didn't think you were serious about getting us into that insane party."

I had to admire her confidence in dragging me out of my rut and into a killer party dress. A smug smile spread across Ivy's face as she spoke, a teasing lilt in her voice.

"You've always underestimated my persuasive talents."

She let out a wistful chuckle, sitting down beside me as I lay motionless on the floor. With a flick of her wrist, her hair turned into a flawless bun with loose curls framing her face. Jossy and I exchanged questionable glances.

"Oh, stop it! A friend owed me a favor, you jerks."

"We're messing with you, Ives." I sat up, taking her hands, then batted my lashes. "We know you couldn't have every guy—"

"Or girl," Jossy interjected with a smirk.

I stifled a laugh. "On Earth, wrapped around your finger."

"You both suck!"

"But you love us," I retorted, a playful smile tugging at my lips.

She pelted Jossy with bras as he swatted them away. "Debatable right now."

"Alright, alright," I conceded, though still hesitant. "For you two, I'll go out."

Jossy flung my comforter over me. I wrapped myself in it on the floor like a burrito. "If you can get me out of here!"

"I'll have to restore these ragged nails. But your outfit and makeup will be my true masterpiece," she declared as she pointed toward the sky. "Challenge accepted."

Ivy created a thick French plait by braiding her hair with intricate patterns, interlacing tiny white blooms and crystals that glimmered under the lights. Lips the color of ripe apples beckoned, ready to entice anyone daring enough to chance fate with her. Flecks of honeyed caramel flickered in and out of her eyes, twin sunflowers. They matched the gilded jewelry dangling from her arms and neck.

A sheer black sequined dress clung to her hourglass figure. The gold stilettos accentuated her height. I shrank back, knowing I'd never rival her beauty, but after a moment's hesitation, I inspected her handiwork in the mirror and smiled. With a gift for making anyone a runway model, she curled my hair into breezy waves. Then, she conjured eyes Cleopatra would envy, false lashes and all.

Deep purple and storm cloud gray eyeshadow played up the silver flecks embedded deep in my onyx irises. She even worked her magic to minimize my scar.

I looked up at her and smiled. "Thanks for doing this, Ives. I know I can be a pain in the ass sometimes."

She rolled her eyes and laughed, light and melodic. "Only sometimes? You're lucky I adore you, Noa."

Little about me was striking except for the scar, a ripple above my lip from the reconstructed indentation. My mom claimed angels loved me so much they kissed me recklessly before I was born. Preposterous. Sometimes I felt like Ivy's charity case, but that was my self-deprecation rearing its head. She never flaunted her affluence or forced it on me.

However, this birthday exemplified how much my friends cherished me. They insisted on celebrating with no rebuttals, so I accepted. A single-shoulder silver glittering blouse showcased my breasts with the help of a push-up bra, and a short leather skirt accentuated my hips. Rainbow-shimmering high heels gave me enough height to meet Ivy's gaze. I was ready for an event she swore would be legendary.

CHAPTER 3

Our ride-share glided into Helena, pulling up the frosted driveway to Crystal Wings Mansion. Decked out in silver for the holidays, it's what I imagined a Hollywood version of Heaven looked like. It beckoned to the entire city as another world materialized when we stepped out of the car.

Snowflake-shaped lamps glittered with silver sequins. Entertainers on stilts juggled huge stars. They welcomed everyone. Scents of cinnamon and vanilla perfumed the air as we ascended the stairs. It was the first time I had celebrated my birthday since Mom died, and I gave in to the allure, beaming as goosebumps prickled my skin.

Once inside the foyer, we left our coats in a room on the right and toured the main floor to take in the décor. I kept a silver-chained cross-body bag, big enough to hold my phone and a few pieces of makeup, with me. Ice sculptures resembling clouds encased feathered angel wings. Icicle-shaped chandeliers hovered overhead, and silver and black velvet draped the tables. Wisps of fake snow swirled around us.

Servers wore white bikini tops adorned with shimmering crystals. Goose feathers fanned across their backs in the shape of wings. Matching hot pants left little to the imagination as they floated through the house, serving drinks and canapés. Silver streamers and white balloons bobbed among the guests, making sounds like popping champagne corks.

"Who owns this place?" I yelled over the music as we made our way to the second floor and out onto the terrace.

Ivy's body swayed to the pulsating beats throbbing through the house. "Some cattle rancher bought it for his daughter a few years back. They donate the money raised from tickets to cancer research every year."

"That's pretty cool." I nodded in sync with the music.

A bold, large notecard marked our reserved spot. It claimed the table's center with the name 'Sazerac.' Jossy walked off to a group in hushed conversation. Their expensive suits and the other guests' deferential glances marked them as important.

The only waitress on the veranda, who made several attempts to catch the DJ's eye, darted around the crowded space. She balanced a tray full of champagne flutes with skill, and I snatched two before she vanished into the crowd. I downed one glass in record time, trying to calm my nerves, and placed it back on the tray with a clink. I regretted leaving my vape at home while I took my time with the second glass.

Ivy requested a song from the DJ and immediately stole his attention. When I looked to my left, the waitress's face turned sour, and I concluded it was due to Ivy's unmatchable beauty.

My breath caught when I noticed Lex standing in a corner across from us.

I struggled to recognize him as the shadows obscured most of his figure and the light touched his face. He stepped out and walked straight toward Ivy. I tucked my hair behind my ear and straightened my skirt in case he looked in my direction.

When I made sure every inch of me looked as good as possible, I decided to join them. The closer I got, the more I noticed his hands balled into fists. His chiseled shoulders bulged at the seams of his leather jacket as his arms stiffened. He whispered something into Ivy's ear. Even angry, he looked beautiful.

On the outside, the three siblings looked nothing alike. Ivy and Jossy embraced lily-white skin, but Lex was my praline fantasy I'd take to the grave. Not realizing the time, Auld Lang Syne boomed from behind me, and my glass of champagne slipped from my hands. Pieces of glass scattered among the crowd.

Ivy stepped out from in front of Lex to see me and smiled. "Happy New Year, bestie!"

As she embraced me, I tried to focus on her words over the blaring music. But I couldn't help but notice Lex, who stood a foot away from me with his jaw clenched. A familiar pang of longing hit my stomach, a mix of yearning and frustration. My heart raced as he turned away to flag down a server, his expression hard and distant. He didn't want to be with us.

Though Lex kept to himself most of the time, I couldn't help but feel drawn to him. When we talked, it felt like there was something there. Was it his kindness?

Maybe it was because I was Ivy's best friend. I used to be his too, but he'd grown distant since he graduated from college. As much as I wanted to believe there was something more, I knew deep down it was wishful thinking.

As Ivy let go of me, I smiled and grabbed a watermelon tequila shot from a passing server. I hoped it would distract me from my thoughts. Then I brushed my hair back and made my way over to Lex, pretending to move to the music as I approached him.

"Thanks for coming, Lex," I said, trying to sound casual.

"Sure thing," he replied, his eyes scanning the room.

I followed his gaze, wondering what or who he was looking for. "Do you have a big date coming?"

"Huh?" His head swiveled back to me, and his jaw tightened. "No. I'm people-watching."

My cheeks flushed hot, and my toes began to curl. I needed to move away from this man before I made a fool of myself. "Cool. Well, I'm running inside to the bathroom," I lied.

He pointed to a party tent set up near the bar. "There's one up here on the roof."

A white canopy and sheer white drapes covered the area. They were so translucent that anyone who liked a good peep show could see through them. The area housed portable restrooms without doors, and a leaky pedal activated the handwashing station. I cringed at the thought.

Disgusting.

"Not even if I were so drunk that you, Ivy, and Jossy all had to hold me up to pee," I joked with a weak smile before walking away.

Lex looked down at me with a smile that didn't quite reach his eyes, and I swore I saw a flicker of a full moon rising against the fog in his pupils. I felt a hand on my back. I turned to see Jossy, and when I glanced up, ocean waves crashed against rocks within his. I shook my head, thinking the alcohol had me seeing things, and I stumbled backward, but Jossy caught me.

"Careful, Noa," he cautioned. "You don't need to spend your birthday in the hospital."

I adjusted my shirt, and when I looked back at them, whatever I saw disappeared. "You're hilarious. Be right back, guys."

"Not without me, you won't."

Ivy shoved her drink into Jossy's chest, and as we walked off, something compelled me to glance back. I kept enough distance so they couldn't see me, yet I heard Lex's every word.

"What are we doing here, brother?" Lex groaned as he raked his fingers through his tousled hair. "You know this is a waste of time, man. She's a good friend, but you two keep trying to force this when it's someone else out there who is the one."

My chin quivered and my shoulders slumped. "Fuck you," I whispered.

I couldn't believe I fell for partying with them, thinking he would finally notice me. Tears threatened to spill, but I held my head high and pivoted away. I grew dizzy, hugging myself, replaying his callous words. He confirmed everything I knew, but it was the first time he had ever voiced it aloud where I could hear.

My feet felt like concrete bricks. I shuffled through the house and down the hall, following Ivy. I had to get past a gauntlet of guys giving high-fives. Hunched over, I was unable to meet their gazes, a ringing humiliation drowning out the party.

I reached the end of the dimly lit hall, and when I looked up, the bathroom came into view, offering a private space for me to cry. But off to the right, an elderly woman smiled at me. She had a wrinkled face and bright, lively eyes.

Set back in a shadowy alcove, she shuffled a deck of round cards at a table. I'd seen those circular cards before, but never used them. They claimed to offer a complete view of one's life and connections. It was intriguing, but I lacked the motivation to learn a new technique for my clients.

Ivy's eyes lit up like a child at Christmas as she pleaded with me. "You need a reading, don't you? It's been a while."

It wasn't the right time for a reading, and I couldn't deny that my mood was less than ideal. Pinching my eyes shut before opening them again, I tried to regain focus. The old woman before me sat tranquil, surrounded by velvet ropes. An antiquated sign sat awkwardly on an easel beside her.

A crystal ball, emanating a gentle glow, was at the center of her display. It looked more like a novelty nightlight than a portal to the supernatural. It felt kitschy but nonetheless amusing in our party setting, and she motioned toward the empty chair facing her.

"Another time, Ivy," I protested and turned away. "I'm not exactly in the best frame of mind."

She shook her head. "What? Why? We've been having fun."

Realizing Ivy didn't hear what Lex said, I took a deep breath and tucked my hair behind my ear. "I still have a tinge of a headache, but you're right."

Ivy tugged at my wrist with encouragement, guiding me closer to the waiting psychic. "It's your birthday and you're killing it tonight." She gleamed as she peered back over her shoulder. "This will be fun for you. Besides, did you see all those guys back there wanting to talk to you?"

"Pretty sure they were looking at you."

She lifted my chin to face her and her throat bobbed. "Those idiots don't come close to what or who I want." Ivy paused and cleared her throat as she took my hands. "Noa, you're gorgeous. Stop putting yourself down. Your bad attitude is what turns people off."

My cheeks flushed with embarrassment under her scrutiny, so I turned back toward the psychic. "Okay, but party readings aren't real," I insisted.

Ivy rolled her eyes and pressed me into the soft fabric chair with a laugh, then whispered, "Says the tarot reader."

Murmurs echoed in my mind, warning against this foolish act. Uno and Dos, my vigilant protectors, were always sensible. Especially since nothing from the other side has helped me. But emboldened by liquid courage and convinced that fate had exhausted all avenues of ruining this night, I threw caution to the wind.

Against all odds, I found a strange comfort in the psychic's crinkled corners and translucent gaze. It felt familiar. There was urgency in those eyes; an eagerness to relay some vital message.

"I have to admit," my tone a chirp of false cheer, "your crystal ball has charm." My forced admiration for its pulsating blue glow didn't mask my nervous anticipation.

Her withered hands traced over mine with a soft touch, gliding across my arm as she examined my mandala wrist tattoo. A small nod, then a brief, silent meditation added mystique to her already foreign expression.

"You carry courage within you." Her assessment cut through the thickening tension. "Good way to express it," she said.

Despite her reassurance, any perceived strength felt

completely absent because I let some drama caused by Lex get to my head. The atmosphere around us turned quiet as the woman's touch sent a wave of electricity through my veins. The vibrations were warm and thrilling, with brewing excitement in my core. She closed her eyes, her expression turning serene, as if she were delving into another realm.

When my eyes met the chalky pools of hers again, they held an ancient wisdom. Whispers, woven from experience and laced with conviction, shifted the energy around us. They tugged at our very being.

"The path you walk holds hidden truths," she murmured.

Curiosity piqued within me despite better judgment.

"Oh, I know how this works," I replied.

Humor crept back, hoping to break some irrational spell woven through last-minute prophecies.

A knowing smile curled her parched lips, amused by my naivety. "In every bend and in every turn, there lies choice— that's where your power resides."

I began to protest and denounce the charlatan. But a surge of electricity coursed through me, and my head jerked back. Time froze as visions of my mother and me played out like a movie reel, starting from when I was a young child. Then, I saw myself on the lawn watching flames engulf our house, with my mother trapped inside.

CHAPTER 4

Shadows loomed as she choked and clawed at the bedroom door. Then, a quick pull sent me into a strange dimension. Voices overlapped in a cacophony, and I collapsed to my knees, covering my ears.

I slowed my breathing, and the air became still, producing a slight hum. My heart skipped as I heard my mother's faint voice, though I couldn't see her. I stood, scanning every direction.

Then I lurched forward, phasing through the ground and emerging on the other side. A scream tore from my throat at the excruciating pain. There she was, extending a hand to me, her ghostly touch caressing my cheek.

"Come," my mom whispered.

I trailed after her graceful, floating form, mesmerized by her fluid movements. Then she halted, turning to face me, as breathtaking as I remembered. Luscious brown curls tumbled over her shoulders.

Then, her violet eyes pierced mine as three shadows materialized in the distance. She pointed to the silhouettes of Ivy, Jossy, and Lex conversing with someone in a field; their presence was haunting.

"Secrets lie beneath the surface, waiting for you to find them," she said.

"What does that mean, Mom?"

I reached for her hand, but she looked toward my friends and pointed.

"There are forces that shape your destiny, Noa. Forces as ancient as time itself. Embrace your power to choose, for it holds the key to unlocking hidden truths within you."

"This is insane." My voice trembled with fear. "What do my best friends have to do with any of this?" My breath quickened, and I felt hot, but I didn't know how to escape the depth of this reading.

"The Baneful are coming for you, Noa. Listen to those closest to you and find the place that keeps the answers, not the secrets. There you will find my killers."

"I won't stop until they're dead," I promised.

My mother's words hung in the air, each syllable seeping into the depths of my soul. A sudden wave of realization hit me as I stood alone in a world full of secrets and unknown powers. The Baneful. The name reverberated in my mind, a sinister echo that sent shivers down my spine.

"Who...who are the Baneful?" I stammered, my voice shaking with a potent mix of terror and resolve.

My mother's features twisted into anxious purpose as she warned, "The Baneful are ancient evil beings, Noa," she explained.

Her image began to fade.

"Wait!" I ran after her, making every effort to hold on to her.

She offered me one last clue. "They seek to harness the power within you—a power that can shape worlds or bring them to ruin."

Without warning, I gasped for air. Then, I flew backward in the chair, knocking over one of the pillars holding up the velvet rope. I stood up too fast and fell into the line of people waiting for their turn.

Baneful? Hidden forces? What the fuck happened?

The entire day inched up the back of my throat, and I ran to the bathroom, choking back the contents of my stomach until I found an open stall. My chest ached from getting sick. This morning and now, so I curled myself into a ball and sobbed until nothing remained. I knew it was a bad idea to go out on my birthday.

"Hey," a man's voice echoed in the bathroom. "Time to go."

I swallowed hard. "I'll be out in a minute."

"No," he insisted. "The party ended an hour ago. Now, get your ass up and go."

"Fine!" I stood and pushed open the stall door, ready to tell him where to go, but he'd left. I stomped my heel on the ground. "Fucking security, assholes!"

I gave myself a once-over in the mirror, then turned on the cold water to rinse my mouth. Monogrammed paper towels sat to my right, so I wet them and wiped my face. At least the water-proof mascara did its job and stayed in place, even though it wrecked my false lashes. Once I peeled them off, I leaned in to fluff my hair and grabbed a mint before heading out to find Ivy and her brothers.

But first, I'd give that jerk a piece of my mind for yelling at me.

Except when I walked into the hall, the house was empty, and the music stopped. All the lights were on, and I didn't see any guests.

I clamored down the stairs and cupped my hands around my mouth when I spotted Jossy in the foyer. "What happened?"

He quirked an eyebrow at me. "The party's over!"

"What? Why?" I stumbled toward them, dodging strewn party favors.

Ivy snapped her compact closed with a snap, then shoved it into her purse. "We've been looking for you everywhere. Where have you been?"

I gaped at her, my tone drenched in skepticism. "Are you joking? It's only been like twenty minutes."

I fished out my phone to check the time - 2:00 AM. The room spun as I looked from the bar to the stairs and back.

"More like two hours, Noa. You sat down with that psychic and I turned around for a second, but when I looked back, you were gone," she remarked.

My chest felt like a thousand elephants were sitting on it, but I shut my eyes hard to think. My mind was hazy from the reading. The echo of my heel coming down on the floor carried throughout the foyer, and Jossy took me into his arms. He rubbed my back in a circular motion.

"Slow breaths, Noa. What happened?" Jossy asked.

I opened my eyes, focusing on his pristine suit that looked as though he'd just put it on. Not a speck of New Year's clung to him. We breathed in tandem as he massaged my arms.

I shook my head as helplessness washed over me. "I did that reading."

"What do you mean?" he asked.

"Some woman near the bathroom was doing psychic readings. Ivy thought it would be fun." My voice quivered, and a sharp pain lanced through my skull.

Jossy's face turned fiery red, like his hair. He glared at his sister. "Are you insane, Ivy? Do you have any idea of the ramifications of your actions?"

Lex sidled over, placing a hand on Jossy's shoulder, then guided him toward the exit.

Jossy's voice echoed with anger through the hall and returned to his sister. "Of course you do!"

"What's he talking about, Ivy?" I looked at her, bewildered, trying to make sense of Jossy's cryptic words.

She blinked those sun-gold eyes at me and winked. "You'll see."

Lex made his way back over to me and Ivy. His face hardened with a tick of his jaw. "We need to get her home. I've got a ride-share outside."

My body went numb, hands tingling. I clawed at my shirt, feeling it constrict around my throat. "I can't breathe. My pulse is gone!"

Ivy cradled my face tenderly in her hands. "You're breathing and talking, Noa. Focus on my voice."

"It's going to be all right," Jossy interjected, steering me outside and down the steps. "But Lex is wrong. You need to go to the hospital."

Lex removed his leather jacket, swaddling me within its folds. "I don't think that's wise, brother. Make the call, and we can handle this."

Jossy rubbed his lips with one finger and exhaled a breath.

He situated himself up front with the driver as a wad of cash appeared in his hands.

"Get us to this address as fast as you can, and this is yours," Jossy urged.

The best birthday I'd allowed myself in years faded into the background in a pile of ruin. What was looking more like a vivid hallucination plagued me. Now, sandwiched between Ivy and Lex in the back of the car, my skin felt like fire and ice bursting from within. I rubbed my arms as Ivy held me close.

Watching streetlights stream past the window, Crystal Wings disappeared in the distance. Our driver earned his pay as he screeched to a halt in my apartment parking lot. We tumbled out, one after the other, and I lost my balance when a writhing pain clawed through my top lip.

This time, I knew something was wrong. Doubled over, the entire night of drinks splattered onto Lex's cowboy boots. Then everything went black.

CHAPTER 5

My eyes fluttered open to an unfamiliar beeping sound. A firm hand, unfamiliar to me, clasped mine. Comfort intertwined with strangeness, its touch both soothed and startled.

"Where am I?" My voice was a parched whisper.

A rich, husky voice met my ears as he tried to soothe me. "Easy there, Noa. You're all right."

My throat felt raw and dry, like sandpaper, and I struggled to take in my surroundings. As my vision cleared, I realized that medical equipment filled my apartment - a blood pressure cuff encircled my arm, and an IV was in my hand. Panic gripped me as I scanned the room in vain for familiar faces, but my friends weren't there. I steadied my breathing with slow, measured breaths.

"Please, may I have some water?" My plea emerged in a fractured rasp, louder than intended.

The man sitting beside me nodded and handed me a bottle

from a nearby tray. Water flooded my mouth, refreshing my taste buds with its crispness. I examined his refined features, finding them both luminous and unsettling.

Tailored jeans and a crisp button-down shirt donned his frame as he uncrossed one leg over the other, his feet clad in loafers. No socks. He stood, and his gentle touch eased me upright to track my breathing.

Yet, his emerald eyes unsettled me. They were arresting. Each time they peered down at me, I felt a mix of unease and familiarity. Something about him set my nerves on edge, but before I could question him, his hand brushed my throat. My pulse quickened under his lingering fingertips.

He chuckled and asked, "Do you know who I am?"

I shook my head as a small flashlight grazed across my eyes, following his gesturing finger. "No," I managed.

Sound from the hallway seeped into the living room, and I faced the door.

"Are my friends out there?" I leaned forward, straining to see if Ivy or Jossy were near.

"Yes," he confirmed, his expression unreadable. "But I need you to listen, Noa."

I shielded my face with trembling hands. "Something's wrong with me, isn't it?"

He settled next to me on the sofa and tilted my chin back as darkness filled his eyes. "Not exactly, no."

My eyes fixed on his, and I bit on my bottom lip. "What does that mean?"

The man rose to check the machine's blinking lights and numbers next to me. As he turned, I opened my mouth to call for Jossy. He flashed a piercing look over his shoulder at me. "Don't bother screaming. You aren't awake," he cautioned.

"Huh?" My eyes widened, uncertain of his implication.

"If your friends looked in now, they would see you in a deep sleep." He walked to the door, opened it, and gestured outside. "See?" he said as he returned to my side.

My fidgeting hands worried the blanket as I tried to conceal my escalating dread. "Why act out checking my vitals, then?"

"You caught me there." He chuckled and settled next to me, grasping my hands in his. "I wanted you to feel at ease, Noa."

Every hair on my body bristled when he uttered my name. His voice was hypnotic yet ominous, concealing something sinister. I swallowed hard. "But you don't. This is anything but comforting."

Disregarding my concern, he continued, "Do you remember what happened last night, Noa?"

I inhaled a quivering breath before answering. If I didn't, I feared what he might do. "I was on the terrace with friends, did a reading, then blacked out. Does that cover it?"

Being rejected by Lex had cut deeper than I cared to admit, and now here I was, trapped in a nightmare with a stranger. He watched me like a lion stalks its prey. Then, he inclined his head. His warm breath brushed my neck as his cedar and vanilla aroma enveloped me.

"Your mother was right," he murmured. "The Baneful will come for you."

My eyes snapped shut, memories of my mother's solemn warning about the Baneful flooding back. Reality struck with chilling clarity. Was he one of them? His body hovered over mine, evoking an involuntary shiver. I wasn't certain.

"Don't be afraid," he said with a sly grin. "I long to see the moment you understand." A slamming door outside made him pause, his gaze never leaving mine. "You're fighting me in your sleep."

I gritted my teeth. "Get out of my head!"

"We're not done. You need to see this." He grabbed my head and pulled it toward his.

"No," I heard myself say, my voice stronger than I felt. "Get away."

I pulled myself from his grasp and recoiled against the back of the couch. He came closer, his hands reaching for my neck. They were strong and gentle as he cradled the base of my skull with a firm grip. His thumbs drew soothing patterns on my skin, countering the fear that seeped through me. My body melted under his.

"I'd never hurt you, but don't move. Breathe," the man instructed.

The man with sparkling emerald eyes curled his fingers around my neck. He pressed his forehead to mine, applying slight pressure. Our eyes converged, and I began to see into his mind, or he was projecting into mine.

A deep scent of earthy grass and lilac filled my senses. It was intoxicating. It settled into every inch of my body, pulsing through my veins like a drug. A tree sprouted from the floor of my apartment, erupting in swirling green vines.

They snaked across the blanket and up to the ceiling, morphing into thick boughs spreading in all directions. I reached out to touch them. They coiled around my fingers and arms with a euphoric sensation. Then, they bloomed into delicate pink petals. My audible gasp faded as the fragile blossoms sifted through my fingers.

"It's a cherry blossom tree," I said.

An eagerness saturated his voice. "Yes. Now, focus."

My body tensed as he fisted my hair, fingers digging into my scalp. I tried to resist, but his touch overpowered me. He searched my mind with his. It was like a tidal wave crashing over me, erasing all control.

An intense pulse rushed from my neck to my lips. Tiny sparks danced behind my eyes as I trembled under his touch. A sharp sensation pierced my head, and I found myself in a field, frozen in time.

Soft blades of blue grass tickled my feet, and the wind played with my hair. I surveyed the endless expanse of the field stretching out before me. It bordered a wide river, and chunks of ice drifted along its glassy surface.

To my left, a waterfall cascaded down a bisected mountain. One half was black, the other half white. Then pressure on my jaw forced me to look right. Across the river, the blooming cherry tree sat silhouetted against the mountain. Set within the rocky face loomed an iron gate; its pull was magnetic.

"Do you see that?" I asked. "It's jammed shut."

"It's locked. Now, open it." Eagerness took root in his voice.

My breath hitched. "I can't. There's no keyhole."

His grip tightened as he applied more pressure with his head and held my gaze. "Try harder, Noa."

A wave of nausea churned in my stomach at the thought of what lay beyond that gate. "I need a key," I pleaded, heart racing as I felt someone's approach drawing near. "They're coming!"

"No. You're—" With a jolt, his head snapped back as a powerful current shot between us, and my eyes closed.

When I awoke, my bones ached, and my hand throbbed.

"Noa, wake up," Ivy sang, pressing something cold and wet to my face.

I felt around and located a damp cloth on my forehead, tossing it aside. I sat up, kneading my pounding temples. My fingers found a needle piercing my skin, secured with tape and connected to an IV.

A soft moan escaped my lips. "What's going on?"

"You fell off the couch," Jossy huffed, arms crossed.

My eyes began to burn and water as I whispered, "I had a nightmare."

"Must have been a powerful one to throw you to the floor." Skepticism decorated his face.

"Can you please help me up?" I asked with a touch of defensiveness.

"Looks like he kicked your ass," Jossy quipped.

I winced while stretching my neck with caution as Ivy helped me to stand.

She turned to Jossy with regret in her eyes. "I'm sorry I wasn't here," she offered, "I only stepped out for a minute to check my voicemail."

I shook my head, scanning my apartment. "You didn't take me to the hospital?" I asked.

"Too much paperwork. And questions," Jossy said with a grave expression.

Massaging my throbbing temples, I let them both help me onto the couch. "It feels like someone took a sledgehammer to my head."

Ivy sat with me, then took my hand and traced my palm. "Yeah, about that," she mentioned. "Your choices are your own, but you've been drinking a lot."

Seated on a nearby chair, Jossy leaned toward me. "More than usual. Hence this chat."

Fear gripped my heart, and I squeezed Ivy's hand. "Is this… an intervention?"

"We're worried about you, Noa." Jossy crossed his legs and gestured toward the equipment in the room. "I ordered an IV service to come here because the amount of alcohol in your system is alarming."

"Okay, Dad," I sighed, feeling drained.

He ignored me and, without missing a beat, said, "And, no anxiety meds in your system? What's that about?"

"I value our friendship, Jossy. Truly, I do. But certain aspects of my life are mine to decide," I replied.

Ivy's face lit up with a warm smile as her hand enveloped mine. "Of course. As your closest friends, we're concerned."

"No," Jossy barked. "This is because of Uno and Dos. They're going to get you hurt if you keep listening to them."

Indignation flickered in my eyes. "Don't insult me because you're scared. I'm not a puppet to spirits, and the decision was my own," I retorted.

"Because they told you not to take them," he argued.

"Can we take a breath here?" Ivy squeezed my hand as she shot a pointed look at her brother.

A small bruise formed around the needle when I glanced at my other hand. Jossy untied his ponytail and raked his fingers through his hair. He sat in the chair beside me, a look of desperation on his face.

"I'm sorry, Noa. We don't want to lose you," Jossy confessed. A vulnerability I hadn't seen in him plagued his face.

I angled myself toward him and squeezed his leg. "You don't have to fight every battle for me, Joss."

A dry chuckle betrayed him, and his throat bobbed. "How ironic," he commented.

"Fine," I conceded, a hint of defeat in my tone, "I'll ease up."

His jaw tightened as he contemplated something. "You mean more to us than you can imagine, and we don't want to find you dead somewhere."

I couldn't ignore the fact that I'd become careless with my drinking. Jossy's gaze bore into me – raw, relentless – a pressure cooker with no release valve. My breath hitched. I didn't know if mental illness had decided to set up camp in my head or if the dark abyss of depression wanted me to fall into its hole. Either way, I needed to get a grip on both.

A knock on the door interrupted us, and I looked down and gasped. I wasn't sure how I hadn't noticed it before, but I realized I was wearing a silky pink tank top and shorts.

"Ivy?" I groaned. "What in the world am I wearing?"

Her eyes brightened. "You're my best friend, and no matter what, I want you to look good and feel good."

She always had a way of taking care of me, even when I didn't want it. I forced a smile even as my body began to reject the outfit.

"Thanks," I mumbled, adjusting the silky fabric against my skin. "But did it have to be pink?"

Ivy rolled her eyes and teased, "You look good in pink."

The knock persisted, and Jossy moved to answer it. "I told you it was open when you texted me, brother."

The room seemed to shrink as Lex walked in with a duffle bag in one hand and dropped it on the floor next to Ivy. His unzipped jacket revealed sculpted abs under his shirt, and he smelled like fresh air. I shrank back, not wanting to see him after what he had said about me.

Ivy jumped up from her spot and embraced him with a grateful hug. "Thank you, and I owe you one."

Lex nodded. As Ivy checked her bag for her toiletries and clothes, he rubbed his chin and eyed me with curiosity.

"I didn't take you for silk or pink, for that matter."

I crossed my arms in front of me. "You're here. Not something I'd take you for doing, either."

Lex slid his hands into his jeans pockets. "I deserve that since I'm not around much anymore."

"No, you don't." I shook my head, then scrunched my nose when I remembered how I puked on him. "I'm so sorry about your boots, Lex."

One side of his mouth rose in a slight smile. "Not a problem, and I'm already having them cleaned."

With my head cocked sideways, my eyes turned to slits as I watched him. "Why are you here?"

He pulled his hands from his pockets and rubbed them together. "I want to help."

"You do? But I thought—"

"You scared us last night." He interrupted me and smiled with a sincerity that stopped me from going down any road that led to him not wanting anything to do with me.

"Myself included," I admitted with surprise.

"Care to share what happened with that psychic then?" Lex asked.

I thought about the Baneful and my mother's warning. My thoughts were in disarray as images and emotions flooded my mind. The weight of their concern pressed down on me, and I took a deep breath. They deserved to hear the truth, even if it meant exposing my vulnerability.

"I had a vision last night," I revealed, kneading my eyelids with trembling palms.

Jossy's shoulders relaxed, but worry lines remained etched across his forehead. "Noa, we know you're seeking answers, but consulting a psychic won't reveal them. Even if our sister coerced you."

"She didn't coerce me, but I did see something," I admitted.

Ivy's gentle touch on my thigh sent a wave of calm through me. "You can tell us anything," she said.

Lex took a confident step forward. "Let's see if we can help you make sense of it."

"I saw my mom, and she was beautiful," I whispered. "Radiant, actually. She wanted me to find out who killed her."

Jossy shook his head, doubt clouding his eyes. "Are you sure you didn't see what you wanted?"

"I'm leaving in a week, Jossy," I confessed, then bit my bottom lip, waiting for him to respond.

His eyes widened as he glanced at Ivy. "And you knew about this, but didn't say anything?"

She shrugged, meeting her brother's startled gaze. "I found out before the party, but now do you understand?" She sighed deeply. "I had to do something."

"Understand what?" I asked, confusion knitting my brows together.

"We knew you would plan this at some point, Noa. But why now?" asked Jossy.

I leaned my head back on the couch and closed my eyes. When I looked at them again, I saw concern covering their faces.

"This isn't as unexpected as it sounds. I'm pretty sure my godparents know something about my mom's death, and I'm going to hire a private investigator to help me."

Lex ran a hand over his chin before walking to the fridge to get a soda, guzzling it in two gulps. He looked back at me with a heavy sigh. "So your job knows?" he asked.

I nodded. "I'll stay at the bookstore until the end of next semester, but Mr. Dell said I could come back."

"So that's why Ivy pushed for the reading," Lex concluded.

"What does that mean?" I asked, feeling as though I wasn't the only one hiding information.

CHAPTER 6

I raked my fingers through my tangled locks. "Y'all are freaking me out."

"We'll come back to you leaving, Noa. Finish telling us what you saw," Jossy urged.

"Um, okay." I squeezed my eyes shut and tried to remember. "I saw the three of you, but the rest was hazy, fragmented... like puzzle pieces I couldn't fit together."

Though I'd been able to trust them, if I mentioned the Baneful, it would get me admitted to a psychiatric hospital. I wasn't ready to cross that threshold, but I wondered if they were already planning a trip for me to a padded cell. I felt a knot tighten in my chest as fear washed over me.

"Damn it!" I winced at nerves firing off like an explosion in my lip again.

"What is it?" Ivy squealed and scooted back from me.

I cursed under my breath and tried to push out the unsettling thoughts about psychiatric hospitals. I focused on the physical pain at hand – my lip.

"I'll be fine," I assured her as I rubbed my aching scar.

Except I wasn't, and despite my efforts, it continued to ache. The uncertainty of why it was happening now terrified me. My anxiety rose no matter how hard I tried to shake it off. Lex furrowed his brow in confusion, his fingers rubbing at the tension in his forehead. He took a long, slow breath and looked at Jossy.

"This is getting out of hand, you guys," he stated.

Ivy shifted a few times next to me, crossing her legs back and forth, then stood when she couldn't get settled. Her voice wavered as she looked at her brothers. "This situation isn't going anywhere, and Noa needs to rest."

"Sit down, Ivy," Jossy snapped. "You've done enough."

She pursed her lips and flung herself onto the couch with a huff. "You're welcome, brother," Ivy shot back.

"Hey there." A woman with a rounded figure and blue scrubs walked in, beaming.

"Hello," I offered, still dazed at my friends' exchange.

"Hi, Mr. Sazerac." Jossy nodded at her. Then, the lady turned to me and said, "My app notified me that your infusion will be done in a minute, so I need to remove it. Then I'll get out of your hair."

"Of course," I managed with a weak smile.

Ivy's demeanor transformed into artificial cheer. "We'll get you some food while you rest."

"Good idea," Lex and Jossy echoed.

My brows twitched, and I shook my head. "Not until you tell me what you know."

Lex's eyes ballooned as he pointed at me. "Rest first, eat second, then talk later."

Their insistence on food and rest compounded my unease. Despite the tension in the room, they seemed unconcerned. They'd leave me alone for a while. I realized that my fears of hospital confinement were a result of an overactive imagination. As the nurse removed the IV from my arm, I felt a sense of relief from its confines.

"Fine, I'm starving anyway." I lifted my arm, and when I turned my head to the right, I pinched my nose. "And I need a shower. So, when you get back, I expect answers."

Ivy leaned over and kissed my cheek. "Absolutely."

The nurse bandaged my hand and had me sign release forms. After that, she gathered her things and left, ignoring our conversation altogether. Jossy paid her and waited by the door with Ivy and Lex.

Jossy tipped his chin toward me. "Rest up. We'll bring back enchiladas."

My stomach roared in response to the mention of food. "Chicken and sour cream sauce," I begged, my eyes wide.

He laughed and started to close the door.

"Oh! And a Dr. Pepper," I called out.

"You got it!" he replied.

I exhaled in relief, relaxing into my now silent apartment, but solitude left me vulnerable. I knew turning to drinking was a bad idea, but I couldn't stand the way I felt inside. It was the only thing that kept my emotional demons away. So, I poured myself a healthy dose of whiskey and gulped it down.

The junk drawer in my kitchen contained a few extra vape cartridges, so I opened one and took a sharp inhale. The minty flavor filled my lungs, a familiar refuge. One I'd relied on over time to help me suppress the chaos in my mind.

I opened the patio door, letting in a crisp breeze. Ominous clouds rolled over the mountains, signaling another snowstorm headed our way. My glance fell to Dust Bunny's makeshift cardboard home. I had been feeding that stray rabbit all winter, and her box needed cleaning.

Taking a few small carrots from the fridge, I brought them outside. Her tiny brown nose emerged, sniffed, then withdrew into the warmth. I placed one carrot inside the box, allowing her to investigate. As she began to gnaw on it, I carefully extracted her and sat her inside the door.

After replacing her fleece bedding, I tucked her back into the makeshift shelter. The last thing I needed was another living being depending on me; yet here I was.

After closing the patio door, I reveled in a rare moment alone. Even Uno and Dos were quiet, but I did tell them to get lost for a while. I started the shower, letting the steam fill the room.

As I waited, I poured one more drink followed by another long drag from my vape. After I escaped from the pink outfit Ivy put on me, it didn't take long to wash away the last twenty-four hours. Stepping out of the shower, I wrapped myself in a fluffy towel.

As light as I felt, a tick in the back of my mind cautioned me not to let my guard down. A wave of drowsiness swept over me once I situated myself back on the couch under my comforter. The alcohol and weed lulled me into the embrace of sleep. Then, a tug in my gut catapulted me into the heart of a snow-cloaked meadow.

A lone cherry blossom welcomed me. Its pink petals fluttered down around the majestic mountains that encircled the field. In the distance, silhouetted against the moonlit sky, stood the man from my nightmare. With his back to me, I took a step closer to investigate as petals floated around him.

My heart fluttered as I crept closer, my bare feet sinking into the powdery snow with each tentative step. The frigid air prickled my skin as he swiveled around in one fluid motion, seeking the source of the sound. His eyes danced like fireflies in the velvet night. He swept his dark hair behind one ear and leaned toward me, cupping his ear.

I could see his chiseled features, with the sharp angles illumi-nated by the faint moonlight. Despite our closeness, he remained blind to my presence. Or so I thought. In a single heartbeat, he stood before me, our breaths colliding.

A deep sigh escaped him as a smile twitched at the edge of his lips. "You're back," he acknowledged.

"How in the hell did I end up here?" I panted.

A shiver ran down my spine as I tried to piece together my reality. Ignoring my confusion, he took hold of my wrist and started inspecting my mother's bracelet. His touch sent jolts of uncertainty through me. Who was this man, and how did he know me? Part of me wanted to know more, while another part was afraid of what I would discover.

"Let's go!" His command echoed in the silence.

But as he pulled me across the field, I yanked my hand away and then found myself upright on my sofa. Remnants of my elusive traveling melted into the cushions. I patted myself down, confirming I was whole, though my feet remained icy and numb.

Uncertain of my reality, I rubbed my arms and waited for someone to barge through the door. No one came. I pushed my hair back and cradled my knees to my chest, wanting to run but paralyzed with terror. Nothing made sense as I rocked back and forth.

Unsure of what was real, I wrapped my arms around my knees, rocking as I awaited some sign I wasn't losing my mind. Only silence greeted me. I leapt up and scurried to the door, peeking out.

The hallway stood empty and quiet. I shut the door and turned the lock, relief washing over me as I steadied my breathing. My mind swirled with questions as I paced my apartment. Then it hit me. Could this man be one of the Baneful?

Anger simmered beneath my skin. I had to leave for Texas— it was my only chance to protect my friends. I rubbed my hands down my face and grabbed my vape, taking a deep breath before releasing a long exhale.

I knew it wouldn't be long before my friends returned. That's if they went to the closest Mexican restaurant and picked up an order to bring to my place. I rushed to shove toiletries and a change of clothes into my backpack.

This was my life on the line. Besides, I couldn't risk theirs for whatever this was, especially if this man was after me. I needed to know for sure before telling them anything. Home was the only place I could think of that held any answers about me or my mom, so that's where I'd go.

"How ya doing, doll?" Uno's voice was a welcome sound.

I choked back tears. "What's going on, Uno?"

Dos cleared his throat. "We aren't sure yet. The Veil is getting blurry, but we'll keep trying for answers."

I rolled my eyes as I searched my apartment for a clean pair of socks, then found a pair hiding in the back of my dryer.

Uno added, "Something is coming."

My lip began to sear in pain like someone held a match to my skin. Whispers filled the air around me with gentle echoes bouncing from one side to the other in my mind. Spirits. I didn't have time for any of them. My stomach dropped as flashes of my mother in my vision warned me.

"That's our sign to leave," Uno said as her voice faded into the distance. "Be careful, doll."

"Wait!" I spun around in my apartment, hoping they would stay.

Dos sniffed, and his voice turned sad. "Take care of yourself, and we'll be in touch soon."

"Fuck," I groaned and threw my head back.

Once I pulled on my socks, I slid on a pair of jeans, a hoodie, and boots. Then, I pocketed my vape and locked my apartment. Dodging patches of ice across the parking lot, I ran as fast as I could to my truck. A stillness hung in the air, broken only by the distant hoot of an owl.

My keys jangled as I unlocked the rust-flecked door of my weathered truck. It screeched open, and I winced at the sound. My heart ached to leave my friends, but I had to do this alone. I punched the directions into my phone and sped off into the frigid darkness.

Fat snowflakes began to pelt the windshield. I flicked on the wipers, and a wave of nausea crashed through me. Rubbing my temples, I blinked hard against the pain throbbing behind my eyes. As I opened them, I thought one of the lights had turned green for me to go. Except when I looked again,

Jossy, Ivy, and Lex were standing in the middle of the inter-section.

I rolled down the window and stuck out my head. "Where the hell did you come from?"

"We followed you!" Jossy yelled.

I shook my head in disbelief. "Of course you did."

Why I thought I could do anything by myself was a joke to the three of them, and I was becoming annoyed.

"Get back in the truck, Noa, and go home," Ivy ordered.

I leaned out even further when I heard them chanting in unison. No way my friends were doing some kind of magic. After putting the truck in park, I joined them in the abandoned street.

Surrounded by a glowing ring of green light, Jossy stared at me in a trance. His lips twitched. He drew circles in the air with each pointer finger, counterclockwise. Ivy stood to his left. Both hands were out, lunging forward as she strained against some invisible force. Lex stood on Jossy's right side, holding his hands in prayer with his head bowed.

Then, Ivy's breath grew ragged. "Do you see it, Jossy?" she gasped. "We have to stop it!"

"What are y'all doing? There's nothing out here!" I shouted through chattering teeth.

Ivy's eyes turned completely gold and beamed like oncoming headlights. I shielded my eyes with my arms, and as I turned to run back to my truck, something tugged at my hair. My blood ran cold, and spiders ran down my back. I spun around to see a monstrous creature.

It had reddish-yellow hair resembling a woman with a face

half human, half pterodactyl. Baring rows of jagged teeth, she lunged toward me. Her hollowed-out eyes filled me with terror as her claws sliced through the air. One ripped through my hoodie, grazing my shoulder.

I fell to the ground as the creature towered over me, teeth oozing with brown saliva, and ready to strike again. As the monster's claws came down for me a second time, I threw my arms up, crossed in front of my face. A deafening explosion sent us all hurtling through the air. Shards of glass and tires whizzed past us as we tumbled through the air.

Enveloped by a rush of wind, the abrasive symphony of twisting and scraping metal echoed in my ears. The smell of burning rubber and gasoline filled my nose, turning my stomach. My back cracked before I slammed into unforgiving asphalt, having the wind knocked from my lungs. I rolled over and retched. Violently. Then, I fell back and hit my head on the concrete.

A snarl in the back of my mind, followed by a sinister laugh, taunted me. I jolted into a sitting position, but steely arms held onto me. I couldn't tell if they intended to save or imprison me. Disoriented, I struggled to escape.

"It's me, Noa," breathed Lex, loosening his grip. "I can't believe you're alive."

"I'm not sure I am," I coughed as I looked around.

Brilliant sunlight streamed through a stained glass window of a church across the street. The snow had even stopped. Where the hell were we in the middle of the day? A few minutes ago, black painted the night sky. I lowered my gaze, then rubbed my eyes with the palms of my hands.

When I looked again, I noticed two wooden doors that formed an archway to the entrance of the church. I scrambled to my feet and spun around. I tried to find where I had landed after whatever had happened.

My head throbbed with questions and confusion. Other than the church across the street, waves of farmland surrounded us. I stood on a two-lane road in the middle of nowhere, not sure how any of us got here.

My eyes hunted for Ivy and Jossy, but my vision blurred. Was this Judgment Day? A hand gripped my shoulder, and I screamed. But it was Jossy, his voice soothing as he folded me into his arms. Fiery pain seared my shoulder.

"You're okay, Noa," Jossy said.

"Oh, Jossy," I choked out, trying to catch my breath. "Are there scratches?" I asked, turning to raise my hoodie up over my shoulder for him to inspect.

"It's not as bad as it seems. They're already healing." His fingers tilted my chin up. Dizziness washed over me as he scanned my face for other injuries.

"Healing from what?" I managed.

"Venom. And your bones are mending." Jossy checked my pulse. "Teleporting can do that."

I shook my head in confusion. "Who the hell teleported?"

He took my hands and took a deep breath. "We did."

My throat bobbed. "Explain that monster and the claws, Joss. You're way too calm."

"I can't believe you survived," he said, confused.

"Why did I? Why did any of us?" I blurted.

For once, he had no words. Then, Ivy burst from the church and engulfed me in a crushing hug, relief etched on her face.

"You're okay!" She set me down gently.

With my feet back on the ground, Ivy squeezed me hard enough to crack a walnut, but I felt nothing. I should've been full of cuts, broken in two, besides the wound on my shoulder. I should've been dead, but I wasn't. None of us were.

I placed my hands on her shoulders and steadied myself. "I might get sick again."

She pulled out her phone and checked the map. "We've landed on Highway Eighty-Seven between Stanford and Windham."

Lex sprang up from the road, brushing off his jeans. "At least we're still in Montana," he called out.

Jossy turned my face back to him. "Lex saved you. It took a lot out of him, but he'll recharge."

My words spilled out in a gush. "What do you mean? What's going on?"

"It's time for the truth," Lex admitted. "We planned to tell you after dinner, but here we are."

Before I could respond, Ivy said, "Let's go inside. Someone might drive by."

Jossy replied, "I warded the area. We're safe." He looked directly at me. "That thing was a demon. Some kind of energy in you repelled it." His eyes darted skyward momentarily. "And you brought us here."

"Wait, I teleported us from the intersection to... the middle of nowhere?" My voice trembled with disbelief.

Lex passed out water bottles from a stash by the roadside. "Yep, because we can't do that. We move quickly but can't just appear anywhere."

As Lex handed me a bottle, I took a long gulp, trying to

wrap my head around Jossy's revelation. The weight of his words felt like heavy chains pulling me down.

A demon? Energy repelling it from me? Teleporting? It all sounded unreal—as if I'd stumbled into an alternate dimension.

CHAPTER 7

My mind reeled in shock. I tasted the metallic tang of blood inside my cheek while I chewed it, my eyes darting between Jossy and the mangled remains of my beloved truck.

"Let's pretend for a moment that's true," I said, my throat bobbing as I forced down a swallow.

Jossy stopped drinking and screwed the cap back on his bottle. "It is." His voice was flat and certain.

"But how?" My voice cracked in bewilderment. "I've never done anything like that before in my life." I gulped down the cool water in relief, draining the entire bottle in a few thirsty swallows.

"We don't know the details yet." Ivy's smooth voice held a note of mystery.

"You said the searing pain in my shoulder was venom." I looked to Jossy for confirmation.

He gave a solemn nod. "It tried to paralyze you."

Baneful. It had to be one of them. They were demons?

I trudged toward the gravelly roadside, straining to hear Jossy explain how the creature appeared in my truck and pursued me. His voice faded behind me.

My phone lay smashed on the sharp rocks; the cracked screen was now dark and useless.

I shoved it into my back pocket anyway and remembered my vape. Still safe, I grabbed it and took the longest, soothing draw of my life to steady my fraying nerves. I had to get a grip before I completely unraveled.

Lex materialized in front of me, his piercing eyes fixed on me.

I exhaled the vapor faster than I had inhaled it. "Jeez! What?"

"Don't go rummaging through the wreckage. It's dangerous," he advised with raised brows.

I waved him off and rolled my eyes. "Yeah, thanks, Lex."

My tone came out more biting than intended, and pain flashed across his gorgeous face. The man I'd pined for now looked as though I'd broken his heart.

I blinked. "Sorry. Um, thank you for saving my life."

Lex's voice dropped to a whisper. "I'm not trying to make this worse for you, Noa, but you should be dead."

"You didn't have to save me," I stated, taking another inhale from my vape.

He shook his head and his voice turned gruff. "I don't want you dead. Quite the opposite. I only want to help you gain some perspective."

I cleared my throat, holding his gaze. "It's difficult to get perspective when my best friends are wielding magic at intersections and battling demons, Lex."

My brain struggled to believe his intentions, but I grasped what he meant. Nothing logical explained the fact that I was still walking, talking, or breathing. I suppressed the thought and pushed it down.

Way down, but I was grateful for his rescue. My stomach churned as I stepped on the glass scattered along the shoulder of the road.

"May I look at least?" I gestured behind him to the crumpled truck.

"Don't touch anything," Lex cautioned.

I inhaled, absorbing the catastrophic scene. The truck was so mangled I couldn't tell front from back. As I drew nearer, I noticed a foot protruding from the weedy ditch beside one of the massive tires, which had rolled closer to the road's edge. A woman lay motionless face down in the dirt, dressed all in black with heavy boots, showing no signs of life.

My body shook as I wondered if she was the thing that had attacked me, or an innocent bystander. I prayed it was the former. I inched closer when Lex's iron grip clasped my wrist.

"Stop!" Lex's voice echoed across the fields surrounding us.

His eyes pleaded with me, and his chest heaved. He wouldn't let me go until I agreed. I nodded, and he released my arm, poised to grab it again if I moved any closer to the woman. His strength astonished me.

I pivoted to see Ivy and Jossy, their eyes resembling flickering lights and expressions taut. My head swiveled back to Lex, remembering what I'd noticed in his eyes on New Year's Eve. I'd thought it was a trick of the light then, but now Lex's eyes churned like fog rolling over a stormy sea. I looked back at Jossy and Ivy, theirs now subdued.

My voice trembled. "What's going on with your eyes?"

"Noa, breathe. We'll explain everything." Jossy stepped toward me, his tone gentle. "But something very wrong has happened here, and we need to figure it out."

I glared at him and folded my arms. "Answer the damn question!"

"Not until I know you're thinking straight," he said.

Ivy shook her head, her curtain of purple hair swaying gently. "I don't think she's ready yet."

"Back the fuck off!" I shrieked and raised both hands for them to stop.

The tension mounted as we stood circled together, everyone on edge. My body shook with adrenaline and fear, and my feet flexed in my shoes. I struggled to keep my trembling hands steady at my sides.

"Stop avoiding this and do not lie to me, Jossy." I kept my eyes glued to him. "I want no part of dark magic, demons, or these Baneful beings. But someone here better start explaining now."

Lex's eyes flickered at me, one brow raised. "But you talk to ghosts and do tarot readings?"

"What I do is not dark magic, jerk. Besides," I lectured, "Uno and Dos took off when all this started."

Lex stood upright, his voice a mere whisper. "I'm not trying to make it worse for you, Noa. Or even more difficult."

He turned away from me with his hands up in defeat and walked toward the church parking lot.

"And another thing," I called after him. "What I do is a spiritual connection with the other side. I was born with this gift!"

He spun back toward me, irritation lacing his voice. "As were we. What exactly do you think all this is?" He flung his arm out, gesturing around us.

My eyes narrowed, holding his gaze. "Not sure, but it can't be anything good. I saw you using those freaky powers."

"The same ones that saved your life, Noa." His voice rang with conviction. "I will do everything I can to protect you. Always."

His words surprised me, and I stood unable to respond. Ivy moved toward me as I glanced back at the woman next to the tire. Jossy touched her arm and shook his head, but Ivy wrapped herself around me anyway. A sense of calm engulfed my body.

"What are you doing?" I asked.

She leaned her head on my shoulder, her silky hair brushing my cheek. "Helping. I don't blame you for the fear and panic, Noa. But we need to talk about it calmly."

"That demon is dangerous," Jossy advised, his tone grave. "And she's the one who scratched you."

I touched Ivy's head as a rush of calm flowed through me and released a relaxing breath. "I'm good. You can let go."

Ivy bounced in delight as I stepped away. "The ability to soothe and ease situations is one of my powers," she divulged.

"Uh huh," I said, my jaw tense. "Are you the Baneful?"

"How do you know about them?" Jossy moved closer, and I took another step back.

"My mom warned me about them," I admitted.

He chuckled, and a deep rumble fell from his chest. "Of

course. You probably thought we would send you to a head doctor."

I rubbed my fingertips together down by my sides and squinted up at him. "You were in the middle of an intervention with me, so yeah."

Standing next to the demon, I placed a foot on her side and pushed hard. She rolled to her back and her head flipped toward me. The snapping beak and teeth I saw in the intersection were larger than I had expected. She choked for her last breaths of air and convulsed against the ground.

Her claws dug into the ground, and I stumbled backward, falling onto the road and scraping the palms of my hands. The gear shift from my truck protruded from her throat, then her head hit the ground one last time with a piercing squeal. Terrified, I crab-walked backward into Jossy's legs, then grabbed my chest.

He reached down to help me stand as her skin began to melt. Tendons sloughed away, exposing black bones. Her body disintegrated into a puddle of thick, putrid disgust, resembling tar.

It didn't take long before the inky blackness faded, transforming into a dull gray hue. I took another step back, my eyes fixated on the grotesque mass that was once a living, breathing something. As if on cue, it cracked and crumbled into a pile of ash, leaving nothing behind but a sickening, sulfurous odor in its wake.

My body shook in terror at what lay in front of me, and before I had a chance to process what I'd seen, the wind picked her up and blew her across the road. I looked for a way out, but my friends blocked my straight shot to the church.

"Get away from me!" I shrieked, my heart pounding like a jackhammer.

I bolted past Lex and Ivy, their faces a blur as I pushed through them. As I reached the steps, what felt like a punch to the chest knocked me backward. Red hair filled my vision as Jossy swallowed me into his arms.

We fell to the ground, and his body hardened like granite around me, refusing to let go. I struggled for breath while screaming to no one. Jossy grew stronger with the strength of a full army, but his pressure on my body was careful, like handling a precious artifact.

He didn't want to hurt me, only stop me from fighting him. I gave up, knowing my attempt to escape was futile.

"Are you done, Noa? Stop before you hurt yourself." His voice was rich and warm.

Tears streamed down my face as I gasped for breath. "Tell me you're not one of them."

He spun me around to face him. I flinched, unsure of what he would do next, but he relaxed and caressed my cheek with the back of his feather-light hand.

"I would never, could never, hurt you," he whispered, his voice heavy with sadness and regret. He slipped his hand to the back of my neck and pulled me into him. "We're not the Baneful."

My fear betrayed me again as I cried on Jossy's shoulder, trying to block out the world.

"We know the truth about your mom," he added. "What happened in the fire. And we know why you're struggling."

I looked up at him to make sense of it all. As Ivy and Lex

approached us, I saw it. Everything I knew about them began to fall into place as his words sunk in.

"You know?" My lips quivered as I stared at them in disbelief.

Jossy nodded, his eyes intense. "We've known all along."

Clutching at his shirt for support, I asked the question burning in my mind. "My mom was right. They're all coming for me, aren't they?"

Before Jossy could respond, Ivy pulled me to my feet, breaking me from Jossy's protective shield. I stood frozen in anticipation as Lex rejoined us.

"I don't care what happens to me anymore," Ivy declared. She looked deep into my eyes. "Yes, they're coming for you, Noa, and you killed one of them."

CHAPTER 8

Jossy stood and brushed dirt from his pants. He tried in vain to straighten his wrinkled jacket, but he couldn't, so he took it off and laid it across his arm.

"Let me do this." His tone was more than annoyed.

Lex scraped patterns in the gravel with his boots as Jossy struggled to find the right words. He folded his arms with a smirk.

"Come on, brother, don't keep us waiting," Lex chided. "We're all eager to hear how you're going to spin this."

Jossy shut his eyes and released a heavy exhale. "Must you always create drama, Lex?"

"Oh, I'm sorry, but we're in the middle of a demon ambush and, if you don't spit it out, one of us will. We have no more time to waste," Lex reminded his brother. "But it's better if it comes from you. At least you can get clemency from Vincent and the Church."

My eyes darted between them as they argued, but Ivy

gripped my hand with reassurance. "It's okay," she whispered. "This is nothing. You should see them when they bust out their wings."

I cocked my head to the side with furrowed brows. "Wings?"

She covered her mouth with a sly smile and raised brows. "Oops."

"What the hell, Ivy?" Jossy said through gritted teeth, his jaw clenched.

She planted her foot and crossed her arms. "I told you before, I'm done waiting."

A rumbling growl vibrated in Lex's chest. "Does free will mean nothing to you anymore, little sister?"

"I'm expediting this so we can proceed." She gestured to me with one hand. "Noa still has the choice to unravel it herself and decide."

I retreated from Ivy and tugged at my hair in frustration. "You said I slaughtered a Baneful, which was also a demon." I pointed at Ivy, and she nodded, a delighted grin spreading across her face. "You also said Jossy and Lex have wings."

"Yes." An ecstatic smile lit up her face, and she winked. "As do I."

I could feel a lump form in my throat as I nodded. "Go on, Jossy."

Jossy's piercing blue eyes met mine as he studied my expression before he spoke again. "Right." He closed his eyes and regrouped his thoughts. "If you connect the pieces, I wouldn't need to ask for forgiveness from our superiors. We're not supposed to interfere with free will." He shot furious glares at Ivy. "Some of us take the punishment no matter what."

A smug look crossed her face. "I'm better off for it, brother. And stronger."

I finally voiced the question that had been nagging at me. "Are you the good guys?" I asked.

"As good as it gets for our kind," offered Lex.

Somewhere deep down I knew. It was always there, but I refused to acknowledge it because of our friendship. And now, facing it head-on was terrifying. They were wonderful, smart, and unbearably beautiful. They showed me endless love and welcomed me into their world and family as one of their own.

"The thing is, Noa," Lex continued, his voice steady. "When we first met you, we weren't certain you were the one we were looking for. Then, after your mom's death, we couldn't track you anymore."

"Track me?" I echoed, disbelief twisting my features. The very notion peppered my skin with goosebumps. I scanned the area for unseen eyes lurking in the shadows.

"Humans put off an energy like a locator beacon," he explained, jerking his thumb toward his sister. "Yours vanished nine years ago. It wasn't until Ivy here," —he gestured with exaggerated air quotes— "sped things up on your birthday."

"That demon sensed me." I scratched my head as I shook it and pulled a leaf from the tangled strands.

Jossy made a steeple of his fingers and added, "Your psychic reading flipped the switch. We sensed you leaving the apartment last night and followed you."

My eyelids twitched at the intrusion of my privacy. "That's... disturbingly intrusive," I managed.

"We're supernatural beings," Ivy interjected, tapping her foot with an edge of annoyance.

"I get it. Powers. Wings. You're angels," I said without hesitation.

"And we fell on purpose," added Lex, his expression hardening as he spoke.

My eyes widened in shock. "Why would you do that?"

Lex raked his hands through his hair, fingers tangling in the tousled strands. "For you."

"Me?" I whispered. The weight of what I had stumbled into pressed down on me. "But I thought fallen angels were demons?"

"Demons are different." Ivy's voice cut through the thick fog of confusion enveloping me. She leaned forward, her eyes fierce. "They're pure evil souls of humans who never believed in the afterlife. They did horrendous things and died wanting to do even more. Once they realize there is a hell, they get their chance."

"Like that bird creature?" I asked, recalling the grotesque image seared into my memory.

"Mhmm," she nodded, her expression grave. "And sometimes they're gifted a human form if they were evil enough when alive."

Lex turned back toward Jossy. "We should focus. You realize that was a Lurker, right?"

Jossy pivoted on one heel, his voice growing louder with each word. "Yes, I know it was a Lurker!" The frustration radiating off him was almost tangible.

"We can't rely on your wards indefinitely, brother," Lex shot back. He paced the confines of the road. "The longer we stay here arguing, the more vulnerable we are to another attack."

I let out a hollow laugh, the sound brittle in the heavy blanket of silence. "Why is this happening?"

Jossy paused and turned to me. His expression softened as he realized how lost I felt amid their revelations. "Noa," he began, "you've been part of something for much longer than you know. Your mother's death wasn't an accident—it was part of something bigger."

Lex stepped closer to me, his eyes earnest now. "You have powers that you don't know or understand. And those powers have drawn attention—both good and bad." He glanced at Ivy before continuing, "We're not here because of your energy; we're here because you matter."

A lump formed in my throat as their words sank in like stones dropped into still water.

"What do you mean by that?" I asked softly, vulnerability creeping back into my voice. My hands trembled, and I felt pressure build in my head as the beating of my heart grew louder in my ears. "I don't have any powers."

Jossy stepped forward again, and this time, his presence felt protective. "You have plenty of power." He lifted my chin to his eyes with one hand, then placed a finger against the side of my head with two gentle taps. "Because of that, our kind wants to get their hands on you. Your existence could tip the balance between good and evil—and that's why we need to keep you safe."

My world tilted, and I was certain I wouldn't recover. "Can we stop them?" I pleaded as my shoulders tensed.

Jossy hesitated, a flicker of uncertainty crossing his features. "We believe we can."

"Reassuring," I bit back as I dragged my hands down my face.

"Do you trust me?" Jossy asked and held out his hand.

Doubts swirled within me, but I gave in and placed my hand in his. "If you promise to be honest with me," I told him.

His expression softened, and he released me. "As much as I can. Some of this they'd have my wings for if I explained it all."

"Then who can?" I sighed, a weight anchoring my shoulders as I let out a breath that felt heavier than the air around us.

Jossy's voice broke the quiet. "An older and more powerful angel, Vincent."

There was a hint of reverence in his tone, a tangible respect that made me glance at him sideways. Did Vincent embody the same noble characteristics as Jossy? I folded my hands in prayer, pressing them against my lips.

I watched how still everything had become. Even the wind and trees followed the angels' lead. It seemed as though each blade of grass stood at attention, waiting for an order.

The world outside our cocoon faded into an eerie hush; I couldn't hear a single car in the distance. It was nothing but dead silence—a silence so profound it felt like an entity in itself.

Jossy moved toward me. I leaned back by instinct, shaking my head to ward off both his offer and the ominous truth hanging over us. But then I met his wide blue eyes brimming with sincerity.

His brow arched in playful challenge. "Come on, Noa," he urged. "We don't bite."

With a groan that spoke volumes of my hesitation—yet also my need for answers—I placed my hand in his and relented.

CHAPTER 9

My heart fluttered. Jossy's touch warmed me, sending tingles across my skin. I realized in that moment he had only revealed a fraction of his true self during all the time I'd known him. They all had.

"How does this work?" I asked, my voice wavering. "Help me understand, Joss. Angels, demons, end-of-the-world prophecies... are not something I'm prepared to handle. Putting killers away for arson, that's doable."

His eyes turned sad. "You don't want to face it because you can't explain what your senses can't confirm. You can rationalize ghosts because you can hear them and sometimes see them."

"They were once human, with physical bodies before death," I argued.

"We existed too, but we forged our flesh when we fell," Jossy countered, intertwining our fingers. "The world is corrupt, and most people don't care about our kind, but you experienced our world for yourself. Did you imagine it all, Noa?"

I shook my head, chilled to think something as sinister as a demon could reach me. "What about vampires?" I asked.

His face puckered as though tasting something foul. "People put more stock in the devil and his loathsome minions. It's absurd."

"Wait. You're telling me vampires exist?" I gasped.

"They're nothing like the movie versions." He said it in such a casual way like it would be easy for me to hear. "Vampires are like zombies, but quite rare."

I scratched my head in shock. "For a mere mortal with alcohol issues, this could push me over the brink," I said.

"We'd never let that happen, Noa," Jossy assured me. "Every woman in your family who came before you knew about us."

I looked at him, searching for a lie. "My mom?"

"And your grandmother." He nodded and began rolling up the sleeves of his shirt. "They tried to protect you."

I rubbed my chest as anxiety swelled. Jossy's voice faded to a muffle, and I struggled to hear him over the pounding in my ears. When I looked up, my stomach twisted in a knot. With an unpleasant retch, I vomited from the uncertainty of my own sanity.

"It's all right, I've got you," he said, reaching for me. I recoiled, signaling him to wait as I shook my head. Still hunched, I met Ivy's eyes as she handed me water.

Rubbing my forehead, I muttered under my breath, "I need a second, okay? This is just... too much."

The fog lifted as Ivy's soft voice broke through. "Puking is part of learning how to portal, but that will wear off soon enough."

"Thanks." I poured water into my mouth before swishing

and spitting it out. I wiped my lips with the back of my hand. "Where did you even find these?"

She shrugged. "An unassuming coat closet inside the church."

My skin prickled at the realization of my best friends as fallen angels. Resolving myself to accept this reality was daunting, but something in me was worth everything to them. Dread gathered in the pit of my stomach, but unlike before, I tamed it.

Isolated, the sun was almost eye-level, with gentle hues of orange and purple coloring the sky. I took a deep breath and fought to make a choice. Trust my friends or continue looking over my shoulder, as demons sought me out while I figured it out alone.

My mother's soothing voice penetrated deep into my mind, urging me to go with them. I glanced up and saw how much more of what they were now. Daunted, feeling several inches smaller in comparison, I wanted to turn heel and run again, but I didn't.

I was suspicious, but I found the courage to ask, "Why did it take so long for you to realize it was me?"

"I don't know," Jossy offered me a smile. "We had a limited role, only to ensure that you were you."

I steeled myself before voicing my irritation aloud. "You knew about this and kept it from me," I huffed. "Well, nothing says 'beaming target' like ignorance."

Jossy's gaze softened, the tension in his brow easing as he regarded me. "Noa, we have to be cautious," he said, his voice low and steady. "Your safety is paramount, and Vincent will explain the other details."

The urgency in my chest ignited a fire in my words. "Get us

a car," I declared, my voice cutting through the charged atmosphere.

Ivy stopped playing with the white tips of her hair, a bored habit I had come to recognize. "Wait a minute," she interjected, her brow furrowing in disapproval.

Lex's eyes flickered, as though he could see the storm brewing within me and wanted to stop it. "What if we could help you disappear for a while? It's possible."

"I didn't take you for a coward, Lex," I challenged, crossing my arms over my chest.

His nostrils flared as his arms remained at his sides. "We need to think this through because they could have a damn army built by now."

"If I have a supernatural tracker in my head, they'll find me, right?" I countered. "I want answers, and I want to know how to fight off demons from killing me."

"Demons and fallen angels aren't ones to mess with, Noa," Ivy warned. "If they catch you, they won't kill you."

"I'm sorry?" I chuckled, certain she meant to say will kill.

"Ivy's right," added Lex. He scanned the area as if they had already found me and Jossy's wards weren't strong enough to hide us.

"You're the last of your family," Ivy continued. "They want you, and they'll do horrendous things to you for eternity when they have you." Her words hung heavy in the air, each syllable a reminder of how vulnerable I was.

"Which is what exactly?" I asked. "To start Armageddon? Bring it on." Defiance surged within me like a tidal wave. "I won't run. Besides, with the three of you, they can't touch me. Right?"

Ivy grabbed Jossy's arm, her voice laced with fear. "No. Please, talk some sense into her."

"You're taking me to Vincent, Jossy," I insisted, refusing to back down.

"I agree with Noa. There's more to this," Jossy continued, his gaze shifting toward the wreckage that surrounded us. "And if that Lurker is dead, then—"

My eyes widened in realization as dread seeped into my bones. "Then what?"

"Its master will know about it soon and come for us," Jossy warned. The weight of his words felt like an iron cloak draped on my shoulders, pressing down with immense force. "You're safer back at the ranch with us," he decided.

Ivy's eyes exposed her worry when she looked at me. "Noa, the Baneful is an entity of the purest evil," she warned.

"I'm not hiding," I declared, my voice stronger than I felt inside. "For years, you made me believe arsonists killed my mother. You knew who I was and lied about it. Now, I want the truth. I'll deal with the consequences later."

Ivy groaned, throwing her hands by her sides. "You always do this."

"Thought this was what you wanted, sis?" Jossy said roughly. Then, nodding at me, he pulled out his phone. "I'll request a car."

"Yes, I am selfish," Ivy snapped with a shrug. "Knowing about us and charging into a cursed war are two different things."

Lex gave a disapproving shake of his head. "Will the wards hold for us to get far enough away from here before demons come looking?" asked Lex. He grew more paranoid by the minute, expecting an evil horde to attack us on the road.

"Long enough to get us to Whitefish," Jossy answered him. He began entering our location into the ride-share app.

"Sorry, but I'm not skilled in how to portal, or else I'd have us there sooner," I announced, a hint of sarcasm rolling off my tongue. "You can find me in the church when the car arrives."

The sun had nearly vanished, casting long shadows around me as I stood in the empty church. I could feel the tension crackling in the air. The solemn silence enveloped me, amplifying the terror and uncertainty gnawing at my insides.

I paced back and forth, my mind racing with questions and doubts. I didn't know how my family got tangled up in this supernatural world or if I was even ready to face the forces that sought to harm me. I took a deep breath, readying myself for what to do.

Then, Ivy peeked into the door and gestured for us to leave. I nodded, my resolve masking what I felt. As I walked down the stairs of the church, the night seemed to press in on us, amplifying the dread.

We climbed into an idling black SUV. I didn't know what ride-share Jossy called, and I didn't care. He sat up front in the passenger seat while Ivy and Lex sandwiched me between them in the back. Their expressions were unreadable in the dim light, and none of us spoke.

The car pulled away from the wreckage, tires crunching on gravel as we headed toward the ranch that my friends called home.

And Vincent.

Ivy unlocked her pink crystal-encrusted phone and began scrolling through social media. Of course, hers was in perfect condition.

I leaned forward to get her attention. "Hey, do you mind if I text Jack and Claire? I've avoided them long enough."

"Sure." She handed it to me, but her fingers gripped the phone longer than necessary as she studied me.

I placed my other hand on her wrist, and she relaxed beneath my touch. "This was going to catch up to me, Ivy," I said, as a flutter of anxiety twisted in my stomach. "Besides, I still need you to keep me safe."

She released a long sigh, her breath escaping like a deflated balloon. "We didn't call first, so Vincent is going to be pissed." Her eyes darted toward the window, watching the blurry landscape flash past us. I could almost see the gears turning in her head, calculating the repercussions of our actions.

Jossy turned in the front seat to look at us both, his expression shifting from concern to strength. "I'll handle Vincent, but it's safer the longer we wait." The driver peered over at him with a raised brow, and Jossy turned his head to meet the driver's gaze. A flicker shot across Jossy's eyes, then the driver focused his eyes back on the road. Jossy continued, "He'll sense us the closer we get."

"What did you do to that guy?" I pointed to the driver, who remained focused on the road ahead, oblivious to our mounting drama.

Jossy faced forward again, adjusting his ponytail with practiced ease. "We can't have everyone know about us, Noa," he clipped.

"You used powers to make him forget," I stated, disappointment creeping into my voice. The thought of manipulating someone's memory felt heavy on my conscience.

He adjusted his position in his seat, his fingers tightening around the middle console. "Text your godparents," he instructed with soft urgency.

I typed out a thank you for wishing me a happy birthday, then lied about losing my phone. I prayed it would keep Jack and Claire satisfied. Shaking my head, I remembered I had a job and my boss would notice if I didn't show up.

"Dammit," I grumbled.

"What is it?" Jossy's tone turned irritated, with impatience bubbling beneath the surface.

I could feel him ready to pounce on whatever excuse I'd offer next. Even though I decided to go with them, it didn't make the choice easier.

"I'm supposed to be at work tomorrow for a book delivery before the new semester starts." My voice came out a cracked whisper.

"Don't you have vacation days?" he asked with a tone that suggested my human concerns were trivial compared to our current situation.

"If I don't show up, that's when people start asking questions and cops get involved." I clapped back. "Do you get vacation, Jossy? Are you even a lawyer?"

Jossy laughed—a rich sound that cut through the tension like a knife. "Yes, Noa. I'm a lot of things," he said, a smirk playing on his lips. "But a lawyer is my focus here. We've been around for hundreds of years, so jobs bide our time and help us keep our home."

"Good for you," I quipped. "So you know that calling off last minute isn't professional." I bounced my knee, but my pulse quickened, and I turned toward Lex, my eyes wide. "Hundreds of years?" I asked.

He arched an eyebrow and smiled. "Yep. A breath for us in the Veil is years and years for you here."

Considering I was in love with him, I needed to know. "How old are you? I know you've existed since 'let there be light' and all, but what's your age in human years?"

"That's irrelevant. We're eternal beings and we don't age," Lex explained, then glanced at Ivy's phone, which I now flipped back and forth between each of my hands. "Call your boss."

I scrunched my nose—an involuntary gesture of doubt— then took a deep breath to steady myself. "I don't want to lie to the man."

"But Mr. Dell likes you," Ivy chimed, placing a hand on my thigh. "I bet he won't have a problem with you needing a few days."

"Tell him it's a family emergency," suggested Lex in my other ear.

I twisted my lips as an idea began to form in my head. "He's always nagging me to take time off, so that could work."

I dialed Mr. Dell's number and explained that I would be leaving town for a family emergency. That wasn't a lie. I was the family, and I was definitely in an emergency.

He agreed and decided to have his daughter cover for me since she would soon be my assistant. It was a relief to have that handled. Maybe this was not an obstacle. It could be an oppor- tunity to find sanity amid the madness.

After my call, Ivy tucked her phone under her thigh and was

asleep within minutes. I concluded she didn't feel there was more she could do to help, except provide moral support. I was exhausted, just like her, but I couldn't fall asleep.

CHAPTER 10

Once we arrived in Whitefish, another car waited for us. We switched into the new ride-share for another drive through the mountains to Saint Mary. This time, I couldn't fight the urge to close my eyes.

When I woke up with a bump in the road. It took me a few seconds to remember where I was, but a gentle hand touched my leg.

"You're okay," Lex's voice affirmed, steady and warm, wrapping around me like a familiar blanket.

The faint rumble of tires on the road matched the rhythm of my anxious heartbeat, each bump we hit a reminder that we were still moving forward.

"Are we almost there?" My voice cracked as I rubbed my eyes, exhaustion clawing at the edges of my consciousness.

He stared out the window, his profile illuminated by the soft glow of the interior car lights. Shadows danced across chiseled features.

"We're coming up the road to the gate now," Lex stated quietly.

The tension in his shoulders seemed to disappear as the familiar landscape unfolded around us.

I let a sliver of hope creep into my voice. "Did we pass Saint Mary's?"

"Yeah." His voice was low and distant.

I thought about our exchange earlier in the day, and I took a deep breath. Biting my lip, I looked at him and said, "I'm sorry about before. You're not a jerk."

Leaning back against the seat with a relaxed smile, he responded, "No need to apologize."

"But I do. I overheard you the other night telling Jossy I wasn't the one." I sat up straighter and turned to him, clenching my hands together. "I thought you were saying I wasn't good enough for you. With everything that happened back there at the wreck by the church, I lost it."

He shifted and pinned his slate eyes on me. My breath hitched at his sudden closeness. I pulled back, but his hand, rough with calluses, clasped mine.

It was the first time he had willingly touched me, and I let him. My emotions churned like a cyclone in my belly, but the flutters I expected didn't come. Odd. Exhaustion must have dampened my reaction, but I wasn't completely sure.

Lex's eyes sparkled as assurance claimed his face. "You're more than good enough for anyone, Noa."

The words I'd longed to hear spilled from his lips, yet I still felt inadequate. "Except I'm mortal. A human."

"We can choose a human, but you were an assignment to us at first. None of us will cross the line of duty." His gaze flicked to Ivy, one brow quirked. "No matter how much one of us might want to."

I sucked in a breath. "She loves me."

"Yes," he murmured. "Hopelessly."

"Damn," I exhaled and turned to watch her sleep.

Lex swallowed and leaned close to me. "She'll kill me if she finds out I told you."

I drew my fingers across my lips in a zipping motion, then smiled. "What did you tell me?" I asked with a shrug.

My heart surged at the sentiment of Ivy's devotion, then turned heavy with the weight of what she masked so well. Surprise and confusion about her feelings for me made me rethink our entire relationship. She knew I was only attracted to men, but it didn't excuse my self-absorption and inability to pick up on my best friend's clues.

In that moment, I decided to banish whatever thoughts I had about Lex to the recesses of my mind. He'd never betray his sister. I didn't think he had a sliver of romantic feelings for me, but his duty wouldn't allow it. If I couldn't return what Ivy felt for me, I'd never hurt my best friend to date her brother.

"How much further?" I asked, my voice carrying a hint of melancholy.

Lex held onto the grab handle and sighed, "A few minutes."

Apprehension pumped through me as I replayed the day's events in my head. I somehow created a portal to keep us alive after a Lurker demon tried to kidnap me, and fallen angels were my best friends. A spasm shot through my neck, recalling the demon's skin melting from her bones.

Lex pointed to the bracelet on my wrist. "That's new," he commented.

"It was my mom's." I ran my fingertip over the etchings, a smile crossing my face. "It's hideous, isn't it?"

"No. It looks unique. Like you." He nodded and turned to look back out the window.

My pulse quickened. A gnawing reminder of the countless moments I had spent dissecting his every move, every glance, and every fleeting smile.

No. I needed to ground myself, to tether my thoughts to reality and not let them drift into the tumultuous sea of memories. He had occupied too much space there for far too long. He wasn't worth losing my friendship with Ivy—our bond was stronger.

Much stronger, I told myself.

As if sensing my turmoil, Ivy opened her eyes and raised her head, her gaze scanning our surroundings with intensity.

"Everything okay?" I asked, my voice laced with concern that only heightened my sense of entrapment.

"Yeah." Her hand found my leg to offer reassurance. "I'm ready to get inside the protection of the gates."

"Why are we safe in there, but not out here?" I pressed, glancing back and forth between her and Lex.

"It's warded from demons. We use a hint of divine power and the help of one family from the Blackfeet Nation," she explained, her tone imbued with devotion.

My curiosity sparked, and I couldn't help but ask, "How did that happen?"

Jossy answered from the front seat, his voice low and contemplative as he continued to stare out the windshield. "When we fell here, it was on their land. After we gained their trust, they let us buy that piece of it."

"But it was Vincent who orchestrated it all." A glimmer of admiration flickered across Jossy's face.

"Is that all it took?" I asked, eyebrows raised in disbelief.

"No, but it helped." Lex laughed, shaking his head. "We come from the stars. The Blackfeet Nation is a spiritual people and believes in a higher power, too. Earth needs protection, and the same goes for the rest of the universe."

Listening to Lex's words made me feel strange—the idea that something so vast and profound entwined with human existence humbled me.

Jossy drummed his fingers on the dashboard. "We don't know why your family was chosen to hold these secrets, Noa," he began. "But, if the wrong hands got your hidden knowledge —angel, demon, or human—we're all screwed."

Ivy leaned closer, urgency threading her tone. "Believe it or not, we aren't invincible, either."

"So, what's the secret formula for the wards? A spell or something?" I inquired, and a hush fell over the car.

A grim expression crossed Lex's face. "That's a story for another time."

"If we're killed," added Ivy. "We go the same way that Lurker did. Except our bones and wings stay behind. Feathers and all."

My face contorted at the gruesome thought. "Why is that?"

"It's something to do with our transition to this plane and the chemical makeup of our bodies when we become human," Lex added. "Our skeletal system is almost indestructible." He paused, searching my face. "How much do you know about volcanoes?"

I nodded and managed a smile. "The basics. I haven't done a science report since high school."

"The easiest way to put it," he said, and his eyes brightened when he spoke, "is that we're composed of diabase rock. It's like magma that doesn't come to the surface. The liquid crystallizes underground and becomes strong and durable."

"We still have the powers given to us in the Veil." Ivy joined in on the science lesson. "Our wings are what contain the power and control it."

Ivy turned to face the window, then raised her shirt for me to look at her back. Two thick black veins, at least an inch wide, emerged, running parallel to her spine. I recoiled from the sight, landing in Lex's lap when they started to pulsate.

"Jesus!" I covered my mouth with my hands.

Ivy chuckled as hers retreated back into her body and sealed beneath the surface of her skin. "That's where we store them. Our wings are in there too, so we can use both if needed."

I massaged my temples, trying to process the information as I readjusted myself in the backseat. "Okay, so your bones are something more science fiction. What happens if someone finds what's left behind?"

Ivy exhaled a deep sigh as she situated herself back in the seat. "There are protocols in place. We emit angelic energy like yours so higher-level angels can find us."

My brain pressed against my skull and slumped against the backseat of the car, yearning for the comfort of my lumpy couch and rundown apartment. The events of the day had left me drained and wanting to escape reality. I'd give anything to put on some Tom Petty and forget any of this happened.

I glanced over at Lex and caught him staring at me. I grabbed my chest when a flicker of fog moved across his pupils.

"That freaks me out." I pulled out my vape and took a deep inhale.

He leaned close to me, flashing his luminous smile, then elongated each word. "It's. Supposed. To."

I pushed at his chest, shaking my head as I exhaled a ring of fruit-flavored smoke in his face. "Uh-uh. Not today and not now."

With a dismissive wave of his hand, Lex drew closer and snatched my vape from me. He flung his head against the headrest. "I can dial it down, but it takes effort. Now that you know, it's easier to just… be."

I held out my hand, palm up. "Can I have my vape back, please?"

"No." He adamantly shook his head. "It's clouding your judgment, and you need a clear head."

"I'll get another one then," I huffed, leaning back in my seat and staring out the window as we drove up the road.

"Go ahead and try," Lex confirmed as he slapped his palm with my vape. "I'll take that one too."

I breathed out through my nose in frustration as I gave him a dirty look. Then I turned away and looked out of Ivy's window into the darkness.

"I like you better when you don't talk so much," I grumbled back at him.

He leaned in close to my ear, making the hairs on my neck stand at attention. "Best intervention I've ever done. You'll thank me later."

I elbowed him in the stomach and smiled. As much as I

wanted to believe him, I still had more to learn about my family. Vaping helped keep me at peace and relaxed. And if I was carrying around insurmountable power that I didn't know how to access or use, then I needed to remain calm.

"You're not playing fair," I protested.

Lex's mouth curled into a wicked grin. "Never forget, Noa. As a fallen angel, nothing about us is fair."

Fog crept over the ground as we turned onto the narrow driveway, and the driver came to a stop. The headlights illuminated a sturdy wooden gate, and when the driver put the car in park, I stepped out in awe at what stood before me. As the car drove off, Jossy walked up and leaned on my shoulder.

"Gorgeous, isn't it?" His sparkling eyes grew wide at the carvings on each side of the gate.

CHAPTER 11

The temperature had dropped even lower, but as much as I liked the cold, I needed more than a hoodie outside. I rubbed my hands together and blew into them for warmth.

"Incredible," I said, breathless.

Some moments in life surprise you in a way you never imagined. Outside of learning the truth about my friends, this was another one of those moments, and I had a feeling it wouldn't be the last. The headlights revealed an enormous wooden swing gate.

Its height was equal to the top of a streetlamp. On each side of the gate, two hand-carved wolves angled toward each other, both howling up to the moon. No matter where I looked, their eyes of midnight blue followed me. I felt inferior to the world as they pierced into my soul.

Around the neck of one wolf, a white collar, with stars of ebony speckled throughout it as deep violet caressed the edges.

The other wolf's collar was an inverted replica of the first. I glanced between the wolves and noticed the moonlight made their eyes sparkle.

They were real gemstones. I stepped back and inhaled a sharp breath when my left foot caught on a rock. Jossy held his hand out for me, and I took it, thankful that the night hid my embarrassment.

"Please be careful," he said.

I walked back and forth in front of the gate as I inspected the wolves while a camera followed each step.

I whirled my body back around to Lex. "Real gemstones sit in their eyes. Aren't you worried about thieves?"

"No one could even get near them, and if they did, they'd get the life shocked out of them if they tried."

"Figures," I said.

I bounced in place on my toes and chuckled with a shiver. "It makes sense with warding and angels having abilities I'm still clueless about."

Wolves began to sing in the distance across the Montana night and grew louder as a sharp twinge shot through my lip. Not again. Chills tap-danced down my spine, and for a brief moment, it felt like a mistake to go to the ranch.

Jossy reassured me, "Even though we aren't inside yet, we're safe here, Noa."

I nodded as I watched Ivy talk on a phone attached to a call box in front of the gate. Her back was turned toward us, so I couldn't hear the conversation.

"Why don't you use your cell phone?"

"Protocol. When Vincent isn't told we're coming before we

arrive, there is a security clearance check we have to go through."

Ivy hung up and walked over to us. "The car is waiting on the other side."

As I glanced at my three friends, I tilted my head when it dawned on me that none of them seemed to feel the chill in the air. "You're impervious to the cold, too?"

Lex grinned and ran his fingers along his chin before sliding them into his front jeans pocket. He began to whistle as if he hadn't heard me.

"This keeps getting more interesting, doesn't it?" I asked them, my voice sharp with annoyance.

He paused and jabbed with a playful tone, "But you're a fan of the cold."

In that moment, the heavy gate creaked open to reveal two imposing guards standing on the other side. Twins. Identical, from their sharp features and piercing gazes to their thick purple braids that cascaded past their waists. Their eyes, a stormy shade of navy, held a hint of something more beneath their stony exteriors. I knew they were angels in their perfection.

"I'll keep foot traffic," Ivy stated, pulling me from my trance.

"Wait." I reached out and took her hand, my grip on her fingers weak. "You're not coming with us?"

"It's safer if I help scout the area while you stay protected in the car." She moved forward and hugged me, then ran ahead of us on the dirt road leading up to the house. The twins followed.

Once I situated myself in the front seat with Jossy behind the wheel, he instructed me to wear my seatbelt, which I ignored. As I turned around to see the gate close behind us, two white wolves paced across the road. My heart sank, wondering what I'd gotten myself into as I searched the dark for Ivy.

"Are you nervous?" Lex asked from the back seat.

"Yes," I said. The admission felt heavy in the air between us. "I'm not sure this is a good idea anymore, and I'm tired of being stuck in a car."

My nails dug into the flesh of my palms as I sought to ground myself. A familiar ritual that had accompanied me through countless moments of doubt. Now it felt more urgent than ever.

"What?" Jossy shook his head, loosening a few mahogany locks from his ponytail. "No turning back now, Noa."

"Why are you so on guard if this place is safe and you have wards?" I rebutted, my voice laced with skepticism as I glanced between them both.

The shadows of the night danced against the glass. For a fleeting moment, I wished I could slip through them and escape from this suffocating uncertainty.

Lex's eyes flickered to mine in the rearview mirror, searching for understanding. "We're hidden from the general public, but the Baneful roam around here; they can't touch the land."

"If you say so," I looked out the window again, searching the night for Ivy.

Jossy gripped the steering wheel tighter. "We aren't taking chances now that you're here," he said, punctuating his words with a slight nod.

Lex leaned forward on the console, sandwiched between me and Jossy. "Now that you're back on the supernatural grid, the Baneful and others will gather."

Goosebumps sprinkled my arms at the thought of being

hunted. "If you're trying to make me feel better," I replied with an edge in my tone. "That's not it."

"Don't forget," Jossy interjected, his voice cutting through my spiraling thoughts. "The Lurker's master should know it's dead by now." His gaze drifted to the road ahead, eyes narrowing.

"You better pray Vincent has his shit together," I shot back, anger tinged with fear bubbling beneath my skin. "Because if he doesn't..." My voice trailed off as an aura flashed across my eyes—a kaleidoscope of colors swirling like storm clouds gathering above. A slow throb began behind my eyes, building like pressure before a storm.

"You found me." A raspy voice coughed across my mind, jagged and broken like glass shattering on concrete.

It slithered through my thoughts and wrapped around my consciousness until it suffocated me. My eyes burned, and I could feel the tension in my head as my breaths came in shallow gasps. I squinted, trying to focus on anything but the bright, swirling crescents that danced across my vision.

I rubbed my eyes with the heel of my hand, desperate to see better. "I can't see, guys. I'm getting a migraine."

"Finally." A coughing fit wracked his body, and the man in my head spoke, his voice familiar. *"You won't get away this time, Noa."*

It was the man infiltrating my mind while I slept, but I was wide awake now. Jossy's face blanched white when he looked over at me and saw the fear I couldn't hide anymore. His foot slammed on the gas pedal, kicking up rocks and dirt behind us on the winding road.

"All I need is two minutes, Noa," Jossy announced.

Wind gusts became stronger, pushing the car back and forth across the gravel road, threatening to tip us over. The sound of wings above us, getting louder by the moment, sent chills down my spine.

"What is that?" I cried, my body jerking with every swerve of the car as Jossy swerved to avoid balls of fire that were now raining down on us.

"Demons," Jossy spat, his knuckles white on the wheel. "Something must be wrong with the wards."

"You can't be serious!" I yelled above their unearthly wails.

I gripped the edge of my seat when Lex pounded the roof of the car. "It's about to get exciting, Noa."

He rolled down the back window and stuck out half his body. The sudden roar of what sounded like jet engines drowned out his words, and the ground heaved and buckled. Clods of dirt and grass spewed into the air around us. Jossy's eyes narrowed to slits as he floored the accelerator one more time.

Lex spun around and perched in the open window, peering up at the inky sky. A blinding flash lit up the night, and for a split second, I saw the silhouette of a massive, bat-winged creature. An earth-shattering explosion followed, hot air buffeting us as flames erupted where the beast had been.

"Got that son of a bitch!" Lex whooped in victory, then leaned back in the car.

A bone-chilling screech assaulted our ears, like claws raking a chalkboard. I clapped my hands over my ears, shuddering and yelling through the pain. Jossy swerved and dodged through the chaos, maneuvering the car with precision and skill.

Demons swooped down from the sky, never touching the

ground while fireballs exploded in all directions. The wind howled around us, carrying with it the stench of sulfur and decay. Sparks exploded against a nearby tree, and I ducked my head into my knees.

"Hold on, Noa!" Jossy shouted over the deafening racket of demonic squeals.

He swerved around a crumbling tree, avoiding a molten burst that erupted beside us.

Lex found his way back into the car, his breath heavy. "Why are the wards going down?"

Jossy's voice was tight with concentration as he fought to keep us on the road. "I don't know, but we're almost there."

As we sped down the road, I sat up and stole a glance at Jossy. His calm demeanor had transformed into a focused intensity. He seemed to be in his element amidst the anarchy.

I, on the other hand, wanted to puke again and again as I fought through the growing pain behind my eyes. I braced myself with one hand on the dashboard as Ivy materialized in front of us. Two other massive angels stood next to her, taking up the road with their size.

Ivy's eyes sparked with intensity as she raised her hands, summoning a powerful gust of wind and then a flash of light. The demonic creatures shrieked in frustration and retreated into the night.

As I closed my eyes again to rub my temples, Jossy slammed to a stop in front of a cabin at the end of the road. My chest collided with the dashboard, and Lex clamored out of the backseat to open my door.

He bent down in front of me, concern etched in his eyes. "Are you all right, Noa?"

I pounded on my chest, gasping for breath. "Water!" I wheezed.

Jossy grunted as he threw a bottle across the top of the car, and Lex reached up with one arm to catch it. Unscrewing the cap, he made me drink. He rubbed my back until I took steady breaths, and when I looked around, all signs of an attack had disappeared as suddenly as they had appeared.

Jossy turned to Ivy with a grateful wave. "I appreciate the assist back there, sister."

Ivy gave a casual shrug as she placed her hands on her hips. "A few demons won't be enough to take us down."

Jossy nodded, and his eyes flickered as he assessed our surroundings. "We can't stay out here for long. More will come."

"They're toying with us." Lex shook his head, his dark eyes glinting with frustration, the muscles in his jaw tightening as he spoke. "We should get inside and talk to Nevaeh."

Jossy shifted, his face flushed with anger. "Where's Vincent?" he asked, scanning the perimeter.

"He bolted to check the wards and make sure they don't fail again." Ivy glanced at me, and her eyes sparked with unspoken fear. "Noa, are you sure you're up for this?"

I took a deep breath, feeling the sharp ache radiate from my chest where the impact had struck me. My heart pounded with doubt threatening to engulf me, but this was more than survival. I had to claim this power in me to stay safe.

"I have to do this, Ivy," I confirmed. "Hiding me won't keep any of this from happening."

Lex placed a hand on my shoulder, offering silent support. When I turned to look at him, he raised one finger to his lips.

CHAPTER 12

I raised an eyebrow, then whirled around, checking each side of me. "What is it?"

Rocks bounced along the ground as something trotted up behind me, and I felt a nudge in the middle of my spine that pushed me forward. I fell knees-first into the dirt. Hot breath seeped through my jeans, and a yelp escaped my throat. A low growl positioned at the nape of my neck provided a warning if I moved.

My fingers dug deeper into the dirt when paws the size of dinner plates began to circle me. My head erupted in fury once more, and the scar on my lip burned in agony as if someone were ripping it open from within.

"Find me!" his strangled voice called out to me.

I didn't know who this man was or what consequences would come if I gave him what he wanted. Electricity crackled across my forehead, and I flipped over, my palms pushing into my eyes.

Tears stung my cheeks as dirt now clung to my lips. "Please, stop!"

A booming howl erupted beside me, then the ground shook as the animal took off into the night. I braced myself against the ground and dug my fingers into the earth, gritting my teeth against the pain. Someone scooped me up in one swift motion, and a cold wind rushed through my hair.

"You'll be okay, Noa. I promise." Ivy held onto me tighter as she sauntered up the stairs of the cabin.

"What. Is. Happening?" My breath panted as I pulled at my face.

Chatter filled the surrounding space, and I tried to decipher the voices, but I couldn't. Another blow hit the back of my head, and I crumpled into the fetal position in Ivy's arms. I clung to her with fingers so tight it would take a crowbar to release me.

Her hold around me grew stronger. Someone shone a light into each of my eyes, then guided us through the house.

Ivy blinked at me. "Was this Baz?" she asked.

"Not likely," a man's deep voice answered. "Lay her on the bed and remove her shoes and socks."

His command carried an urgency that settled over us like a thick fog, leaving no room for debate. I looked deep into Ivy's eyes, searching for a glimmer of reassurance, but all I found was a mirror of my own turmoil.

"Please don't leave me!" My voice cracked under the weight of desperation.

The thought of being alone in this moment was suffocating —another nightmare I couldn't bear to face.

She fought against the pull of his authority. "I can't let her go like this, Nakoma," Ivy insisted, her brows knitting together.

"Ivy, this is what I do," he said, his gaze steady and compassionate.

"Let her go, Ivy." Jossy stood beside her now, pulling on her arm before she did something reckless.

Ivy's face contorted into a mixture of fear and shame as she peered down at me.

"Drop her now, Lieutenant!" Nakoma's voice rang with urgency. "Consider that an order."

The authority in his command resonated through the room like thunder, demanding compliance.

"Yes, doctor," she snapped back, her tone sharp.

Then she released me from her grasp.

The sudden absence of her warmth left a chill in its wake, amplifying the sense of isolation that seeped into my bones. I instinctively wrapped my arms around her tighter, pulling her into my chest. I needed to anchor us both from the storm brewing within me. What felt like a hot iron singed the space between my lips and nose.

Ivy pressed her lips against my ear and whispered, "I love you and I'm so sorry."

"Ivy…" I started, but the weight of emotion caught in my throat. I wanted to tell her that I understood—that love often meant making difficult choices, but all I could manage was a shaky exhale. "I love you, too."

With a sharp tug, she tore my hand away from her sleeve and wiped a tear from her face. She turned away, and the sound of the door slamming echoed through the room. Bursts of heat engulfed my legs as my shoes and socks fell to the floor with a soft thud.

The man attempted to assess my eyes for a reaction, and I

sensed a cold wipe against the inside of my arm. I remained rooted to the spot as if time had frozen and my body had turned into ice. My gaze remained fixed on the ceiling, unable to tear away from its dull white surface. Every cell in my body felt like it was on fire, yet I couldn't move a muscle.

"This might hurt for a second, but you'll relax soon," Nakoma said. He tried to sound encouraging, but doubt filled his voice. I think the pep talk was for both of us. "I'm giving you a small dose of medicine that will help you. You're safe here."

But I wasn't safe.

A few minutes ago, demons tried to kill us to get whatever secrets and powers lay hidden deep in my mind. I felt a pinch in my skin. Could I keep the promise to myself that I was strong enough to fight them off?

A warm sensation moved through my body. The excruciating pain in my head started to dissipate, and I wiggled my fingers and toes. My body soon relaxed into the mattress.

I turned to rub my arm, and Nakoma came into focus. He wore aqua-colored medical scrubs and clung to a stethoscope with slim fingers. The smooth, rich brown tone of his skin accentuated the lines of his muscles and chiseled jaw. And his long black hair was pulled back into a braided pony-tail.

His soft chestnut eyes penetrated mine, refusing to let go. I slunk back from him as he observed me. They all wanted what I had, but I didn't know how to reach it. Within two days, I became part of a world I never knew existed and was uncertain about my future in it. How would I ever protect myself?

"Rest, Noa. I'll be back to check on you later," he stated with a pat on my arm.

As the door closed, a heavy silence settled in the room. I was alone, trapped in the darkness with only my racing thoughts for company. My purpose, whatever it entailed, weighed heavily on my mind, casting shadows of doubt and fear.

I tried to steady my breathing, willing myself to remain calm amidst suffocating uncertainty. But the grip of anxiety tightened around my heart, along with slumber. The unknown can be a cruel companion when facing the prospect of death.

CHAPTER 13

My eyes shot open as morning screamed through the window. As soon as I pulled the covers up over my head to block the light, Lex stepped into the doorway wearing black fight training shorts and a sleeveless t-shirt. His muscles bulged sideways from all the training he had done.

Time to wish away any thoughts that perked my desires for him as I hid in my blanket cave. He was lethal with that body, but I made a promise to my friendship with Ivy. I wouldn't go back on it. After two deep breaths, I peeked out from under the sheets.

Damnit!

He caught my eye and walked closer. He also carried a glass with him and set it on the nightstand. I felt every ache slice through my bones and sat up.

I didn't know what on earth I'd gotten myself into by following them here. I could barely lift the rim of the cup to my nose, but when I did, the smell of eggs and licorice punched my nose.

I gagged and slammed the cup down on the nightstand. "What is this?"

"Consider it immunity support." He stood with arms crossed, and every muscle flexed out in the open as the light caught each line of definition.

On his right thigh, an intricate tattoo of a triangle encasing an eye stared back at me in the middle of a dream catcher. Black feathers cascaded around it, falling from the sky. I focused harder, and a tree blooming with small pink flowers rose up behind it as the roots branched out below it.

I sucked in a sharp breath at the similarity of the tree compared to the one that the man hijacking my mind had shown me.

Lex rolled his eyes and pointed to the cup. "Drink."

"I'm getting to it." My fingernails tapped the side of the glass, and I gestured my head in an upward motion. "Interesting tattoo," I said.

"Oh," he smiled. "It's the all-seeing eye. We each have some variation of it."

"What is that tree?" I asked, trying to memorize every detail.

Lex traced the lines of his tattoo and smiled. "It represents the tree where we fell. The one I told you about in the story."

I nodded, praying he couldn't see my mind racing at what it might mean for me, but his reaction didn't tell me he did. Something told me I should keep the mystery man and his brain chatter to myself for the time being. It was possible if he would stop trying to give me an aneurysm.

I grabbed the mug and brought the drink to my lips, trying

to find the courage to swallow the rotten sewage. Uncertain of how I felt about the new information, I needed to see if I could get to that tree somehow. I pinched my nose and held it as I swallowed in one chug and coughed hard.

"Disgusting," I choked and stuck out my tongue, wishing the taste away.

He took the glass and inspected the contents with a smile. "Good."

"My vape would help me the same way, you know." I flung myself back onto the bed.

Deep lines formed between his eyebrows as he tilted his head down at me. "Don't even think about it. We need your brain firing on all cylinders, so alcohol and weed are no longer part of your vocabulary."

"You can't be serious about me having to stop vaping," I said with disbelief.

"I am. You need a clear head with demons after you." He was stern, as if he were speaking to a child.

My lips pursed as I looked deep into Lex's eyes. "Fine," I said, my tone firm. "I'll give up the vices if that's what it takes to survive."

"You said you were ready for this, Noa. It's time to learn what that means."

I met Lex's unwavering gaze. "So, teach me."

"Get a shower, then meet us out in the living room. Make sure to inspect your entire body and let me know if you see anything unusual."

"Angels are a pain in the ass," I groaned.

"Fallen ones, yes. And you're welcome." Lex gestured toward the other side of the room to a small closet. "You'll find clean clothes in there, and new bras and panties in the dresser."

I turned back to look at him, but the door closed before I could speak. I fell back on the lumpy mattress and smothered myself with a pillow, then screamed. Safe in the moment, I let the tears roll back into my hair, then threw the pillow at the door. After a deep breath, my eyes fixated on the ceiling with its rough-hewn cedar planks. Its raw color resembled how exposed I felt.

I forced myself out of bed when a shock of cold struck my feet. I crossed the wooden floor and scurried over to a small rug placed in front of a wooden dresser dotted with pine knots. A wood-framed mirror accented with thin gold leaves hung above it.

I pushed my hoodie back over my shoulder to inspect the scratches left behind by the demon who attacked me. I held my breath when tiny scar lines were all that I could see. My skin healed itself, and I didn't know why or even how.

As I ran my hands through my hair, my fingers caught on every knot. Turning sideways, I shuddered at the shape of my body. For someone who protested the gym, my image reflected that. I was a limp noodle compared to my friends. I'd never survive if I had to defend myself.

Drops of sunlight began to dance with the shadows of trees across the mirror and the floor. I glanced out the window, then touched it. The chill stung my fingers.

I pushed the latch with all my strength, but it wouldn't budge. Sealed shut, I rested my face against the windowpane, enjoying its relief.

I blinked, adjusting to the light, and noticed the fence

stretched on for miles. It was difficult to see where it stopped. Beyond the thick tree line were snow-covered mountains. The grass was light brown, with scattered snow patches. I stood in awe of its beauty, then investigated the rest of the room.

The closet held jeans, t-shirts, and sweaters. Even a puffy green snow jacket hung toward the back. A pair of tennis shoes, two sets of hiking boots, and snow boots lined the floor, and when I checked them, they were all my size.

Everything anyone on a camping trip to the mountains could use filled the space, and it was mine. They prepared this room for me. I convinced myself it was for my protection, but something about it didn't feel right.

Ultimately, I settled on a white tank top, an oversized plaid flannel shirt, and fitted jeans, then laid them across the bed. The hiking boots would be my best option if I figured out a way to explore. I wasn't about to let some stalker mess with me when I had too much at stake. Better to figure him out first and keep myself alive. Then I could move on to finding my mom's killers.

"I hear you, Mr. Mind Stalker," I sang in a low whisper. "If you could stop attacking me, that would be great."

I waited for a response, but it didn't come. As I chose my underwear and socks, I noticed dirt and blood crusted up under a few of my fingernails and winced when I tried to pick it away. I found the contents of the cabinets in the bathroom stocked with bubble bath, peroxide, a box of adhesive bandages, and an unopened pack of elastic hair bands.

Once I discarded my clothes, I filled the tub and then sank into what felt like a spa bath. The scent of lavender foam caressed my skin. Noticing a few broken nails from scratching at the ground last night, I soaked the dirt away.

After rinsing the last couple of days down the drain, I looked at the bracelet I still wore. It was atrocious, but it was a connection to my mom. I wrapped myself in a towel, then gazed at the beautiful designs carved into the wooden crown molding.

Phases of the moon rose and fell across the trim, while intricately carved wolves howled into the sky from each corner. Red and blue towels dressed a gold towel bar above the toilet, and a painting of an orange and purple sunset behind a strange rock formation hung above the bathroom door. I kept my focus on the detailed carvings that resembled the wolf statues at the front gates while peroxide sizzled on my fingers.

Once the pain stopped, I wrapped bandages around the two worst fingernails. Then I pulled up my hair into a quick bun and secured it with a hair tie. After dressing, I took in the fresh floral scent of the fabric softener in my flannel shirt and smiled.

Time to get the truth.

CHAPTER 14

The smell of bacon frying hit my nose when I opened the bedroom door. Stepping into what resembled a hectic family holiday, angels scurried back and forth in front of me, dressed in identical black pants and gray sweat-shirts. They looked like gladiators at boot camp. Voices echoed across the living room into the kitchen.

The screen door off the porch bounced back and forth as they grabbed paper plates filled with scrambled eggs, bacon, waffles, and fresh fruit. Carafes of coffee and orange juice sat at the end of a counter, and my stomach lurched me forward to eat. The twin guards from the previous night stood drinking orange juice together like auto-synced robots.

Chills scurried across my skin when a man seated at the kitchen table looked up from his plate and stopped eating. I swallowed hard as his deep brown eyes bore into me. I offered a slight wave, but he got up and exited through the front door, leaving his breakfast unfinished.

The twins followed him. My mind struggled to process its surroundings, and I understood Dorothy's desire to get home from Oz. Only, I didn't see my slippers anywhere. Faces I didn't recognize, some with different scars on them, looked in my direction as I inched further into the kitchen.

Another man, securing a black eye patch, struggled to focus as purple and blue swelled over his other eye. I wondered if whoever he fought even survived, based on his injuries. Considering what he was, what they both were, the answer was yes.

More fallen ones moving in and out of the house began to look at me, letting their eyes linger. I slunk back until I saw Jossy lounging across a couch, reading a sports magazine. He traded his suit for dark jeans and a white button-down. His lava-colored hair was not in a ponytail, either. He set the paper down as soon as he saw me, with my mouth hanging open in shock.

"How are you feeling?" Jossy stood and walked over to me with his arms open for a hug.

"Not sure yet." I laughed as I squeezed him. "I like this look on you, though."

He held his hands out with a tilt of his head. "I can relax here."

"Where are we?" My eyes took in the warmth of the cabin as a fire roared in the living room.

"This is Vincent's place, but he likes to serve our meals and hold meetings here in the mornings. Now, let's get you something to eat."

I nodded, and he stepped aside and gestured with his arm out for me to walk into the kitchen before him. Lex leaned over the stove, now wearing a sweatshirt and black sweatpants. He stirred oatmeal while an elderly woman with soft copper skin dashed sugar and cinnamon into the same pot.

She turned, her russet eyes sparkling. Deep-set lines caressed her face. She offered a smile, then clapped her hands twice to gain the attention of a few remaining angels. Those who finished tossed their plates in the trash, and others carried their food to the porch.

Wearing a long denim dress and a red and white paisley waist apron, she faced me. "Hi, Noa. Feeling better?"

"I think so." I pressed my hands against my head. "My head doesn't hurt anymore, but I can't say the same for my body."

"You can thank my grandson for that." She brightened with pride, and I smiled. Her raven hair, parted down the middle, spilled down her back. She took a paper plate from the bar and filled it with waffles and fruit. "I'm Nevaeh, by the way."

"Nice to meet you." I grabbed a few grapes and chewed quickly. Hunger overcame me.

"Likewise." Excitement sang out in her voice. "Bacon?"

"Yes, please." I took a bite of a strawberry while she guided me to a seat at the bar where others left plates behind. "I'd like to thank Nakoma. Is he around?"

She watched me and rubbed the gray and white beads around her neck. They seemed to bring back a long-forgotten memory.

"He goes where he's needed around here, but you'll get a chance." The screen door slammed, and Nevaeh patted her hands on her apron and sighed. "You need to talk to them, Jossy. Look at this mess. And slamming doors? I won't have this house disrespected, no matter their feelings."

"They're processing everything, but I promise I'll remind them of the rules," he pledged.

Jossy walked out onto the porch, where voices grew louder in frustration. I turned back to watch Lex fill containers with leftovers and oatmeal. He stacked them into brown paper sacks, then labeled the bags with names. I ate faster, then gulped down two glasses of orange juice, savoring each burst of flavor left on my tongue.

What my mind craved was answers. About myself, the demons that stormed in last night, and my mother. I knew it would be challenging, but Jossy's assurance about Vincent having all the answers gave me hope.

Something shifted inside me as I pondered it, and fear morphed into courage. I wiped my sweaty palms against my jeans, feeling anxious, and pushed my plate away. Realizing I hadn't seen Ivy, I looked around.

Lex glanced up while wiping away remnants of breakfast from the counter. "She's not here," he offered with a smile.

"Not to worry. Ivy will be along." Nevaeh's tone indicated there were other important things to take care of besides me.

I forced a smile as she filled a percolator with freshly ground coffee. Two thermoses sat on the counter, and when she looked over, her eyes gave me solace. When the coffee finished brewing, I stepped down from the bar chair to join her, and she pointed to the thermoses. She took them with a smile as I pretended to keep my nerves in check.

Lex reached for a coffee mug at the back of the cabinet next to us and poured a fresh cup. He handed it to me.

"Cream and sugar?" he asked pointing to each on the counter.

"Wow, your choice to give me this and live for another day is impressive, Lex."

I nodded with a smile and gestured with my coffee cup. The intense aroma of vanilla wafted toward me, causing my body to collapse in contentment.

He dropped two spoonfuls of sugar into my mug, followed by a dash of creamer. Handing me the spoon, he said, "It's the only high you're allowed to have."

"And you love reminding me, don't you?" I shot a disgusted glance at him before reclaiming my spot at the bar, as Lex chuckled at my expense.

My unease about the situation only grew stronger. I debated whether to reveal the truth about the man in my head. He could be a demon for all I knew, but in the end, I kept quiet. My eyes flickered from Nevaeh, who gazed out of a tiny circular window above the sink, and back to me.

She reminded me of my grandmother, whom I'd never met but had only seen in pictures. I'd never met any family on my mom's side and knew nothing about my dad. Not even photos of him existed.

Ugh! My memory box. I'd have to figure out a way to get it back.

I sipped my coffee and Lex walked past me, then winked. He carried the paper bags full of food and the thermoses out to the porch, then returned to wash the dishes.

"Lex?" I blew into my coffee mug, cooling it before taking another sip. "What turned you into such a domesticated, er—"

"Angel?" He chuckled, nodding toward Nevaeh. "No one says no to her. We earn our keep and keep our lives."

Nevaeh flapped her hands at him, then gave him a side hug. "Do you like the coffee, Noa?"

"It's fantastic, thank you." I raised my mug with a smile.

"It's my own special blend. It's a hobby, but I have a few coffee bean plants in my greenhouse on the property. I spend a lot of my time in there these days."

"And the vanilla?"

"A supplier ships those to me in bulk."

"Nice!" I ran my finger around the edge of the coffee mug, inhaling again, then I smiled.

Jossy closed the front door and walked into the kitchen to plant a kiss on Nevaeh's cheek. "Her coffee is one of many reasons we keep her," he chirped, and she swatted him with a dishtowel. "They'll be on their best behavior now."

A twinge of jealousy stung my heart as I watched how close they were. I was close to my friends, too, or at least I thought so, but their connection with Nevaeh was different. I began to miss my mom as I watched them.

In that instant, a husky voice trailed down the hall from the other side of the kitchen. "What do we have here?"

A man rounded the corner, taking up most of the doorway. My mug slipped from my grasp and fell to the floor, but his quick reflexes caught it before it made a mess. Not a drop spilled, and he flashed me a gentle smile as he placed it back on the counter.

He towered over me like a bear with thick, inky waves of hair that hovered over the top of his broad shoulders. I wanted to grab it and run my hands through the sheen of it. Drawing a deep breath, I inhaled the heady scent of mountains and cedar that clung to his skin.

He helped me down from the barstool. "We didn't get a proper introduction last night. I'm Vincent." He extended a hand and I shook it, my pulse quickening at his touch. With a gentle hand on my back, he guided me to the couch. "Let's sit."

Vincent looked back at Nevaeh and gestured to the porch. When I glanced outside, two enormous wolves materialized on the porch. Their fur was as white as snow, threaded with glimmers of copper and flame. What struck me most was their staggering size as one occupied the entire doorway, its fiery orange eyes boring into me.

My body quivered as Vincent cupped my chin. He tilted my gaze up into eyes that blazed with the same feral intensity as the wolves. The door clicked shut, sealing off the beasts outside.

My throat tightened as I pointed a shaky finger toward the door. "What are those?"

His expression remained unruffled. "A special type of wolf."

"Are they yours?" I whispered.

"Yes," Vincent chuckled. "They help provide security here."

"Those aren't ordinary wolves," I murmured in disbelief.

Vincent shook his head and chuckled. "You're right. They're not."

We sat on the sofa. The fabric of the couch was smooth and cool against my skin. As I leaned against the arm, my fingers grazed over the armrest, feeling the slight give of the material. Jossy and Lex sat across from us on the hearth of the oversized stone fireplace.

"Was it one of those wolves that came out to greet me last night?"

Nevaeh brought over a tray of coffee and handed us each a cup. "Would you like more, Noa?"

I waved a hand at her. "No, thank you."

Nevaeh poured one cup, then doctored it with cream for Lex. Jossy drank his black. Once we were comfortable in the living room, Nevaeh grabbed her coat from a hook by the front door. She then stepped outside to give us privacy.

"Yes," Vincent told me.

"Why was it angry with me?"

"Akta wasn't angry with you." Vincent rested his eyes on me with a half-smile. "The chaos wound him up, then after you fell and had your episode, it concerned him," he clarified.

I wasn't sure I believed his explanation, but it seemed plausible. "Where did they come from?" I asked.

Vincent's voice hinted at a sound of regret. "Some of us begin to die as soon as we touch the earth," he said. "We don't know why, exactly, but there's a ceremony we can perform that allows us to save them. The wolves are fallen angels, too."

My skin prickled with goosebumps as I tried to process his words. "Although I'm not surprised, that's amazing."

Vincent's brows crinkled between his eyes. He eyed my wrist, his gaze lingering on my bracelet. His eyes flickered with a million fireworks as they searched mine for an answer I didn't have.

Air seemed to catch in his throat, and he blinked the colors away. "I haven't seen that in ages."

"You've seen this before?" I held up my wrist, and Vincent reached out to touch it. He inched closer, then pulled his hand away.

"It was your grandmother Sasha's," he confirmed as his lips formed a tight smile. "It's ancient. Someone gifted it to her many years ago."

"I've always wondered where it came from." I stroked the etchings with my finger and smiled. "My mom gave it to me before she died."

Vincent's shoulders tensed a fraction, his focus shifting from the bracelet to my eyes. His throat bobbed when he swallowed. "It's nice to see it has stayed in the family."

My eyes narrowed as I watched him lean back against the couch. I was happy to know the bracelet had meaning and wasn't something my mom found at a yard sale. That it meant more than junk.

I hunched forward, adjusting the sleeves of my flannel shirt, ready to dive into my past. "Can we discuss what's going on here, please?"

"Straight to the point. I like that." He placed one foot over his knee and stretched his arms across the back of the couch.

My voice trembled when I addressed him. "Vacation doesn't last forever."

Vincent's gaze softened as he spoke. "This will be over soon."

Jossy placed his cup on the serving tray in the middle of the coffee table, then sat in a recliner next to me. "We hope."

"You'll stay for a couple of weeks," Vincent began.

I shook my head and waved my hands. "No way. I have responsibilities."

"Your safety is a top priority," Vincent said as he inclined his head sideways. "Ours too, for that matter, so you can't leave until this is all sorted."

My heart felt like it was about to beat out of my chest. "Nothing was safe about the demons penetrating the wards last night," I insisted.

"All fixed up." He smiled, but his eyes seemed to hide something when I looked at him.

I looked over at Jossy, then at Lex. They both nodded in agreement before I said, "How do you plan on fixing me?"

Uncrossing his legs, Vincent edged forward. "It won't be easy, Noa, so patience is key."

Despite the turmoil inside me, I held my voice steady. "I know there's power locked inside me, and there's a demon master looking for me."

"His name is Maros." He rubbed his eyebrows with his finger and thumb.

"I killed one of his Baneful Lurker demons." My breath shuddered, but pride swelled inside me at the thought.

"He's a typical demon thug who wants your world for his own," Vincent remarked. "Maros and my brother Vallen plotted this together."

A heavy awareness settled on my chest. "But they'll torture me if they find me," I said after a moment.

CHAPTER 15

Vincent's mood quickly shifted to aggravation.

"My brother lost his way," he said through clenched teeth. "Angels should watch over humans, but sometimes they wonder why you're the chosen ones. It's an ache that eats at them like a plague. They'd do anything to switch positions."

His jaw ticked as his gaze seemed to drift through memories too painful to relive. My gut knotted like a warning. When he glanced back at me, his eyes reflected a well of sympathy.

Skepticism laced my words. "What could an angel do to change things?"

Vincent's expression turned dark as he leaned in closer. His voice dropped to an intense whisper. "Some angels have the power to rewrite destinies, to alter the fabric of reality itself, but such acts come with a great cost."

I picked at the bandages on my fingers when it dawned on me that whatever was happening was on a much bigger scale than I'd imagined. "Humans didn't choose this life," I reminded him. "Why would you care about us so much, then try to eliminate us?"

Vincent nodded in agreement. "Some angels don't feel that humans are worthy of the choices they get."

"Last time I checked, it wasn't up to your kind to decide." The disdain in my voice was evident as I rolled my eyes. "How are you even allowed to do things like this?"

He fixed his eyes on mine, unyielding and grave. "We're not only messengers, Noa. We help keep order and we're given gifts and the power to do that. We can change worlds, but angels take reckless chances sometimes."

My face contorted in confusion at the implications of his words. "Because Lucifer wasn't enough of a wake-up call?" I asked.

"He wanted to be in charge of it all. That's a different story. Angels, in general, want to shake you and help you get your life together." Vincent's expression softened, but his words hung heavy.

"So we're puppets. Great." I shook my head in disbelief.

"Are you listening?" he bit out. Then, he stood up, his movements purposeful as he crossed the room to a bookshelf lined with old journals. Dust swirled in the air as he ran his fingers over the spines. He selected one bound in cracked leather. "We don't control humans, Noa. We assist."

"Vallen believes otherwise," I retorted. Terror coiled in my chest like a slumbering beast.

Vincent returned to the couch and opened the book. Symbols filled its pages and stirred my mind. "He was noble once," he explained, his voice tender. "And dedicated to protecting human souls before their journey here."

"Is this yours?" I asked as he flipped to a section where two angels faced one another and their wings spread wide. They held up a bright golden ball.

Vincent nodded and continued, "I'd get the soul and whisper half of our knowledge into it. Then, Vallen would whisper the other half. He'd seal the soul—"

"With a kiss," I interrupted him, touching my top lip lightly. "My mom told me bedtime stories, but I thought they were folklore."

He smiled at me as I ran my finger over the pages of information. "Yes," he confirmed with a slight chuckle. "But not the way you're thinking, Noa. Your lip could be genetic or environmental, but even that isn't definitive."

"I know." My voice was soft, but my face turned red, and I lifted one shoulder. "That was the legend. So, what's the truth?"

"Once a soul becomes attached to the body, the knowledge seeps in over the course of a human life," Vincent shared. "It helps to guide your choices and assists you in finding your purpose."

"It seems too simple," I whispered with a tilt of my head.

"There's no grand revelation here," Vincent lectured. He closed the ancient book and brought it back to the shelf. He turned around and crossed his arms. "Vallen grew bitter and cynical."

"What happens if a human isn't given the secrets?" I blurted out without considering whether I truly wanted the answer.

His eyes flitted to Jossy and Lex, who sat engrossed in our conversation like they had never heard it before. He continued,

"Without the guidance of divine knowledge, that you call a conscience, humans become the worst versions of themselves. They're lost and confused as they claw their way through this place."

My knee bounced as I cradled my head in my hands, working to process it all. "Don't you have a celestial HR department to help unhappy angels find new careers?" I glared at him. "It seems odd that he decided to play keep-away one day without any clear reason, like a spiteful child."

Vincent shook his head with a weary sigh. "It wasn't random or impulsive. Watching humans across eons wore on him. In his eyes, they had yet to evolve in their humanness."

"Taking away a person's conscience is worse." My eyes turned to stone as I challenged him.

"That's irrelevant," he stated as he rejoined me on the couch. "The knowledge you carry has the power to reshape universal existence."

I felt pressure building in my head and untied my bun. Rubbing my scalp, I squeezed my eyes shut. "My mom hinted at something similar in my vision."

"There's more," Vincent revealed. Lex and Jossy both seemed to squirm at what was coming next.

"That's not ominous," I mocked, growing impatient with his storytelling.

"When your great-great-grandmother died," Vincent drew out, "we learned she only possessed fragments of the secrets. Each woman passed them down until only one descendant remained to hold them all."

"And here sits the last one," I muttered, my palms held up in frustration.

"Yes," Vincent confirmed. "But the secrets are too immense for an ordinary human mind to contain. It would rupture at the seams."

I chewed my bottom lip, scrutinizing his stoic expression for any clue to his meaning. Vincent's lips pressed into a taut line, his body coiled tight as a spring.

"Where are you going with this?" I inquired, as I arched my brow.

A shadow of uncertainty crossed his face before he answered. "It's only a matter of time before you set off a bomb, destroying everything as you know it."

The air left my lungs as I processed Vincent's words. "How do we stop it?"

He shut his eyes and bowed his head. "We can't. Our best option is to postpone it," he told me, his voice barely loud enough for me to hear. "Nothing detrimental has happened yet because Vallen hid your soul in the Veil."

A chill ran down my spine, and for a moment, the world seemed to spin around me. "I don't have a soul?" I whispered, unable to believe the magnitude of what he was saying.

Vincent nodded. "We can get it back, but it will need participation on your part."

A nervous laugh escaped me as I felt a sense of terror snake over me. Events of my life began to fall into placc as I thought about my past and my current situation. I didn't have a soul, but I still had most of the secrets since my mom died. They must have helped me in life to some degree. I remained calm, even though I was certain my face revealed a different emotion.

"What twisted carnival ride do you have planned for me next?" I asked.

Vincent hesitated before answering, uncertainty flickering in his multicolored eyes. I didn't move or say a word. I rubbed my hands together, feeling like a pawn in a twisted chess game between angels and demons.

"With the help of Nevaeh's granddaughter, Ena," he admitted, "we can retrieve the secrets and then transport them back to the Veil."

"If we perform the ceremony with precision," Jossy interjected, "we have a chance to replace your soul at the same time, Noa."

I stood up and paced in front of Lex with my stomach in knots. "I'm hearing too many maybes about this situation, and now you're involving magic?"

"It's spiritual." Lex jumped up, taking me by my shoulders to face him. "This world connects Ena's people and us as celestials. We assist Ena, so it's possible for her to perform the ceremony," he explained.

I stepped back from him and fixed my eyes on Vincent. "What happens if I die? If the bomb in me decides to go off?"

Vincent rose from the couch and walked over to look out a window above the front door and leaned one arm against it. "I don't want any of you to think about that right now."

"Too late," I said with gritted teeth to his back. "What happens, Vincent?"

Lex gave my hand a reassuring squeeze, but I couldn't bring myself to reciprocate. Instead, my face contorted, and I crossed my arms over my chest. I didn't know what Vincent was holding back, but I would explode sooner than he imagined if I didn't get an answer. Nothing happening with these secrets was good.

Vincent dropped his arm and turned back to me. His throat

bobbed before answering, and I knew I wasn't going to like what he was about to say.

"If you still hold the secrets and you die," he started, "everything behind the Veil and the angels here on Earth vanish. You included, so it's you that turns to mist. Everyone else becomes trapped here as your world becomes forgotten. It becomes uninhabitable. Feeling nothing. Knowing nothing."

My arms dangled at my sides. "Oh my god. Children and babies, too?"

Vincent nodded, confirming my fears. "They will go mad, as they age with all the decomposition that comes with death, but they will never die. There would be no end for them, Noa, and the most horrendous torment anyone could go through." He cleared his throat before continuing and said, "That is the punishment for my brother's actions."

I sat on the hearth in disbelief as grief began to wash over me. "Once again, a supernatural creature's dumbass decisions are punishing humans."

Vincent squatted down in front of me at eye level. "If we succeed in retrieving the secrets, but are unable to return your soul," he continued in a voice meant to keep me calm, "then you're the only one who suffers."

My mouth turned to cotton. "How do you mean?" I croaked out.

"Hell, Noa," Jossy said, resting his elbows on his thighs and folding his hands together. "You go to hell when you die."

I felt like I was going to pass out. "I go to hell because your dickhead brother decided to play a god's game." My breath hitched as I thought about my family. "Are my mom and other relatives in hell too?"

Vincent sat next to me as the pieces fell into place. He didn't look at me as he rubbed his chin. "Yes. But I need to tell you something else. Vallen and Maros are the ones who killed your mother."

The room began to spin as I struggled to process his words. I stood, but stumbled forward over the coffee table, and Jossy grabbed my arm to catch me. The walls began to close in, and beads of sweat formed on my forehead. Lex ran into the kitchen, and I heard the ice machine, but my legs grew weak.

"Sit down, Noa." Lex offered me a glass of water and pressed a cold, wet cloth to my head.

Panic rose inside me, and I choked back the bile forming in my throat. I wasn't going to stand there and let any of them strip away another minute of my life. I slapped away the glass, and water drenched the floor.

My head snapped up and I glared at Vincent. "Where are those two murderous pieces of shit that sent my mother and the rest of my family to hell?"

The corner of Vincent's mouth twitched as he stood, but my eyes narrowed even more while waiting for his answer.

"We know Maros is the one after you," he admitted. "They caught Vallen years ago. He's locked away for his crimes."

Wrath crept through me like icy tendrils. "Is he back in the Veil, or is he here somewhere?" I pressed him as my eyes refused to leave his.

"Noa, you can't get to him." Vincent blinked. "He's untouchable and, more importantly, warded by powerful angelic runes. Impenetrable ones."

"So he's here." I squared my shoulders. "What I want to

know is, how are they both still breathing?" The electricity in the room seemed to crackle with my anger.

Vincent stilled as he looked around at the flickering lights, then back to me. "A master of demons isn't easy to kill," his voice was calm. "Maros is like an unhinged demonic Hitler with an endless supply of resources." He dragged his hands down his face. "My brother lives because, as much as I wanted to rip his wings off, it's a crime and an atrocious obscenity in our world. Trust me, he is suffering."

I let out a feigned laugh and threw my head back in wonder. "This is unbelievable. And how will you protect me from an unhinged ancient demon?"

Vincent looked at me with hardened resolve. "Maros is consumed with a desire to uncover the secrets and to kill you himself. It's why he stays hidden. And now, he'll use the Baneful to seek you out. He did it last night, but that gives us an opportunity."

What felt like centipedes skittered down my spine at the thought. "Using me as bait is your plan? I'm better off out there alone."

"If you leave, you put every human outside of the ranch at risk of torture and death. You'll end up the same as your mother."

My eyes narrowed as I clenched my fists, and my fingertips pressed into my skin. "Vallen and Maros will burn the same way they burned my mother," I snapped at him. "Your rules don't govern me, Vincent. They will die."

He disregarded my statement, likely thinking it was a panicked outburst. "We can contain this, Noa. If you want to stay alive, you need strength, which isn't always physical."

Lex placed a gentle hand on my shoulder, his expression soft. My head jerked in his direction. "We'll get Maros," he said. "But for now, the best course of action is to strengthen our defenses and prepare for what's coming."

Jossy's eyes filled with empathy, and he walked around the coffee table. "We need to keep you alive, Noa. If you die before we extract the secrets, we're all doomed." He stood in front of me, offering what he thought was a sliver of comfort as my heart shattered. "And when we catch Maros, you can light the match yourself."

Sobs overcame me and I shook my head. "No. I will kill them both. Vallen's wings are mine, and once he turns to ash, I will saw them off and nail them to the fucking wall!"

A tidal wave of emotions crashed down on me, and I could sense their worry about my next move. Then, the ground beneath us began to quake. A piercing howl erupted with another rumble.

I lost my balance, but steadied myself by grabbing the mantle above the fireplace. Then, as quickly as the tremors began, they stopped. We all looked around at one another as Nevaeh burst through the door. Right when I noticed an opportunity to make a run for it, a rush of wind blew me back into Jossy's arms.

CHAPTER 16

A deep growl vibrated the cupboards, and dishes shattered onto the floor. I shielded my eyes with my hands until the room fell silent. When I peeked out from behind my fingers, I swallowed hard as Nevaeh stood face-to-face with a massive black wolf in the doorway.

Bigger than the white wolves I saw earlier, its head was the only part that could fit in the house. With bared jowls, it growled at Nevaeh, but she stood her ground.

"We were coming to get you," she said, her tone annoyed.

It sniffed the air, then settled its sapphire eyes on me. My heart raced as sweat formed on the back of my neck. The wolf chuffed and bobbed its head before retreating outside.

Nevaeh's smile was gentle as she ushered me to join her on the porch. I stepped outside and watched the wolf walk away from the house. It turned around and waited by the fence line.

"He's been waiting for you," Nevaeh whispered, her eyes glistening with a hidden fire.

I gasped in amazement as I leaned on the railing for support. "Me? I don't understand."

Vincent, Jossy, and Lex stood behind me, their faces etched with a mix of awe and anticipation. As I took one step down the stairs, I couldn't help but pause. My breath caught in my throat as a sudden pull carried me toward the wolf.

"Go on," Jossy said, his voice tinged with urgency. "He belongs to you."

My head swiveled back toward him, then back to the wolf. "Belongs to me?" I asked.

The wolf fixed its unblinking gaze on mine, as if it held a secret that only I could unravel. Then, a strange connection formed between us, like a silken thread woven from the very fabric of the universe, binding me to him. He felt like home.

He stood again, and patches of melting snow dotted the expansive field behind him, making my throat bob. He was majestic as he stretched and shook out his fur. I inched down the steps and approached him, careful not to make any sudden movements.

I shivered as the wind picked up and cut through my shirt, but with a deep breath, I went to him. His fur shimmered under the sunlight, revealing hints of silver and blue intertwined in a mesmerizing pattern. It illuminated the contours of his magnificent wolf form, accentuating the powerful muscles rippling beneath his sleek black fur.

My heart skipped in awe as I extended my hand, and he allowed me to touch him. I ran my fingers along his side before facing him. With a sudden gracefulness that belied his size, he lowered his head to nuzzle my outstretched hand.

In that moment, a rush of images flooded my mind—flashes

of memories I couldn't quite grasp. The bond between us was unbreakable. A surge of warmth and energy coursed through me at his touch.

"You're one magnificent type of angel," I breathed, my voice a whisper. Speaking too loudly could have disrupted the magic swirling between us.

"Thank you." His voice was low and gravelly, a sound that rumbled deep within me like distant thunder, sending shivers through my entire body.

I dropped my hand and took a step back, pulling away from the warm, inviting fur and creating some distance between us. "Did you—"

"Don't draw attention to us. They don't need to know I can talk to you. Keep petting me," he grumbled, his eyes narrowing as he glanced toward the porch.

"How are you in my head?" I whispered, my curiosity bubbling over as my mind struggled to comprehend the impossible.

"The easiest explanation—I'm your guardian angel," he replied, his tone both playful and serious.

"Holy shit!" The words escaped me in a gasp, an involuntary reaction to the revelation that felt exhilarating.

"My name is Baz," he offered. *"And keep quiet before they all come down here. They don't know I can talk to you, and it's rare."*

I turned back and waved at everyone on the porch. "His teeth are like a foot long!" I called out, my laughter mingling with the frigid air.

"Thank you," Baz said, his tone shifting to something more focused.

"But I found you. Or you found me," I stated when I looked

up at him again. "You look different as a wolf, but the black fur makes sense because your hair is black." I rambled on, trying to piece together this surreal encounter. I barely took a breath before asking, "Can all the wolves shift into a human?"

"Noa, this is the first time I've ever spoken to you." Baz paused and shook his head. *"There has only been one account of a guardian angel shifting back into human form."*

I stepped back again, dropping my hands to my side as reality crashed over me like cold water. "That's not possible. Then who—"

The sound of approaching footsteps caused Baz to shift backward into a sitting position. I turned to see Lex standing behind me, his hands jammed into the back pockets of his training pants. He was confidently casual. It clashed with my turmoil, and I felt annoyed that he interrupted my one spectacular moment in this disaster.

"What is it, Lex?" My tone bordered on resentment, not wanting anyone to disturb us.

"This is amazing, right?" he chuckled, amusement dancing across his features as he gestured toward Baz. "That wolf could swallow you whole."

"I wouldn't dare!" Baz shot back with certainty.

I coughed back a laugh, unable to stay mad at Lex for any length of time. "So, you guys have been hiding him from me?" I asked, tapping my foot.

"Only a couple of weeks." He tilted his head with an expression of mock innocence. "The wolves start out as young pups."

I turned and collided against Baz's belly, inhaling a mouthful of fur. Heat rose in my cheeks from the sudden physical intimacy. I wiped my face and looked up at him with wide eyes. "Why did you do this?" I questioned him.

Lex tapped me on the shoulder as if trying to ground me in this bizarre reality. "He can't exactly answer you, Noa."

I lowered my gaze and turned back to Lex, pretending to seek clarity. "Good point." I faked a smile and folded my arms across my chest. "How do you know he's mine? Did he come with papers, or did Angels 'R Us drop him off with an adoption certificate?"

Baz lowered his snout and released a low growl against my neck. It sent goosebumps racing down my arms. *"That was unnecessary,"* he told me.

I pinched the bridge of my nose and said, "After dealing with everything thrown at me for the last couple of days, that was me being nice."

"Baz told us before he transformed," Lex stated with an annoyed shake of his head. He leaned past me and eyed Baz with an analytical gaze. "Trust me, we know he shouldn't be here," Lex said to Baz. "Since Noa's still alive."

Baz growled, stood up, and circled Lex, ready for a challenge. He blew out an oversized breath in Lex's face before sitting next to me again.

"Alright, brother," Lex conceded with his palms facing out. "But you know I'm right. It's bad enough other guardian angels have fallen for the Drake women, but now that Noa is the last one, it could put you both in jeopardy."

"Isn't it better he's with me here?" I implored, wanting to cling to this newfound connection despite the danger it might stir up in our lives.

"We don't know," Lex replied. His expression turned curious as he met Baz's gaze once more.

"What is it with this place? For angels, you don't have a clue about what you're doing." I leaned my head back for a second and shut my eyes.

"It's the truth, Noa," Lex insisted with a gentle yet firm touch on my arm.

"I don't know what to believe," I admitted to Baz, feeling adrift.

"You can trust Lex." Baz's voice resonated within me again.

My eyes widened. *"I just talked to you without talking."*

He chuffed in amusement. *"Because you relaxed."* His cobalt eyes sparkled with something akin to mischief mixed with genuine affection.

But I wasn't relaxed. In awe, yes, but the thought of that Lurker trying to kidnap me yesterday gave me chills. The man in my head who wasn't Baz sent a different kind of worry through my core. Not to mention Vallen and Maros, the bastards who killed my mom, were still out there breathing.

"Lex, could you give us a minute alone?" I asked, shading my eyes from the sun with my hands.

As he turned to leave, Baz's body went rigid. He moved closer to shield me when a piercing shriek tore through the sky. I fell to my knees, covering my ears.

"Ivy's coming," he bobbed his head and used his body to cover mine.

Ignoring the cold, I took off my shirt, then wrapped it around my head to block out the deafening shrieks, but not a chance. They grew stronger with each passing second, and I covered my ears. The ground rumbled beneath us, sending rocks and debris flying into the air.

"Crawl under me!" directed Baz.

I fell to my knees and tucked myself under Baz's stomach, lying flat as he stood over me. Through trembling fingers, I looked into the sky and saw storm clouds churning like the formation of a hurricane.

My heart felt like it was going to burst out of my chest, and my eyes expanded like saucers as I turned to look at Lex. "What in the name of all that's holy is that?"

"It's the Baneful!" Lex confirmed over the incessant noise, his eyes never leaving the sky.

Jossy and Vincent leaped off the porch, and in less than two strides, all the angels surrounded me. They were ready for a counterattack, but the wards held strong this time. Just then, the sounds faded into the distance, and the clouds returned to normal. I lifted my head as a sleek black car drove up the gravel road.

It screeched to a stop a few yards from where we were, and Ivy tumbled out of the open door. She fell onto her back, coughing. What looked like spatters of blood covered her shirt, and one eye was swollen shut. I didn't know what could cause that much damage to a powerful angel, but I imagined it was a powerful one.

Maros.

Without hesitating, I rolled out from under Baz and ripped my shirt from my head as I sprinted to Ivy's side. Panic rose in my chest at the sight of her injuries, and I prayed they were not as bad as they looked.

My face twisted as I shouted, "What happened?"

Ivy clutched her throat as terror flashed in her eyes. I knelt beside her and brushed pieces of blood-soaked hair away from her face.

Coughing, she rolled onto her side and spat out a tooth. "You don't have much time," she stated before her gaze shifted past me and focused on Vincent. "Maros is coming for Noa."

Baz stretched his mouth wide and howled a primal cry that echoed off the mountains, then was joined by the distant cawing of crows. Lex and Jossy dashed over to me then hoisted Ivy up, each of them supporting one of her arms. She had endured a beating from that sadistic bastard.

Vincent's brows snapped together as he waved for Nevaeh. "Get Nakoma here, please. And fast!" He turned to Jossy and Lex. "Let me have her."

My eyes filled with tears as I scrambled to my feet and followed them. "Is she going to die?" I questioned Vincent.

Vincent avoided looking at me as he carried Ivy across the path, his face warped with rage. "If the injuries are bad enough and she doesn't get enough time to heal, then yes," he yelled back to me.

My body locked up as I wrapped my arms around myself. "This is wrong on so many levels. Vallen… he caused this!" I shouted.

"Jossy, follow me," Vincent ordered, his tone clipped.

I rushed after them, not wanting to leave Ivy when Lex stepped in front of me with my flannel shirt.

"You dropped this," he said, then followed Vincent and Jossy into the house.

As I slipped into the shirt again, someone who resembled a younger version of Nevaeh appeared on the porch. I hesitated when my eyes caught a glimpse of a rifle in her hands. She smiled and raised a hand, but it didn't matter. I needed to help

Ivy. When I reached the top of the steps, Nevaeh stood in front of me with a camouflaged coat.

"Take it," she offered, then placed her hand on the small of my back and guided me closer to the other woman.

I pressed the jacket against my chest and shook my head. "No, Ivy needs me."

"What Ivy needs is for you to be safe, Noa. And that is not in this cabin," she insisted.

Baz stood on the other side of the railing waiting for me, his eyes following my every move. *You're exposed here, Noa; an easy target.*

A rusted truck with a significant dent in the front fender came around the corner at a ridiculous speed. As the truck pulled to a stop, Nakoma jumped out with a medical kit in his hand. He left it running, but offered a slight nod as he rushed into the cabin. I whirled around to follow him, but Nevaeh side-stepped in front of me.

"Let's go," Baz demanded, then sauntered toward the truck.

"I can't leave her," I argued while keeping my feet planted on the porch. "Besides, the wards are fine. Nothing got through them."

"You need to get out of the open, then we can assess the situation." His tone left no room to argue. *"If it's safe, you can come back."*

"Noa, this is Ena. My granddaughter and Nakoma's sister." Nevaeh gestured to the woman who now held the gun with a finality that was almost unsettling. A flicker of apprehension flashed across my mind—one more stranger thrown into this chaotic mix.

Ena's smooth raven-braided hair brushed the top of her butt

as she searched the sky. "Nice to meet you," she said with bright eyes.

"Ena's going to take you to my house," Nevaeh advised. "My husband, Dawson, is waiting there."

My best friend needed me, and I needed her. My skin flushed, and my feet turned to concrete bricks.

"Please," I begged, with an ache ripping through my heart.

"This is new to you, Noa, but angels can endure more than any human," Nevaeh assured me with a soft smile. "She'll be okay. Besides," she added, "you want answers, don't you?"

I sniffed and wiped tears from my cheek. "Yes."

"Then go. Trust your gut, Noa." She raised a brow and gestured her head over her shoulder.

Without realizing it, I was somehow standing on the passenger side of the running truck. Baz nudged me with his snout. *"I'll lead the way."*

I climbed inside as Ena secured the rifle to the gun rack above our heads, then drove us toward the back of the property. I couldn't shake off the image in my head of Ivy's battered figure. Guilt gnawed at me; she had suffered because of me, because of a world I didn't know or understand.

Maros was coming, and I didn't care how powerful he was. I had to stop him. Especially, since he started attacking the ones I loved. If he could do that much damage to an angel, then what else was he capable of doing?

It was evident he only kept Ivy alive to deliver that message. And as much as I hurt leaving her behind, Nevaeh wanted me to know something that seemed like Vincent wasn't ready to share.

CHAPTER 17

We drove until the cabin was out of sight. Anytime the wind picked up or the rocks popped up under the truck, I focused on Baz running ahead of us to ease my fears. Ena had a shotgun, but she was still human. The wards seemed okay, but I didn't trust that to last either.

I looked out of my window up into the sky. "How do the wards work, Ena?" I asked.

"Oh. Um." Her brows rose as she hesitated.

"Are you not allowed to tell me?" I inclined my head in her direction, keeping the hunting jacket close to my chest.

"I'm not," she said, her voice disappointed. "Vincent determines who can know the specifics."

I sank back against the seat. "Interesting," I sighed. "So, not all of your family knows about everything going on here, then?"

She shook her head. "They know about the angels, but the wards don't extend into our land because the demons won't go there," she said with a grateful smile. "Besides, most of us don't see a need to get involved in angel business."

I shook my head, laughter tinged with nervousness escaping my lips. "I understand if you can't share details about the wards, but I hope they don't weaken again."

Ena gripped the steering wheel tighter, her smile faltering. "Don't worry. Vincent made sure of that last night."

"Yeah, he mentioned that." I adjusted my body against the door and prayed that Nakoma would heal Ivy. Dawson should have an update when we got there. I inhaled, filling my lungs with air, and then said, "Vincent said you would help with the ceremony to save my soul. What will you do?"

She hesitated before speaking, then her words almost got lost in the hum of the engine. "The ceremony... it's a sacred rite, and Vincent... he keeps the details shrouded in mystery. Even from me," Ena admitted, her eyes flickering with uncertainty.

"Are you serious?" My annoyance spilled out.

"He believes that the less we know, the safer we are from prying eyes and dark forces." As Ena navigated the winding road, her gaze turned distant. "He's careful."

Vincent seemed paranoid, and his mysterious ways were starting to wear thin on me. Ena's evasive answers only stoked my impatience. I leaned my head against the window, staring out at the passing landscape.

The dirt road curved to the right before splitting into two paths. One led into the woods, but a locked cattle gate blocked the entry. The other continued on toward the mountains, fading into the distance. We pulled up in front of the gate, and Ena shifted the truck into park.

"We walk from here," she said, and turned off the engine.

"Ena," I pressed, my voice firm, "I need to know more about this ceremony. How can I prepare if I'm kept in the dark?"

She glanced at me with a troubled expression. "Noa, you have to trust Vincent. He knows what he's doing."

"I want to," I replied with sincerity, "but this is about my soul." I won't sit back and let angels or anyone dictate my fate."

Silence shrouded us as Ena stared at the barbed wire fence that twisted between the tree line. Was it meant to guard against real threats, or was it an illusion of safety? Sunbeams filtered through clouds overhead but failed to pierce the chill settling over me. I slipped into Nevaeh's coat, letting its warmth envelop me as I wrapped it around myself.

"Hey," Ena offered in a soft voice. "As soon as I learn anything new, I'll tell you."

"I appreciate that." I nodded, but something in me said I should find more answers on my own.

A slush puddle full of mud greeted me as I opened the door, and I leaped over it. Ena hurried around the front of the truck, and I stumbled into her, but she caught me before I fell.

"Thanks." Embarrassment flooded my cheeks as she handed me a pair of crumpled brown gloves. I turned them over to inspect them. "What are these for?"

She gestured to the locked gate, also wrapped in thick rope. "To help me open that."

The gloves were thick. The type a rancher would use to snag up barbed wire fences. The same fences installed throughout the forest around us.

Ena waved me in her direction as I slipped them onto my hands. She showed me where to stand and instructed me to pull on a rope fastened to the middle of the gate. She pushed from the other side.

Baz exhaled a deep breath and shook his jowls. The loose skin flapped as he attempted to shake off the weight of worry that hung in the air.

"I'm going to circle the outskirts and meet you on the other side," he declared. *"Stay close to Ena."*

"You can't leave me!" I protested, my pitch rising like a string ready to snap.

Baz took a step closer to bridge the distance between us, then lowered his head to look into my eyes. *"She can protect you, Noa,"* he reassured me, nodding in her direction.

I glanced at Ena. She was sifting through a retractable belt loop key ring to find the right key to unlock the gate. Unfortunately, when I looked back, Baz had sauntered off, nowhere in sight.

"Don't want to annoy you or seem impatient," I interrupted her as I strode toward the gate. "But Baz took off," I said, exasperation trickling from each word.

She threw her hands in the air, losing her place on the keychain. "That damn wolf has been nothing but a pain in the ass since he got here."

I shot her a curious glance. "How so?"

Ena's eyebrows pinched as she searched for the key again. "He's gone for all hours and disappears without telling anyone."

I squinted under the cover of my hand as I looked around the property. "Maybe he's been getting familiar with his new form and the lay of the land."

"Who knows?" Ena shrugged with a sigh and found the right key.

I exhaled a deep breath and walked over to her. "How far is the house from here?" I asked.

She looked at me over her shoulder, jiggling the key into the lock. "Right through here," she said with raised brows. "And you're not annoying me, by the way. You've been thrust into this world without any warning. I probably would've shit myself had I not grown up with it either."

My jaw dropped at her candor. "Really?"

"Hell, yeah," she continued and jerked her fingers hard to the left. The lock popped open, and she smiled.

"It's wild and a little freaky," I replied, feeling the gravity of my situation bearing down on me. "Like a mythical legend, except it's flesh-and-bone reality now."

She nodded, a flicker of pride igniting in her eyes. "Most days it is," she said, pausing for a moment as a shadow crossed her features. "Except my mom doesn't think so."

"Why not?" I asked, curiosity piqued.

Ena sighed as her fingers wove through a loose strand of hair that had slipped across her forehead. "She saw it as a burden rather than a blessing. She couldn't handle the expectations and the responsibilities," she murmured with a hint of dissatisfaction. "Living under a spotlight felt to her like always being watched and having to uphold this image."

"Not to mention all the secrecy," I interjected, sensing the weight of her mother's discontent on her shoulders. "So she never helped out here?" I pressed, wanting to understand this legacy that both fascinated and haunted her.

"She passed on it, but I found it fascinating," Ena confirmed, with a sparkle taking over her eyes. "When I got back from nursing school, I had my own ceremony with them."

My skin tingled, and a shiver of delight raced through my veins at the thought of another human learning to navigate this world.

"And when I took the angel's sacred offering," she continued with her eyes closed. "It was a weird experience and I had a panic attack."

She clapped her hands together and then blew into them for good luck. Pulling hard on the gate, she said, "Lex helped me through it, though. Help me open this, will you?"

Ena showed me how to wrap my hand around a thick rope hanging from a pipe in the center of the gate. When she gave me the cue, I tugged hard with my hand in the loop. We both groaned, and the gate opened a few inches more.

"Are you allowed to tell me about the offering?" I squeezed my eyes shut as my strength tested me.

"They left you with me because I can help protect you, so I'd say yes." She grunted as she pulled harder. "I received the essence of an angel."

My grip loosened on the rope, and I straightened, curiosity blooming within me. "Vincent mentioned the essence to save Ivy. What exactly is it?"

"Keep pulling, Noa," she said, her voice taut like the rope in our hands. "That rock closer to you," she pointed with one hand, "kick it as hard as you can while pulling at the same time."

Securing my hands in the coarse rope again, I tugged with all my strength. It held me while I lunged at a stone wedged between the crumbling dirt and the gate. I struck it many times with my steel-toed hiking boots.

"You don't open this gate often, do you?" I asked with a ragged breath.

Ena's forehead creased as she shook her head. "Not anymore. And to answer your other question, angel essence is the very blood flowing through their veins."

My eyes widened at this revelation. "Fascinating," I murmured, my mind racing to comprehend that detail.

"And if depleted," she continued, her voice dropping to a rough whisper, "they die. Like us, but it takes longer." Her gaze met mine—piercing and profound—offering a glimpse into a mystical world I had only begun to grasp.

"Why would they give it away?" I asked, dropping the rope.

I walked over to the rock and used the tip of the boot to make an indentation around it. Ena didn't complain, which surprised me. Due to the way she leaned against the gate, I could see she needed a break.

"The angels need a human connection to our land," Ena noted. "It all comes together in their formula so that the ceremonies will work."

After scooping out what dirt I could from around the rock, we summoned one final burst of exertion to wrench the gate open. I wedged my boot under it and overcame the stubborn rock's tenacious grip on the soil.

"Finally!" she exclaimed with fervor and punched the air.

My mouth curved into a smile. "Not bad."

Wrestling with the gate left my skin flushed and damp. I peeled off the gloves and jacket, then swiped my gritty hands across my jeans. The brisk wind kissed my skin, and I closed my eyes, savoring the moment until Ena's voice stirred me.

"You gotta help me close this thing from the other side, Noa." She laughed, nearly breathless.

"Aren't you forgetting something?" I panted as I looked back toward the truck, nervous that she had forgotten to grab the gun.

"We don't need it through here, and by the time we reach Dawson's, we'll have all the protection we need."

I decided to trust her, so I laid my jacket and gloves on the rocky ground to help close the gate. Once we tied it up and padlocked it again, I felt trapped. We were two vulnerable humans surrounded by a forest brimming with guardian wolves and other wild animals.

CHAPTER 18

"Let's move on," she said, urging me forward with an outstretched hand.

I took a deep breath and followed her along the worn dirt road. Its once-distinct tire ruts were now obscured beneath lush grass and tangled underbrush. Demons could be anywhere, and even if the wards had returned, they had failed before, meaning it could happen again.

Not to mention real wolves that could jump out at any moment. Even with angel essence, how could Ena, another human, protect us?

"So, the essence helps you perform ceremonics," I stated for confirmation. "Does it let you do anything else?"

"A few rules," Ena declared, ignoring my questions and treading ahead.

My pace now matched hers, and she removed her work gloves and shoved them into her back pocket. I threw my head back and groaned when I realized I had left mine back at the gate. She produced another pair of gloves from the inside lining of her coat.

These were different and made of a thin rubber-like material to match the russet hue of her flawless skin. A group of three small bumps gathered on the tip of each finger. She pulled them on, then peered over at me.

"What in the world are these?" I asked, taking her hands without asking, flipping them over to inspect them.

"Silicone gloves." A coy smile spread across her face, and she continued forward.

"If you're going to wear them, at least tell me why," I implored her.

"You asked if I could do anything else by having angel essence, so I'm going to show you." She stopped and faced me, taking a moment to study my reaction. "Many people think we are magical. We're not." Her lips pursed as she eyed me like she was making sure I was willing to listen. "We are spiritual, and we have a deep appreciation for the universe and all beings."

I acknowledged with a nod. "Yes. Of course."

"What we do and how we celebrate our existence is important to our heritage. It keeps our ways and culture alive." Her eyes glinted as she stared at me.

"Absolutely." I beamed. "We should admire and respect it all."

"Nakoma and I are both medicine people. But I can't perform the ceremonies for the angels without their essence," she continued, worry crossing her face.

"What is it that you do for the angels?" I asked with a flutter of excitement in my stomach.

Her eyes lit up with pride. "With guidance from the spirits

and the angels, I created a ceremonial bundle to use during the wolf ceremony."

"I've heard about sacred bundles for Native celebrations."

Ena shook her head. "Sacred bundles are for my people. The one I put together is not the same, but it is similar and sacred for the angels."

I swallowed hard, my throat felt dry, and I blinked as my eyes stung. "You helped save Baz."

Ena's big smile illuminated her face. "It's beautiful to watch the transformation every time it's done." She raised her gloved hands, allowing the thin material to catch the light. "And these keep me hidden," she said.

My eyes narrowed as I ran my fingers across the thin material. "These are what, silicone?"

"There's an old priest who has lived on the ranch for decades," Ena explained. "He's also a scientist. And since my abilities produce an energy that's like runway lights for demons, he and Nakoma made these gloves to mute that energy."

As she spoke, I couldn't help but reflect on the energy in me and how it sent out a locator signal to both angels and demons. I let go of her hands and took a few steps back. "What other powers do you have, Ena?"

She grinned with infectious enthusiasm. "I can manipulate the air for one. I call them enhancements."

I laughed softly, a sound that danced through the air. "So that's why we didn't need the gun."

"To some extent, yeah." She walked down the path to Nevaeh and Dawson's house. I watched her go as she rattled on about the wards and the cover that the trees provided.

A moment of envy flooded my chest. Her beauty and her

intelligence were captivating, a stark contrast to my own sense of purposelessness. Ena embodied her heritage and powers with ease, whereas I still struggled to find my place in the world.

I was a curse from a petulant angel who was hell-bent on destroying humans. He, or the demons, were going to use me as ammunition to end us all if I didn't find a way out of this. Once I caught up to her, we walked in silence for a few minutes and I began to think about how much of a family Ena and my friends had become.

My relationship with Jossy, Ivy, and Lex wasn't genuine like I'd thought. They befriended me to see if I had divine secrets tucked away inside, and now, what was I to them? Not only Vincent, but Jossy and Lex made it clear that my safety was a priority so the world wouldn't go boom.

"It must be nice to have a connection to who you are and where you come from," I said, wanting to delve deeper into what she knew about this world.

"Sure, but learning that I could manipulate air wasn't easy," she mentioned with a whisper. "But aren't you here to figure out those things for yourself, too?"

"I'm not sure how far I'll get if I don't get my soul back, especially with demons after me. Not to mention this guy in my head—"

She stopped walking and pivoted with her palm up. "What guy is in your head, Noa? Nobody said anything about that."

Realization hit me straight in the chest because I got too comfortable with her. "Forget I mentioned it, Ena. Please." I walked ahead, but she caught up and grabbed my arm.

"I need details," she pressed. "With Maros and his demons attacking us, I need to know who's in your head."

Frustrated, I grabbed at my hair and let out a groan. "I don't know. And I haven't told the others, so you can't say anything."

"You didn't tell Baz?" she asked, giving me a curious look.

"I haven't had a chance. Two days ago I was going to my birthday party and now I'm in the middle of fucking Oz." A sharp jolt of pain shot through my skull, and I doubled over. With wide eyes, I turned to Ena and choked out, "We need to run."

She stood tall, and her expression turned grim. "Why, Noa?"

"He's coming," I admitted as shakes ran through my body.

"Who's coming?" Ena looked around with her palms out in front of her. She began circling me, darting her eyes in every direction.

My scar throbbed, and my mouth twisted as I strained. "The man in my head, and unless you want me to pass out right here, we need to move now."

I took off running at breakneck speed through the forest, Ena struggling to keep up behind me. The memories of a cherry blossom tree and a raging waterfall flashed before my eyes like a warning sign, igniting sparks of fear in my mind. With every stride, I pushed myself harder, determined to outrun this terror. But as we approached a fallen tree and tangled brush blocking our path, the fear set in.

"On it!" Ena called out and thrust her hands forward, launching the tree deep into the woods.

She'd somehow summoned a gust of wind so strong that it picked up scattered underbrush, giving us a cleaner path out of there. We rounded a small curve as I continued to blink through images flooding my mind. As soon as I stepped into a wide-open clearing, mowed into a perfect circle encased in a line of trees, the images stopped.

The pain in my scar subsided. Uncertain of what it meant, I continued to run out into the field until I finally slowed down to a jog.

"What gives, Noa?" Ena ran up next to me, then stopped to lean over. She hugged her stomach while taking short, deep breaths.

"Not sure." I shook my head as I scanned the clearing. "I don't feel anything now."

Bent over, she planted her hands above her knees. "You," she panted, "don't?"

I shook my head as I looked over at an old, weathered totem pole standing tall in the middle of the clearing. Each part was hard to make out from where we stood. From what I gathered when I examined it, there was a bear paw and a fish carved into it.

Three rows of wooden benches and rocks fanned out in a half-circle with an aisle down the middle. To my left stood a white house remodeled from a two-story barn. It had a red metal roof and a bricked silo that remained attached to the front right side. The front had floor-to-ceiling glass-paned windows and a red-stained, oversized wooden door that matched the roof.

A loud crack echoed through the forest, and I turned to scan my surroundings. Dark shadows emerged from behind the trees, followed by another. My heart seemed to stop as two intense pairs of piercing lavender eyes fixed on me with predatory focus.

As they stepped out from the cover of the trees, their silver fur shimmered with each slow and calculated move. I tumbled backward into Ena, uncertain of their intentions, but this time I fell into a pile of gravel. My hands broke my fall, and I rolled over, spitting dirt from my mouth.

"Dawson!" Ena cupped her hands around her mouth and called out toward the house. "We're going to need an ice pack!"

"You okay, Noa?" Baz called out to me, his breathing becoming faster with each quickening step.

"I'm fine," I grumbled, feeling more humiliated than anything else. "Your friends scared me."

"Holy night, girl. What the heck is goin' on?" An aged hand appeared in front of my face to help me up.

I looked up at the sun and squinted, not quite able to make out the figure of an elderly man. He wore denim overalls over a white t-shirt, and mud covered his work boots, showing signs of wear and tear.

"On top of freakin' demons and oversized wolves jumping out at me like I'm in a never-ending haunted house? And my best friend fighting for her life," I snapped, grabbing his rough, calloused hand. "I damn near peed my pants in those woods."

"The name's Dawson," he offered, helping me back onto my feet unaffected by my outburst. Then, he gave a curious glance at Ena. "That true about the woods?"

Ena shrugged one shoulder, and her eyes begged me. "Kind of, but you should tell them, Noa."

I looked away, ignoring her intentions and saw the truck we left back at the gate parked next to the house. The front door slammed, and Jossy and Lex came running across the path. Nakoma trailed behind them, offering a wave to the other wolves. My heart was in my throat as worry for Ivy took over any other fears I had.

Baz darted out from between the house and a row of stables to the right.

"What happened to you?" asked Jossy.

"Nothing," I insisted. "How's Ivy?"

Ena shook her head, then blurted, "Yes and no, right, Noa?"

My eyes widened and I chewed my bottom lip. It was a situation I wasn't ready to explain. "Damn, Ena."

"What is she talking about?" Baz asked with a questioning look as he sat down next to me. His head towered at least a foot above mine, and I shrank back into myself.

The other two wolves joined us, and I felt the world closing in on me. I couldn't breathe. Now, I had no choice but to tell them about the man infiltrating my mind since Ena had outed me.

"The pain in my head," I said, annoyance boiling up inside me. "My scar is bothering me and the headaches. There's a reason, and it's—"

"Maros," Lex interrupted me before I even started. I shook my head in disagreement as he pointed to the sky. "Everybody, inside!"

CHAPTER 19

We spun around, eyes magnetized to rolling clouds that erupted with darkness across the sky—a clear omen of Maros's arrival. Time stood still, and there was no room for doubt. We bolted across the field and headed down the gravel path.

Amidst the chaos, I tripped over an unseen rock and tasted the sharp sting of gravel against my lips.

"Fuck!" I was getting tired of running for my life and was ready to end him.

Baz appeared beside me like a protective shadow, his canines bared and ready for attack. Leaning on his sturdy leg, I pulled myself back to standing as a lightning bolt launched Jossy and Lex backward.

Their landings resembled a cat's grace. Massive wings unfurled and shimmered with ethereal colors. Jossy's flaming crimson and gold contrasted beautifully with Lex's marbled slate and ivory. Yet, the sight did little to temper the dread gnawing at my insides.

The storm raged overhead like an angry beast, and when I peered over at Nakoma and Dawson, they struggled up the porch steps against the onslaught. My heart sank as I wondered how we would survive this. But Ena turned and planted herself firmly on the ground beneath her. She raised her hands, fingers swirling through the air as if capturing invisible threads.

Gathering momentum, Ena channeled the very essence of nature, drawing upon its energy. Her unexpected display of power briefly countered Maros's destructive winds. It allowed Nakoma and Dawson a chance to escape inside the house. I looked at Baz, who nodded at me in reassurance.

"I thought Maros couldn't get through the wards!" I yelled, using the wolves to block out the wind.

"He can't! Unless…" Baz's voice trailed off, his eyes narrowing and a ground-shaking growl rippling from all three wolves. He swiveled back to me. "There's a traitor among us."

Before I could process his insinuation, a voice boomed from above as Vincent and Nevaeh appeared at the edge of the tree line that had been our refuge a minute ago. My mind raced to Ivy. Where was she in all this chaos? A cold dread strangled me, and I clutched my chest.

"Now that we're all assembled!" Maros's words dripped with a sinister glee. A maniacal laugh punctuated each syllable and echoed through the clearing like a haunting melody.

His hands tamed the winds as he loomed over us. A shadowy figure clad in ornate ebony and cardinal robes that swirled around him like a cyclone of smoke. His ruby-red eyes bore into mine—gleaming with superior amusement.

"You are quite the spectacle, Noa," he grinned with malice, as if he were savoring an unseen feast. "I do regret your little stunt yesterday—taking out my daughter—but don't worry, pet, we will have our reckoning, you and I."

Nausea surged within me, and the wolves formed a protective barrier to guard me from Maros's gaze. But through a narrow gap between their bristling bodies, his menacing face was still in my view. I noticed the way his hooked nose twitched, a telltale sign of his frustration simmering below the surface, and realization struck me.

"He can't step on the ground," I whispered, tugging at Baz's leg.

"We know," Baz replied, his voice low and edged with impatience. *"It's sacred land."*

"Then what is he doing?" My heart raced, each beat echoing louder than the last in my ears.

"What demons do best. Playing twisted games," Baz snapped, the weight of his emotions evident from having to hold back and not intervene.

"Can't we do something?" I pleaded with him, worry crawling up my throat.

Baz's snout lifted as he scanned the sky above us. I followed his gaze and felt my stomach drop as I saw them—creatures lurking in the clouds, their shapes a grotesque fusion of bats and dragons.

It was impossible to discern their features from this distance, but the sight of their elongated hind legs was terror-inducing. Each time they dove to attack the invisible shield, their talons screeched like banshees. It made my entire body recoil.

"Maros brought reinforcements and we're outnumbered," Baz added as he looked up, tracking the sky.

Sprinting back into the frenzy, Nakoma now held a sleek silver bow that almost matched his height. Maros looked down on Nakoma as if he were a nuisance he could flick away. Maros lifted his lips into a wicked smirk, revealing a hint of his sharp teeth as Vincent strode into the middle of the field with assurance.

"Oh, it's the hero cherub I came to see," Maros said, his voice dripping with mockery, as if savoring the moment like fine wine.

Vincent's eyes blazed with fury, threatening to consume everything around him.

He stared up at Maros, searching for any hint of his intentions behind the demon's vacant gaze. "Whatever you're thinking of doing, Maros, don't."

Maros wagged his finger and shot back with a flourish that echoed across the field. "Afraid I'm going to spill your little secret, Vinny?" he probed.

"You won't make it out of here alive today," Vincent spat, hatred igniting within him as he unfurled his wings and rose to meet Maros mid-air.

"We'll see about that." Maros crossed his legs and took a theatrical bow. The angel with the eye patch from breakfast appeared below. He was carrying someone in his arms.

My mind raced as I tried to piece together what was happening. Was Vincent lying to us? Or was Maros setting him up? Either way, I couldn't stay hidden anymore.

Baz growled low in his throat, his fur spiking in fury. *"That son of a bitch,"* Baz barked. *"We should rip Jax apart right here."*

My chest clenched, and it felt like someone had stolen my breath. "Is it Ivy?" I cried out, trying to push through the wolves.

"No," he confirmed. "It's someone else. Now, stay still."

I placed my hands on Baz's side, unable to contain the frustration of my inability to see.

"Move!" I demanded, and a flash of static electricity shot through my fingers.

Baz jumped and shook his head as the other wolves glanced at me with a look of annoyance in their eyes.

"What was that, Noa?" Baz's confusion was clear in his question.

I stared down at my hands for an answer. "I don't know," I admitted. "I only wanted to see what was happening for myself."

Baz chuffed in amusement and stood beside me as he focused back on Jax walking across the field. My eyes darted back and forth between Vincent and Jax.

As Jax approached the center of the field with a woman whose life now dangled by a fragile thread, Vincent's wings gathered strength behind him like a storm. Jax dropped the body to the ground with the casual disdain of flicking away an insect. The soft thud of her form hitting the earth echoed in the stillness, and I swear Vincent stopped breathing.

The entirety of his skin drained of all color as he retreated backward from Maros. Vincent turned and dove toward the woman's body, hitting his knees, and agony took over. Jax stepped back and held out his arms with a smug smile across his face, proud of having helped to end the woman's life.

Out of the corner of my eye, Nakoma released an arrow at Jax. It sliced through the icy air with a piercing whistle before embedding itself deep within him. Brilliant flames now engulfed Jax. They licked at his flesh, seeking to consume him. Then, he turned to ash before us. His bones and wings remained, like a forgotten myth.

"No worries, pretty boy," Maros taunted. "I have more where he came from. But for now," he hummed and gestured a kiss to Nakoma. "I'll let you have that one."

Vincent's wings collapsed like wilted petals. He lifted the woman's head, wiping away the blood from her mouth with jittery fingers. Nevaeh ran to him, and her hands flew to her mouth with a gasp.

Maros laughed at Vincent as he spiraled in the air. "Did you honestly think I'd hand over half of everything to you?" He rose higher toward the top of the trees, clapping erratically. "Not to mention that I believed you wanted to share it all with me. What a naive fool you are!"

"Is Vincent in on this, Baz?" I asked him, terrified of the answer.

His tone was serious as he replied, *"It could be a ploy. Remember that."*

Maros reached his hand out and pulled at the air as if it bore an invisible enemy. Whatever it was, he grasped it by the throat with his talons. Then, a thunderous crash shook the earth as dark tendrils of smoke erupted around him, curling back toward us like living shadows. Baz and the other wolves stood tall, barking into the air and ready to attack.

"Stand your ground, Lex!" Jossy's voice cut through the chaos across the field.

Dawson stepped onto the porch with an assault rifle slung over his body and aimed at Maros. Ena remained ready if needed. When I looked back at Maros, he raised his arm high and, with a snap of his free hand, Ivy appeared ensnared in his grip.

"I'm keeping this one for good measure," he purred, clutching her tighter.

"Ivy!" I shrieked. Without thinking, I ran for her, Baz on my heels.

Before Baz could reach me, Lex materialized next to me and then enfolded me in his wings.

"Stop, Noa!" Lex pleaded in my ear. "You can't help her now, and this is what Maros wants."

"Then let him take me," I said, sobbing against his chest.

Ivy thrashed erratically, her wings flapping uselessly against Maros's unshakeable arm. I balled Lex's shirt in my hands as I struggled against the urge not to run to her again. Though Ivy's wings were on display, they remained motionless, pinned to her sides.

Ivy released a guttural scream as she slashed at Maros's face, her sharp nails glancing off his skin, leaving him untouched. Jossy and Lex exchanged a glance. Then, Lex released me. He and Jossy flew up, circling Maros like vultures ready to descend.

"Notice anything, boys?" Maros grinned while stroking Ivy's midnight wings. She'd turned entirely dark. "Don't worry, I'll take good care of her for you," he snarled.

"You're going to die!" Jossy bellowed, then twirled in the air like an acrobat. He dove, slicing at Maros with the razor-sharp edge of his wing.

Maros dodged him, using Ivy as a shield, and a gash opened across her stomach. Scarlet droplets began to fall like rain from the sky as Jossy landed in a puddle of her blood. Lex reached for his neck, but sensing him, Maros used his free hand to strike him, sending Lex tumbling to the ground.

"And when I'm done with you, brother," Maros cackled down at Vincent, "I'll pick off your toy soldiers here, one by one."

"But I'll save my favorite morsel for last. She'll bleed for me, and I'll relish every secret I wring from her frail human mind."

Maros blew me a sardonic kiss. I shuddered with revulsion as his malevolent laughter rang across the ranch. He snapped his fingers, and they vanished without a trace.

The wolves unleashed a murderous howl. Baz stayed close to me as the other two prowled the forest's edge. Vincent fretted over the mystery woman's lifeless body, and the wards continued to flicker around us.

We were all exposed and vulnerable. My eyes darted about, uncertain of where to look or how to breathe.

Nakoma fashioned his bow across his back to a sling, then ran to Jossy, wrapping him in a fierce embrace. Their lips met, fusing with an intensity that threatened to consume them both. A bittersweet revelation for me among all our pain.

And as much as I wanted to share in Jossy's happiness, my world had fallen to ruin in mere minutes. Ena and Dawson ran toward Vincent and Nevaeh, who were sitting around the mostly dead woman with the other wolves. Nakoma and Jossy released each other and sauntered toward the group.

"We need to get you someplace safe," Lex urged, taking my hand as his wings released me. "This is too dangerous and we don't know who's turned on us."

My body stiffened and I trembled with fear. "But Ivy. She just—"

I dropped his hand and stumbled toward Vincent and Nevaeh. The answers I'd longed for were here and staring me in the face. Taunting me to make a move before they did. Challenge accepted.

"Think about Jack and Claire, Noa," Lex called after me, staying on my heels. "Maros will go after them."

"No." I stopped and turned to him, placing my hands on his chest. Shaking my head, I added, "I'm staying right here, and I will fight this."

Then I joined everyone else in the middle of the field. Endless thoughts looped in my mind. What was Ivy's true motive? Did she join Maros because I couldn't love her the way she needed me to? Ivy couldn't have done it alone. She needed help, or Vincent forced her to do it.

Although Jax betrayed Vincent and the rest of his family, there had to be more who knew about the attack. I glanced down at Vincent, who now cried over the woman dying in front of him. Something about him and this woman, only he and Nevaeh seemed to know, stirred my suspicion.

I knelt on the ground to get a better look at her.

CHAPTER 20

Dawson inched closer and wove an arm around Nevaeh's waist, his rifle now dropped to the side.

"Who is it, sweetheart?" His voice was low, but the concern etched on his face spoke volumes, a protective instinct flaring to life.

Nevaeh lifted her head. Her tear-filled eyes met his for a moment. Then, she buried her face in his side, her sobs muffled against his shirt. "It's Sasha," she whimpered.

"But that would mean—" Dawson's voice trailed off as realization washed over him, leaving an unsettling void in its wake.

"Impossible," Jossy challenged, standing close to Nevaeh as if his presence could somehow change the reality we faced.

My grandmother was alive.

Sasha wasn't young, but she wasn't old either. Frozen in time, wisdom flickered behind her once-bright eyes. Yet now, her eyes were fading—losing their light.

Blood seeped from her lips, painting a stark contrast against her pale complexion. Vincent situated one arm underneath her and pulled her close, his head hanging low in despair. He stroked her cheek with trembling fingers as if trying to soothe away the pain that refused to relent.

"I'm so sorry, my love," Vincent cried, anguish lacing his words. "It wasn't supposed to happen like this."

Baz lowered his head close to my ear, making it look as though he was inspecting the scene.

"Noa, I know you need me and this isn't the best time," he said. *"But stay close to Ena and Lex."*

Fear gripped my body like a vice, and I whirled around to face him as another one of the wolves got up and walked over to us.

"Where the hell are you going?" I asked in a terrified whisper.

"I'm taking Seraphina to gather help. I won't be long." They retreated backward into the woods, their movements deliberate and cautious as they slipped away without drawing attention. *"Stay here,"* he insisted one last time, then disappeared into the shadows.

The angels looked like they'd seen a ghost as they studied Sasha—faces pale and eyes wide with disbelief. The one wolf who remained let out a horrific cry of anguish that reverberated through the air before lying down beside her. Nakoma turned without a word and sprinted back toward the house.

The blood drained from my face as I fought to process what was unfolding before me. Dawson pulled a pistol from the holster on his hip, its metallic glint catching the dim light. He aimed it at the back of Vincent's head with precision.

The danger dawned on him too late. Vincent's gaze fixed on Sasha's limp form, a haunting image I couldn't take my eyes off.

"Wake up," Vincent pleaded under his breath. "You can't be gone."

Dawson's knuckles turned white as he gripped the gun tighter, ready to squeeze the trigger.

"Drop the gun, Dawson," Jossy shouted in desperation.

Dawson didn't move. He stood guarding a threat I'd yet to see. "Not gonna happen, son," he replied with sturdy defiance.

A gurgling noise erupted from Sasha's mouth. Blood gushed up like a crimson sea, and she choked.

"Turn her on her side!" My words echoed through the clearing.

Worry guided my hands as I carefully grabbed Sasha's arms and legs to flip her over. I sat next to her and rubbed her back. Ena rushed to help make Sasha comfortable. Her brow furrowed as if willing life back into Sasha's frail form.

Moments later, Nakoma arrived with a medical kit clutched in his hands. Ena checked Sasha's vitals—her fingers dancing over the pulse points—then shook her head with a grave expression. Each shallow, ragged breath Sasha dragged in sounded like the last one she'd ever take.

Sasha strained to squeeze my hand. It was a faint warmth in the encroaching darkness, but her body was giving in to whatever fate awaited her. Nakoma drew up a syringe from a vial of clear fluid, its contents almost invisible in the fading light.

"It's a sedative," he offered as he injected a shot into her arm. A small act of mercy before rejoining Jossy by his side.

The end was coming for Sasha. But it felt too slow. Each

moment was an eternity of dread and despair. My stomach knotted as tears spilled down my cheeks.

"How is she even alive?" I pleaded, searching for answers in the faces surrounding me.

Vincent's face twisted in terror as he leaped up, ignoring Dawson's gun trained on him. He grabbed fistfuls of his own hair in torment as if trying to pull himself back from some precipice of despair. I didn't know if a gun could kill angels or if bullets had any power against them, but Dawson seemed convinced. His pistol never wavered from Vincent's trembling frame.

"Start talkin', Vincent," Dawson demanded with an edge of fury. "Is what Maros said true?"

"Dawson, lower the gun, please," Jossy begged. He stepped forward as if attempting to close an irreconcilable gap between them. "I'm sure Vincent can explain everything."

Dawson's eyes remained fixed on Vincent. "Oh, he'll spill his guts," he hissed, then pushed past Jossy, placing the gun against Vincent's chest. "How's a woman who killed herself the same night Scarlett died, layin' here now?"

My head snapped up as a surge of clarity hit me. Lying protectively over Sasha's lifeless body was the other wolf, and it dawned on me that he was her guardian. Somehow, he remained here while Vincent kept Sasha alive.

Vincent cursed. Strangled breaths escaped him as his eyes narrowed to slits. They were feral.

"You won't kill me, Dawson," he spat.

"Try us," Nevaeh challenged. She drew her own pistol from its holster with practiced ease and pointed it at Vincent. "Sasha took her own life the night of the fire," she said. "What is this blasphemy?"

Lex stepped behind me, expanding his wings wide enough to cast a shadow across where we all stood. "Vincent won't touch you, Noa," he assured me.

The Earth began to tilt as understanding set in that Maros was telling the truth. It was Vincent who'd wanted all the power for himself. With my friends watching my back, I pleaded in silence for some way to ease Sasha's passing but found no answer. My words fell flat against cruel fate, and my hope shattered like glass.

As I looked down, Sasha's eyes overflowed with ceaseless tears. "Please. Somebody help her," I begged again.

"We can't, honey." Nevaeh's voice wavered as she spoke to me over her shoulder, but her eyes never left Vincent. "If Vincent did what we suspect, there is only one way to release Sasha from this."

I swallowed against the lump forming in my throat and shifted my gaze toward Vincent.

"What did you do?" I sneered.

Nevaeh stepped closer to Vincent and looked up at him, determined to get answers. "You gave her your essence, didn't you?" she accused him.

Vincent wiped his nose with the back of his hand. "What of it, human?" he snapped back with contempt and spit on her shoes.

"There are rules here, Noa," Dawson said to me, sympathy filling his voice. "If you wanna end Sasha's torment, you have to do it."

"No." I shook my head in denial. "No," I said again. It was the only word I could manage to get past my lips.

"Yes, you do," Vincent stated, devoid of warmth as his body leaned into Dawson's gun. "It's called a blood kill, Noa. Once a human receives an angel's essence—"

"An already dead human, defiled by a dark fallen angel," Dawson remarked with contempt.

"If the angel dies or rejects the human," Vincent continued, "then the only way for the human to die is by the hand of another in the same bloodline."

An unbearable weight seemed to crush my lungs. "You're a monster," I seethed. "You did this, so you finish it!"

Before anyone could react, Vincent released a dagger in my direction. Lex caught it in his hand before it delivered a lethal strike to my heart. Vincent's lip curled back, knowing he didn't expect me to die yet.

"You asked too many questions this morning, and Maros knew you'd be a problem," Vincent snarled.

My lip quivered as I looked up at Lex, betraying my effort to keep my emotions in check. I found myself trapped in an abyss of despair.

My body pulsed with an ache that consumed me, and I cried, "Why would you do this to her?"

He peered down at me, his husky voice cutting through me. "Sasha, not you, should be the one harboring the secrets."

"No," Jossy added, surprised by Vincent's admission. "None of them should."

Vincent scoffed with mocking laughter. "Always a good little soldier boy, aren't you, Jossy? Sasha and I were destined to rule over this godforsaken place and the cesspool of humans. I did what was necessary."

I blinked back hot tears pooling beneath my lashes. "Did she know that, you piece of shit?"

Vincent pointed at Sasha, whose eyes now begged for someone to end her suffering. "I helped her see reason as she died! I saved her from going to hell because she was mine.

"And once I arrested Vallen," Vincent proclaimed, shoving Dawson aside and pointing at me, "I made a deal with Maros for Sasha to take half my essence.

"He and I would divide the secrets. Then he would drag your sorry ass away for the rest of eternity."

Jossy helped Dawson regain his balance, then hung his head in disappointment. Vincent laughed maniacally at the sky while his honor crumbled around him. He was too far gone to care about the consequences.

"All three of you plotted to steal this world, but you cheated your brother," I wheezed as my senses overwhelmed me. "And Ivy. How did she get caught up in your bullshit?"

"She loved you," Vincent criticized as anger painted his face. "But as the selfish human trash that we all know you are, you would never love her back.

He crossed his arms as his eyes narrowed on me, then paused, savoring one final moment of power over my life.

"When Ivy grasped the fact you'd never choose her, the decision for her to join us was easy."

I clenched my fists, my nails digging into my palms, trying to calm the fury boiling within me.

"I'm straight!" I yelled as I squared my shoulders. "But I

loved my friend with everything in me, and you fucking destroyed her."

Lex shook his head and lifted his chin in defiance. He handed me the dagger, which I took willingly now.

"There's no way Ivy went along with this," Lex said. "You threatened her and used her love for Noa against her."

"Believe what makes you feel better," Vincent chided with a smirk on his lips. "But it's the truth. Convincing Noa to do that reading on her birthday was a work of art by Ivy."

"You love my grandmother," I whispered and brushed back Sasha's hair. She began to lose her youthful appearance, transforming into what I imagined a grandmother should look like.

"Loved," he stated, stressing the last syllable. Vincent stomped his foot, enraged, and the ground shuddered with the impact. "She's no good to me now. What are you waiting for, Noa?"

"Fuck you!" I screamed, then stabbed the earth with the dagger.

Scooping Sasha into my arms, I gently rocked her back and forth as reality swallowed me.

Dawson reclaimed his place in front of Vincent with his finger ready to squeeze the trigger. "What does Maros have planned?" he demanded.

"It seems you've mistaken me for someone who actually cares." Vincent unfurled his wings and struck them against the earth with rapid force.

Dawson had no choice but to retreat and shield his eyes from debris as the wind picked up.

As Vincent ascended into the air, he roared down at me. "I will take back what's rightfully mine, Noa!"

Vincent's eyes remained fixed on me with a flicker of temptation, as if he might snatch me away, but he wavered.

"And in case you were curious, Noa, Maros and I lit the fire that killed your mother. But it was Vallen who finished her off," he confessed, his tone cold and lifeless.

Then, he launched into the sky. At that moment, Dawson and Nevaeh fired their guns. A barrage of gunshots filled the air.

"Go on," Vincent yelled over the sound of gunshots, using his powerful wings to deflect the bullets. "End your grandmother's suffering!"

Then he was gone, leaving me clutching Sasha's hand as the truth sank in. She gasped for air, coughing up more blood. I searched around, praying for deliverance from anything in the universe that would listen.

In that moment, Baz appeared from the trees, carrying a mysterious figure dressed all in black. Once close, the stranger dismounted and knelt beside us.

CHAPTER 21

Sasha was on the brink of death. But she wouldn't die, not unless I granted her the mercy of a swift end. Maros and Vincent had ensured I'd be her executioner.

When I peered over at the man Baz brought to us, I saw wrinkles etched like a roadmap on his face. He began praying over Sasha as everyone formed a circle around us.

After he finished speaking, his voice shook. "I need to administer the last rites to her."

"O'Neil, wait." Lex's voice was firm as his eyes flickered a warning.

"I'm giving her what she deserves, young man." Ignoring him, O'Neil moved to sit across from me, taking Sasha's weathered hand in his.

"You're the priest," I said in a hushed whisper. "Can you help her?"

Jossy huffed and rolled his eyes. "This is for show now, old man."

"I'm doing what's right." O'Neil's tone was severe as he glared at Jossy.

"It's a damn insult," Jossy retorted. He grabbed Nakoma's hand, and they walked off toward the house. He turned back one more time to address me. "I detest this for you, Noa. We'll find them both and end this."

Agony seized me as I swayed back and forth, grappling with the air that refused to stay in my lungs. "This. Is. Wrong."

Nevaeh holstered her gun, then settled next to me and Ena, who refused to leave my side when Vincent broke down.

"Noa," she said, trying to hold back her tears. "None of us could've imagined any of this, and Vincent will pay for what he's done, but Sasha—"

A regretful sigh escaped Lex, cutting off Nevaeh. "When word about the fire reached us," he said, his voice heavy with sorrow, "Sasha thought you and your mom both died that night. She couldn't bear it and—" He paused, not needing to say more.

The world spun as I took in Lex's words. Guilt washed over me, twisting my gut. I was prolonging her pain. Anger surged, directed at Vincent for causing this.

Nevaeh placed her hand on my back and whispered, "She already knows where she's going, Noa. You have to—"

The atmosphere suffocated me.

"None of that makes this any easier," I countered.

"You're right, but it's time." Lex pulled the dagger from the ground and clutched it in his palm. He grabbed one of my hands and closed my fingers around the hilt of the dagger. "Take this, please."

"Why does it have to be me?" I cried, the weight of the world threatening to crush me into nothingness.

"She's sufferin' girl." Dawson stood over me, his gun still drawn and uncertain of our safety.

Nevaeh looked up at him, horrified. She shook her head fiercely, her lips pursed in a silent plea for him to stop and not to make the situation any worse.

"Where was he hiding her?" I demanded, shaking with rage.

"We don't know, honey," Nevaeh said with helplessness in her tone.

"Help me do this, Baz," I begged him, pushing back the bile rising in my throat.

With a low, warning growl, Baz made it clear I needed space. He sat next to me, and I leaned into him for support.

"Turn the dagger around, Noa. I won't leave you," he promised.

Sasha's wolf let out a torturous cry, and my body stiffened as I felt it pulsate to my core. Ena offered her hand to Nevaeh so they could both stand.

Nevaeh turned to Dawson and whispered, "Babe, why don't you check the perimeter and prepare the pyre? That's best, considering."

Dawson gave her a soft kiss on the cheek. "Of course, my love," he agreed. Then he looked down at me with regret. "I'm sorry for this, Noa."

I nodded, tears falling onto Sasha. I laid my head on her, and as I pressed my cheek against my grandmother's chest, her heartbeat grew weak beneath my ear. Time was running out for me to end her torture.

The weight of the dagger in my palm grew heavier with each passing moment. I knew what needed to be done, but could

I bring myself to kill my grandmother? Sasha's eyes fluttered open, clouded with pain but still filled with understanding.

Another weak squeeze from her gripped my hand. It was a soft plea for release that shattered what little remained of my resolve. I hesitated while Nevaeh, Ena, and Lex stood with Father O'Neil, who prayed quietly behind us.

Their voices were a steady murmur in the background of my turbulent thoughts. I could feel Sasha's weakening pulse beneath my fingers, her breaths growing shallow and labored.

Every fiber of my being screamed for me to end her suffering. With trembling fingers, I squeezed Sasha's hand one last time and swept stray hairs away from her now-aged face. Her skin was cool to the touch, a stark contrast to the fire burning in her eyes.

"Please forgive me," I said, patting her shoulders lightly.

My heart pounded in my ears, and I gritted my teeth, begging the merciless universe to help me. There was no answer, only the sound of crushing silence. I wiped each of my cheeks and sniffed. Then, as if someone else were in control of my body, I raised the dagger over her heart, my fingers struggling to keep hold of it.

A strangled sob caught in my throat as I plunged the blade forward, piercing through flesh and bone. Falling onto my grandmother's lifeless body, I pleaded for her forgiveness. Then, consumed by guilt, I tore out the dagger and hurled it across the field.

A blinding light erupted around us. It seared my vision and blasted me into the cold, damp grass. My body writhed in agony as I struggled to regain my senses. Through blurry eyes, I saw Father O'Neil darting across the clearing in my direction.

"Noa," he gasped, crouching next to me. "Are you injured?"

I groaned and tried to sit up, but my body refused to cooperate. Instead, I pressed my hand to my head and let the ground consume me.

"The secrets." O'Neil took his thumb and, in a gentle sweeping motion, drew the sign of the cross on my forehead. "You have them all now."

"Oh, thank god," said Lex, as he hovered over me with fear in his eyes. "I thought that was it for you, too."

"It was her body taking in the secrets," O'Neil remarked. "The most powerful reaction we've seen."

"She's the last one," confirmed Lex as he stood looking around the field.

I forced myself to turn to my side, ignoring their exchange. The lifeless body of my grandmother and the image of her sweet face were imprinted in my mind. She was gone, and I had killed her. Dead for the second time. Shivering, I rolled onto my back again.

Lex reached a hand down to help me sit up, but I shook my head. O'Neil stood and looked around for any threats, but there were none. At least, not yet.

"Vincent is a dead man," I finally muttered. "I'm killing that prick. Vallen and Maros too. The nerve of angels thinking they can fuck with humans like this." O'Neil cleared his throat, and I looked up at him, squinting with one eye closed. "Sorry, Father."

He nodded with a polite smile. "You're forgiven, child, but there's still a lot for us to figure out."

"Plot away, but that's the endgame. They're all dead," I reiterated with a little more force this time.

I glanced to my left and saw Nevaeh and Ena absorbed in a

conversation. I was confident it was about what took place and how to bury Sasha's body. I would let them sort it out and I'd help if they needed me. Baz and Sasha's wolf bounded toward me.

"*Are you all right?*" Baz asked, a tinge of worry in his voice.

I rubbed my eyes with the heels of my hands. "Yeah, just need to figure out where they imprisoned Vallen," I replied. "I have a hit list of my own."

Across the field, Dawson ran up the steps into the house and slammed the door. Nevaeh and Ena looked our way, then turned with heavy footsteps to join us.

"Are you able to sit up now, Noa?" Lex asked, regret filling his stare.

I nodded with a half-smile and lifted my hand for help. He grasped my forearm and lifted me to my feet. I dusted off my hands on my damp jeans and immediately craved a shower. What I needed was sleep, but that would have to come later.

I gestured toward the house with a nod of my head. "Where are they taking her?"

Ena's eyes flitted to Father O'Neil as she avoided my gaze. "They're going to gather Sasha for a cremation ceremony."

"Oh." My tone went flat. I looked down and started picking at my fingernails. "I thought I heard the word 'pyre' earlier, but it didn't register."

"Yes," said Father O'Neil with a nod. "I should help them. Then we make our plans, which include scouring the books in the vault room." He glanced at me and warned, "You're the last one, Noa. I don't know what that's going to mean, but there might be more than fallen angels and demons after you now."

My eyebrows rose. "What the hell are you talking about?"

"Yeah, care to fill us in?" asked Lex, shifting his weight from one foot to the other. He was still wearing his sweatshirt and pants from earlier, and I could tell he needed a shower and was starting to feel uncomfortable.

"This ought to be good, but I figured it was coming," quipped Baz as he released a deep breath and lay next to me.

O'Neil released a long breath. "The Vatican," he murmured.

I shook my head as the three of them surrounded O'Neil, hurling information back and forth. They lost me when I heard someone mention the Roman Curia. Lex threw up his hands, and I swore a vein bulged in his neck.

The Catholic Church was foreign to me other than the television shows I'd seen about secrets and conspiracy. Apparently, secrets were real. Maybe it wasn't about conspiracy so much as it was about protecting humans, but I wasn't sure, and I didn't have the strength to listen to them argue.

Then, my grandmother's wolf walked up next to me and lowered his head. I reached up, cupping one hand under his chin and stroking his snout with the other. It was a calming distraction from the group chaos.

Baz stood close as we watched Dawson, Nakoma, and Jossy wrap Sasha in white sheets. They tied pieces of rope around her to hold them in place. Then, the three of them hoisted her up and carried her to the funeral pyre at the foot of the totem pole.

They composed it of wooden boards, firewood, and branches of trees they found lying around the side of the house. They placed wildflowers they found on the edges of the trees on top of her, then tucked bundles of sage around her body. As beautiful a gesture as it was, I couldn't watch, knowing my grandmother was in hell.

I looked back toward the house, then twisted around to scope the area of the field behind me. My grandmother's wolf peered at me with his deep amber eyes and followed my movements. Studying him, my heart broke as I wondered if he would stay with us since Sasha died.

"Can he understand us?" I asked Baz.

"Yes, and the pack communicates through telepathy as well," he informed me.

It dawned on me that this other wolf, a fallen guardian angel, had heard every agonizing word before I let my grandmother go. He had likely been comforting her somehow. Hot tears streamed down my cheeks again. I couldn't bear to dwell on what I'd done. The taste of iron still coated my tongue.

"And he talked to Sasha." It wasn't a question. I stroked the wolf's coarse fur to comfort us both.

When I glanced back at the altar, Jossy and Nakoma stood entwined, while Dawson doused the top with lighter fluid. Ena strode toward them, leaving Lex and Nevaeh embroiled in a heated debate with Father O'Neil. Dawson struck a match, and flames engulfed the pyre with a roar.

I let out a deep sigh and returned my gaze to the wolf. "What's your name?"

"Callum," Baz answered for him, his voice low.

My heart ached for all of us. Because of selfish angels who decided to rip away souls to hide ancient secrets within humans. So many lives were lost between the Veil and here. I wrapped my arms around Callum's sturdy neck, embracing him, but he went limp and fell to the ground.

"What's happening?" My breath shuddered, and I froze where I stood.

"He's decided to leave." Baz's tone was oddly tranquil.

Lex halted mid-sentence, wheeling around to face me, eyes wide. "Callum, wait," he pleaded.

My muscles tensed as Callum lifted his head with a whimper. "Where are you going?"

"Back to the Veil." Baz stretched his neck toward the inky sky, releasing a long, mournful howl.

My confused eyes darted to Baz. *"I thought your punishment for falling was eternal damnation, too?"*

"We can't reenter the Veil, but we can serve by guarding it from the outside," he explained. *"Falling is unforgivable, but if we don't completely succumb to the darkness here, we're allowed to join the army in the Veil."*

"Brother," Lex edged closer and sat down next to Callum. "We still need you here."

Callum lifted his head for a moment, heartache shining in his eyes. Forcing him to stay would only prolong everyone's agony. "He's in pain, Lex," I murmured, recalling Dawson's same words to me about Sasha.

Lex raked his hands through his hair. "Fucking Vincent," he growled.

Nevaeh and O'Neil kept their distance as I stroked Callum's head. Cosmic electricity surged through my hand, crackling against his fur. I stared at my hand in bewilderment, then back at Callum.

"What's happening?" Lex asked, his voice rough with emotion.

"I don't know," I answered honestly, continuing to stroke

Callum's fur.

Callum released a long, anguished howl, then slowly morphed from wolf into man, then dissolved into shimmering energy. My pulse quickened as his presence swirled around me. Amidst the glimmering mist, rugged features crystallized. A strong jaw, flowing snow-white hair, and sparkling amethyst eyes.

His radiance caressed me before he disintegrated into what looked like stardust. In a single movement, he wrapped around me, raw energy jolting my body. Callum's essence fused into my veins, mingling with the potent secrets harbored inside me.

As he faded into my being, the scent of pine mingling with euphoric lilacs embedded itself in my nose, and a thought fluttered in my mind. Baz stared skyward, then he dropped his snout to the ground. I scanned the empty field, feeling consumed by the cosmic flames of the universe.

Lex was so still that I thought he'd shed his mortal form and travel somewhere beyond. Glazed, his eyes flickered like strobe lights. I waved my hand before his face, breaking the trance. Lex jumped back to the present.

"What... What happened?" My faint voice trembled.

Lex's brow pinched together. "Callum was saying goodbye, but he decided you needed a fighting chance."

"He…he gave me his essence?" I studied my open palms in wonder.

Lex nodded. "He did."

Father O'Neil approached, face etched with concern. "Let's get moving, everyone."

Baz snarled in irritation, making O'Neil's eyes bulge. *"There's time, and we need to talk,"* said Baz.

"Wait," I breathed and blew out my cheeks. "I need a minute."

A surge of emotions threatened to consume me. It all weighed on my shoulders, and my lips turned numb. The realization I had taken my grandmother's life, because it was the one way she could die, was a burden too heavy to bear. It would haunt me for whatever time I had left here.

O'Neil fidgeted with his rosary beads, eyeing the sky. "Don't linger. I trust nothing, and we don't know when Maros or Vincent will be back."

"Come," Nevaeh linked her arm through the priest's, leading him to the porch where the others waited. "We need to get out the maps and strategize."

Father O'Neil nodded as he lifted a finger. "Yes, we need to find a way to check the wards."

"Then we need to find ourselves a tree," she confirmed and patted his arm.

Lex began to follow them, and I called out to him, "Stay with us."

He cocked his head and eyed me curiously. "Sure."

I gazed down at the faint shimmer of Callum's essence lingering on my skin. The comforting yet unsettling warmth radiating from it was a stark reminder of Callum's sacrifice.

Feeling a gentle nudge from Baz, his fur brushing against my leg, grounded me in the present moment. My guardian wolf's eyes held a depth of understanding that spoke volumes without uttering a single word.

Lex admitted, "I'm as hard on Father O'Neil as anyone else, but he does have a point."

His words pulled me back to reality as he looked off into the tree line. I turned to Baz and whispered into his ear, *"You said Lex was trustworthy."* Baz nodded in agreement, eyes narrowing as he weighed my words. "Let me tell him I can talk to you."

He chuffed and lifted his chin. *"Pretty sure you're going to, no matter what I say at this point."*

"We need him, Baz." My eyes pleaded with him. *"I need you both, now."*

Baz's eyes softened as he blew out a deep exhale. He nuzzled my hand to offer me silent comfort. A reassurance I desperately needed.

Lex's gaze shifted between us, confusion creasing his brow. "What is going on between you two?"

"Baz and I," I glanced up at Lex with my stomach doing flips, "share a connection deeper than what you might think. We can communicate."

Lex's eyes darted between us as if searching for some rational explanation. "But... how is that even possible?"

Exchanging a knowing look with Baz, I tapped my temple twice.

CHAPTER 22

Lex's hands slid down his face. "This is unexpected," he acknowledged.

"Let's move closer to the house," Baz advised as he strode ahead.

"Follow, Baz," I said with a slight smile and nodded in his direction.

We reached the porch, and Lex leaned on the rail. Baz settled close to me, and I rubbed his shoulder, knowing I would never get used to how massive he was or the comfort he brought me.

"Explain this connection to me," Lex urged, his voice heavy with contemplation.

"I figured if anyone would understand, it would be you," I stated with a shake of my head. "He's my guardian angel and you're an angel. Demons and magic roam here. This was bound to happen, Lex."

His brows knotted together as I retreated into the maze of

my own thoughts. I'd now become the sun around which our worlds turned, like a soap opera. The weight of universal survival now rested on my shoulders, which disturbed me.

Baz rustled beside me, a subtle intrusion pulling me back into reality, and I looked at Lex. His eyes lingered on the bracelet on my wrist, a shadow of realization crossing his face.

"What?" I raised my brows, unsettled as unease skulked across my skin.

Lex stepped closer, gesturing for my hand. He traced the etched designs, then cleared his throat. "Your bracelet has something to do with this," he said.

My eyes turned to slits as I pointed to the bracelet. "This piece of junk?"

He stroked his forehead with his thumb. "Think about it. You killed the Lurker and sent us through a portal. That happened when you shielded yourself while wearing the bracelet."

My disbelieving chuckle echoed around us before I fixed my eyes on Lex's, stating each word with utmost certainty.

"Vincent and Vallen disrupted the order, and because of that, and the secrets in my head, I can talk to Baz. Also, I'm walking around soulless." I nodded and glanced at each of them. "This bracelet means nothing."

"Maybe." Lex elongated the word and shook his head like he didn't agree with me. He lifted his chin toward Baz as skepticism crossed his face. "Why did Noa wait to tell me about you two?"

"Don't take offense." I scrunched my nose and placed my hands together in prayer in front of me. "It was a measure of precaution, Lex."

Lex grumbled in annoyance as his jaw ticked. "Could Callum talk to Sasha?" he asked.

I glanced at my feet, then back at Lex, and nodded. "Yes," I murmured.

Lex moved forward, poking Baz in the chest. "Tell me you didn't know Sasha was alive, brother," he challenged.

Baz snarled and tossed his head. Lex retreated, a disappointed look crossing his face. My eyes grew wide as I looked at Baz with fear in my heart.

"Did you know, Baz?" I probed further so Lex could hear.

"No," he confirmed as he bowed his head and looked into my eyes. *"Callum didn't either. His connection with Sasha severed on the night she died."* Baz exhaled and lay down on the ground next to me.

My head swung back toward Lex, and my eyes pleaded with him to forgive Baz. "None of them knew," I stated. "Until today."

Lex stepped back as relief crossed his face, and he swept his hands through his hair.

"Is that what you were going to tell us before Maros showed up?" he asked me. "This connection."

My lip twitched, and I shook my head. "No. That was something different."

Baz shifted his weight and craned his neck in my direction. *"What was it?"*

Lex cocked his head, noticing Baz's shift toward me. "Go on because he," Lex said, pointing at Baz, "doesn't know everything that's going on in your head, does he?"

I thought about it for a brief moment, then fixed my eyes back on Baz. "You don't read my thoughts, right?"

Baz now towered over me, staring down at me suspiciously. *"No,"* he confirmed. *"That's offensive."*

Reassured, I relaxed my shoulders. "No listening in. We talk with our minds."

Cold air stung my cheeks as the wind picked up. The temperature had dropped even more as the sun set over the mountains, but I felt comfortable without a coat. Which was unusual, even for me loving the cold.

I rubbed my arms for comfort, hoping it would distract Baz and Lex so we could go inside the house. I was wrong. Gingerly licking my dry lips, I winced at the sting from my cut, but their eyes never left me.

"Don't be mad," I warned them, holding up my hand.

A low rumble escaped Baz's throat. *"Don't count on it."*

"Let's get one thing straight," my tone irritated as I placed my hands on my hips. "You have known about me since the beginning of time, but I barely found out about this in the last couple of days." I shook a finger at both of them. "Shame on you for expecting every detail from me while I navigate this supernatural shitstorm. I've needed a few minutes to wrap my head around it."

Baz's glacier eyes shifted down at me, and pride flashed across them. *"Understood,"* he said.

"We get it." Lex shrugged, then squeezed my shoulder for assurance. "Take all the time you need. All we ask is that you don't make decisions that could put you or us in danger."

My brows pinched together, and I dropped my hands to my sides. "That's it? Nothing else?" I asked, puzzled.

Lex leaned in, lowering his voice. "We don't expect you to

skip around here like we live in a land of rainbows and sparkles."

"Yeah." A smile slipped onto my lips as I waved my hand dismissively at them. "Exactly. Thank you."

"All of this," he gestured toward the vast open field, "is way cooler."

My shoulders dipped. "Glad my soulless secret-keeping vessel amuses you," I murmured.

"No, no, no. Don't do that." Lex reached for me and took my arm. "We're getting your soul back and you're not just a vessel housing our destinies."

My eyes flicked to his beneath my brows. "You mean that?"

"Of course." He smiled and pulled me into him for a hug. "You're family, Noa."

"I've been wondering about it," I admitted, burying my face in his chest.

Leaning back, Lex gripped my chin and tilted it, forcing me to look at him. His moody gaze almost dropped me to my knees, but I shook away the thought, knowing it was nothing more than his angelic presence.

"Humans come first and you're the key to saving them," Lex smiled. "But we'll protect you and keep you."

Baz interrupted us with a grunt. *"We need you to tell us what happened in the woods before Maros showed up, or I'll drag Ena out here myself."*

The front door slammed open with a crack that splintered through the cool air, and Ena stepped onto the porch. Silhouetted against the warm glow of the porch lights behind her, I groaned and threw my head back in resignation.

"Great." The word escaped my lips like a bitter pill.

"Perfect timing, Ena." Lex's eyes brightened at the sight of her, the stormy gray in them momentarily clearing like clouds parting after a downpour.

Ena smirked and bounded down the stairs, her voice replicating wind chimes as she spoke. "Sounds intriguing. What are we planning?"

A revelation shot through me as she took Lex's hand and he helped her down the steps, her fingers interlacing with his. Lex was the one who gave Ena angel essence. The familiar pang of jealousy I expected didn't come. Instead, when I thought about the feelings I once held for him, seeing them together made me happy now.

When did that change?

He deserved someone good, and from what I'd seen of her, Ena was worthy. The thought settled in my chest, not entirely comfortable but true nonetheless.

Baz shifted beside me, his shoulder brushing mine. The contact sent a jolt through my system, like static electricity but warmer, more intense. His scent—leather and cloves and something else I couldn't name—invaded my senses.

Focus, Noa.

"We were asking Noa what happened in the woods with you," Lex began as Ena joined us, the gravel crunching beneath her feet.

The late afternoon light cast long shadows across the yard. In the distance, a crow cawed, its harsh cry echoing through the trees. My mouth went dry.

"We? You and Baz?" she asked, raising an eyebrow as her gaze flicked between them. A knowing smile tugged at the corners of her mouth.

"It's not that serious," I scoffed, rolling my eyes. I swallowed hard, trying to ignore the heat rising in my cheeks.

"Noa and Baz can talk with their minds," Lex divulged, crossing his arms over his chest.

Goosebumps prickled along my bare arms, and I rubbed them absently, my fingernails scraping against skin. A huge grin spread across Ena's face, her eyes widening in wonder.

"That's amazing!" Her voice pitched higher with excitement.

If only she knew how overwhelming it is to have someone else inside your head. Two someones now.

Then Lex looked back at me, his expression hardening. "Start talking." Not a request—a command. The fallen angel in him surfacing.

Ena crossed her arms and flashed me a hard gaze and the temperature between us quickly dropped. "Tell them, Noa."

My heartbeat picked up, a drum in my ears. I could taste copper—had I bitten my tongue? No longer able to suppress the truth or hide it from my friends, I gulped down the lump forming in my throat and decided on honesty.

They deserve to know. All of it.

"The day after my birthday," I mumbled and glanced up at them, the words sticking to my tongue like peanut butter. My fingers trembled slightly, and I pressed them against my thighs to steady them. "And it's only happened a few times, but a strange man showed up while I was asleep."

The yard fell silent as Lex balled his fists by his side, knuckles whitening. "I'll kill him," he fumed, his voice a low growl.

An involuntary laugh escaped me, sharp and brittle. "Interesting that you say that, but you can't."

He looked at me like I'd forgotten who he was and shook his head as he pointed to his chest. The tendons in his neck stood out, a roadmap of anger. "Fallen angel, remember?" he reminded me, the words clipped.

"Yes," I replied with a sigh that came from the very depths of me. "But he's in my head. Lex—he got through somehow last night too on our way to the cabin." Those last words fractured under pressure as my emotions threatened to spill over. My throat tightened, and I swallowed hard against its force.

Don't cry. Not now.

Lex's eyes darted between each of us before landing back on mine. Those stormy clouds flickered within them again, lightning in a bottle. His jaw set tight enough that I could hear his teeth grinding. "No. He's out there. Once we figure out how to find him, then I'll kill him."

The air around him crackled with barely contained energy. I'd seen what he could do when pushed—the memory made my skin tingle.

"Why didn't you say anything earlier?" Baz's stern voice broke in as he began pacing the yard, rocks shifting beneath his paws. Each step was deliberate, predatory. His shadow stretched long across the ground, distorted and threatening.

"I wanted to," I said through unshed tears. A knot formed in my stomach, twisting tighter with each passing second. *"But when we met this morning, you said it was the first time we'd spoken."*

Ena studied my interaction with Baz, concern etched on her face. She leaned toward Lex, her lips barely moving. "What's happening with them?" she whispered, but the breeze carried her words to me.

"I'm frustrated and Baz is irritated with me," I blurted, and pushed away a tear from my cheek with the back of my hand. The moisture felt cold against my skin.

Understatement of the century.

"Okay," she stuttered, trying to find the right words. Her eyes narrowed, calculating. "But he's not the one in your head?"

I sighed and shook my head as tension settled at the base of my skull and the pounding in my temples intensified. "When Maros showed up, I thought it was him, but he's just... repulsive." Taking a deep breath that smelled of pine and the possibility of another snowfall, I confessed, "I don't know who it is."

"Do you know what he looks like?" Lex pressed with urgency, stepping closer. His shadow fell across me, blocking what little warmth the sun still offered.

Baz sat down in a flash beside me—too close, not close enough. His focus sharpened on my next words, his pupils dilating slightly. *"Describe him,"* he instructed, his voice deceptively calm.

With a casual shrug, I began recalling fragmented details. Pieces of a puzzle I couldn't quite assemble. "Dark hair and wild green eyes..." The memory skipped like a damaged film reel. "He comes to me while I sleep—showing me visions..." I hesitated before continuing. "...My scar burns like someone is holding a match to it right before he appears."

My fingers traced the outline of the mark on my lip, the skin hot to the touch. The pain was a phantom now, but the memory of it made me wince.

"Visions of what, Noa?" Ena interjected, her eyes narrowing at me. Her posture had changed—alert, defensive. Ready for a fight.

I racked my brain trying to sort through the jumbled images, fragments that refused to form a coherent picture. My temples throbbed. "There's a field," I said, struck by sudden clarity like lightning illuminating a night landscape. "And the tree. Lex, your tattoo!" I exclaimed and pointed at his thigh. "It's the same tree, and he insisted I find him there. Do you think he's waiting for me?"

Lex stroked his chin, his voice tinged with contemplation. "No," he said, shaking his head. His eyes darted briefly to Baz—a message passed between them, too quick for me to interpret. "Doubtful."

They're hiding something.

Baz remained silent for a moment, seeming to wrestle with the question. He glanced at me, a look of struggle in his eyes that made my heart stutter. *"There's nothing at the tree for you, Noa,"* he agreed, but there was a hesitation in his voice that raised my suspicions.

But what if there were? Something more lurked beneath our conversation, currents running deeper than any of them were willing to admit. Why ask me about the man, then tell me I'm wrong when the clues are there? A nagging instinct told me to push harder, the same instinct that had kept me alive so far. I couldn't let them decide for me. Especially when it was my mind under attack.

I hugged myself, desperate for a breakthrough, my nails digging half-moons into my skin. "What if he's been trying to warn me about this?"

"Why would he do that?" Ena's forehead crinkled with confusion as she glanced at Lex. Another silent exchange. Another secret.

"Why not?" I shook my head, my hair whispering against

my back. I looked at each of them in turn, challenging them with my gaze. "I have all this stuff going on inside me, so he's trying to tell me I'm in danger."

What felt like a drop of rain, not snow, fell cold against my skin, then on my lip. Rain wasn't expected, but I tasted its freshness anyway, a stark contrast to the bitterness of our conversation.

Ena's tone carried a weight of sorrow as she explained why my idea was wrong. She stepped closer, her shoes sinking slightly into the softening ground. "Two fallen angels remain at the tree. One guards it while the other nourishes the tree to sustain its abilities. They would have to be severely injured, but too much to speak to you telepathically."

The rain fell in bigger drops, pattering against leaves on the ground. No one moved to seek shelter.

"They'd most likely be dead," added Lex, rain darkening his shirt in patches. "Vincent wouldn't let them live to guide you there, Noa."

His name sent a chill through me that had nothing to do with the weather. Vincent. The puppet master pulling all our strings.

"Angels nourish the tree? With what?" I questioned, feeling a sense of dread sink into my bones, settling there like lead.

Lex cleared his throat before answering me. "Their essence."

My stomach churned in turmoil as water trickled down my neck and under my collar. "But they'll die!"

"Over time, yes," Baz acknowledged, his voice low in my mind. His fur was flattened now, water dripping from his enormous eyelashes. *"But it's to keep the portal open and the wards intact, Noa."*

"Why is the portal still open?" My mind reeled at the gravity of the situation, and I rubbed my temples, smearing rainwater across my face. The pressure behind my eyes intensified. "Let me guess, Vincent's idea."

Ena stepped forward, her jaw tight, water running in rivulets down her face. She looked fierce trying to get me to understand. "It took years to figure out how to keep it open," she confessed, raising her voice to be heard over the rain. "And the lower-ranking angels are the ones who feed the tree."

I shivered with displeasure at what I was hearing, goose-bumps rippling across my skin—a chill of realization, of horror. "I don't see how any of you are okay with this."

How many more will die because of me?

"Sometimes," Baz said, his voice barely audible against my thoughts, *"survival requires sacrifice."*

"The angels choose to fall, Noa and we know it comes with responsibilities," Lex said. "Besides, with the portal open, we can return the secrets and gain access to your soul."

"Keeping it open is saving our world too, Noa," Ena emphasized as she looked in my direction.

"I get it," my tone soft as I nodded and pushed the hair back from my face as the rain let up. "And that's exactly why I need to find it and talk to this angel. He's alive."

Baz yelped at me in disagreement and shook out his coat. *"It could be a trap."*

I turned into him and leaned my head on his shoulder. *"Do you really believe that?"*

"Of course I do," he insisted. *"Vincent and Maros could've faked the wards failing earlier to lure you there and kidnap you. When you didn't go, Maros got impatient with Vincent."*

I rolled my eyes, then withdrew from him, stepping back to

face Lex and Ena. "Baz thinks Maros is trying to kidnap me. He makes a good point. However, I disagree because Maros already showed up here and left me."

Dawson leaned out the front door with a scowl on his face at how wet we all were. "Y'all comin' or what? Weapons aren't gonna prepare themselves."

"We'll be right there," I called back and smiled before he disappeared inside again.

As soon as Dawson was out of earshot, I turned back to my friends. "So, who's coming with me to check out the tree?"

Lex started climbing the stairs to the porch. "Absolutely not," he objected with a raise of his hand.

"Listen to him, Noa." Baz's body tensed, and he stood tall in agreement.

"Isn't Callum's essence providing me protection?" I asked, raising a hand in question. "Ena has enhancements," I said. "So it makes sense I would too."

"We're all targets now," she nodded, agreeing slightly.

Lex turned back to face me, ready to counter, but I shook my head.

"I'm not waiting for trouble to show up here again and drag me to hell," I insisted. "Vincent and Maros don't know what Callum did, and we can use that to our advantage."

Ena tapped her chin as she nodded. "If it's an angel at the tree warning, Noa, we can get answers to help with the ceremony to retrieve her soul."

Lex's fingers tightened around the cool iron railing, the other hand sweeping across the rough stubble on his face.

"We'll go, but we need a logical plan," he said in a measured and deliberate tone. His eyes shifted to Baz. "You know damn well she'll go off on her own if we don't help."

A smirk tugged at the corners of my mouth. I pulled my shoulders up to my ears with a grin. "I'd rather you go with me, Baz, but Lex isn't wrong," I sang.

"Fine." Baz released a deep, irritated growl. *"But get inside before I change my mind,"* he ordered.

"He's in." I gave Ena and Lex a thumbs-up, then I sauntered up the steps with them.

Baz trotted to the corner of the house, pausing as if weighing his next steps. *"You'll need a weapon,"* he declared.

Giddy with anticipation, I clasped my hands behind my back. "And I get a weapon."

"Don't get too excited, Noa." Lex leaned in with a teasing expression. "The tree is warded, so we'll need to find it first."

"I'll go around and come through the back," Baz sighed, done with the conversation.

I cast a doubtful look at Baz, but before I could ask how, he was gone. Lex opened the door for Ena and me, ushering us inside.

"Besides," Lex added. "You might get a dagger at most."

Dagger.

I turned and ran back down the steps toward the empty field. Smoke curled upwards from the remnants of the totem pole, reducing Sasha's body to ash. Tears blurred my vision; I needed the dagger—the one Vincent had forced me to wield against Sasha.

There was no sign of it anywhere. Not even the glint of a hilt. I sprinted into the house, shock painted on Ena's and Lex's faces.

CHAPTER 23

"Where is it?" The sound of my voice reverberated off the towering walls.

Jossy flung open a pair of majestic oak doors to my left as I was about to step into the living room, water trailing behind me. "What's wrong?" he inquired, concern etching his brow.

Desperation surged through me as I grasped his shirt. "Where's the dagger, Joss? I need it!"

He clasped my trembling hands, his thumb tracing soothing circles in my palm as he guided them away from his chest with care. "Breathe, Noa. We have it in here," Jossy assured me.

He led me through the grand foyer, the air thick with the scent of aged wood and dried herbs. The whitewashed wood floors creaked beneath my feet as we walked, the sound echoing through the house like ghostly whispers.

I trailed him deeper into the house, my eyes darting to every shadowed corner. Ena and Lex followed closely behind, and as we entered the expansive living room, Nevaeh met us with towels to dry off, and a bottle of water extended toward me.

"You could use this." She offered a warm smile as I gulped down its contents.

"Thank you," I replied, my hands still trembling as I wiped my parched lips.

"There's bannock bread on the kitchen counter, and I opened a jar of my homemade chokecherry jam. Help yourself if you're hungry," she added.

I nodded in appreciation as the towel soaked up the water on my body as best as it could. I would need fresh clothes. Nevaeh glided to the center of the room to join Dawson, where he was sorting ammunition. Knives and an array of medieval weapons were strewn across the floor in front of an oversized stone fireplace. There were maces with intricate designs, various war hammers, and what appeared to be several customized firearms.

A metal garage door had replaced a section of the floor-to-ceiling glass windows that comprised the back wall of the house. My understanding deepened when I spotted Baz standing beside the fireplace, focused on Dawson's work.

To my right stood an imposing wooden table that once hosted family dinners but now lay strewn with ancient maps and tomes steeped in history. Father O'Neil paced back and forth, thumbing through one of the worn volumes, clad in white gloves that contrasted against the pages' yellowing edges. He peeked over his glasses and smiled before returning to his reading—a picture of scholarly dedication.

Behind O'Neil hung a painting of The Last Supper, timeless and poignant on its canvas backdrop. Jossy approached the table and reached for the dagger resting precariously on its edge. I hadn't realized he was offering it to me hilt-first until it warmed my palm. I'd been too caught up in my inner turmoil.

The dagger was carved in the shape of a wolf's head—something I had overlooked before releasing my grandmother from her pain. The sheath encasing the blade was crafted from weathered leather adorned with delicate engravings on either side. Leather ties dangled from its top.

I unsheathed the blade and set the empty case back on the table, mindfully running my finger along its spine while avoiding the sharp edge. No traces of blood marred its surface. Any evidence that I had used this very weapon to end my grandmother's life remained absent, rendering Jossy's act of cleaning it a compassionate gesture.

I'd keep the dagger close to serve as a reminder that adhering to my plan was paramount. Reach the cherry blossom tree to help the angel and learn the steps of the ceremony, then hunt for Vallen. After that, Vincent and Maros were mine.

I didn't know how, but I was grateful for the few angels who hadn't betrayed me. I prayed we could find a way. As I tucked away the weapon in its case, Nakoma rounded a corner, clutching another map in his hands.

"I think I found it," Nakoma gushed with excitement. He lifted it high with gloved hands before spreading it across the table and beckoning us all closer.

"What is that?" I asked, peering at markings no one but Nakoma seemed to understand.

With raised brows hinting at his amusement, he replied, "One of the earliest maps of this land."

Dawson and Nevaeh halted their organizational efforts and

ambled toward us while Baz took his place beside me. He scrutinized the timeworn paper with an intensity that intrigued me.

"Let's get to work," Dawson declared as he retrieved a clear map case alongside erasable markers. He glanced at Jossy and Lex before asking, "Do either of you have any idea where we should begin?"

Without warning, Uno's cheerful voice jolted me from my thoughts. I was close to dropping the dagger in surprise when she chirped, "Hiya, doll! Is this a bad time?"

I instinctively scanned above as if she had materialized from thin air. "Not a bad time at all!"

"Dos and I weren't sure if we should interrupt or not," she continued in a rush. "But we've gotta."

The room fell silent as every gaze turned toward me as though my sanity were in question. But Lex and Jossy dismissed their scrutiny and returned their focus to the map. Father O'Neil and Nakoma slid the map into the protective case as I walked toward the front of the house for privacy.

"Anyone talking over there?" I implored under my breath, desperate for insight into Vincent or Vallen's next moves.

"Well," she began casually amidst what sounded like gum smacking against her teeth. "It's bumpy on this side, doll. Things aren't thrilled you're all juiced up with the cosmos now."

"Things?" I sounded it out deliberately and with emphasis for clarity. My experience talking to ghosts in the past educated me on never leaving anything to chance.

"Things," she reaffirmed before cautioning me further. "Watch your back, doll."

"You can't elaborate more, Uno?" Panic clawed up my

throat as fear tightened around me like a vice while I clutched my dagger.

"Sorry. I'm risking myself as it is to warn you." She smacked her gum again, then I heard her take a breath and blow it out as the pop of a bubble followed. "But you're in good hands there. Trust your friends, and I'll catch ya later."

Before I could pry for more answers, she vanished. Nausea grew in my stomach, forcing out an exasperated sigh. Trusting my friends is what got me into this mess. It was bad enough that angels, demons, and the church of all churches might be after me. Now other creatures were out hunting for blood.

If there were any chance for me to stay alive, without other entities siphoning me off for all eternity, I needed to reach that tree sooner rather than later. When I rejoined everyone in the living room, I couldn't see Ena anywhere, and someone had drawn a circle on the map.

Father O'Neil scratched hasty notes into an old journal as Dawson combined weapons into several duffel bags on the living room floor. Lex and Jossy leaned over Nakoma, comparing markings on the map to some recent satellite images they had found online.

As I stepped closer, I saw the ranch property with sections marked and a legend scribbled out on paper. Vincent's cabin, the totem pole, and Nevaeh and Dawson's house served as landmarks. They were all woven together with dashed lines representing the fence lines placed around the land. The circle was northeast of Vincent's cabin and close to the mountains.

"How's the spirit world?" Lex asked as he offered me a cup of coffee, and the aroma of hazelnut hit my nose.

I shoved the dagger at his chest and half-smiled. Letting

the mug warm my hands, I mouthed 'thank you' to him. "It's turbulent over there, so we want to find that tree soon."

In a heartbeat, Baz was next to me, worry deep in his voice. *"What's wrong?"*

"Uno mentioned we may have greater threats beyond Vincent and Maros." Sipping leisurely while digesting the flavors, the coffee flooded my cheeks with warmth.

Jossy drew in a deep breath, sensing the weight of the information. "And what does that entail?"

"She didn't elaborate," I began and placed the coffee mug on the table, "but things know what's going on with me over here, and they aren't happy."

"Then that," he said and turned back toward the map schematics, "doesn't give us a lot of time to find the tree."

"I don't like the sound of that," Baz suggested as he cautioned, shaking his head.

"Me neither," I stated and leaned into him for support. "None of you know where the tree is?" I asked Jossy.

"Vincent warded it and after we fall, we're never allowed to go back. The ones chosen to guard and nourish never leave it until it's their time." Jossy pointed to the circle drawn on the map. "We believe it's in this area close to the Valley of the Fallen."

"Valley of the Fallen?" My expression shifted when I heard this information.

Lex moved my dagger back and forth between his hands and said, "Remember when I told you about that burial site? That's the valley."

I cleared my throat and stepped up to the map to get a

better look. "So, you want me to walk through a fallen angel burial ground to find this tree?"

Lex handed me back the knife as his lip curled into a teasing smirk. "You can always wait around here for hell to drag you under."

I snatched the dagger from him and slapped his arm with the back of my hand. "Not funny."

Ignoring us, Jossy placed my coffee cup on the kitchen counter and walked back over to the map. "There's nothing but mountains around our burial ground."

"Lovely." I threw my hands up in frustration. "Now what? Because if the wards aren't stable, we're exposed, and if that angel dies," my breath shook. "I'll never get my soul."

"You will, Noa." Lex raked his hands through his hair as he stared hard at the map. Then, turning to Jossy, he asked, "Will you and Nakoma stay here and help guard the house?"

Jossy nodded and gave Lex a reassuring pat on his back, letting his hand linger. "Of course, but what are you up to?"

"We need to split up. The wards failing isn't safe for any of us, but if there is a lull we may have an opportunity to see the tree," Lex admitted with a smile.

"And that's why you're one of the best leaders we have here, Lex!" Jossy slapped his brother's wet back with a nod.

"Nevaeh," said Lex, walking away from us and into the living room. "I need you and Dawson to assist Father O'Neil. Secure everything back in the vault downstairs and add whatever supplies you can muster."

"Sure," she acknowledged, pulling one last gun from a bag. "But I'm telling you, only one other angel ever knew the location of the tree and the steps to perform the soul ceremony."

"Who's that?" asked Jossy, tilting his head with a quirked brow.

Everyone stood tall as we waited in suspense for her to tell us.

Nevaeh glanced at me, her eyes worrisome. "Vallen," she said.

"Fuck!" I exploded and started pacing, clasping my hands behind my neck. "I'm screwed. We're all screwed."

"Breathe, Noa." Baz stood in front of me, his breath of pine and lilacs brushing against my skin.

"Not that easy," I argued as fists formed at my sides. *"Dark angels and demons have completely ruined my life and my family's lives, Baz."*

"Noa," Lex interjected, "Ena should be back any minute with some clean clothes and a coat for you."

"I don't need a coat," I said, walking back and forth in front of them.

"Didn't look that way to me earlier," Baz remarked.

"Chilled, yes, but it's like sitting in an air-conditioned house. I'm not freezing," I retorted.

"Strange, but it could be everything you've experienced today," offered Jossy with a smile. "It's got your blood pumping."

"Regardless," Lex continued, "Baz will take you to his camp for the night while I get changed and we plan the trek."

Nakoma placed his hand on Jossy's arm. Inclining toward him, Nakoma whispered, "I'm going to prep Lulu. Let me know when you need me." He smiled and walked off, leaving Jossy and Lex with me and Baz.

Lex wrapped his arms around me and placed my head under his chin. The sudden shock of our cold damp clothes against our skin made me gasp, but it stopped me from pacing and stilled the twinges of electricity running through my body.

"Ena and I will meet you both in the morning and head out," he reassured me.

A calm settled over me, and I began to think of Ivy and how she calmed me after I killed the Lurker demon. But she betrayed us because I couldn't feel for her the way Jossy and Nakoma felt for each other.

She was the key for me to open my mind to these secrets and learn about my family. As angry as I was, it terrified me to think about what Maros had done to her. But it was Vincent and Vallen I needed to focus on destroying first.

CHAPTER 24

Lex released me as Nakoma emerged from around the corner, carrying another duffle bag full of weapons. He had the long silver bow he used against Jax earlier draped over his shoulder.

"You're pretty good with that thing," I admitted as he stopped in front of me to hand Jossy the duffel bag.

"This is Lulu." Nakoma swung the bow around to the front and caressed its sleek silver limb. "You were informed about angel wings. This beauty here allows me to pin them down."

He brought the bow to his soft brown lips, placing a kiss on her, then winked at me. I watched his fingers glide over the bow with precision as he adjusted the grip and tested its pull.

"Pin the wings." I repeated his words back to him, my face painted in horror. "Then do you bury them once they die?"

Nakoma closed his eyes and sighed before staring right into mine. "The dark angels are different, Noa. Some of them get buried, but most of them aren't."

My brows pinched together. "What do you do with them?" I asked.

Jossy passed a cylinder-shaped quiver to Nakoma, their eyes meeting in a silent exchange. Nakoma nodded, pulling out a single arrow before handing back the container.

"They're used for the betterment of science," Nakoma admitted as he inspected the arrow's shaft.

A jolt of recognition ran through me. My gaze found Father O'Neil, remembering Ena's words about a priest. He now highlighted different parts of the map, then went back to scribbling in his journal. I'd never known of such a combination for career choices; then again, I wasn't sure how many priests knew about the angels.

Nakoma continued, "O'Neil and I created the arrows from the ground-up bones of the dark angels."

Jossy patted my arm and lightly touched the tip of the arrow Nakoma held. "It's a good thing to grind up their bones. Trust me. Because the darker we go, the stronger the bones become."

"Gross," I muttered with a shiver that ran across my skin.

My body tensed with unsettling thoughts as Nakoma handed Jossy the arrow. Instinctively, I shoved my hands into my pockets for comfort. What would keep a fallen angel from going completely dark?

Maybe finding someone to spend their life with, like Jossy had with Nakoma. Was it all about hope, or was it something else? Jossy pressed a minuscule lever at the base of the arrowhead. My eyes grew wider as three more blades sprang forth from its center, adding to the already daunting display of torture tactics.

"We still have our powers, and those can't be taken away,"

Jossy pointed out. "So if one of us turns dark, things become amplified."

He handed the arrow to me, and I carefully removed my hands from my pockets to hold it. I inspected each side with its unusual etchings adorning every inch of the shaft's surface. They reminded me of the ones on my bracelet.

I handed Jossy the arrow, asking, "Are the dark angels stronger than regular fallen ones?"

Jossy and Nakoma glanced at one another, then Nakoma turned to me with a sigh.

"Somewhat," Nakoma stated. "The black magic of demons enhances their powers."

"Which makes their bones great arrows," Jossy added as he filled Nakoma's quiver with more arrows.

"And what about Lulu? What is she made out of?" I inquired further.

"She," Nakoma lifted Lulu, lining his fingers on the grip, "was crafted from an ancient Kauri tree long before the Church gifted her to me."

Then, in one swift motion, he drew back the string with his right hand and anchored it against his cheek. Setting his middle finger at the corner of his mouth, he closed his left eye and pretended to shoot at a target.

I imagined him shooting arrows into Vincent and Vallen. And the moment he did, I'd have them both. I'd cut out their fake angel hearts and torch them while I sawed off their wings. Then I'd mount and display them on the walls of my living room like works of art.

I shut my eyes, imagining my plan when Jossy walked by and

grasped my wrist. "Why haven't I seen this before?" he questioned while twirling my bracelet between his fingers.

"O'Neil!" Jossy yelled. "Come over here and take a look at this."

"What's wrong?" I asked as my heartbeat grew in my ears. "It was my mom's. Besides, Lex saw it, and he didn't think anything of it."

O'Neil gave a weary rub of his eyes before pushing his glasses back into place on the bridge of his nose, leaning in for a closer look at the bracelet. "Ah, yes. I don't know where he got it, but Vincent gave it to Sasha after your mother was born."

"It looks like someone made this in a kindergarten pottery class," I remarked, eyeing the bracelet with cynicism.

"Unique as it is," Lex acknowledged as he walked back toward us with a slice of bannock bread slathered in jelly, "I don't put things under a microscope like Joss."

With a sigh that seemed to carry the weight of long-held regrets, O'Neil shook his head. "Vincent wasn't one to explain himself," he remarked.

"He lied to us," Lex stated, then swallowed his last bite of bread. "About everything."

"And the symbols," I interjected. "What do they signify?"

I rubbed my wrist and realized the bracelet was one of the things Vincent would return to claim. The other was me.

"They're angel runes," Jossy explained. "But, with any language, their order means something different for everything, like hieroglyphics."

"What if they're protection runes?" I posed as I tapped each one.

Baz grumbled with skepticism as he settled onto the floor in the living room. He crossed his paws, then laid his head down while we tried to decipher the runes.

"Can I take a better look at it?" Jossy asked me.

"Sure." I gestured with a casual flick of my hand as I moved to remove the bracelet from my wrist. "It has to mean something to Vincent if he needed to lie about where Sasha got it."

Jossy extended his hand, waiting for me to place it in his palm. "You and Baz need to get going, Noa. Come on."

"I'm trying," I chuckled, feeling a flutter of anxiety as I met his ocean gaze. "It slid on easily the other day, but it's like my hand is too big now or something. It won't come off."

"I guess that's a good thing. Later then," he commented.

I watched as Jossy walked over to Nakoma, planting a light kiss on his lips. Nakoma closed his eyes and relaxed as Jossy pulled his forehead to his. "Are you ready to canvass the area, babe?" asked Jossy.

"Let's do it," Nakoma answered. He pushed Jossy's fiery hair behind his ear, then kissed him back. This time with more force.

My eyes lingered on their tender moment, and a wave of happiness washed over me. Jossy deserved this love, this companionship that seemed to fit him like a glove. And the way Nakoma held Jossy, it was clear he cherished him. As they parted, Nevaeh cleared her throat behind me and brought me back to my reality.

The front door opened, and Ena walked in with a backpack and a snow jacket. She held the door open for Jossy and Nakoma, and once they left, she placed the backpack at my feet. I took the jacket with a forced smile.

Stepping toward Lex, he placed a hand on her lower back, and she breathed, "I still can't believe Vincent and Ivy did this."

"I can," said Dawson as he loaded bullets into a magazine. "Always walkin' around irritated with her nose in the air."

"I don't think it was that, honey," Nevaeh countered and holstered another gun at her side. She looked at me with a soft smile.

"Oh yeah? What then?" Dawson asked, and, placing his hands on his hips, waited for a response, but he added, "The nonsense about Noa being unable to love Ivy is ridiculous."

It stung me to my core to think I was the reason for Ivy's betrayal. It also pissed me off that she chose to fall here to help, then went off and joined Maros because she couldn't have a human.

She couldn't have me.

Bullshit!

"Let that anger fuel you because you're going to need it," Baz interjected as his warm gaze met mine.

"Not right now, Baz," I snapped in frustration. *"Besides, I thought you couldn't read my thoughts?"*

"You said that out loud in your head to me." He stood and tipped his head back. A gesture for me to come stand with him by the garage opening.

I groaned, but hoisted the backpack over my shoulders and joined him anyway.

"I'll enlighten you on how to shield your thoughts so they don't come out as a spoken voice in your head," he offered.

I laid the jacket on a small end table next to him.

"Can we do that?" I asked, trying not to sound too eager. I didn't want to reveal all my vulnerabilities to him.

As I crossed my arms over my chest, I observed the group getting ready for battle. I had no experience or training in fighting. With any luck, Baz and my friends would be able to defend me.

"For brief periods of time, yes," Baz confirmed as I fidgeted in place before finally resting my head on his leg. *"Remember, the purpose of my fall was to help restore your soul, so our connection should stay open as much as possible."*

Nevaeh continued talking to Dawson behind us. I tried to ignore it, but it was impossible as I reeled from the loss of my best friend.

"Ivy lost faith after waiting so long, Dawson," I heard Nevaeh say. "Vincent preyed on her for it."

Dawson huffed, then grabbed a trucker hat from a rack by the back door. After placing it on his head, he holstered his pistol on the side of his jeans, then strapped a tactical knife to his leg.

"Whatever the reason, she sure as shit mucked it all up," he sniped.

I still felt a sense of loyalty to Ivy no matter her issues, and I made sure to let the others know.

"Ivy was collateral damage and, like Nevaeh said, they used her." I scowled at them, then turned my attention back to Baz. "Can we go now?"

In that moment, an ear-piercing blast outside rattled the walls of the house, causing everyone to scatter in a desperate attempt for cover. Baz shielded me with his body as another thud echoed through the room, this time near the front door.

We lifted our heads and saw Dawson slouching against the wall next to the fireplace. He wrapped his hand around his ear while crinkling his brows in discomfort.

"I'm all right!" Dawson called out, then took a finger and jiggled the inside of his ear.

He stood up, then stumbled into the kitchen. The sound of running water filled the air as he washed his face with agitation. A fist slammed down on the counter, and I jumped.

"We prepared for this, old man!" Nevaeh called out to him.

"Yeah, yeah," Dawson groaned.

He walked back out to the living room when another tremor shook the ground beneath us. I jumped up and met Baz's fierce gaze, a silent exchange of understanding passing between us. He nudged me with a feather touch and bowed down for me to climb up his leg and secure myself to his back.

As I climbed up for the first time, I realized there was enough room for two people, and I prayed I'd stay on.

"What do I hold onto?" I asked, flashing my black eyes at him.

Lex grabbed a thick leather belt from a hat organizer attached to the wall by the back door. He passed it around Baz's neck and buckled it.

"Grab onto the strap, Noa. You can hook your arms through it and lie down," he advised.

As I tried to steady my racing heart, Ena tossed me the jacket, which I promptly slipped my arms into backward as O'Neil secured a dagger holster around one of my thighs. He shoved two daggers into it - their wolf-head pommels glinting in the dim light. He placed the other dagger I had left on the table in my palm.

"Hang onto him, Noa," O'Neil ordered.

As the threat of demons capturing me began to set in, my bones rattled. "I'll try," I said, tucking the sheathed dagger into my bra.

"You will do more than try, Noa," Baz countered with a seriousness that sounded as if he were scolding me.

Lex turned and met Ena's gaze, his eyes scanning her disheveled hair and stained shirt before asking, "Are you okay?"

Ena nodded, then Lex placed her hand in his, and they stepped through the garage door into the backyard. A sharp, sulfuric stench hit my nose, nearly making me gag. In the distance, Jossy fought fiercely with fallen angels who had once been his family. Nakoma and Lulu turned them to ash from the ground.

As Ena put on her gloves that acted like a talisman to hide her energy, a tremor shook the house. My stomach twisted, a knot of fear threatening to choke me. As I reached for the leather strap around Baz's neck, my grip tightened with such force that I thought I felt fur ripping out from between my fingers.

"I'm so sorry!" I winced, then loosened my hands to check my palms.

"Hardly felt it. Put your head down, and do not let go," Baz directed, and stepped one paw onto the patio.

He crouched down, ready to run. I peered into the darkness, then glanced back into the living room one last time.

Nevaeh patted my leg. "You're all right. Don't do anything stupid, and stay alive."

A laugh caught in my throat as she stepped back. "You got it," I promised her.

Lex stood close to me and Baz and said, "It's Vincent's crew, so keep your head on a swivel, Baz."

"Ready?" Ena asked, and I shook my head, indicating I was not ready for any of this. She raised her hands, then looked up at me. "I'm going to create a diversion. Whatever you do, don't look back."

She closed her eyes and began to hum with her arms stretched out, palms up like she was offering something. The wind picked up and the windows rattled. A chill ran through me as her hands began to dance in front of her. A tree to the left shook, and the roots began to break free from the ground.

"Hold on tight, Noa," Baz instructed as his body readied beneath me.

Grasping onto Baz with all my strength, I buried my face in the hood of the jacket. The wind felt like a hurricane force as he took off into the night. His powerful strides covered ground faster than I ever thought possible. Baz snarled as I heard a Baneful one lunge for us, but with the shrill it unleashed, I knew Baz had killed it.

CHAPTER 25

Wind bit at my face, and I could feel the temperature dropping as we made our way across the property and into the woods. Branches of the trees slapped against our backs, and I was never more grateful for the backpack protecting me. Baz knew his way through the undergrowth, but it wasn't until we were deep inside that he began to slow down. Once he thought we were safe, he turned back to make sure nothing followed us.

A strange sense of relief washed over me as we escaped, or fear had numbed me. Either way, we were out of reach of Vincent and Maros. It didn't stop the rumbles of the fight from easing into the woods around us.

Baz reached out to me and said, *"Almost there, Noa."*

"Please tell me they'll be okay." I touched my thigh, making sure the daggers were still strapped to my leg.

"They'll be fine," he assured me. *"It was a distraction to see if we were prepared to fight."*

He turned in another direction and began walking at a steady pace. I lifted my head and noticed it had to be well after midnight the way the darkness took over. I couldn't see my hand in front of my face.

We finally reached a hidden opening in the trees where the flickering light of a small campfire beckoned against a wall of bedrock. The muffled sounds of voices and laughter carried through the trees, as did the intoxicating scent of burning cedar. We walked by at least ten tents lined along the camp's edge.

Baz stopped in front of a large round one with blue canvas walls. They remained unmoved as the cold wind blew, holding steady against its force. Baz lowered his body to the ground, and I climbed down, removing the jacket and backpack from my shoulders.

He used his teeth to untie a thick leather rope to the left of the entry. Then, using his head, he pushed open the flaps of the tent, and I followed him inside. The space was well-lit by candle-light, casting a golden glow on the wooden beams that formed a perfect circle around the tent.

The flickering flames from the wood stove provided a cozy ambiance. Two rectangular plastic windows on either side of the entryway revealed glimpses of trees and moonlight. The wood flooring had some give, and when I bent down to inspect it, I noticed it was interlocking rubber mats.

A king-sized bed with a fluffy comforter invited me over, and I sighed in relief. When I glanced left, a chest-high iron table with a mosaic top sat in the center of the room. The assortment of cheeses, fruits, meats, and breads on display made my mouth water.

Baz nudged me toward the food with a gentle push, his eyes

full of concern that I'd missed out on eating some of Nevaeh's bread. Coffee was the only thing I'd had since breakfast the day before. I dropped the backpack and jacket on the floor and hesitated with my choices.

My mind was still reeling from the past two hours, and the worry for my friends grew. There weren't any wolves back at the house and no way for Baz to communicate with them, so I had no idea if everyone was okay.

"I don't think I can eat yet. We don't know—," I started out loud and turned back to him.

"You need your strength, then you need to sleep. They know what they're doing," Baz assured me with another nudge toward the table.

Trusting him, I looked over the food again, then took a deep breath. I picked up a chunk of homemade cornbread and a slice of smoked cheddar cheese. I devoured it, savoring the creaminess and saltiness of both in my mouth.

Next, I grabbed an apple from the table. As soon as I took a bite, the flavors and juices satiated me. It wasn't until I swallowed that I realized how hungry I had become.

Baz watched me with intense focus, his black fur glowing in the dim light. I smiled, uncertain of how much longer I could hold it all together, and swallowed another piece of cheese.

A deep sigh escaped Baz, and it ruffled my hair as it brushed past me. *"Finish eating and get comfortable,"* he said.

I picked up a croissant next, and buttery flakes fell onto the floor, but I didn't hesitate. With my mouth full, I asked, "You wouldn't happen to have some wine or whiskey around here?"

"No," Bazz huffed.

I bit into what remained of the croissant and then grabbed the backpack and jacket. After tossing both onto an armchair next to the bed, I continued eating, but frustration bubbled up in my chest.

"So no one drinks around here?" I complained, pulling out some drawstring sweatpants and a long-sleeve t-shirt.

The name of Ena's nursing school was on the pocket of the front left, and the worry returned. When I twirled back around with the shirt in my hand, Baz stalked toward me, but I didn't budge. His large head loomed over mine as he peered into my eyes.

"I'm telling you," he warned, *"now that you're full of essence and our cosmic secrets, if you drink, you are susceptible to demons getting into your head. So, if you're thirsty, drink water."*

I raised my palms in a gesture of understanding, then tossed Ena's shirt onto the bed. If I was honest, I loved his protection. Even if he scared me a little. Walking over to the table, I grabbed the filtered pitcher and poured myself a glass of water, then another. My body sang with relief.

"I wouldn't call needing a good shot of whiskey because of all the shit I've dealt with thirst, Baz," I complained with a roll of my eyes. "Besides, I've never been susceptible to anything getting in my head before, and I was born with some of the secrets."

He turned to leave the tent, refusing to engage with my protest, but he looked back. A softness filled his eyes.

"The bed is yours," he announced.

"You're leaving?" My brows furrowed in confusion.

"I need to check in with the others, but I'll be back."

I set the glass down and walked over to him, finding comfort as I rested my head in the middle of his chest. Hugging him in a way that let him know I was sorry for acting like a pain, I asked,

"Where will you sleep?"

He turned his head, brushing the top of mine to return the hug. *"At your feet. Just as I've always done."*

I stepped back in awe of him. He fell for me, and as I contemplated his sacrifice, guilt enveloped me. I didn't deserve that kind of loyalty, compassion, or protection.

Baz had been by my side since the beginning of time. I couldn't help but feel disappointed in myself for how little I'd done with my life. Always obsessing over who killed my mother and hell-bent on finding her killers plagued me.

How could it not when I could talk to Uno and Dos? The spirits always knew it was murder, and so did I. If I were being honest, knowing that information brought me enough comfort to push me to attend college.

At least for me, getting a degree in criminology helped so I wouldn't end up in a complete downward spiral. It occupied my time, and I worked to save money. Then I planned to go home to Texas and investigate.

But now, I knew who killed my mom. I could make her proud once I killed Vincent and Maros; then, I would take Vallen's wings with pleasure.

"Thank you, Baz," I said, and squeezed him hard again.

"No problem," he said and chuffed. *"Try to get some rest."*

He left through the tent opening, then I scanned the room, seeing two quilts and a fleece blanket folded inside a metal bin. I craved sleep now, so I walked over and chose one of the quilts to sleep with.

My body thanked me as I undressed, pulled on the t-shirt and sweatpants, then placed all the daggers into my backpack. I wrapped myself in the quilt, not wanting to get under Baz's covers. Something about it felt strange to me. As I settled into the cocoon of warmth, exhaustion washed over me.

When I woke, it felt like I'd slept for a thousand years. I flipped over when I heard chatter outside of the tent and rubbed my eyelids. I sat up and slid out of the bed, placing my feet onto what was supposed to be the ground.

Then, I tripped over someone, hitting both of my knees on the floor. A sharp pain vibrated through my kneecap as I screamed and woke the naked man in front of me.

A man and a woman ran into the tent, swords drawn like they were preparing for battle. Except the man wore only jeans and the woman a black unitard. They looked down, mouths wide open in shock, and lowered their weapons. I stood and limped toward the table without assistance.

"Get him out of here! Where's Baz?" I yelled while searching the tent in a panic.

The door flap opened and Lex stepped inside, and seeing me, he offered his arm to help me regain my balance.

"Thank heavens," I said and grabbed his shoulders. "You've gotta get that guy out of here. I don't know how he ended up in this tent, but please find Baz," I pleaded.

The human tree with blonde hair looked at us, stunned, then grabbed a blanket from the bed to cover himself. He gestured to the others to leave before he stood up.

"Noa," Lex chuckled as the disheveled man walked toward me. "Meet Baz."

I ran my fingers through my tangled hair with a free hand as I clung tightly to Lex for support with the other. Swallowing hard, I examined the man who stood towering over us. Intricate tattoos and symbols covered his entire body, stopping below his collarbone. Some of them replicated the runes on my bracelet and Nakoma's arrows.

The most prominent tattoo that I couldn't take my eyes off was the face of a wolf that covered most of his chest. Its mouth was open as it bared all its teeth against his bulging muscles. They tightened even more as he reached out his hand to shake mine.

"How is this possible?" I whispered as I shook Baz's hand.

Then I took a quick look at Lex, confusion evident in my expression. He let out a hearty laugh, showing his amusement at the situation.

"It more than likely has something to do with your current predicament," Lex reasoned.

Baz cleared his throat, his eyes warming as he glanced at me. "I didn't mean to scare you, Noa." His voice was deep and soothing when he spoke.

I felt the heat rising to my cheeks as he kept a tight grip on the blanket that had inched its way down when he stood. He was a Greek god. I licked my lips and tore my eyes from his to find the right words.

"I'm okay now," I lied. "But I need a minute." Unhooking my arm from Lex and placing one hand on the table, I dropped the other to my side.

Lex eyed the food, now covered with a mesh lid to protect it from bugs. He lifted the lid and piled strawberries into his free hand. I peeked at Baz, who opened drawers from a canvas dresser and pulled out jeans along with a short-sleeved shirt.

I remembered the wolves' and angels' body temperatures were higher than humans'. Baz dropped the blanket so he could get dressed, and I turned away.

"When did you get here, Lex?" I whispered, hoping to take my mind off of the insurmountable male beauty in the tent.

"A couple of hours ago," he said with a nonchalant expression, then ate a cube of cheese. "Ena's here too."

"So everyone's okay?" Relief spread through me with that information.

"Yeah, and there's been a development," Lex shot me a quick smile. "But we were waiting for you two before discussing it."

"You should've woken me, brother," Baz said as he walked up behind Lex and squeezed his shoulders with both hands.

"I peeked in," he admitted, "but I wasn't about to miss Noa finding you like this."

I gasped and slapped Lex's arm. "Jerk!"

A flicker of emotion flashed across Lex's eyes, then a smirk pulled at the corner of his lips. He was beautiful, but so were all the fallen angels, which, in all honesty, unnerved me. Since they were damned to spend eternal life here, I suppose they deserved that much ethereal beauty.

"Where's the coffee?" I groaned and pulled at my hair.

"I'll make you a cup," Lex offered with a laugh.

Folding my hands and resting them on the table, I said, "That's the least you can do."

Shaking his head, he walked to a small area across from us where a single-serve coffee brewer sat. After placing a pod inside, then a paper cup underneath it, he pressed start. I watched him for a moment, then turned my attention to Baz. He inhaled a banana, then walked back over to the bed and sat down. He pulled on a pair of hiking boots with a huge smile plastered on his face.

When I tried to put weight on my foot to walk to him, pain shot through my kneecap. Leaning my back against the table seemed like the better option until I had my coffee and Ena could look at my knee.

"What's with all the human clothes?" I asked, ignoring the throbbing eruption down my shin.

"They've been here," he said while tying his laces, "in case we stay human."

But you didn't, and you've been stuck as a wolf. What idiot angel does that for me? I thought to myself.

"This idiot angel." He winked and stood, walking over to me.

I pointed my finger at him. "No. No way," I declared. "You don't get to do that now. Talk to me like a regular person."

Lex's eyebrows furrowed as he took huge bites from a chocolate muffin while waiting for my coffee. "This ought to be fun with you two," he snickered.

"Noa, you and I are what's called signati," Baz's tone was firm as he met my gaze.

"Signati?" I asked, my eyes darting between him and Lex.

My knee screamed for me to sit down, but I wasn't sure if I could make it to the bed without falling on my face and embarrassing myself.

"It means you're sealed for life," said Lex with raised brows as he poured two packets of sugar and one single creamer into the cup. "It's a covenant," he added, setting the cup in front of me on the table.

"Our bond sealed when you were born," Baz added, placing his arm around my shoulder. "But when I fell, I couldn't be with you all the time like a guardian angel should, which damaged that seal. So for us to be signati here is epic."

"How nice for me," I mocked. I hated this gorgeous, intrusive angel in my space. "If there's any other way for angels to torture me, tell me now, please."

Baz pulled me into him and rested his chin on my head. "I would never have fallen if it hadn't been for you in this situation," he stated with regret. "You need me."

"How does this even happen?" I propped my elbow on the table and rested my head in my hand.

Baz's hand rested softly on my shoulder. "It might be due to the secrets," he said. "Or that bracelet, now that we know Vincent has a need for it."

"Or Callum's essence could be a factor," Lex proposed with his mouth full of grapes. "He juiced you up good."

He chuckled, and my hands slapped the table. My coffee splashed over the edge of the cup, and I grabbed a napkin to wipe it up.

"Sorry," I grimaced. "But I can't believe you're acting like this is funny, Lex."

He placed a hand over mine and shook his head.

"It's amazing for you and Baz," he acknowledged. "Signati represents everything to a guardian angel and provides significant benefits for a human." Lex smiled and took a proud breath. "Who else gets an angel that can shift into a wolf at will and offers unwavering protection? This guy is yours until you die, Noa."

My mind scrambled to make sense of something I would likely never understand. Right then, Baz wrapped one arm around my waist. Cradling my legs, he hoisted me up in his strong arms, and my stomach dropped at his closeness. He placed me on the edge of the bed, then touched my knee, careful not to inflict any more pain.

"I can see it hurts you, but it doesn't feel dislocated," he offered with a reassuring smile.

I shut my eyes, feeling uncomfortable with him fussing over me. "I'll be okay if you get me an ice pack."

"That won't do it." Baz shook his head. I watched as he brushed his forefinger against my knee. A tickling sensation ran through me, followed by a warmth that spread across my kneecap. "Done," he said.

"You fixed it?" I rubbed my knee, and the pain was gone.

"I did. Now, you should get cleaned up." He stood and stretched his arms over his head, then shook them out by his sides.

"Thank you, Baz," I said, then stood up, dying for a shower.

"There's a bunkhouse up the path on the other side of camp." Baz gestured with his thumb toward the door of the tent. "We'll take you and Ena up there. She can stay with you while Lex and I get our packs ready to go."

"I can shower and dress without a guard." I folded my arms and glared at Lex, who shook his head at me.

"We're not letting you out of our sight," Lex confirmed. "We have no idea what Vincent or Maros have planned next." He took the top off the filtered water pitcher and drank the entire canister. "It's too dangerous for you to be alone, Noa," Lex added. "Even in places with extra security."

Annoyed with so much protection, I yanked up my boots from the floor and put them on. Placing my hands on my knees, I gave them both a fake smile. "Fine, but at some point, dads, you're going to have to let your little girl venture out on her own."

"We'll see," Lex said, patting my head. I pushed his arm away, but all he did was laugh.

Baz reached for my hand and I let him take it. "Let's walk, Noa."

"What about these clothes?" I hesitated and went to grab my backpack so I could change.

Lex snatched my backpack before I could reach it, then slung it over his shoulder. "You change after you bathe, but you should put your jacket on."

The corners of my mouth lifted and I inhaled a deep breath through my nose. "I don't need the damn jacket," I stated, shaking my head. "But thank you."

"Okay, then. My mistake," he said, a doubtful tone in his voice. "How are you not freezing to death?"

"Maybe it's all the angel juice." I hissed, and Lex quirked a brow at me, unamused.

Baz led me out of the tent with Lex close behind. A circle of angels and wolves had gathered outside. As they clapped and cheered as we emerged, I saw Ena standing front and center, a warm smile on her face. Every ounce of tension in me melted away as she embraced me.

CHAPTER 26

"How are you?" Ena examined me, her eyes brimming with genuine concern.

"I'm not sure," I whispered, trying to push aside the whirlwind of emotions churning inside me.

A cluster of people gathered around Baz as the brisk mountain air nipped at my cheeks. I rubbed my hands together for warmth, waiting for him to weave through the crowd.

"I'm relieved you made it out of there last night," she said softly.

I slapped a hand against my forehead in frustration. "I'm sorry, Ena. I'm a twit for not thanking you for saving my ass."

She chuckled, biting her bottom lip while sneaking glances at Baz. "You have bigger fish to fry. Besides, uprooting trees and summoning gale-force winds is another Tuesday for me."

"Right." I raised an eyebrow and fixed my gaze on Baz. "What's the story behind those tattoos?"

"They're etched during the ceremony I perform," she replied matter-of-factly.

"That's mind-boggling! How does that work?" I leaned closer, lowering my voice so we wouldn't be overheard.

Ena squinted against the rising sun. "When I utter the incantations during the ceremony, Lex's essence ignites something within me. Tattoos materialize on the angel before he transforms into a wolf." She inhaled a deep breath, then exhaled gradually. "They connect him to both his wolf form and his celestial nature. But I can't believe he's standing here as a human."

"Stop drooling," I nudged her playfully with my shoulder.

She beamed and giggled. "Do you blame me? He's mesmerizing, Noa."

"But don't you have your own angel?" I teased, nodding toward Lex.

"Maybe," she sang with a wide grin and tossed her long black hair over her shoulder.

"What do you know about the signati bond?" I asked.

"He's tethered to you in every conceivable way now," she explained, emphasizing its importance.

"Wait." I raised a hand to halt her words, as my brows shot up. "Not every way, right?" I asked, terrified with raised brows. Even if Baz had a level of gorgeousness that hurt my eyes, we were linked for life, and that would be strange.

Ena shook her head in amusement. "Not at all. You can have a relationship; he won't."

"That's unfortunate," I sighed as I watched him embrace his family, then my shoulders sagged in concern. "Oh no, please tell me he isn't a eunuch."

Ena erupted into laughter so hard she doubled over. I turned

my head to avoid drawing attention to us, but it was too late—
Lex shot us a disappointed glare, resembling a parent disapproving of children interrupting a serious meeting. We both turned away, keeping our backs to them.

"Look," Ena said between gasps of laughter, "guardian angels don't crave romantic connections. You are his world and his sacred duty to protect," she added with a hint of envy lacing her voice.

"Wonderful," I muttered, and wrinkled my face.

"Are you honestly going to hate having that delicious piece attached to you?" She fanned her face and laughed.

"You're killing me, Ena! Focus, please."

I looked over my shoulder and Baz's eyes flickered with concern. He and Lex broke off from the group and walked toward us, both with questions dancing in their eyes. I tapped Ena's arm with the back of my hand before we turned to face them together.

"Everyone okay over there?" I asked, rocking back on my heels.

Baz reached his hands out to guide me up the path. "Everyone knows what to do when the time comes."

"What are you doing?" I protested, trying to pull my hand away from his firm grasp as he continued to lead me forward.

"Protect and guard—remember?" He looked down at me with an endearing softness I'd never seen before as I stood still, refusing to budge.

"You were okay with being close to me when I was a wolf."

"I need some time to adjust, okay?" I smiled at him with a soft expression, and he nodded, understanding my desire for space. "I'm going to walk with Ena."

Baz and Lex moved ahead while Ena fell into step beside me with a light elbow poke in my arm.

"Swoon." She laughed as we made our way down the path toward the bunkhouse.

"Stop." I hugged myself for comfort while keeping my eyes straight ahead. "How's everyone back at Dawson's?"

Ena zipped her jacket closed and looked at me as though she were noticing for the first time that I wasn't wearing one myself. "You aren't cold, Noa?"

I turned my head and shrugged. "No idea why, but more than likely it has to do with Callum's essence flowing through me. That's my guess, anyway."

"Maybe," she said, then put her eyes back on Lex as we kept walking. "There isn't much damage at my grandparents' house. Vincent's angels knew when you left."

"Figures, but I thought we'd have more time to plan." I bit my bottom lip as I tried to think of a way to save my life and everyone else's.

"Yeah, but my grandmother and Dawson are pretty badass with Jossy's help. And of course, Nakoma and Lulu." Ena laughed with a shake of her head, as if she were remembering their efforts from the night before.

"I'm glad you're all safe." I nodded, then I adjusted my pace to catch up with Baz and Lex. I tapped Lex's arm. "What's the new development you were talking about back there?"

Lex's eyes shifted to Ena, then back to me, and we all stood motionless on the path. A wry smile crossed his lips as he said, "Dawson and two other angels saw the tree."

Baz stopped on the trail and grabbed Lex's shoulder with one hand. "You're certain?" he asked.

"Yes," he confirmed. "They took off in the wee hours of the morning and radioed back from the edge of the burial grounds."

"We need to go now," I urged, grabbing Lex's arm. "That angel showed me the tree and the damn mountain with the icy river."

Baz stepped closer to me. "You didn't say anything about water."

A shiver crawled down my spine, and I rubbed my face in irritation. "Yes," I said with certainty. "I told all of you."

Baz shot me a skeptical glance before turning his questioning eyes to Lex. "No," he countered, his tone soft yet sharp. "You only mentioned the tree."

Lex nodded in agreement before meeting my eyes head-on. "He's right, Noa."

Frustration simmered beneath my calm facade as I retorted with a biting tone, "Why does that matter? The tree is what's important."

Baz sighed with a deep breath before placing a guiding arm around me. "It is," he agreed. "But it's better if someone else checks it out before us. In case it is a trap." His voice softened with an edge of caution. "Deep breaths, Noa."

Each step seemed heavier than the last as we continued our ascent up the path.

My eyes drew together. "So, Dawson or Father O'Neil gets to die because of me?" I argued.

Baz pulled me into him as we walked, but I clenched my fists and stormed ahead, furious. I knew they meant well because I needed to stay alive, but not at the cost of others dying. The thought twisted something deep within until I halted mid-step—facing back toward them all.

"How much further?" I called out, my tone edged with impatience. "I'm ready to shower and brush my teeth."

Baz pointed ahead to a shipping container, painted red and transformed into a house. It even included a built-on deck. "Fortunately," Baz announced as he caught up with me. "We have arrived."

"Charming," I offered with indignation coating my words.

"Noa, hold on," Lex said before we stepped inside the house. "You walked away before I could tell you, but Dawson and the angels only saw the tree from a distance. Something is keeping them from crossing the fence line."

My face brightened with excitement and I clapped my hands together. "A barrier! So, that means we're still going?"

"I don't think you should be too thrilled about it," Lex stressed with a shake of his head. "But, yeah, we're going."

I fist-bumped the air as Baz opened the metal door with a ceremonial flourish. As we stepped inside, the one-room structure radiated a surprising coziness. The smell of aged wood mingled with a faint hint of lilac sprinkled the air.

To the left was a small living space. Two oversized chairs faced a small electric fireplace that cast flickering shadows across the room. The kitchen to the right had a short, worn wooden counter.

It had a mini fridge, an ice machine, and a microwave. Nothing more, not even a stove. A foldable card table with four fold-out chairs around it was the dining area.

One bathroom across from where I stood in the entryway had a stand-up shower, sink, and toilet with a small shelf above it holding a few towels. I didn't say another word to my friends as I grabbed my backpack from Lex and left them to their own devices. Grateful for the opportunity to escape into a few minutes of privacy, I locked the door and then turned on the shower.

I grabbed my toothbrush and toothpaste out of my bag, then stepped into the cascade of liquid heat, brushing my teeth first. The tension melted away with each passing minute, and the steam created a cozy sanctuary within the small area.

What I wanted most was to find Vallen, but the visions of the cherry tree meant something. Whether it was about me or the angels, I wasn't sure, but I pushed that aside as I pulled the curtain back and tossed my toothbrush into the sink. I poured soap over every inch of me and began to scrub.

My grandmother's bracelet bounced along my wrist, and I noticed a different inscription, in another language, on the inside of the band. I tried tugging it over my hand again to get a closer look, but it refused to budge. Once more, I loaded my hands with soap and rubbed my wrist, making it as slick as possible.

I pulled at it again and again, but still had no success. The water splashing around my face made it difficult to read the cluster of letters. I lifted my wrist to the light, letting it catch the engraving when there was a knock at the door.

"Lex and I are headed back down to camp, Noa," Baz announced to me through the door.

"Okay... yeah... sure," I mumbled, my eyes glued to the inscription as I struggled to focus.

Then the letters began to rearrange themselves. I rubbed my eyes as the water continued to run across my body. When I opened them, I could read the quote.

My entire body jolted in shock as I whispered them out loud. "The blood forgave. The line remains. The one he loved forever stayed."

In the span of a single heartbeat, the ancient bracelet bit into my wrist like a too-tight rubber band. Struggling against its iron grip proved pointless. My tendons and muscles writhed beneath my skin, appearing eerily bloodless. A hot tremor tumbled down my spine, spilling me onto the shower floor. I opened my mouth to scream, but only silence came out.

Winded, with nothing but sharp inhales for company, I stared at the horror unfolding as the bracelet merged with my bones. With each frantic blink that screamed 'no', it accepted an adamant 'yes'—becoming a permanent part of me. The mysterious designs etched into its surface were now tattooed over my once bare skin by some unseen cosmic hand.

Rubbing my skin, the runes and words mocked me with their permanence. The bracelet had claimed me.

"Baz!" I cried, backing myself into the corner of the shower.

Breaths of air lodged in my lungs between uncontrollable sobs. Overwhelmed with fear, I curled up into a ball, tucking my face into my arms as my wet hair clung to my skin like strands of seaweed. In an instant, splintered wood flew across the bathroom, some landing in the shower.

Baz strode across the tiled floor, his enormous frame casting an imposing shadow over my trembling body. He reached past me to shut off the shower. I flinched at the sudden silence, only broken by my ragged breathing.

"Hey, it's okay," Baz said in a low voice, bending down to eye level with me. "Tell me what happened."

His piercing blue eyes met mine and softened with genuine

concern. Ena slipped into the bathroom, her eyes darting between me and Baz. With a deep breath, she began to channel her magic, drying the soaked floor with each gentle gust.

She swept the wood up against the wall into a pile, then leaned against the bathroom counter, her head hung low. Ena was desperate to help, but in that moment, it was one thing she was powerless to do. She reached for a towel and handed it to Baz.

"Please, Baz," I whispered through chattering teeth, my eyes welling up with fresh tears. "I don't know what's happening to me."

"What do you mean, Noa?" His voice was steady as he helped me stand and wrapped the towel around me.

As I looked into Baz's eyes, I hesitated, then extended my arm with caution, revealing the inscription tattooed on my wrist. The words seemed to dance before my eyes, taunting me with their cryptic message.

"I don't know what it means," I sniffed. "It just appeared, then the bracelet... after it—" I choked back a sob, unable to finish the sentence.

Ena's eyes widened as she walked over to examine my wrist. She studied the tattoo, her fingers tracing the air above my skin. "The bracelet is under her skin," Ena whispered as concern plastered her face, and she offered my hand to Baz.

As our fingers touched, a sudden surge of electricity erupted from my palm. A direct strike to the chest propelled him across the room, causing his back to slam against the wall with a sickening thud. Then, he crumpled to the floor.

"Baz!" I screamed, my hand flying to my mouth in horror, and the towel forgotten on the floor. I caught myself on the counter as my feet slipped out from under me. "I'm so sorry. I don't know what happened," I stammered, tears streaming down my face as I reached out to him, afraid to make contact.

Ena rushed over to Baz as Lex burst into the room. "What's going on?" He flashed a look at me, then turned his back in a swift motion. "You're naked, Noa."

"Shit!" I yanked my towel off the floor, then quickly wrapped it around myself. "You can look now, Lex."

Baz groaned, his hand clutching his stomach as he sat up and leaned against the wall. His eyes now glowed and pulsed the way the other angels did. "I'm all right," he managed to say.

Despite the pain etched on his face, I wanted to believe him, to cling to the hope that we could find out what was happening to me. But as I looked at the troubled faces of my friends, I couldn't shake the feeling that this was something far more terrifying than I had imagined.

"We need to get you out of here, Noa," Lex urged, his voice rising. "Vincent is bound to know this was a possibility, and Maros will follow suit. You're not safe here." He looked down at Baz and held out his hand to help him stand.

A cold fear gripped my heart at the mention of Vincent and Maros. The thought of facing either of them again sent a fresh wave of terror through my body. I wanted to fight them. I wanted to stay alive, but I didn't know how.

Lex helped Baz stand, then they walked out into the living room while I got dressed. Ena stood with her back to me in the doorway as I zipped into a fresh pair of jeans and a sweatshirt. My hands didn't want to work because I kept dropping my clothes no matter how fast I tried to get them on.

I assured myself that what I did to Baz was a fluke, but I couldn't let anyone else get hurt because of me. Once dressed, I retrieved the belt of daggers from the backpack and slid Vincent's into my back pocket. After securing the belt to my leg again, I turned Ena around by her shoulders and made her face me.

"Forgive me, please," I begged with all sincerity.

I pushed her to the side with more strength than I meant to, sprinting toward the door on the side of the container. My only goal was to escape before anyone could stop me. But before I could make it out of the doorway, Baz caught me and held me close.

I struggled against his solid hold, my mind reeling with the need to escape, but it was futile. Ena looked at me, annoyed, as she rubbed her arm. I expected her to be angry with me, but she shook her head in disappointment.

"Seriously, Noa?" she asked with a glare, then glanced at Baz.

Baz released me from his embrace, but kept a steadying hand on my shoulder as his eyes hardened onto mine. "You have to give us a minute to gather our backpacks before we can leave."

"No," I objected. "You're safer if I go alone, so let me." I pleaded and held my wrist up to his face.

Lex cracked his knuckles as he drew in a sharp breath. "This is the exact type of thing I said not to do that would get us all killed."

As a tear ran down my cheek, Baz lightly wiped it away with his thumb. His eyes never left mine while he spoke.

"Ena," he calmly requested. "Take two of the wolves and get

back to Dawson's. There has to be something about this bracelet in the vault somewhere."

"On it." She nodded and started to open the door, but Lex stopped her.

"And grab one of the satellite walkie-talkies to stay in touch, please," Lex added with wide eyes.

My eyes broke from Baz right as Ena hurled a glare at me, and my heart dropped. "I like you, Noa," she sighed. "So, please get a handle on this before you wipe us all out. Forever." She kissed Lex's cheek and walked out the door.

"We have to move fast," advised Lex as he walked into the bathroom, picked up my clothes, and stuffed them into my backpack. Handing it to me, he asked, "Can you handle this?"

"I want to, but Lex—" I began, and I looked at the floor.

"You have the strength, Noa." He placed a hand on my shoulder. "I've seen it every day since we met."

I nodded in agreement, taking deep breaths to try to steady my nerves. Baz cleared his throat and touched my jaw with gentle pressure, prompting me to meet his gaze.

"It's time for me to change," he informed me, then strode confidently toward the fireplace, removing his clothes with ease.

CHAPTER 27

First went his shirt, then he unzipped his pants. His chiseled torso caught my eye, with muscles rippling beneath his skin. I instinctively turned to Lex, shielding my gaze from Baz's transformation into a powerful beast.

Despite my reluctance, I couldn't resist sneaking a peek at the stunning display of nature's power. His skin rippled, and he fell to the ground, quickly transforming into a massive wolf. His dark fur glimmered with shades of silver and blue that danced in the shadows of the fire.

"It's almost unfair how all of you look like perfect statues," I remarked with a hint of frustration.

Lex chuckled, his chest rumbling beneath my hand. "Would you rather we look like those pudgy cherubs in the store? No one would take us seriously then," he joked. "Besides, you're a strong woman. You can handle it."

"Creep," I muttered into his arm, trying to hide my smile.

As Baz padded towards the door on powerful paws, I turned

around, mesmerized by the sheer magnificence and primal beauty of him. We stepped outside into the cold afternoon air, and three others from camp greeted us, waiting with backpacks.

One was a hiking pack for Lex and a sling backpack for me. The other was a saddlebag that one of the angels secured to Baz, along with an even bigger neck strap than the one Lex had secured to him last night.

"Did you call for them?" I questioned Baz.

"I did," he divulged with a grunt as the angel tightened the saddle on him.

I raised my eyebrows as I swapped backpacks with an angel who had tattoos covering her entire body, making sure to keep Vincent's dagger with me. Her all-seeing eye tattoo glared at me from the middle of her throat. The delicate cherry tree design inked onto her skin extended up to her jawline, adding to its beauty.

"How long are you expecting us to be gone?" I dared to ask, unable to avert my gaze from the angel's neck.

"Overnight," Lex confirmed. "It's better that we're prepared."

"Especially with the uncertainty of the wards remaining intact," added Baz, now lying next to me, his back level with my shoulder.

As I stood next to Lex, waiting for him to finish securing his pack, I slung mine over my shoulder. An unusual sensation ran through my body like a live power line. It was a strange feeling, almost as if something had awakened inside me. Maybe I would be useful and have a shot at fighting off Vincent and Maros since I seemed to have my own enhancements like Ena.

I still felt guilty for shocking Baz, but whether it was the bracelet or Callum's essence, I was grateful for it. But what did the bracelet fusing to my bones mean? The uncertainty almost made me sick, wondering if it needed the last remaining person from my family who held the secrets to complete the transfer back to the veil.

My thoughts drifted to the inscription on my wrist, the words that had appeared when the bracelet fused to my bones.

The blood forgave. The line remains. The one He loved forever stayed.

They had appeared without explanation, a permanent reminder of something I couldn't understand. It taunted me every time my skin twitched, and I felt like ripping off the bracelet even though I couldn't. My thoughts turned back to Vincent and what he might know about this.

He had given the bracelet to Sasha—but why? Was there some deeper meaning behind his actions? Or did he not realize the power it held at all?

Regardless of the circumstances, it was crucial to uncover the truth behind the jewelry that had bonded itself to me. Especially if we had any chance of saving me and everyone else. And as we prepared for our next move, my mind was buzzing with questions and theories about its true nature and purpose.

"Ready to ride?" asked Lex, bringing me back to the present, and Baz nodded for me to climb up onto his back.

I secured Vincent's dagger inside one of Baz's saddlebags, then readied myself on top of Baz.

"Are these supposed to be reins?" I laughed as I inspected two additional leather bands attached to the belt around Baz's neck.

"They'll work for now," Baz assured me with a huff. *"We'll get O'Neil and Nakoma to make something more suited to you later."*

"I've never ridden a horse, so how the hell do I ride a wolf?" I asked both of them. The inflection in my tone was skeptical as I fiddled with the handles.

"The same way you did last night." Lex glanced at me with a smirk. "Hold on."

I rolled my eyes, then slid my hands through the middle of each one and held the straps with my palms. Baz's powerful legs propelled us forward at an incredible speed, and Lex kept our pace while running alongside us. The wind whipped through my hair as we raced across the terrain, leaving the bunkhouse and the camp behind.

As we emerged from the shelter of the trees, my breath hitched in my throat. Before us lay a vast meadow, filled with lilac bushes in full bloom. The sight was breathtaking and ethereal, as the delicate purple flowers swayed in the gentle breeze.

"Pit stop," Baz murmured, indicating for me to dismount.

My eyes lit up at the beauty of it all. "How is this possible?" I whispered in surprise. "It's not even spring yet."

Baz answered me as he stretched his legs out in front of him. *"The lilacs are the land's way of giving back to us when we lose one of our brothers or sisters."*

I walked forward, my fingers brushing against the silky petals of the flowers. The scent was intoxicating, a sweet perfume that filled the air. For a moment, I let myself get lost in the beauty of it all and forgot about being hell-bound once it was over.

"Is this where you bury the fallen?" I stopped to smell the flowers.

Lex's tone teemed with honor as he removed his pack. "The valley is on the other side of the fence ahead," he pointed toward a roped-off part of the fence not too far away, "but our bones and feathers fertilize this field."

"It's gorgeous," I announced.

The aroma of vanilla and roses enveloped me in its lush embrace, and I smiled. But my peaceful contemplation was interrupted when my wrist began to tingle, and the etchings on my skin glowed with intensity.

I raised my arm to show Baz and Lex. "What's happening?"

Lex's expression mirrored my confusion, and right as I stepped forward, the sound of beating wings filled the sky.

"Get down!" Baz's plea echoed in my ears. He bit my jeans and pulled us into the grass below, seeking cover under the lilacs.

I dropped into the bushes, covering my head like a tornado was ready to run us down. In a mere heartbeat, Lex tossed his pack into the field a few feet away. He army crawled to it, keeping as low as possible, unzipped a pocket to remove something, then crawled back toward me and Baz.

Baz growled into my head. *"Don't say a word,"* he ordered me, his words laced with urgency.

"Is it Vincent or Maros?" I asked, my wrist burning like it wanted me to fight back. I didn't expect to hurt Baz, but I didn't know how to control any of the electricity radiating through my body.

Lex whispered as he lay down next to me, "Maybe both."

"Noa, please stop talking," Baz begged me, with a growl coming from his throat.

"We could easily outrun them," I griped at him, my tone sharp from the pain stinging my skin.

Baz huffed a hot breath of air in my face, his frustration evident about my idea. *"The point of hiding is so they don't find us."*

I lifted my head and made an annoyed face at Baz, then asked, "They can't touch the ground here, right?"

Lex shook his head no. For the first time, it was he and not Jossy who grabbed a ponytail holder from his pocket. He tied back his auburn hair to see better. Baz nudged me under my arm, and I carefully turned onto my back.

When I looked up, two angels with monstrous black wings hovered like vultures above us. The lilacs and grass in the field provided enough cover from them since they couldn't get as close as they wanted to scan the area.

Staying close to me, Lex rolled to his side and opened one of the saddlebags attached to Baz, pulling out a small, yet functional, modernized war hammer. The black rubber handle was short enough for throwing if needed. It had a tapered, talon-like blade on one side, and the other side was a round, flat head. Sticking up from the top was a three-leaf spike.

"Hold onto this, Noa," Lex said, placing the hammer in my hands. "Just in case."

"What am I supposed to do with this?" I asked, shock obvious in my tone.

"If you need to," he stated, shaking his head like I'd had years of practice. "Swing. Then swing some more."

Although the wards did not have full power, they limited the angels' scope of the area. I gripped the weapon with a firm hold, and a crackling sensation flickered at the tips of my fingers like I was a superhero.

"We need to get out of here, guys. Something isn't right with this bracelet that has decided to glue itself to me," I worried, holding the hammer and gesturing for them to look at my hands.

"The wards are down," Baz stated as he looked up at the sky.

"Yeah, and we need to get to that tree before it's too late," I demanded. My heart leaped into my throat before I added, "I've been thinking about how Vincent wanted this bracelet. It has to do with Vallen."

"Why would he do that?" questioned Lex with a puzzled look on his face, inching closer to me. "Isn't it better for Vincent if Vallen stays locked up?"

"Not if they need him to retrieve the secrets," I said, and closed my eyes to think.

Wings of the dark fallen beat in the sky with a force that could lull one to sleep under different circumstances. I steadied my heartbeat and searched my mind, feeling the energy of the secrets, Callum, and the bracelet pulsing through my veins.

"I feel you. Come to me," a raspy voice demanded.

My eyes popped open as goosebumps covered my body as I released a silent scream. "The guy in my head made contact," I panted. "He knows we're close."

Lex's eyes grew wide, and I could tell he was trying to find a way to get up and leave without us getting caught. Baz noticed too because he looked at Lex and growled, then shook his head.

I squeezed tighter to the handle of the hammer. "Oh my god!" I exclaimed in the quietest voice possible.

"What is it now?" Lex asked, a look of displeasure covering his face.

Releasing the hammer into the grass, I stared at the sky, my eyes gliding with the angels who searched for me. "It's a key," I revealed as I felt the bracelet move with my bones.

Then, as one angel swooped down to get a closer look at the field, it vanished into thin air. A breath caught in my lungs, and I waited for what felt like hours, but in reality, it was a mere second before I jumped to my feet. Our invisible protection had returned.

"The bracelet is a key to Vallen's prison!" I yelled, handing the hammer back to Lex, then readjusting my crossbody bag. I began pacing back and forth, running through my thoughts out loud. "It has to be here somewhere. There's no reason Vincent would lie about owning the bracelet and say we couldn't get to Vallen if this thing wasn't a key."

Lex already stood next to me, holstering his pack again, and I looked down at Baz. "Get up! What are you waiting for?" I said, moving my hands in a hurried motion.

I started walking and left Lex to finish securing his pack. Baz trotted beside me at a quicker pace. *"You need to think about the fact that Vallen is not without power. If you find him, he could obliterate you."*

"Lights out. I know." I stopped in my tracks, spinning around to face him with a hand pressed against my forehead. *"Vallen won't let me die. It's all part of his twisted plan to retrieve the secrets for the veil. And with my soul in his grasp, he thinks he holds all the power."* I raised my hands to the sky in gratitude. *"That could be the one thing Vincent didn't lie about."*

Baz leaned in closer, his voice skeptical as he pressed further. *"Which is what, exactly?"*

I swallowed hard before answering, my head spinning with enthusiasm, and I smiled. *"The colossal task of getting my soul back."*

Lex caught up to us as excitement rose in me and my thoughts drifted to my mother. A heavy pressure settled in my chest, a constant reminder of her absence. I missed her gentle smile and the way she always knew what to say to make every-thing better when it wasn't.

But now, she and Sasha were in hell, getting tortured by demons. Probably by Maros, if he had his way. If I could get their souls back too, they could rest in peace.

"Noa," Lex said as he studied my face. "We have an inkling of where the tree is. How are we going to find an invisible, not to mention heavily guarded, angel prison?"

I halted at the edge of the field, where twisted ancient trees marked the beginning of the angel burial grounds. Their gnarled branches were like skeletal hands reaching out.

"Well," I breathed. "I'm pretty sure the angel at the tree will tell us if you guys would quit stopping and avoiding getting there."

Baz stood next to me, his blue eyes meeting mine as he shifted back into his human form, letting the saddlebags and the belt fall to the ground.

"We're not avoiding it, Noa," Baz said, his eyes narrowing at me. "But throwing yourself into a snake den without any clue of how to handle it will kill us all, not only you."

I couldn't bring myself to look at his exposed body again. It was too raw and overwhelming. My gaze frantically searched for something—anything—else to fixate on. Hiding my eyes with my hand, I turned to face Lex, then heard Baz digging through his bags.

"Next time, give me a heads-up before you shift," I snapped through gritted teeth.

"She's got a point, man," Lex agreed as his mouth quirked, stifling a laugh.

"Sorry, it's not intentional," Baz sighed. "But my emotions get the better of me when Noa starts going off on ideas that will get us all exterminated." I heard a zipping sound and huffing. "You can turn back around now."

"Baz," I pleaded, "What if...what if there's a way to get their souls back? Not just my mom and Sasha, but everyone taken from my family? They could leave hell."

"Enough," he commanded. "Noa, I understand how much you hate Vallen for killing your mother. And stealing your souls, but getting them back is impossible. Your mom... she's gone. So is Sasha. They all are."

"Do you even hear yourself?" I challenged, growing frustrated with each of them dismissing my decision. Shoving my wrist in both of their faces, I said, "Looks like I've got the upper hand here. And trust me—I can do a lot more than bargain."

"You can't bargain with a sociopathic, soul-stealing angel of one of the highest orders," Lex added with a heavy breath. "We need a solution to keep you alive."

"That's exactly what I'm doing." I proceeded to unhook the rope that separates the lilacs and the Valley of the Fallen, then looked back at both of them. "Y'all coming?"

Baz nodded reluctantly, his gaze locking with mine. "Lead the way," he commented, still unsure of our decision or what I would do once we found Vallen.

After shouldering his saddlebags and securing the belt to Lex's hiking pack, Baz stepped onto the pathway we would follow through the valley. With a final glance back at the lilac field, I turned and then crossed a threshold onto ground that shook my body with all the ancient energy it held.

CHAPTER 28

As we walked through the Valley of the Fallen, a worn path led the way. With each step, the vibrant green underfoot dulled to lifeless brown. Charred ground crumbled beneath our feet; the air was thick with the scent of ash.

A shiver ran through me, and not from the frigid air. The valley felt wrong somehow—eerie and unsettling in a way I couldn't quite define. I hugged my arms across my chest as I glanced up at the sky, now an ominous gray. Another snowstorm was headed for us.

"You okay?" Baz asked, noticing my unease.

I didn't have the opportunity to respond, as he inched closer and wrapped an arm around my shoulders, pulling me against his solid warmth.

"Yeah," I mumbled, unconvinced. "This place gives me the heebie-jeebies. I'm feeling buzzy, and it's a different kind of cold here."

As if on cue, a gust of icy wind whipped past us, cutting right through me. I shuddered again and burrowed deeper into Baz's side, and he rubbed my arm as he tightened his hold on me.

"That's hellfire cold," he said. "A temperature of fire so high that it turns cold and invisible."

Lex looked back at Baz and shook his head in what I assumed was a gesture to not tell me more than I needed to know about hell. He was right about my not wanting to know.

"We'll be through here soon," Lex said over his shoulder. He scanned the perimeter, ever vigilant. "Stick close and don't let your guard down."

I sprinted ahead of Baz and stayed between him and Lex as we walked. An otherworldly hum emanated from the ground through the soil as we walked farther, and I stopped Baz.

"I need Vincent's dagger," I requested and held out my palm.

Once Baz located it and the knife was in my possession, we continued down the path. My gaze drifted once more to the charred half of the valley. The blackened soil seemed to writhe in my periphery, as if tormented by unseen phantoms of the fallen angels.

I blinked hard, telling myself it's a trick of the fading light. Still, I couldn't shake the feeling that something watched us - something sinister lurking beyond the shadows, biding its time. Biting my lip, I matched my steps to Baz and Lex's brisk pace. But as we walked, the unease in my gut grew stronger.

We needed to get out of the valley—and fast. Before the shadows gathering at the edges of my vision took form and the whispers on the wind became something far worse.

"Why did we have to come this way?" I asked, my gaze darting between the charred wasteland and the vibrant purple of the lilacs. "Couldn't we have gone around?"

Baz's jaw tightened, his eyes scanning the horizon. "It's the fastest way to the tree."

"It won't matter." I swallowed hard, my heart hammering against my ribs. "Vincent and Maros are bound to be waiting for me now."

"They don't know about what's happened with the bracelet," Lex reminded me, kicking a rock out of our path. "And they don't know you think Vallen's prison is here."

My stomach churned at the thought of facing Vallen, and the horrors I had to traverse to get there were beginning to weigh on me.

Baz's hand found mine, his fingers lacing through my own. "I know it's a lot to take in, Noa. How are you doing?"

"Her enhancements will help her out," Lex said as he turned around to face us but kept walking backward. "She'll be fine."

"You don't know that!" I yelled back to him. Spinning the dagger sideways in my hand, I flipped Lex the middle finger.

Baz cleared his throat, his voice low and hesitant. "Do you want to talk about the bracelet? What it's doing to you?"

I glanced down at my wrist, and the memory of it sinking into my flesh, of my bones shifting and reforming, sent a wave of nausea rolling through me.

"It was like something out of a horror movie," I whispered. The thought of it made my hair stand on end. "The way my skin just... ripped open. And the bracelet, it didn't just attach itself, it... it became a part of me."

Baz's hand tightened around mine, his thumb stroking

soothing circles on my palm. "I can't even imagine what that must have felt like."

Lex approached us, his brow furrowed with concern. "Noa, may I see your wrist?"

I hesitated, then released Baz's hand and held out my arm. The strange, foreign script tattooed into my skin seemed to shimmer in the dim light of the valley. Lex studied the markings and inscription, his fingers tracing over the now-scarred lines with great focus.

His eyes widened with recognition. "I've seen this somewhere before," he murmured.

"Yeah, it's for protection," I confirmed with a nod.

"I'm sorry I didn't pay closer attention until now," he apologized, shaking his head. "But this is in some of Father O'Neil's tomes from around the time of the crucifixion."

My heart skipped a beat with that information. "What does it mean?"

"I can't remember all of the details," Lex admitted, shaking his head. "But it has something to do with the crucifixion. With the apostles, and how they stayed behind after Jesus ascended."

A shiver traced my spine as we listened to Lex's story. "What do the apostles have to do with me?"

"How could Noa's family have any connection to them?" Baz echoed my thoughts with his question.

"Really, brother?" Lex responded sarcastically. "All humans have some connection to them."

He walked behind Baz and me this time, amused at what he thought was a big discovery. He pressed the buttons on the walkie-talkie in a hurry to get Ena on the radio.

"I'll let her know I had an epiphany," Lex laughed. When Ena answered, his face lit up.

The valley seemed to stretch on forever, an endless expanse of death. But finally, we reached the edge, marked by a towering iron gate. And then I saw it.

Beyond the gate, a massive cherry blossom tree rose from the ground, its pale pink petals a stark contrast to the dark blue grass that surrounded it. A waterfall cascaded down a mountainside in the distance, half black and half white, like in my vision. The realization hit me like a physical blow, stealing the air from my lungs.

I swallowed hard as different emotions warred inside me, but there was no turning back.

"This is it," I breathed. "The place from my vision after my birthday."

I scanned the gate for some kind of lock or latch. But there wasn't one. Only unbroken iron bars guarding the path.

"You won't find a lock," Baz said, standing next to me. "It's not sealed shut. Go ahead and push it open."

With a dismissive huff, I pressed a hand to the gate. It swung outward with a low creak.

"Fingers crossed," I muttered, looking at Lex.

The first time I saw the gate, I couldn't get in no matter how hard I tried. It was an impenetrable barrier. But visions are subjective, I reminded myself. Maybe being locked out symbolized something else entirely. An obstacle of the mind rather than a physical one.

"I don't see anyone," Baz whispered. Then, he stepped over the threshold and toward the center of the field.

"That's a good thing, right?" I asked as I took one step forward. Unlike Dawson, I was able to get through the gate, and I followed Baz. Shoving the dagger back into the pack, I said, "Not a trap."

Lex offered me a silent nod as he joined me and Baz on the other side of the gate. "Vincent might think you're on the run and nowhere near here. Especially since his groupies didn't see us back there."

I flashed him a smile. "Why don't you let Ena know? I'm sure she wouldn't mind hearing your voice again." I tipped my chin at him with a quick raise of my brows.

"Let's keep moving," said Baz, unamused at our exchange. "I don't want whoever is feeding the tree to alert anyone besides us."

We made our way into the grove as green grass turned a deep ocean blue, and our footsteps muffled in the thick carpet of fallen cherry blossom petals. I stared at the trunk and branches lit up from the inside with a golden glow. The veins of the tree were pulsing. As I watched in awe at this living and breathing heart of the fallen, a sharp, searing pain cut through my upper lip.

I gasped and pressed my hand to my scar flaring in pain. Then, a cough full of phlegm and irritation filled my mind, and I gagged at the sound.

"Hurry," the ragged voice choked.

"What's wrong?" Baz whipped his head toward me.

"The angel," I gritted through clenched teeth. "He senses me somehow, and if this is some supernatural game of hot and cold?" I forced a mirthless laugh. "Consider me burned."

I rubbed the sting away, scanning the delicate pink blossoms.

They seemed to twinkle in the evening sky. A strange sensation washed over me, raising the fine hairs along my arms. As I took another step forward, Lex's hand shot out, grasping my elbow.

"Careful," he warned, pointing to a fallen branch on the ground.

Stepping over it, I approached the tree and swore it sang out to me. The leaves began to pick up and play around us as I moved closer. The petals seemed to glow against the evening sky. It was as though the tree wanted me to touch it, so I reached my hand out in front of me.

"Don't!" yelled Baz, who ran in front of me. "We don't know what will happen."

"Fuck, Baz. You've got to relax," I groaned and walked around to the other side of the tree. "I could've stabbed you if I'd been ready."

"But you weren't." His lip curled up as he chuckled while following my every move now. "I'm glad the knife makes you feel safe, but when we're done with all of this, you will get the training you need."

Around the tree, lying face-first on the ground, was one angel, not two. A pool of shiny liquid surrounded her. I stepped back as Lex bent down to check her pulse. He shook his head and looked around for another angel, but there wasn't one.

"So, if she is dead, then who's in my head?" I asked, terrified of the answer.

Baz scoped the area around us as Lex walked around the tree again. My eyes followed the pool of liquid into the grass behind us and over toward the river separating us from the river. I walked the line, taking my time to follow its path, which led to the edge. Lingering for an instant, I shook my head, angry with myself for not realizing it sooner.

I could feel Baz and Lex staring at me from behind. I should've been shocked, maybe even afraid. But I was growing used to the impossible. I shoved the dagger into my back pocket, then shook out my hands, trying to dispel the tingling in my fingertips.

"Let's not keep Vallen waiting," I called back to them over my shoulder.

Baz caught up with me and stood next to me as I stared at chunks of ice passing by us. "Are you feeling okay? You said Vallen," he remarked.

"Feeling a lot of things," I muttered, more to myself than to him. I struggled to put words to the jumble of emotions coursing through me. "It's him, Baz," my voice cracked. "Vallen's in my head, and I'm pretty sure he's the one feeding the tree."

"Whoa, what?" Lex interjected as he rubbed his temples, hearing the news.

I squared my shoulders and took a deep, fortifying breath. Looking up at both of them, I snapped, without regard for either of their feelings. "It's him and he's in this fucking mountain. Don't ask me how I know. Let's get across, because I've got an angel to interrogate."

Another sharp pain shot through my lip, and my foot slipped on the slick riverbank. Strong arms wrapped around my waist, halting my fall. I found myself pressed against Baz's muscular chest, those glowing blue eyes filled with dread as he steadied me.

"Careful, Noa," he cautioned, his breath warm against my cheek.

"Y-yeah," I managed with a smile and straightened myself. "Thanks for the save."

Baz nodded and stated to me without missing a beat, "I'm going to lift you into my arms. Then Lex is going to help you climb up for a piggyback ride."

I hesitated, thinking it was the dumbest idea possible and I'd drown under the river current, except I knew they wouldn't put me in a life-threatening situation. I wrapped my arms around Baz's neck and nodded for him to hoist me up. Lex moved to Baz's side, ready to catch me if I fell.

The icy current swirled around Baz's legs as he waded across, and my arms grew tighter around his neck. He tapped my arm to give him some breathing room.

"I'm behind you, Noa. I'll catch you if you fall, but loosen up," said Lex with a chuckle. "Let's not strangle Baz to death."

Baz's steps remained steady, his hold on me secure. I marveled at his strength, both physical and mental. What must it be like to be so certain of one's purpose? To have an unshakable duty to another person and make sure they're always safe.

There was nothing about me that could take on that amount of responsibility. Returning these secrets to their rightful home as soon as possible would be best for us all.

Baz glanced back at me, a brief smile tugging at his lips. "Almost there. Doing okay?"

I managed a nod, tightening my grip. "Yeah. Let's get this over with."

After a few tense minutes, we reached the opposite bank. Baz set me down, his hands lingering at my waist a moment longer than necessary. I felt the loss of his warmth as I slid from his back, but the cold at the mountain didn't match that of the hellfire. Callum's essence was a lifesaver.

To the left, the waterfall roared between the black and white mountains, the icy spray creating a fine mist in the air. If my interpretations of my visions were correct, then Vallen was imprisoned in a cave somewhere behind the wall of water on the other side.

CHAPTER 29

Despite the butterflies in my stomach, I walked in sync with Baz, while Lex trailed closely behind us. We skirted the edge of the mountain to the other side, and I was grateful we didn't need to climb.

We came to a stop, and a thunderous crash of water on rock above grew deafening. Icy gusts buffeted us from all sides. Finally, we reached a dead end, and the mountain face rose up in an impenetrable wall before us.

"Now what?" I shouted over the roar of the water.

Lex ran his hands over the slick black stone, searching for any hidden mechanisms. "Nothing here to indicate an entrance, Baz."

"Look up." He pointed to an overhang situated three feet above my head. "You can get Noa up there to crawl inside and check."

I shook my head and walked away. "No way. You're insane."

"It's our only shot, Noa," said Lex, grabbing my arm and pulling me back.

I swallowed hard and took a deep inhale. "I can't believe I'm doing this."

Lex unfurled his wings and handed me a tiny flashlight from the backpack. "You've got this."

"You're lucky it's not that far up." I scowled at him as he wrapped his arms around me. "Also, I want my vape back since I'm doing this," I advised.

He laughed knowing he'd never agree, then hovered above the ground. Lex lifted me to a small tunnel in the side of the mountain, and I crawled inside. I took off my sling pack, handing it to him, then placed the flashlight between my teeth.

Climbing inside the crawlspace on my stomach, I searched for the opening to Vallen. Pulling the flashlight from my mouth, I pointed it down the tunnel and to each side. "There's nothing here, and I've touched everything with my wrist."

"You sure?" Lex sounded skeptical as he hovered outside the entrance.

"Yes!" I yelled, irritation coating my tone. "Do you want to get in here?"

I moved further into the tunnel to where my feet were no longer visible. It grew wider, and I was able to turn over onto my back. Taking a deep breath, I scanned the walls, but still nothing. Looking up, I noticed a small hole above me, and I had an idea.

"Anything?" Lex called in after me, his voice sounding anxious.

"I'm probably going to regret this, but hold on!" I called out to him.

Keeping the flashlight in one hand, I raised my other arm

where the bracelet sat beneath my skin and placed it in the open space above me. I prayed that nothing would eat my hand or rip my arm off.

Feeling around with my fingers, there wasn't a lever or any type of button, but there was an odd groove in the rock. Taking a deep breath, I set my wrist inside, and a needle-like pain shot through my arm.

I squeezed my eyes shut, only to pitch forward as the stone beneath me gave way. The world tilted and I slid down, then tumbled forward hard on my hands and knees, loose gravel biting into my palms. Beside me, Baz and Lex stood startled as I looked up at them, water misting into my face.

Breathing hard, I raised my head, hardly daring to hope. My eyes widened as I turned around to see the mountainside open. I scrambled to my feet as Lex picked up his hiking pack and then handed me mine. Baz looked around to see if anyone was watching us, but he pointed forward, and we hurried inside the small doorway.

"Where's the flashlight?" Lex asked as he swiftly searched the area.

"Lost it at some point," I said, "but it has to be here somewhere."

Placing my back against the entryway, I leaned forward, using the light from outside to help. Bending down, the cylindrical blue glint caught my eye, and I pointed.

"At your feet, Baz," I said and pointed to the floor.

Baz picked up the flashlight and tapped it in his hand to get it to turn on again. "Shall we?" he asked, using the light to guide us forward.

I placed my arm on the wall for support, and the mountain

began to grow dark. The roar of the waterfall had faded to a muffled hum; the air around us was still and musty. Darkness pressed in from all sides, thick and disorienting as the flashlight flickered. I blinked rapidly, trying to make out my surroundings, but it was like staring into a void.

"Let me see it," Lex muttered. I heard him rummaging through his pack, then with a click, he turned on the flashlight. "Extra batteries for the win."

The beam cut through the cavernous shadows, illuminating rough-hewn walls of black stone. We were in a tunnel, narrow and winding, disappearing into the depths of the mountain. Lex moved forward, the flashlight bobbing with each step.

Baz and I followed, our footsteps echoing in the confined space. As we walked, I noticed strange markings etched into the walls, angular letters that seemed to shimmer in the dim light. They were angelic runes, but they looked as though they were a different language altogether.

"I've never seen anything like this." Lex traced his fingers over the symbols, his brow furrowed. "Some kind of ancient angelic language I've never been privy to."

Baz leaned in for a closer look, his eyes narrowed in concentration. "And these words here look like a different version of Latin. I recognize some of them, but I'm not sure what they all mean."

I struggled to hear him as my attention focused inward. With each step deeper into the mountain, a growing sense of unease coiled in my gut. I could feel the weight of the stone above us, crushing and immovable. Each breath came in short, ragged gasps, echoing in my ears as my heart pounded a frantic rhythm against my ribcage.

"Noa?" Lex's voice seemed to come from far away. "Are you breathing?"

I shook my head, struggling to form words. "I can't—I don't think I can."

The tunnel expanded into a wider path, and Baz stopped. He unscrewed the cap of a water bottle and handed it to me. "Here, drink this. Try to take slow, deep breaths through your nose and out of your mouth."

Taking small sips, I fought to calm my racing heart. Gradually, it slowed, leaving me drained and shaky.

"I'm sorry," I whispered, embarrassed by my moment of weakness. "I don't know what came over me."

"Don't apologize," Lex insisted. "This trek could very well be leading us all into complete and utter destruction."

I managed a small smile at his feeble attempt to help me feel better. Taking a deep breath, I straightened my shoulders and nodded for Lex to continue. Lex's flashlight cut through the gloom, illuminating more faded Latin inscriptions etched into the stone. Baz paused, his brow furrowed as he studied the ancient words.

"Can you read those?" I questioned. My words bounced across the confined space.

"It's something about guarding, protecting..." He leaned back and glanced at me. "And a prisoner."

A chill raced down my spine, and the thought of confronting Vallen sent a wave of nausea rolling through me. I swayed on my feet, my vision blurred at the edges.

"Whoa, easy there." Baz's arms encircled me, holding me steady.

I leaned into his embrace, drawing strength from his solid presence. "I don't know if I can do this, Baz. What if—"

"Hey, look at me." He tilted my chin up, his eyes finding mine in the dim light. "We'll find the answers we need and figure out how to return the secrets, get your soul, and all will be right with the world."

I nodded and released a long breath. "Okay. But I don't believe you about the world getting set right."

"I know." Baz flashed a soft smile and nodded.

Lex laughed too loudly for the tunnel. "Did my brother crack a joke? The world really is ending."

"Focus," I said as I exhaled another deep breath. "Please."

We followed Lex deeper into the mountain, the beam of his flashlight guiding our way. The air grew colder with each step, our breath misting in front of our faces. After what felt like an eternity, we reached a dead end—another wall.

"Are you fucking kidding me?" I screamed and kicked it as the frustration in me boiled over. "We're supposed to be here! Why is nothing going right?"

"There's got to be a way through," Lex muttered, running his flashlight over the surrounding walls.

A glint of silver caught my eye, and I moved closer, my palms sweating as I tried to make out the words etched into the stone. "Guys, over here!"

I grabbed the flashlight and directed the beam of light onto the inscription, illuminating the Latin phrase. Baz stepped forward, his brow furrowed in concentration. He held up a finger and read it aloud.

"Sanguis qui manet aperit et aere. It's the inscription from your bracelet, Noa," Baz revealed.

Both men looked at me, waiting, and I lifted my shoulders. "What do I do?" I asked.

"Recite it and see if that works," instructed Lex while pointing at the wall.

Looking back and forth between the stone and my wrist, I recited the lines. "The blood forgave. The line remains. The one he loved forever stayed."

Baz looked around when nothing happened. "Hmm, you might have to speak in Latin," he advised.

"Before I butcher a new language, maybe there's another way," I suggested, placing my hands on my hips. "Earlier I slid my wrist into another opening. Look around for a hole or somewhere my wrist will line up and connect with something."

I waved the flashlight around, but nothing else stuck out. Then it hit me. I raised my arm again and laid my hand flat against the wall, letting my wrist connect with the Latin inscription. Heat flared beneath my skin as the bracelet pulsed against my bones.

Then, a soft blue glow emanated from the phrase, tracing a path along the wall until it reached the middle. With a spark and a pop, the rock crumbled, giving way to another iron door.

"You did it, Noa!" Baz exclaimed, his face breaking into a grin.

Lex let out a whoop of joy, and the two of them pulled me into a tight hug. For a fleeting moment, I allowed their embrace to comfort me, forgetting my fears in the wake of our success. I laughed while pulling down on a lever embedded in the side of the mountain, feeling a wave of anxiety.

Lex held onto the flashlight, its beam piercing through the suffocating darkness of the underground cave. As the beam swept across the space, it illuminated a figure chained to the far wall. A man with a long, matted beard and dark hair that hung in tangles around his face slumped against his restraints.

"I can't tell if he's breathing," I moved my head from side to side and noticed a faint rise in his chest.

"If so," Lex noted. "It's not much."

Baz's sharp inhale beside me caused me to flinch. "Is that...?" he asked.

My stomach knotted as beads of sweat formed on my forehead. I took one step closer, and he raised his head with gradual movement. Those green eyes that haunted me flashed with hatred in my direction. I couldn't tear my eyes away, even though I knew finding him alive came with monumental consequences.

We found him.

We had found Vallen.

CHAPTER 30

Obscure shapes reflected off the light onto Vallen's body as I stood there, rooted to the spot. The sight of him shirtless and restrained had me shaking. Baz and Lex, both equally unnerved, stood beside me, their mouths wide as they struggled to process what they were seeing.

"How can ordinary chains hold an angel like that?" I expressed, my voice close to a sigh.

"Angel bones, like Nakoma's arrows," Lex suggested, his eyes never leaving Vallen. "But I wouldn't worry. He's practically dead."

Baz noticed torches hanging on either side of the cave wall and pulled them down. "Lex, grab some matches from the hiking pack so we can get these lit."

While Baz and Lex busied themselves with the torches, I took the flashlight and began to explore the circular room. No other inscriptions were visible as the light passed over the walls.

As I approached Vallen, I noticed a pool of glacial water in the center of the cave. Small holes in the mountain ceiling dripped water down into the basin, and I breathed in the damp, cold air, grateful we wouldn't suffocate.

"Noa." Lex glanced over at me as he struck a match against the rough cave wall. "We've got the first torch lit!"

"Great," I replied, forcing a smile to hide my unease. "How are you feeding the tree?" I asked myself, keeping to a whisper.

The cave seemed less foreboding with two torches casting a warm glow. But I kept the flashlight on and circled back to Vallen, each step heavier than the last. A wooden crate on the floor close to him held a silver ladle. Was it left to mock him because he'd never get a drink from the water so close to him?

I took another step to get a better look, and a low moan escaped from Vallen's lips. His chains rattled with difficulty from what little movement he could muster, and I jumped. My reaction was so quick that the flashlight slipped from my grasp and clattered to the ground.

After retrieving it, I looked up again, and Vallen's emerald-green eyes seemed to glow in the dim light of the cave, desperation in his expression. He blinked faster than a camera shutter, trying to get his eyes to focus again. Anger throbbed in my chest, wanting him to see the one who would end his life.

"Easy there, princess," Vallen rasped. Amusement danced in his eyes despite his weakened state. "Didn't think you'd be so easily frightened."

Baz and Lex walked up behind me, brandishing the torches like weapons.

"Everything okay, Noa?" Baz asked, his voice steady as he tightened his grip on the torch.

Vallen raised his head, and his thick, seaweed-like hair clung to his face, mingling with his unruly beard. "You brought groupies. How sweet," he mocked.

"Fuck you," I seethed, spitting at his feet. "You're in no position to insult any of us."

"Neither are you," he retorted, pulling against his restraints. "You sure are an angry one."

"I'm not the one chained to a wall and left for dead," I countered before shutting off the flashlight.

"Not yet," he wheezed, expelling mucus with a cough.

Taking Baz's torch from him, I held it tight and tried to drown out the pounding of my own heartbeat.

"I know you're the one in my head," I accused him with a look of revulsion. "Why did you call me here?"

I stood tall despite the fear scratching at the fringes of my mind. Intrusive thoughts of what this confrontation could mean for each of us flooded my head. Vallen was powerful, even chained and wimpish.

"What?" he mused with a forced laugh. "No formal introductions?"

"Don't test me, Vallen, because I'm more than ready to take your wings," I threatened as I raised my arm, pointing to my wrist.

Vallen's eyes darkened as he coughed up more phlegm. His muscles had wasted away, and he resembled a skeleton.

A small lift formed at the corner of his mouth. "You're fun. I've missed my playtime with angels."

"What angels?" Lex scoffed. "This place is a fortress, and I'm pretty sure they left you here to die."

Vallen took deep breaths with each word and gestured his

head toward the pool of water in the middle of the cave. "If you," he exhaled again, straining this time. "Want answers. Then water."

I wavered, not wanting to give him any comfort. But Lex saw the opportunity and took it. He grabbed the silver ladle from the crate, then dipped it into the icy water on the ground. He poured it into Vallen's mouth with precision, and Baz's eyes flashed to mine. I shook my head and gave a little shrug.

"He's right, Noa," Lex agreed as he continued to quench Vallen's thirst. "If we want to get anything useful out of him, water can't hurt."

"Better?" My eyes turned to slits as I stared down the imprisoned angel. "Talk, Vallen."

His voice was only somewhat stronger after he drank. "Remember, princess, you might not like what you hear."

"I'll be fine," I replied, clenching my fists with sparks of electricity dancing between my fingers.

The cold air in the cave seemed to sharpen as Vallen's voice, low and gruff, broke through the tense silence. "Don't worry. We'll talk about the sparks you're igniting between us later."

Baz stepped between us and pulled me to the side. "Noa, he's baiting you, and you're taking it."

I yanked my arm from Baz's grip. "Do you realize the strength it is taking for me not to fry him where he hangs?"

"Yes, but—" he started.

"No," I interrupted him with a raised palm. "I won't let him have any kind of power over me."

"But he does," Baz insisted, looking over at Vallen. I couldn't help but feel a twinge of hurt with his comment. Then Baz turned his head back to me and whispered, "In order for you to do all the bad things to him, you need to live. We need to live."

I looked up and saw Vallen watching us with a smirk playing on his lips. Even though I knew Baz was right, my emotions got the better of me, and I pulled a dagger from the belt around my thigh and lunged toward Vallen. He didn't flinch as I held the dagger against his throat.

"You should save the romantic chats for later," Vallen snickered.

"He's my guardian angel, jackass," I said through gritted teeth.

"He's human. Signati," he growled. "You fell for her!" Vallen fought to escape his chains.

I pulled the dagger away, then folded my arms across my chest with a raised brow. Stepping back, I quipped, "Did we strike a nerve or put a dent in your plan?"

"Nothing I can't handle once I'm out of these chains." He tossed his hair out of his eyes and stared over at Baz and Lex, a twisted smile on his face.

"That's not happening," I stated with certainty. "But how about this? For each answer, you'll get water," I offered, hoping he would agree.

He raised his hands, still chained to the wall, in mock surrender. "Ask your questions, princess."

"We'll unpack and wait over here," Lex offered and pointed to the wall across from us. He glanced at Vallen and said, "I know I'm hungry."

I watched until they were far enough away, and hung their torch back up on the wall, then looked back at Vallen. "Tell me what happened with my mother and why you called me here?"

"One question at a time." Vallen's eyes studied me, and my chest clenched in fear. He shifted slightly against his chains, then began, "Your mother… Scarlett. She was in the wrong place at the wrong time."

I whistled, then shook my head. "You mean our home? Don't give me that crap. You killed her!" I roared, shaking with fury.

He continued, unfazed by my outburst. "I saved her," he stated in a genuine tone through his scratchy throat.

"You sent her to hell, Vallen." I eyed him, my free hand itching to dagger his chest.

"It's not what I wanted." He looked at the ladle, then made his demand. "Water."

I didn't move, waiting for him to give me more than what I was willing to give him.

"So impatient," Vallen noted beneath puckered brows. "Water," he insisted.

"Fine," I gritted my teeth and found another notch in the cave wall to hang my torch. I filled the ladle with water from the pool, then brought it to him. I only allowed Vallen one drink. "I said you could have water," I noted. "I didn't say how much."

"Clever." He licked his lips and let his eyes linger on me too long. "I love that in a woman."

I tossed the ladle onto the crate and stepped forward, dagger still in hand. "Tell me about her death," I requested, teasing the blade along his jawline.

Vallen laughed with a warning, unphased. "You're playing with another fire here, princess."

This time, I pushed the blade into the skin right under his

chin. "Tell me the fucking truth, you used-up, good-for-nothing piece of trash."

Vallen's tone turned hard when he replied, "Your mother's death was necessary and collateral damage in a much larger game. A game in which you, Noa, are the winning prize."

"She was standing in your way, you mean!" I screamed, trying to control my rage, but everything in me wanted to cut Vallen from navel to nose. "You, your brother, and Maros, using humans as playthings."

"Believe what you want," Vallen spat, and his eyes locked on mine. "It's the truth. By the time I got to your house, she was pleading for me to kill her. So I did."

I stared at him, struggling to process what he told me. Was this some twisted mind game, or could there be some truth to his words? My hands shook with electricity as I fought to control my emotions. Vallen's words hung heavy in the air, threatening to choke me.

I clenched my jaw, feeling the tension spread through my body. I forced myself to take a deep breath, willing myself to remain composed. "Continue, if you're so desperate for another sip of water."

"You're not going to like what I have to say," Vallen warned.

"Try me." My fingers twitched as I played with electricity between my fingertips. "I'll even sheath the dagger."

Vallen leaned forward, pulling against the chains, watching me fulfill my promise with the dagger. His voice was gruff and deadly serious as he professed, "I fell to help your family." He sighed, leaning back against the wall.

I glanced over at Baz and Lex, who had settled against the

cave wall on sleeping bags with sandwiches waiting for me. They seemed to trust my judgment, but they knew how volatile my emotions were when it came to Vallen, so both of them remained alert.

"Vincent told me everything." I groaned, realizing Vallen was useless to any of us. "All three of you were in on it from the beginning, then Vincent and Maros turned on you. So, if you can't return my soul without me dying, then I choose to stay alive. I'm pretty sure my puppy or any other angel can help with that."

Vallen's eyes bore into me with a cold, unrelenting stare. My body shook with rage as I turned to leave, but his voice halted me in my tracks. "I would make the same choices again," he declared boldly.

My heart twisted in agony as I stared back at him, numb and speechless. "I already know that," I managed to choke out. "But you're in this prison, and Vincent is out of control. He became obsessed with my grandmother and kept her alive in a revolting and unnatural way."

He dropped his chin to his chest. "Water," he demanded dryly.

An irritated sigh escaped me, but I did as I promised. I grabbed the ladle and retrieved more water, letting him have two sips. He had me curious now so, I nodded for him to continue.

"My brother fell centuries ago. Before me, even," Vallen claimed. "He waited, befriending the people here and placing angels throughout Montana to do his bidding across the land. He waited so he could pretend to save everyone."

Baz and Lex perked up and leaned forward against the wall. Vallen's eyes flicked to them, then back to me.

"Vincent's the one who teamed up with Maros in the Veil to steal the secrets and take your world," he revealed. "They're on a damn crusade to take more than this one. Vincent didn't expect me to interfere and he sure as hell didn't expect to fall for Sasha."

I stared at him in shock, my breath catching in my throat. "No," I wavered.

"I tried to stop it," Vallen admitted. "That's why I stole your souls and placed parts of the secrets in each of you. If I could turn Vincent and Maros into the Seraphic government before they destroyed everything, then I'd be able to put back your souls and the secrets."

"But you didn't," I reminded him. "You used us like pawns."

"Vincent and Maros knew what I was doing the entire time." His head snapped up and he said again, "Water."

I tipped the ladle, which was a quarter full, into his mouth. "How did they catch you?" My tone turned serious as I dug further.

"I stole the bracelet from Sasha and gave it to your mom," he stated. "Stopping them depended on it, but after your mom died, I led them away from you. Except I ran into trouble at a fallen angel biker bar outside of Houston. I've been feeding the tree to keep the portal open. An open portal gives them infinite access to the Veil."

"Well," I laughed with a sudden burst of amusement. "You must've done something else because Maros called off his deal with Vincent."

"That deal was a charade. My brother is a fool for ever thinking otherwise." He lowered his voice to a whisper. "More water."

This time, I allowed him to drink what was left in the ladle, and then I stood back, waiting for anything to help me understand.

Baz must've sensed my unease, because when I looked over at him and Lex, I saw concern etched in his features. He smiled at me, saying, "Deep breaths. You're doing well."

I forced a weak smile and nodded. Except my world was crumbling around me, and I couldn't afford to show weakness to Vallen. I turned the ladle over in my hand, then stared at the imprisoned angel. Carefully examining his face, I held his gaze, and resentment shot through me.

Grief clouded my mind, and my heart broke for the betrayal I felt. I thought about using the ladle on Vallen's face for a second, but what he said next surprised me.

Vallen's eyes softened, and for the first time, I saw a flicker of emotion cross his face as he watched me. "We can use the bracelet and return your soul to you."

My heart hammered in my chest, the rhythm of it almost deafening in my ears as his words sank in. My soul. The prospect left me stunned, and I almost couldn't move.

I twirled the ladle in my hand and said, "Fifty points to house Sazerac. So, that part is true."

"Water," he growled.

I cast a glare at him while gripping the ladle with both hands. "Needy little thing, aren't you?"

"We have a deal, princess," Vallen snapped, so I let him drink the entire amount from the ladle this time.

Baz and Lex exchanged puzzled looks before joining me.

"Are you lying, Vallen?" Baz questioned with a sharp tone, echoing my own silent doubts.

He shook his head and leaned back against the cave wall. "But it comes with a price."

"And what's that?" asked Lex.

Then Vallen's words cut through my temporary hope as he said, "Noa's life."

CHAPTER 31

I searched Vallen's face, battling the burning tears that threatened to spill from my eyes. My chest tightened like a vice grip.

"You've gone against the entire order of the universe, and to fix it, I have to die?" I screeched, the ear-splitting scream echoing through the cave.

Vallen's expression stayed impassive, his eyes revealing nothing. It only fueled my fury as my words bounced off the rocky walls. I spun on my heel and stormed away, boots crunching on loose stones.

Behind me, the clank of metal reverberated through the cavern as Vallen strained against his chains, reaching for me. The force of his struggle sent a tremor through the cave, causing me to almost lose my balance. Baz and Lex stumbled beside me, quickly finding their balance on the shaky ground.

Vallen yelled at me, demanding my attention. "You have the power to fix this, Noa! Fix this mistake and save everyone."

I froze mid-step, his words punching me in the gut. The notion of saving humankind seemed absurd coming from the lips of the one who had stripped me of the very essence of my humanity. My hands clenched into fists at my sides as I turned back toward him, meeting his cold gaze head-on.

"You ripped away my soul without a second thought." Bitter laughter snaked up my throat. "You've made human existence meaningless and unstable for me. If I make this right, I won't even get the chance to live."

The rawness in my throat was undeniable. Baz and Lex's gazes bore into my back, but all I cared about was confronting this infuriating fallen angel before me. With a surge of rage, I punched the wall next to Vallen's face; rocks crumbled all around us.

"You won't be able to contain them, you know?" He threw his head back with an ominous laugh. "That power you hold is knowledge of creation—before and after. Everything in between too. You're a vessel housing them, and they will consume you until you die."

Hiding my trembling hands, I thrust my wrist forward again so close to his face that he could kiss it if he dared. "I have Callum's essence in my veins. Besides, this bracelet has soldered itself to me."

"Callum's essence will eventually disappear," Vallen taunted with a sinister smile. "As the last remaining descendant of your family, that bracelet is meant to attach itself to you—it's a conduit for performing the ceremony and returning that knowledge to the Veil."

Baz squared his shoulders defiantly. "How long does she have?"

"I'm parched," Vallen replied before coughing and licking his cracked lips.

Baz spun on his heel only to whirl back and punch Vallen squarely in the mouth. "How much time does Noa have until she dies—and we're all screwed!"

Vallen spat a drip of blood on the ground and sneered. "A few days. A week," he said. "I haven't been able to keep track, but don't worry, pup; once she gets her soul, neither of you will go to hell."

"Shut up!" I rubbed my eyes with the heel of my hand. We couldn't afford to waste any more time arguing with him. "He isn't going to help because he's locked up and we're the entertainment."

Vallen smirked, his eyes glinting with mischief. He lifted what he could of his wrist chained to the wall and pointed at my face. "I gave you the ability to hold the secrets, Noa, so you could stay alive. Don't you want to be a hero?"

A gasp escaped my lips as I exchanged horrified looks with Baz and Lex. I shook my head and turned away, refusing to play his game.

"Maros is no ordinary demon," Vallen insisted as he chuckled darkly. "He will devour and violate you in every gruesome way you can imagine once he has you." Leaning back, he looked at the ceiling and began listing the ways out loud. "Rape. Sodomy. None of it is out of the question as he drains those secrets from you as he needs them and destroys humankind."

I turned, unleashing the entirety of my anger at him in the chest, screaming, "Die, asshole!"

A bolt of electricity slammed him back against the wall, but it didn't injure him. He hung there, laughing at each of us. All I could do was back away, knowing there was no hope left. But it didn't stop him from delivering verbal blows again and again.

"Maros will give what's left of you to his devil pests so they can take turns," Vallen added. "For eternity, Noa!"

His muscular form was hard as steel as he yanked the chains away from the wall to reach me. His voice cut through every inch of tension in the cave as it turned into a rumble.

"Water!" Vallen thundered across the cave.

I unsheathed a dagger from my thigh again and held it to his throat, clipping the skin right under his chin. "What do you mean, you want water? I'm not giving you another fucking sip. So unless you want me to end your misery now, give me something useful." My eyes flashed to Baz and Lex. "Or I will watch you burn alive, still chained to this fucking wall."

Vallen flashed me a wide grin and barked, "Give me something, too."

My eyes never left his. I studied his face, hard and tired. Then, a quick breath slipped out of his mouth. He was ready for just as much vengeance as I was, and my breath hitched. He didn't fool me.

"You want out," I revealed with a laugh.

"The way you understand me, Noa," he slurred and tilted his hips in my direction. "Makes me—"

My hand moved on its own, reaching for his cheek as I brought down the dagger, leaving a deep cut. But my excitement turned to disappointment in an instant as the wound healed within seconds.

"Pig!" I hollered, slashing his face again even though I knew it wouldn't hurt him.

He raised his hands, palms open and fingers splayed. "Oh, I

wouldn't dream of touching you, but think about Maros," he reminded me. "I can help you and your little doggie stay out of hell."

Lex began pacing in front of the pool. "Hell no."

Baz's fingers tightened around my arm, his eyes narrowing, while Vallen's lips curled into a frustrated grimace. "I don't like this. We came for answers, Noa, not to help him escape," Baz whispered as he dragged me to the other side of the pool.

"Escaping isn't an option," Lex agreed, walking up to us.

Vallen's chuckle reverberated through the damp, shadowy cavern, bouncing off jagged rock walls that seemed to close in on us. "I see your fear is getting the better of you."

Baz scoffed, then turned to me. "We don't have much time, Noa, and I don't know about you, but I'm not in the mood to negotiate. We can still make it back to Dawson's tonight."

"Let's get out of here," Lex agreed. "We'll figure this out with O'Neil and the others. We have enough to go on."

"And how do we leave? We're trapped." I stared up at them and shook my head. "He has my soul and, according to him, if I die without it, Baz and I both go to hell."

Baz eyed Vallen suspiciously, then took a deep breath before speaking to me. "You caught that, did you?"

I shoved his chest hard enough to make him stumble back. "You omitted that little detail," I snapped, as the weight of our predicament pressed down on me.

"We're signati," he muttered, knowing he goes where I go. Dead or alive. He raked his fingers through his hair in exasperation. "And you're right, we can't leave until he tells us how," Baz conceded.

"I can make him think he's getting out," I added with a wink and a tilt of my head.

"I'm here if things go south," Lex chimed in with a heavy sigh. "But think fast and move faster."

We separated and I turned back to face Vallen. "Since you're the only one who can tell us how to get out of here," I admitted. "We'll help you."

"Honey to my ears," he moaned with closed eyes, then licked his lips.

"You're sick," growled Baz. "If it weren't for needing to save Noa, I'd rip your throat out."

"And you should be playing watchdog back in the Veil!" Vallen bellowed, the sound echoing off the stone walls.

"This isn't helping, Baz," I complained as the tension in the cave grew. I needed to focus on the most important questions.

"Other than the typical 'bad guy trying to take over the world' scenario, why is Maros so damn invested in this?" Lex asked, eyes narrowing.

"It's personal for him. Noa's bloodline is old and sacred. He intends to end it and enslave all humans," Vallen explained, his voice weary. "Christians. He's wanted this for ages."

"I knew it!" exclaimed Lex with a bittersweet smile.

"Except Maros and your brother bested you and there isn't a backup plan," I bit out at Vallen, my irritation bubbling up.

"Concealing you and the bracelet was the backup plan, Noa." Vallen rolled his neck, his gaze settling on Lex as he mouthed, "Water."

"Good to know my waterboy skills are coming in handy," Lex grumbled as he refilled the ladle.

"What makes this bracelet so special?" I asked while rolling my wrist back and forth, feeling the cold metal melded into my skin. "Jewelry doesn't typically slice through skin and adhere to people's bones."

Vallen took a deeper drink than we had previously allowed, then continued. "It's a nail from the crucifixion."

My arms fell to my sides as I gazed at him, examining his expression for any trace of dishonesty. "Wait. You're saying that there's a nail from the cross inside my body?" I questioned with doubt.

He nodded, stretching as if to emphasize his point, muscles appearing more defined under the flickering torchlight. "Water," Vallen requested again.

I touched Lex's arm for him to wait before allowing Vallen another sip. Walking up to Vallen, I studied him from head to toe. His once gaunt abdomen now showed slight indentations of muscle, and his hair looked thicker and fuller under the flickering torchlight. Although it was still a tangled mess because his beard was overgrown with knots like twisted vines.

Yet, despite everything, he definitely seemed stronger. Lex approached us with a ladle full of the pool's liquid, and I slapped it out of his hand. The metal clanged against the rocky floor as the contents splattered everywhere.

"What the hell, Noa?" Lex shouted, raising his hands in question.

"You deviant son of a bitch." I chewed the inside of my cheek as I tapped my foot glaring at Vallen. "That water isn't water at all, is it?"

"What are you talking about?" Baz stepped over and dipped his finger into the puddle, then placed it on his tongue after a moment of hesitation. "Holy shit! It's how they're draining you to feed the tree."

Vallen's face hardened as I stood so close that each breath he exhaled brushed against my eyelids like a whispering breeze every time I blinked.

"I see your backup plan now. You're using us to help you regain your essence, then kidnap me to fulfill your ceremony."

Without thinking, my palm connected with Vallen's cheek in a resounding slap that echoed through the cave like a crack of thunder. He let out a guttural roar, but I didn't back down. My fury bulldozed any sense of self-preservation with him.

Baz and Lex tried to pull me back, but as their hands closed around my arms, an unexpected surge of electricity erupted from my palms, sending them flying across the damp cave floor.

I raised my hand for another slap—but this time he was ready. His manacled wrist shot up and collided with the bracelet on my wrist in a blinding flash of light. Agony exploded through my arm as bones met unforgiving chains; our connection felt like touching raw nerves drenched in liquid fire.

The force of the impact sent me reeling backward, my body slamming against the rocky ground. I struggled to remain conscious, my head throbbing with each labored breath. A sudden clatter of metal on stone indicated Vallen's chains had shattered. The ancient wards binding him were finally broken.

He slumped to the ground, no longer supported by the unyielding restraints. Darkness edged into my vision as I struggled to stay awake, clinging desperately to consciousness. It was a futile effort.

A sudden flurry of movement and raised voices pierced

through the void. Baz's worried face appeared above me, his features tight with concern as he cradled my head in his lap.

"Noa? Can you hear me?" Baz pleaded, his voice strained. "Please, stay with me."

I tried to answer, but my tongue felt leaden and uncooperative. My response came out as little more than a pained groan.

Baz turned to Lex, who hovered nearby. "We need to perform CPR. She's not breathing," he begged.

Vallen's voice sliced through the havoc like a knife. "Move aside," he ordered, his tone permitting no argument.

Baz and Lex hesitated, their gazes darting between the newly freed angel and me. I could sense their fear with the realization that they were in the presence of an angel of much higher authority. And power.

Vallen lifted me with little effort while Baz and Lax stood by, their hands clenched at their sides. Even through the haze of pain clouding my thoughts, I couldn't help but feel awe at Vallen's presence. His power crackled through the air like a gathering storm.

His expression unreadable, Vallen gently brushed hair from my brow. "You have no idea what you've unleashed, Noa," he murmured, his deep voice vibrating through my very bones.

As he turned to carry me in his arms, I fought against encroaching unconsciousness. I wanted to protest—to tell him not to touch me and that I could walk on my own—but my mind refused to form words. My limbs lay limp and unresponsive despite all efforts.

He walked toward the center of the cave, and I could see the pool of frigid water we had been letting him drink. Its surface was still and reflected the dim light from above with an almost invisible glitter. Vallen strode forward, his bare feet making no sound on the rocky ground.

We reached the edge of the basin, and his piercing stare met mine once again. "Trust me," he whispered.

Even though every part of me wanted to resist, I found my head nodding in agreement. Then, Vallen plunged into the water, submerging us both in its icy depths. I gasped at the shock of it, the cold stealing the breath from my lungs, but Vallen's grip on me never faltered, and I didn't drown.

As we sank deeper, I felt a sudden warmth blossoming from the inscriptions on my wrist, its lines pulsing with a warm blue light. To my amazement, the glow began to spread, enveloping my entire body in a shimmering silver aura.

My vision blurred underwater, but as I looked up, Baz and Lex stood at the pool's edge, their faces twisted in terror as they gazed at us. My lungs didn't seem to need oxygen as I clung to Vallen's back. Then, his powerful legs propelled us upward.

As we broke through the surface, the water retreated, every drop flowing back into Vallen's body. I blinked in astonishment as I took in Vallen's transformed appearance. Gone were the matted hair and tangled beard, replaced by neatly trimmed locks and a well-groomed face.

His green eyes sparkled against smooth amber skin, once marred by years of grime and neglect. Vallen stood before us, beautiful once more.

Unconcerned by his lack of clothing, Vallen passed me to Baz and said, "Get her dry."

Lex searched the hiking pack and pulled out a towel for me and a thermal blanket. He handed the blanket to Vallen, who quickly wrapped it around his waist with a grateful nod.

Lex followed him to the other side of the cave to question him.

As I lay in Baz's arms, he rubbed the towel along my skin, but my thoughts reeled from the events of the past few minutes. I felt a strong connection with Vallen, whether it was because he helped me or his essence was now part of me. Either way, I did my best to block out what that meant.

"You scared me, Noa," Baz whispered. He cupped my cheek with his hand, then traced the curve of my face with his thumb.

A soft sigh escaped me as I sat up. "Sorry," I coughed.

Vallen purposefully sat close to the spot where he had been chained. For a long while, he said nothing, his eyes distant as he watched us. I came to the conclusion that he didn't want us to see him as a threat. At least, not yet.

Finally, he spoke, his voice low and measured. "Once Noa is warm and in new clothes, we'll talk. For now, focus on her."

Baz gave my hand a gentle squeeze. "Lex, do you have some extra clothes for her?"

Lex handed me a bundle of clothes and smiled. "How do you feel?"

"Okay, I think." I raised my head and smiled. "Thanks."

"Here," Baz said, guiding me to a secluded spot behind a rocky outcropping. "You can change here."

Baz left me alone, and with numb fingers, I untied my daggers and placed them on the ground. I stripped off my wet garments and pulled on the dry ones, relishing the feeling of dry fabric against my skin. Once dressed, I grabbed my belongings and rejoined them. I placed my daggers by my side as I sat down on the cave floor.

I turned to Vallen, who was watching me from across the

area where his essence once remained. A flicker of relief crossed his face as he spoke. "We need to leave and get somewhere safe."

I thought for a moment, my mind racing through the options, then it dawned on me. "My apartment," I stated after a brief pause. "I doubt Vincent would check there again."

Vallen nodded with a firm expression, a touch of approval in his gaze. "Your apartment it is, then," he declared. His focus on survival was notable in his tone.

Lex stepped forward, his face etched with concern. "Hold on, are we actually going to Noa's apartment? If not Vincent, then Maros will still track us."

"Not since that bracelet fused to Noa's wrist," Vallen confirmed. "They're likely frantic, wondering why they can't find her."

I looked at him, a sudden fear gripping my heart. "Is it possible to get the secrets out of me without..." I swallowed hard, then finished the thought. "Without killing me and Baz?"

Vallen's eyes met mine, and for a moment, I saw a flicker of emotion cross his face. He knew I had a full understanding of the signati bond.

"We need to get off this mountain. That's our first priority," he instructed.

CHAPTER 32

None of us slept well. Baz and Lex took turns keeping watch on Vallen, unconvinced he wouldn't try to kill me. Or kidnap me, then kill me. I sat up and rubbed the back of my neck with a yawn.

"Any ideas on how to get to Noa's apartment once we get out of here?" Baz's skepticism was evident in his questioning as he stood gazing up at the small openings of the cavern.

Lex rose, excitement lighting up his face. "You can teleport us, Noa."

"Teleport?" Baz's eyebrow arched, showing his intrigue at the possibility. "She's done it one time."

I shook my head, dismissing the idea, "And that was by accident," I reminded them.

Vallen trained his eyes on me with unnerving curiosity that sent shivers down my spine. Uncertainty clouded my mind. What was he thinking? I would usually dismiss such intrusive scrutiny, but a prickly awareness heightened my senses. It felt as though he was dissecting me like a science experiment. A sickness he was determined to cure.

If I didn't hate him for screwing up my life, stealing my soul, and killing my mother, he'd be the epitome of what I'd take home from the bar to quench my desires. And gods, did I need some quenching. But a romp with a ridiculously gorgeous fallen angel, along with everything else in my life, was on an indefinite hold.

Fucking angels.

Vallen's entire body changed like magic once he took back his essence. Not something easily ignored, even if I wanted to gut him where he sat. He caught my eye, and a smile tugged at one corner of his mouth.

I instantly averted my gaze and offered Baz a polite smile. "It was a fluke. I don't even know how it happened unless Vallen had something to do with it."

"Your lineage has something to do with it," Vallen stated, his observation of me unwavering.

He would need to stop staring at me, or I would consider stabbing him before we left the cave.

"You broke through the shield I created and," Vallen declared with assurance, "if you were wearing the bracelet when you teleported, then it absolutely helped."

My eyebrows furrowed as I examined my skin, trying to make sense of how a rusty nail from the cross had chosen me. "But it wasn't fused to my bones the other day."

"Even better," Vallen chimed in. "The fusion makes you stronger along with mine and Callum's essence flowing through you. But the essence will wear off. And when they do, princess —" He cocked his head sideways, not needing to say it.

Vallen's tone was lethal, and I couldn't help but feel satisfied that Callum gave me something to help save my life for the time being. I didn't want to acknowledge that Vallen had anything to do with it. The more it angered him I got to live, suited me fine.

He shoved the chains lying next to him against the stone wall and stood. My eyes widened at the sight before me. What was once a thermal blanket had transformed into thermal... pants.

"How the hell did you manage that?" I inquired, turning to Vallen with a look of curiosity. I nudged Lex's arm playfully, urging him to join the conversation.

Lex swiveled around, adjusting his backpack with practiced ease. "Well done," he praised Vallen with a smile.

"I have my ways," Vallen replied, his voice smooth and confident.

His eyes held a spark of mischief that made me wary. What other tricks did he have up his sleeve that he hadn't revealed yet?

Baz snorted, unimpressed. "Can we focus on getting out of here instead of playing dress-up?"

I shot Baz a warning look before turning back to Vallen. "Is there a way for us to leave this cave without alerting anyone outside of our presence?"

Vallen's voice remained steady as he considered the question. "They can't track you, but Vincent knows where I am, so I'm sure someone is checking around the mountain," he cautioned. "We'll need to move fast and work together."

I exchanged a wary glance with Lex and Baz, but took a breath. "Alright," I managed to say. "Let's hear the plan."

Vallen tilted his head back once more and peered up into the opening where water dripped into the cave.

"Once your wrist is through there," he informed us. "The

last of the runes will disappear and the opening will expand. It will allow us enough time to get to the edge of the waterfall. From there, you'll portal us to your apartment."

"And how will Noa get up there?" Lex inquired, shifting his weight to get a better view.

"I'll lift her," Vallen stated matter-of-factly. "Once opened, we can pull you both up there."

Baz crossed his arms, a scowl deepening on his face. "You're not going to touch her."

Vallen stood composed beside him, arms relaxed by his sides as he tried to rein in his emotions. "Tell me how you want it done. Remember, your abilities are not the same as mine."

Baz stepped up next to me and flashed a smile as he motioned toward Lex. "He can lift her."

Lex shook his head with impatience. "It's too small an area in here for me to unfurl my wings, brother."

Vallen's jaw ticked, almost pleased. "Lex is right. This space makes it impossible, whereas I don't always need my wings to fly."

Recognition dawned on Baz's face, and he turned towards me. "I don't trust this, Noa."

I looked up subtly, aiming not to draw attention to our private exchange. "He can lift me. Don't worry, He can't kill me yet, remember?"

"Yes! That's why I don't trust him," Baz persisted.

"He won't do anything until the essence has made its way out of my body, so smile and play along." I feigned contemplation with varying expressions.

"Vallen can lift me, Baz. It's fine," I finally reassured them and sheathed my dagger.

Vallen rolled his eyes and remarked, "It's adorable that you two pretend like I don't know you're having a conversation in your head."

Baz hesitated, his gaze shifting between me and Vallen before finally nodding in reluctant agreement. I looked at Lex, who found our decision-making skills boring.

Lex cut in, patting Baz's arm with a sense of urgency. "Can we get on with this, please?"

"Let's do it," I said with a confident nod.

"We need rope, Lex," Vallen pointed out, eyeing the backpack. Lex rolled his eyes.

"You couldn't have mentioned that before I was ready to go?"

Lex pulled off his backpack and located a bundle of light yellow climbing rope. Vallen knelt down in front of me, hands hovering above my waist as if waiting for permission. I hesitated, searching his eyes for any hint of dishonesty.

But his expression was sincere, making me feel like I could trust him, at least for this task. He took one end of the rope and tied it around my waist with a tight knot. Lex and Baz unwound the rest, leaving enough for Baz to stay on the cave floor until I reached the top.

Once Vallen and I were through the opening, Baz would secure himself to the rope still connected to me. Then Vallen would pull him up while Lex brought up the rear. I braced myself and nodded, trying to ignore how his touch sent an electrifying jolt through me.

A fleeting look of pain crossed Vallen's eyes as he hoisted me up, his movements fluid and graceful. His hands were strong but gentle enough not to bruise me. For a moment, I felt almost invincible as I raised my arm so that my wrist could break through the final barrier.

The runes lining the opening began to glow, and the distant sound of rushing water grew louder. The cave trembled as if waking from a long slumber—time was running out.

With a sudden whoosh of air, the opening widened and granted us access to the outside world. We landed on an expanse of grassy terrain near the top of a roaring waterfall's edge.

"Let's move!" he yelled down to Baz and Lex.

A strong gust of wind almost knocked me over, but Vallen reached his arm around my waist and pulled me into him. "Not your time," he whispered.

"Yet," I said, sarcasm evident in my response. "Not my time yet, is what you meant."

I narrowed my eyes at him, then pushed myself away, planting my feet on the ground. A rumble below us made me jump, and I decided that lying face down on the ground was the better option. Vallen knelt down on one knee and placed a hand on my back, showing concern for me rather than ensuring I didn't die before the ceremony to replace my soul.

I was kidding myself to think there was any other reason. As I looked into the cave, Baz tied himself off and tugged on the rope. Vallen began hoisting him up when a faint screech carried across the mountains, and I jumped. Then, what felt like a small earthquake shook the ground. I turned my head and looked at Vallen.

"Hurry up!" Dread filled my body as I tried to reach for the rope.

The piercing sound drew nearer, and I knew Vincent and his angels were almost at the mountain. Small rocks tumbled into the opening, scattering around Lex. Baz shielded his face as Vallen made two quick moves to haul him out. He hopped over me and joined me.

"You okay?" he panted, his eyes scanning my body for any injuries.

I nodded, swallowing hard, then looked back down into the cave. "Lex's turn."

Vallen gripped my arm with a firm hold, his expression tense as he surveyed our surroundings for any signs of danger.

"What are you waiting for?" Baz snapped at Vallen, fear coloring his voice that he might run off with me.

Vallen didn't respond but looked down at Lex and waved him up. As Vallen pulled on the rope again, the mountain shook violently, and Lex slipped from his grasp.

"No!" I reached for Lex, but he bounced in the air and smiled up at me.

"All good, here," he called out, with one hand cupped around his mouth, holding on tightly to the rope with the other.

I repositioned myself on my knees and placed a hand on Baz's shoulder. "Will you please scout around the area and let us know if we have company?"

Baz pinched the bridge of his nose and took a deep breath. "You're right. I'll go check things out."

In one move, Baz was on his feet. As I turned my head back to Lex and Vallen, I heard Baz shift.

"Don't take your eyes off Vallen," he said. *"I'm going to get in contact with the others now. The cave blocked me from communicating with anyone but you."* He sauntered off to check the mountain from all directions.

Watching Vallen was easy. The simmering rage I felt toward

him made sure of that. Even though it seemed like his essence was messing with my emotions, that confusion didn't matter now. I shook my head and paid attention to Lex getting pulled up out of the opening below.

Once he was safely on solid ground beside me, I leaped up and wrapped him in a tight hug. "I'm glad you made it," I said with a relieved squeal.

"Me too," Lex smiled, then untied himself to return my hug with equal warmth.

I let the rope drop from my waist in time to see immense shadows passing above us—there had to be at least ten of them, their wings beating rhythmically and sending gusts of wind around us. Vallen moved in front of me like a human shield while Lex pressed his back against mine, scanning the opposite side of the mountain for threats.

A strangled cry pierced through the chaos. *"Noa!"*

"Baz! Where are you?" I strained to locate him, dashing toward the source of the voice around the rocky terrain.

Vallen grabbed my arm, yanking me back to face him. "You'll die if you go."

"And he'll die if I don't!" Desperation fueled my fists as they collided with his stone-like chest.

"You can live without him, but we can't survive without you, Noa!" Vallen's voice boomed, compelling me to meet his fierce gaze.

"Until you've gotten what you need from me, right?" Energy crackled at my fingertips as I sent jolts into Vallen's muscles. Tears blurred my vision as anger turned into anguish. "You piece of shit! This is your fault; you should be the one dying!"

"Noa," Baz called to me, his voice strained. *"They torched Dawson's and—"*

An excruciating howl erupted from his throat. My head snapped to the other side of the mountain as Vallen freed me. He, Lex, and I all stared up at Vincent hovering above us, Baz clutched by the throat with the claws of his wings.

"Run, Noa," Baz choked out, his wolf form dangling hopelessly.

With a flick of his wrist, Vincent tossed Baz across the mountain. I heard him squeal as he landed with a back-breaking sound, then a splash into the waterfall.

A guttural scream escaped me. "Baz!" I clutched my chest, unable to breathe. "Baz! Baz!" There was nothing but silence, and I fell to my knees.

"I've missed you, brother," Vincent purred down at Vallen with his crimson wings spread wide.

"I bet you have," Vallen commented as he stepped forward, unfurling his gorgeous emerald-green wings with black-tipped talons.

"Shouldn't Maros have taken you to hell by now?" yelled Lex, who now unleashed his wings. The white and silver feathers began to form a cocoon around me, still allowing me to see Vincent.

Vincent's lip curled back as he scoffed. "Maros and I had a little talk. I made him realize that only someone with angel essence could activate the bracelet, but Noa's lineage could bring forth the powers and secrets."

"You won't win this, Vincent!" I shouted up at him as his dark wings flapped menacingly.

He clapped his hands and smiled as though I meant nothing.

And to him, I didn't. "Kindly hand over, Noa," he said in that chilling voice of his, "and I'll let one of you live."

A maniacal laugh erupted from him because we knew he meant that I would be the one to live.

We were surrounded; the hovering angels couldn't land but swooped close enough to make my body shake with terror.

"Lex," I said, glancing back at him. "Please unwrap your wings from me. Go to the camp and alert the others. Baz," I paused, choking on a sob, "Baz told me Nevaeh's house is gone."

"What!" Lex dropped his protective wings like I had asked.

"Baz didn't get a chance to tell me everything, but he managed to tell me enough." Then, I looked up at Vincent. "You will never have me!" I spat.

Vincent watched, amused, as Lex ran his hands through his hair, worry coating his face. A cruel smirk spread across Vincent's face. "You won't make it, Lex," he sneered calmly.

Lex's gray eyes danced with fog and rain, something I hadn't seen since my birthday, and it made my stomach lurch. He searched Vincent's face. "You revolting, lying son of a bitch!"

Vallen's arm shot out in front of me, his grip firm as he pushed me behind him.

"What the hell, Vallen?" I twisted against his grip, my frustration boiling over.

"Lex, I want to thank you for your service," began Vincent mockingly as he pranced and fluttered higher above us.

"No!" Mly voice cracked with desperation. Vallen's arms were vice-like around me, unyielding, and I felt my strength float away.

Vincent's wings beat twice as he shifted to the left, eyes

locked on mine. "If it weren't for you, Jossy, and Ivy…" His voice dripped with menace. "Remember her, Noa? She loved you, but did you love her back?"

"I did love her, you piece of shit!" The tears burned hot trails down my cheeks as I thrashed against Vallen's iron grip. "She was my everything—my best friend."

He looked back to Lex, bored as his eyes glazed over as if he couldn't remember why we were there. "If it weren't for the three of you finding Noa and setting up the New Year's Eve party," he praised Lex with a nod of respect. "We wouldn't be here now."

"Don't listen to him, Lex," I ordered, my hands balled up at my sides.

"Anyway," Vincent shrugged nonchalantly, his eyes shifting briefly to meet mine before flitting away. "Thank you." He gave a powerful flap of his wings, sending a gust of wind swirling around us and rustling the leaves in nearby trees. Then Vincent's angels descended like a well-coordinated flock, their wings slicing through the air as they circled around Lex.

Vallen grabbed me and slung me over his shoulder as we sprinted.

"Lex!" I shouted, watching him turn and give a quick wave before launching into the sky to fight.

Time seemed to crawl as another fallen angel swooped in, snatching me from Vallen's grip. I almost hit the ground, but Vallen caught me at the last second, holding me tight against his chest with one arm. With the other, he reached out and crushed the angel's throat. She disintegrated into ash upon hitting the ground, leaving only bones and ripped wings behind.

I spun back toward the mountain where three of Lex's

former allies hovered menacingly in the air. Within seconds, they seized Lex by his shoulders and flung him into a dark cave below, boulders crashing down on him. Tears streamed down my face as I went limp in Vallen's arms. He swiftly lowered me to the ground.

"We have about ten seconds before Vincent and his horde get here, Noa," he said urgently, though his voice was distant as my ears began to muffle. His hand gripped my shoulder firmly. "Focus! We need to get to your apartment."

My body turned to lead with every motion feeling cumbersome, and I couldn't think straight. A wave of panic hit me as I wondered if I should go back for Lex. I made another attempt to contact Baz, but there was still no response.

Tears streamed down my cheeks as I struggled for breath between sobs. "He...he won't answer me."

Vallen pressed his palms against his temples, his breath trembling as he fought to keep calm. "I know," he murmured. "But please, stay with me. We need to reach your apartment."

My nails dug into my palms as I whipped around to face Vincent, the legion of angels looming behind him like an impending storm. Electricity crackled through my veins, setting off a wildfire of rage that blazed hotter with each heartbeat. Bolts of searing orange and yellow erupted from my fingertips, disintegrating two guards mid-flight before they could even react.

With an earth-shattering roar, Vincent launched himself at us. His claws flashed ominously in the dim light as he closed the distance with terrifying speed.

CHAPTER 33

I closed my eyes, feeling a torrent of heat surging from my core to my fingertips as I stretched my hands outward.

"Bring it, you devil scumbag!" My lips curled back in a snarl, teeth grinding against each other.

As I summoned the energy within me, rough hands gripped my arms like iron chains. My rage boiled under captivity. The audacity of Vallen to prevent me from ending Vincent ignited the fire within me, like molten rage.

With a violent jerk, I slammed my head backward toward his face while driving a fierce kick to his shin. He didn't flinch; instead, he hoisted me effortlessly off the ground. My heart pounded with terror and rage as he lifted me like a ragdoll. Dangling helplessly in his grasp hammered home one grim truth —I was outmatched.

Vallen's voice thundered through me—each syllable crashing like an earthquake. "Apartment now!" The command left an echoing ache in every bone.

My body hummed, and an unexpected surge of energy coursed through me. The bracelet on my wrist pulsed rhythmically under my skin, each pulse faster than the previous one—an ominous countdown ticking away. My mind instinctively focused on the image of my apartment—the familiar haven where I had spent countless evenings in silent solitude.

It was a stark contrast to the chaotic whirlwind that had now become my life—a life that felt foreign and detached from the person I once was. Once again, Vallen had invaded my mind, and this time, I was powerless to resist. As the searing pain in my wrist swelled, images of my living room from every angle and corner flashed in my head.

Orange couch.

Record Player.

Dust Bunny.

Suddenly, it felt as if the solid ground beneath me had given way, replaced by an abyss that sent my stomach spiraling into a free fall. Then, as abruptly as it all began, it stopped.

My eyes snapped open, and I found myself sprawled on the carpet of my living room floor. Flipping over, I blinked rapidly, trying to process a nauseating feeling bubbling in my throat. A feeling all too familiar when I escaped the Lurker demon the night after my birthday. A time when I had no idea what waited for me beyond my bookstore job and my best friends.

Best Friends.

Doubling over, everything in the depths of me came up until dry heaves were all that remained on my carpet.

"Noa," Vallen stated with a hint of suspicion in his voice, looming over me. "The patio door is open."

I sat up and heaved again and gasped for air. "I hate you," I muttered while glaring toward the patio.

Embracing my knees tightly, I met his gaze. "I may have forgotten to close it. People know about my bunny, so they usually don't pay attention," I confessed.

He peered out onto the patio while I savored the comforting scent of home enveloping me. Everything seemed undisturbed, yet a subtle unease lingered within me. I rushed to the patio, my heart pounding in my chest, fearing the Baneful or Vincent had snatched her away.

But nestled in her box, slept Dust Bunny, blissfully unaware of the upheaval that had unfolded since I'd last seen her. Relief flooded through me, and I couldn't help but give her a soft smile and a scratch on her head.

When I walked back inside, Vallen was draping towels from my dryer over the spot where I had vomited.

"Why are you doing that?" I inquired, taken aback by his kindness.

With a weary sigh, he replied, "It's just a towel to conceal it."

Running my hand through my disheveled hair, attempting to regain composure, I found my apartment unchanged yet strangely different. A weightiness hung in the air, almost suffocating. The whirlwind of recent events left my head swimming in a sea of emotions. Guilt being at the top of the list.

Lex, Baz, and my grandmother were all dead now, and I couldn't stop it from happening. Vincent and Maros had me on a hit list until they captured me, and everything in me wanted to kill the one angel standing in the middle of my living room. But he was too powerful.

Even with his essence flowing through me, I couldn't defeat

Vallen. The power he'd given me was fading fast, and I knew Callum's was already gone. Accepting the inevitable, I resigned myself to my fate.

"You can have them." I walked into the kitchen and grabbed a glass from the cabinet.

"What?" He raised an eyebrow at me and stood up, his head nearly reaching the bathroom door frame.

I opened the freezer with a creak and pulled out a bottle of peppermint vodka. Setting both items down on the counter with a resounding clank, I shot him a deadly glare.

"Take these fucking secrets and be done with it," I sneered, forcing a fake smile. "Now, I need a drink. And if you say one thing about it not being good for me or whatever, I swear I'll find a way to stab you."

Vallen glanced around my dimly lit apartment before sinking into the sagging couch cushions. "You do what you need to do," he remarked calmly as if this were all normal.

The soft hum of the refrigerator underscored our silence, blending with the faint traffic noise outside. My fingers brushed against the cold glass of vodka, its chill almost biting—a sharp contrast to my frayed nerves.

I took a shot and let the peppermint punish my senses. The sharp mint flavor hit my tongue first, followed by the burning alcohol that made me wince. Then it melted into warmth. After taking two more, I eyed him curiously as he continued to stare at me.

His composed demeanor irritated me more than it should have—the epitome of indifference amidst chaos—while everything inside me felt like it was unraveling. I tried desperately to hold together some semblance of sanity. He seemed satisfied with my decision, but he was also still shirtless. And as much as it stirred something in me, it was wrong, and I needed to find him something to wear.

"Okay," I whispered sharply and set the glass on the counter louder than necessary. "I know I have something around here for you to put on so you don't look like you just left a frat party."

Creases formed between his eyebrows as I stalked toward the clothes hamper, vodka bottle in hand.

"Too many men are in and out of your life," he declared, not an ounce of emotion in his voice.

"It's not a concern of yours," I quipped, taking a swig from the bottle. "Never has been and never will be. Understand?"

"You deserved better, Noa," he admitted, then went back to studying the room I once called home.

A hollow pit formed in my stomach. Ivy spoke the same words to me a few days ago in this same spot. I didn't believe it then, but she was right.

I inched toward the man who made me just so I could die and shoved a hoodie and sweatpants into his chest. He didn't move as I challenged him. After drinking down a few more gulps of vodka, I launched the bottle into the kitchen, glass shattering across the floor.

"Maybe if your goddamn family weren't a bunch of fuck-wads and you hadn't stolen my soul, I would stand a chance," I seethed. Then, my knees gave out, and I dropped to the floor. "I sure as hell deserve better. My poor mother deserved so much better!"

He swallowed hard as his green eyes danced with bursts of gold, and my apartment rumbled when he spoke. "I will not apologize for trying to save the human race and all the other worlds out there," Vallen stated, his tone composed. "You and your family are a microscopic issue in the bigger scheme of things. I was doing my job."

"What about Lex? Or Baz, huh?" Sobs came in waves now as he watched me crumble into oblivion. "Sasha? Ivy? Vincent made me kill my own grandmother, Vallen!"

He sat on the floor next to me, but maintained a respectful distance. "That is war," Vallen explained, his words measured and logical. "The sooner you grasp war is never-ending, and there will always be collateral damage, the better you will handle this." His voice carried a hint of regret as I lay on my side with my hands under my face and watched him now. He released a long sigh. "When you're called, you do what's necessary, Noa, and I'd rather lose a few angels and humans than watch complete evil destroy your world and mine."

Tears streamed down my face as I sniffled and wiped my nose on the arm of my shirt. I rolled onto my back and looked up at Vallen. "You wouldn't let me end him," I accused, my voice thick with bitterness.

Vallen's expression softened slightly as he turned to face me. He leaned over, his breath hot against my cheek as he spoke. "Because I will not allow him the satisfaction of taking your life," he growled.

I turned away from him, facing the other direction now. "Because you want to do it," I spat, my words laced with venom. "To be the hero and watch as my life slips away."

He delicately brushed the hair out of my face, his touch sending tingles up my neck, causing my hair to stand on end. "I take no pleasure in having to kill you, princess," he whispered.

"But I promise you won't suffer. I'll be there with you every step of the way."

A sob escaped my throat as tears continued to fall. He truly believed he was doing me a favor.

"Every girl's dream, right?" I managed to choke out through sobs, unable to hold back bitter laughter at the absurdity of it all.

What did he know about humans or their dreams? His job was all that mattered. Whether he didn't know what to say or he didn't have the nerve, he sat there letting the silence speak for him. The quiet unnerved me, so I stood to face my bathroom and took a deep breath.

"I need a shower," I said, wiping my face with the back of my hand. As I stood, I snatched up a pair of jeans and a sweater from the top of my laundry basket, then left him sitting on the living room floor.

I closed the door for privacy and cursed the angels and the universe. War. What did I know about war? Nothing, and I was going to die without a chance to fight for anything.

My entire life had been a sham. Standing in my bathroom made me wish Uno and Dos were here, but they hadn't reached out since Callum's death. I missed them and how simple my life was before angels ruined it.

I yanked back the shower curtain, expecting nothing but an empty tub. Instead, my heart seized. There, in the tub, lay Ivy. She lay curled up like a discarded doll, bruises painting her skin in grim hues. Her left eye was swollen shut, a grotesque bulge of purple and black. A deep gash ran from her split lip up into her jawline.

Where luxurious white curls once cascaded down her back,

now only patches of hair clung to a bloodied scalp. Her once radiant beauty, now marred in purple and blue, lay there, wheezing shallow breaths—a broken shadow of the friend I'd once known.

My hands trembled uncontrollably as I grabbed a towel to drape over Ivy's violated form. The faint metallic tang of blood mixed with antiseptics churned my stomach. Bile surged up my throat while tears stung my eyes, blurring Ivy's broken form even further.

Staring at Ivy's shattered body, it felt like all the air had vanished from the room. A scream—raw and filled with terror—ripped from my throat as my world tilted.

The bathroom door flew open as Vallen rushed in, his eyes wide with alarm. "Shit," he cursed under his breath, taking in the horrific scene before him. "Wait out there," he ordered, and I ran into the living room, panic tearing at my chest.

Moments later, he emerged carrying Ivy's limp body in his strong arms. He laid her gently on the couch, his expression fierce.

I shook my head grimly. "She's not going to make it."

"I know," Vallen said, agreeing that there was no hope for her.

I wanted to hold my friend and let her know that everything would be okay. Fear of her crumbling in my hands prevented it. "Why is she here?" I asked.

"Maros could've brought her here," he stated plainly.

I shook my head. "What? That's ridiculous," I argued.

"Demons are known to do worse. Even to their own kind, Noa." Vallen shook his head in frustration. "She joined them, but she loved you, Noa. She didn't feel there was another choice. They see her as a traitor regardless, and they used her."

A thousand thoughts raced through my mind as I saw my once-confident and vibrant friend now shattered both physically and spiritually. I knelt beside Ivy, tenderly brushing a strand of hair away from her face. Despite the pain etched on her features, there was a flicker of recognition in her eyes when she gazed up at me. It was a silent plea for forgiveness, understanding, and perhaps even redemption.

"We should try to clean her up," I forced out as Vallen retrieved some water and towels.

Together we began to carefully wipe away the crusted blood that covered Ivy's face and head. I was determined to give my friend as much respect as I could before she died.

"Is there anything you can do to heal her?" I asked hesitantly. I didn't know if Vallen was even willing, but I had to try.

He looked at Ivy with a pained expression, shaking his head. "I'm sorry, but once an angel falls for good, there's no helping them with the essence of another who hasn't."

"Fucking Maros," I cried under my breath as I took Ivy's hands in mine and kissed them. The anguish in her eyes mirrored the pain gnawing at my own heart. "This is a warning. He's baiting me."

As Vallen wiped away the last traces of dirt and blood, I couldn't help but remember all the good times Ivy and I shared – the laughter, the late-night talks, and dumb drinking games. Now, all that remained was a shell of the person she once was, and it tore me apart.

The soft glow of the evening sun filtered through the window, casting a melancholy light on Ivy's pale face. Her breathing slowed, her chest rising and falling in a weak rhythm. Then, her eyes fluttered open, unable to focus as they found mine.

"Noa... I'm so sorry," she rasped, tears shimmering in the corners of her tired eyes.

"Sh, sh, sh," I whispered. "Don't talk."

"I didn't want it to end like this," she pressed. "But I had nowhere else to go. I just... I hope you can forgive me one day."

"Of course. I forgive you, Ivy," I told her kindly, choking back more sobs.

In the quiet of that moment, she released one last breath and was gone. The little essence that remained left her body, and as it did, her flesh turned to ash, scattering across my couch and the carpet. All that remained was her skeleton.

Tears flowed freely down my cheeks, each drop carrying the weight of unbearable loss. A surge of disbelief gripped me as I whispered, "Where are her wings?"

Vallen turned her bones slightly, his gasp echoing the horror in my own heart. Ivy's wings were cruelly absent, severed from her in a despicable act.

"That sick fuck sawed off her wings," I sobbed, my voice faltering. "While she was still alive!"

"Most don't survive past the first wing if it's done," Vallen added. "She was strong, Noa. She held on for you."

I batted away my tears, but the sight of Ivy's mangled form twisted my stomach. The stench of death was suffocating, and a bitter taste surged up my throat, bile threatening to spill. How could it have come to this? My thoughts spiraled as I tried to piece together what was left of my shattered world.

My breath came in ragged gasps as I tried to make sense of

what had just happened. I fled to the bathroom, slamming the door shut behind me and locking it. The cold tile floor beneath my bare feet grounded me, a small comfort in the face of overwhelming grief. But I couldn't stay in there forever. I couldn't outrun reality.

I stripped off my clothes and turned the water on, rinsing away Ivy's blood. Then I let the hot spray wash away the ash that clung to my skin, each droplet feeling like a tiny lifeline in a sea of despair. In my cocoon created by the steam and white noise, I forced myself to think about how to move forward, how to survive.

Pulling on the clothes, my body began to feel even hotter now, the secrets pleading to go home. When I emerged, Vallen had changed his clothes, leaving the last remnants of his prison in a pile on the floor. He stood over Ivy's bones, staring at the ash, his face a clear picture of vengeance.

"We need to get her back to the ranch." I swallowed hard, my voice barely above a whisper. "She needs to be buried in the valley."

"You'll need to teleport us again," Vallen murmured beside me, his breath warming my ear as he extended his hand.

"I know," I choked out and gestured for him to wait. "Hold that thought."

My stomach churned at the thought of Vincent and his band of fallen angels. Their faces haunted me, reminders of endless agony. As I moved toward the patio, Dust Bunny bounded into the living room, her fur brushing against my ankles.

I scooped her up, cradling her close to my chest. "You're coming with us," I whispered fiercely and closed the door.

Vallen's eyes narrowed at Dust Bunny, a flicker of doubt crossing his face. "She may not survive the trip."

"She's mine." I cupped her tighter to my chest. "She'll survive."

He nodded in understanding, then stooped down and lifted Ivy's bones into his arms. It was a somber sight, but it only served to remind me of how much was at stake. Portaling back to the ranch would be no easy task given my emotional state, but if I channeled the hatred for Vincent and Maros growing inside me, I would get us there.

I placed my hand on Vallen's forearm and closed my eyes. Focusing on the familiar hum beneath my wrist, its rhythmic pulse invaded my senses as the world around us dissolved into a swirl of colors. When the dizziness subsided, we stood in the middle of camp—a hundred eyes fixed on us—ready to fight.

CHAPTER 34

Every muscle in my body tensed as we braced for an attack, my heart pounding in my chest. Dust Bunny nibbled at my finger, and I breathed a sigh of relief right before she spit up in my hand. Portaling must've changed her molecular structure, because from what I'd read about them, rabbits don't puke.

"Come on!" I groaned, then shook off my hand.

I bent down to wipe it on the ground, and Vallen didn't move. He scanned the crowd, searching for an ally.

"Stand down!" Jossy's voice rang above them all as he walked through the middle of everyone huddled around us. Once he saw me, a flash of relief washed across his face.

I tucked Dust Bunny under one arm, then flung myself at my friend, wrapping the other around him. Jossy held onto me so fiercely that I thought I would burst, but I didn't care.

Then, behind him walked Dawson, Nevaeh, and Nakoma. I

searched the faces of my friends until I landed on the one I was most excited to see and hugged her next.

"Welcome back," Ena smiled as she released me. But her eyes flicked to Vallen and began to fill with concern. She now stood paralyzed, looking at the skeletal form Vallen held.

"Noa?" Ena swallowed hard. "Who is he holding?"

Vallen stepped toward us and held out Ivy's remains. "I'm sorry for this."

"It's Ivy," I sighed and closed my eyes while stroking Dust Bunny's head.

Everyone sighed in relief, which shredded me up inside because they didn't seem to care that she was missing her wings. They looked grateful she was gone. All they saw was her betrayal, but it wasn't the time to discuss it. Vallen handed Ivy's remains to two angels who stood to my left as Jossy doled out instructions to take her to the Valley of the Fallen. At least he would give her a proper burial and not use her to make arrows or gods only knows what else from her bones.

"Wait." Ena squinted and said, "We thought Lex was with you."

A lump formed in my throat as I realized I had to break the news about Lex. "Can we go inside Baz's tent to talk, please?"

Dawson held open the flap of Baz's tent, his face drawn with concern. Ena, Jossy, Nevaeh, and Nakoma walked in ahead of us, their steps heavy with anticipation. Vallen and I followed after Dawson. My chest tightened as I glanced at Ena, who clung tightly to her grandmother.

Once we gathered inside, Dawson looked down at me, a small but genuine smile crossing his lips. "Glad you're safe, Noa."

I guess my portaling skills are improving," I said with a choppy laugh that did little to hide my discomfort.

Vallen glanced down at me, and his lips twitched. "You did well."

My breath caught, and I blinked rapidly. "Was that... a compliment?"

"You're embracing your responsibility. That's all." He lifted his head and watched everyone's faces as they studied him.

"That was a compliment," I whispered into Dust Bunny's ear, tracing her soft fur with my thumb before planting a gentle kiss on her head.

Ena stepped closer, her eyes wide with anxiety. "I'm trying to reach out to Lex on the radio, but I'm not getting a response. Is he doing something to help us?"

The last time I was in Baz's tent, my guardian angel and I forged our signati bond somehow as we slept. I felt sick now, unable to hear his voice in my head. A pair of boots sat next to the bed and all his things were still in their place.

I almost crumpled at the sight of them, but what was worse, I had to tell everyone that Lex didn't make it back with us because Vincent killed him. I looked around and noticed Father O'Neil wasn't there.

"Where's the priest?" I asked with a nervous hitch in my throat, wishing he was available for support.

"He's up at the bunkhouse with a few of the other angels," Nakoma said. He planted a soft kiss on Jossy's lips, then squeezed his shoulder as he turned back to me, his dark eyes dancing. "It's good to see you, Noa, but I should get back to O'Neil."

"Nakoma, wait," I urged, and my eyes met Ena's, full of agony for her. "It's about Lex."

Ena's grip slackened, and the walkie-talkie slipped from her hand, clattering to the floor as her lips began to quiver. I thrust Dust Bunny into Vallen's arms and sprinted toward Ena, my heart pounding as I wrapped my arms around her, feeling her shaky breaths against my chest.

"I'm so sorry, Ena," I sobbed, my voice trembling along with hers as her arms fell limp at her sides.

"Lex?" Jossy shook his head slowly as if trying to clear a fog. "Where is he, Noa?"

As I guided Ena to sit on Baz's bed, Vallen replied, "Vincent... Vincent killed him."

I grabbed a tissue from the small bedside table and handed it to Ena. My hands were shaking as I spoke softly, "He ambushed us during our escape from the cave... they threw him back inside."

Ena doubled over, clutching her stomach with such force that it seemed she might tear herself apart. Her wails pierced the air. "No! Please!"

"I'm so sorry," I begged as my voice cracked under the weight of guilt that felt like an anchor around my neck.

"We'll gather a team to retrieve Lex's body when it's safe," Nakoma said softly, gripping Jossy's hand tightly, planting them both in reality.

"I'm still in shock," I murmured, my mind reeling and vision blurring slightly as I stroked Ena's back.

Nevaeh walked out of the tent, but quickly returned with a burlap sack. Uncertain of how she felt, I knew she loved Lex. We all did, but the look on her face was one of fury. She pointed at Vallen to secure Dust Bunny in the bag for safekeeping, then handed me the sack. With an air hole up top for her to breathe, it gave me time to find a crate for her later.

"We finish this now," Nevaeh stated as she grabbed Dawson's arm and left the tent.

Ena's breath trembled as she sat next to me, her eyes full of curiosity. "Can you... tell us what happened out there?"

I tucked my hair behind my ears and sat Dust Bunny behind me, then stared at my fingers for what seemed like an eternity. "The three of us found Vallen," my breath caught when I thought about Baz, and I hesitated. "The bracelet helped, but once we were out of the cave, all hell broke loose," I revealed sadly. "I'm guessing it was the same for you."

Jossy nodded as he took a seat across from me and rubbed one hand down his face. "We had maybe a two-minute warning from the wolves. We tried to reach you, but couldn't get through."

"The cave prevented communication to the outside," Vallen added as his gaze fell on me. "It was warded by angelic runes."

"That demon burned our house down and took over our land," Nevaeh announced as she strode back into the tent, her voice laced with anger. "They can stand on it now."

My head turned toward Vallen. "Do you think it's because your essence no longer feeds the tree?" I asked.

He nodded with a sigh and confirmed, "Just another reason Vincent wanted to find the bracelet and kill me." Then he added, "No one knows how many angels he's turned for this fight, but the portal is closed. They're free to wander the grounds."

My brows furrowed at Vallen, and I asked, "What does that mean for the ceremony and getting the secrets back to the Veil?"

Vallen glanced at the ground, then back at me. "Whatever Vincent told you was all lies," he sighed. "I'm the portal for the secrets to return."

"Oh," I said, my eyes wide. "That's what you meant by me not being alone when I die. We go together."

Jossy's features twisted into confusion out of the corner of my eye. "You want to do that, Noa?" Jossy interjected as he leaned against the table in the middle of the room. "You're just going to let him take the secrets and die?"

"We have to stop them, Jossy," I demanded. I prayed my anger would finally get through to him. "Ivy was beaten into oblivion and tossed into my bathtub like trash." I tucked my knees up under my arms and pulled at my hair. "You saw her skeleton, but you didn't see her before she died. That fucker sawed off her wings!"

Jossy's jaw twitched, and a storm began to rage in the depths of his blue eyes. "Vincent is closer to becoming a demon and not just a dark fallen one," Jossy admitted, his tone sounding as though he regretted following Vincent for so long.

Vallen arched a brow and reminded us, "He and Maros will come for Noa and that bracelet. They're not done, and they're gathering their forces as we speak."

I pointed a finger at Vallen as my eyes flashed to his. "That's right," I said, my eyes wide. "You and Vincent mentioned something about the bracelet needing the essence of an angel and someone from my ancestral line."

Ena chimed in before Vallen could respond. "We found some interesting information about that," she offered.

I shook my head and took her hand. "You don't have to do this right now," I assured her.

She blew her nose, stood up, and threw away her tissue, then pointed to a bag on the table in Baz's tent where the food once was. "I want to show you," Ena sighed as she washed her hands and dried them.

She pulled on a pair of white gloves and opened the bag. When she removed the book, I expected it to be ancient like some of the ones Father O'Neil was looking at back at Dawson's, but it was a fairly new leather journal.

"I'm going to make some tea," Nevaeh announced, then walked back toward the opening. "Dawson and I will devise a strategy."

I nodded as I stood to join Ena at the table. For a moment, the memory of us looking for the cherry tree seeped in, and I smiled.

"I need to do this. For Lex," she said, then turned to the pages she wanted me to see.

"That's Vincent's," Vallen gasped, and his eyes widened. "Wait, let me do this."

"According to this paragraph right here," Ena started, ignoring Vallen and pointing to a sentence on the page, "the bracelet was made for a woman using a nail from the crucifixion."

I nodded. "I know. Vallen spilled his guts. Figuratively speaking of course. Because apparently he can't be harmed." I flashed him a quick, sharp smile. "Although I tried."

Vallen cleared his throat. "You weren't doing it right."

"She was John the Apostle's wife and your ancestor," Jossy interjected. "Her name was Elizabeth."

"I don't understand," I confirmed as I looked at Vallen curiously.

"John was Jesus' cousin, Noa," Ena explained, and goose-bumps peppered my skin. "He followed him even after the crucifixion."

"Maros is the incarnation of Domition," Vallen interjected and all our eyes landed on him. "A Roman emperor who tried to kill John, but due to divine intervention, he couldn't, so John was banished to the island of Patmos."

Ena nodded, then continued, "Think about the inscription on the bracelet. If blood forgives, that represents Jesus, and the line remaining is John's." She lifted her head with a smile. "That's you."

"What about the one who stayed?" I questioned with furrowed brows.

"That is in reference to Domition failing to kill John," Vallen professed to us. "It's why I always knew where this bracelet was so I could use it, but Vincent and Maros used it against me and sealed me in the cave."

"But that's not the best part, Noa," Nakoma's voice cut in as Ena turned the page.

A huge smile broke across Ena's face and she sighed. "The only way it could have fused to your bones like it has," she paused. "Is because you're part angel."

My heart pounded, my thoughts a chaotic mess as I struggled to process what she was saying. The tent fell into a hushed silence around me, but inside, my mind was a raging storm. Could this really be true? I couldn't wrap my head around the idea that I might have angelic blood flowing through my veins, but the undeniable evidence on my wrist begged to differ.

My mind was a jumbled mess, unable to form coherent words as I stammered out, "Are you absolutely certain? How could this even be possible?"

"It comes from one of your parents," Ena replied, her gaze sympathetic. "And since we know your mom is a descendant of John, it has to be your dad."

I stumbled backward and fell onto the bed, shocked as my gaze darted between Ena and Vallen. Her confession sent shockwaves through me.

"You knew," I accused Vallen as a fresh wave of fury crashed through me.

As the weight of her words settled on my shoulders, I realized that my identity – and my role in this now – was far more complex than I could have ever imagined.

I leaped to my feet and charged toward Vallen with furious steps. "You've known since before I was born. That's why you took my soul," I hissed, poking at his chest.

His eyes pierced into me, filled with a torment that mirrored my own. "If you would've kept your soul, you would've died," he threatened. "It wasn't just about the secrets. I took your soul to save you from becoming what we search and kill, Noa. Nephilim are a human and angel hybrid disgrace, but you, an Elioud, are an abomination in the universe."

I shuddered and closed my eyes, trying to calm my racing thoughts. This was all too much to take in at once – my connection to John, a devout follower of Jesus, the secrets raging in me that could turn the tide of any universe, and I was part angel.

It meant I could live.

CHAPTER 35

Rubbing my temples, I opened my eyes to the suffocating weight of silence that filled the tent. Everyone watched me, their eyes heavy with expectation that made my skin crawl. The entrance blew open with a gust of wind that sent a shiver down my spine, spurring me into motion.

I bolted up the path toward the bunkhouse, heart pounding in my chest as I pushed past guardian wolves with fur like midnight and eyes glowing eerily in the dim light. When I finally reached it, just as I turned the knob to walk inside, two hands grabbed each of my shoulders and spun me around. Nakoma stood with Jossy, shaking his head.

Jossy's eyes were wide with concern as he pleaded, "You can't go in there like this."

"Leave us," Vallen demanded, and stepped in front of them both.

Jossy stood to the side, waiting for my signal that it was okay for him to go, but Nakoma walked around me and slipped into the bunkhouse. I nodded at Jossy that it was okay for him to head back to camp.

Vallen's finger cupped my chin and tilted it upward until his chest brushed gently against mine. "Look at me, Noa," he commanded.

My pulse spiked as I found myself caught in the mesmerizing pool of viridian fire that was his eyes. I blinked rapidly, trying to shake off the spots in my vision, only for those hypnotic emerald orbs to morph into a swirling abyss of gold-leafed ivy vines. But the tears wouldn't stop.

Following the trail of his own touch, he traced the scar above my lip, then wiped away a tear, a dark hunger clouding his eyes. "Yes, I found a way to get your mother and father together. But your dad was a Nephilim," he explained solemnly. "It was the only way to make this work, but they loved each other."

"That doesn't help," I moaned in agony at what my life had become.

He sighed and thumbed the top of my lip. "I stripped your soul and created this mark on you. That is my scar, Noa." My chest tightened under his touch. "I carved it into you so you would survive," he went on as though his reasoning made the outcome better. And to him, it did. "It's what gave you the ability to stay alive and hold onto the secrets until it was time to return them to the Veil."

My body shook so close to him, and he took my hands in his. I looked up at him and wished I could blink him away. "But you want me dead," I confirmed through my tears. "And it's not just because I'm the carrier of secrets. It's because of what I am, isn't it?"

Vallen's voice dipped low as he entwined his fingers with mine. "I want to trust you, but you don't know what you are or what you're capable of, and—"

"And," I cut him off, not giving him the opportunity to finish. "You don't want to take a chance even when I said you could have the secrets back. Return my soul, but kill the Elioud, right?"

He closed his eyes and I pulled my head away from his. "If you choose my way," he remarked sternly. "Not only will I get your soul for you, to breathe life and fulfillment back into your body, but together we'll wipe out every last one of those bastards who thought they could touch you - including Vincent and Maros."

I felt faint, uncertain that I had heard him correctly. "What are you saying, Vallen?" My eyes narrowed.

His voice dropped an octave lower, sending a shiver down my spine as energy thrummed beneath our wrists. "You'll rise like the goddess you are to claim your true purpose. And you will save your kind, mine, and what's beyond the Veil."

"I don't understand. You want me to keep the secrets?" I asked with a shaky breath.

"I didn't expect you to be so stubborn," Vallen replied, his voice firm as I stifled a laugh. "Or fight so damn hard. Eliouds turn into something more grotesque than a demon's plague. Killing you was supposed to be the easiest task I completed. But you've fought with the conviction of an angel."

"And the heart and soul, if I had one," I chuckled. "Of a human."

He stroke the sensitive skin between my fingers and thumb. "If I kill you now," he admitted with a flicker of gold in his eyes, "I'm not convinced that something worse won't come of it."

"You mean I might follow Maros and Vincent willingly into hell?" I asked quietly.

"The thought has crossed my mind." His eyes darkened as he glanced down at my lips. "But that's not what I mean."

"Oh." My throat bobbed as his eyes consumed me. Those feelings of attraction brewing in me ever since he saved my life with his essence began to mean something.

"The moment I laid eyes on you in the cave," he divulged, his deep voice a whisper. "And you challenged me, it woke something in me, Noa. It brought back the fight in me and a respect for you."

"Vallen, don't," I pleaded, squeezing his hands tightly. "I can't take this up and down of whether I will live or die."

"You will live," he promised and pulled me into his solid chest. His hands played with my hair as he whispered into my ear. "It's the only way to know for sure that our worlds, and others, won't succumb to the demons or worse."

"Well, that's good to know." I laughed uncomfortably and felt the slow drum of a heartbeat beneath me.

"And," he added with an intensity I wasn't expecting. "It's the only way to make sure I wouldn't beg to be chained up and tortured again for all eternity."

I stepped back from him and leaned back against the bunkhouse door. I had been so caught up in killing him that I couldn't think straight. I didn't want any of this, much less feelings for this angel, with the entire universe on the brink of annihilation.

My heart raced, and I swallowed hard. Vallen and I were

connected on a deeper level now, and he knew I felt it too. A sudden, undeniable desire coursed through me – that pull I felt before now became a push.

"Well," I said with a light laugh, "I don't want to die and be the one to send you back to an eternal prison."

"Noa," his gravelly voice whispered in my ear.

"Don't. Because I hate you," I murmured, pushing aside the tingling sensations growing low in my core.

He drew me in again, planting a soft kiss on my forehead. "I know," he expressed, an understanding in his tone.

Then, my eyes found his, and those gold starbursts shot across his pupils. He tilted my chin up and leaned down, inching closer to my lips. I closed my eyes, ready to become his fool. Ready to welcome him into my mouth, but right as our lips touched, the door of the bunkhouse opened and we stumbled inside. Vallen caught me with one arm behind my back, and I leaned backward with Father O'Neil gazing down at me.

"Oh, my," O'Neil said with a raised brow, and he cleared his throat. "Quite the development."

We stood, and I adjusted my clothes as we stepped inside.

Nakoma blocked my view in front of the fireplace. "Welcome," he said as a smile danced across his lips.

On my right, a smaller wooden dining table replaced the card table I'd seen the day before, covered with books and relics salvaged from the attack on Dawson and Nevaeh's home.

"The angels are working when they can to get into the basement for more, but it isn't safe," said O'Neil. He looked at Vallen with raised brows. "Welcome back."

"Father," Vallen replied and offered him a nod.

My head turned to the left, and Nakoma shifted, matching

my line of sight, keeping me from whatever was on the other side of the room.

"Noa, there's something else, but before you can see it, I need you to take a few deep breaths."

My brows furrowed as a skeptical interest swirled within me. "What is it, Nakoma?" I asked.

Bowing his head, he stepped to the side and my mouth dropped. My stomach lurched, and I darted over to where another table had replaced the chairs in front of the fireplace.

"Baz," I said to him, wanting to fling myself across his body.

But he was propped up on a pillow with an IV coming out of one arm and a blood pressure cuff on the other.

I looked back at Vallen, who remained in the doorway just as stunned as I was.

"How is he alive?" Vallen asked, wrinkles forming across his forehead.

Nakoma walked up beside me and replied, "Do you honestly think the other guardians wouldn't come running when they heard their alpha's cry?"

I rubbed my hand down my face, wiping away the tears. "This is incredible. Will he live?"

"We aren't sure," Father O'Neil offered from behind me. "It's touch and go, but we're trying."

Nakoma slipped his stethoscope off from around his neck to check Baz's breathing. "Vincent's claws contained some kind of venom that got into his bloodstream."

Vallen stood over me, looking down at Baz in his human form. "That damn wolf is fighting for you, Noa, and deserves to be your signati."

I glanced up at him, regret now covering Vallen's face. "It's not our fault," I reminded him. "But we can't let him die. I couldn't bear the thought of him getting sent to hell to be tortured by Maros."

Vallen stepped back and walked toward the door. He leaned his head back, then looked at me without blinking an eye.

Brushing his hands through his hair, he told Nakoma, "You need a branch from the cherry blossom tree. Get its petals, grind them up to make a paste with any type of carrier oil, then feed it to him. The venom will leave his system, and he should recover if you do that."

Nakoma gasped, his eyes widening in surprise. "We've been searching for anything that could help," he said. "Thank you, Vallen."

"Vincent and I..." He trailed off, biting his lip and looking away for a moment before finally planting his gaze on Nakoma, "we're the only ones who know."

"And he was hoping you'd be dead and unable to tell anyone," confirmed Nakoma bitterly and pulled the walkie-talkie from the clip on the back of his belt. "I'll radio someone down at camp to get on this."

The chair next to the table where Baz lay healing scratched against the surface of the floor as Father O'Neil settled into it. He carefully opened an aged Bible and began reading to Baz. A feeling of relief washed over me as I made my way back to Vallen, a genuine smile tugging at my lips.

"I saw how hard that was for you," I commented, placing my hand on his chest.

He released a nervous laugh and shook his head. "He's your signati, Noa. I can't interfere in that bond. But he's going to freak when he finds out about you and me."

My laughter echoed around the room as I tossed my head back, earning me a glare from Father O'Neal. "Sorry," I whispered. "Is there a you and me?"

Vallen's eyes took on a playful glint as he lifted the corner of his lip. "Could be, but we need to finish this with Maros and Vincent. Tonight."

"I'm ready, but I have a question." I gestured for him to step outside with me, and when we were alone on the path, I took a deep breath. "You said I can hold the secrets, but I'm pretty sure I don't have Callum's or your essence in me anymore."

Vallen cupped my face in his hands, and his eyes bore into mine. "Our essence helped you, but your human and angel sides are competing against each other when they need to work together."

"I can do that without essence?" I asked, leaning into him.

"You have your own essence," Vallen offered as his thumb brushed against my jaw.

"And to think you strung me along and were going to kill me," I teased with a sigh. "Just to keep that information to yourself."

His eyes began to devour me, and he closed the small gap between us. Pressing against me, his craving hardened against my belly through the sweatpants he wore. Then, without waiting a moment longer, Vallen crushed his lips to mine.

His scent of cedar and lilac filled my senses, and my lips instinctively parted for his. I welcomed him with my tongue, and he obliged with a sly flick and swirl of his. I eagerly matched his fervor by exploring every inch of his mouth, while one hand found its way into my hair and the other around my waist, pulling me closer.

A small moan escaped me as his touch sent volts of electricity between my thighs. His taut muscles flexed under my touch, and the desire radiating from him tempted and terrified me at the same time. Sparks shot across my skin as I traced the rugged contours of his face, then down his chiseled chest.

Each graze of teeth across my bottom lip sent a wave of raw pleasure over me. We were lost in each other when my hands released a jolt against his skin, matching my excitement. He jumped back in surprise, eyes wide as he studied my body from head to toe.

"Vallen!" I screamed, horrified at what I had done to him.

"I'm all right." He winced and, as he rubbed his face, a mischievous smile formed on his lips. "You'll be able to handle this just fine."

My vision began to blur, images flashing through my mind like vicious lightning strikes. The past, present, and future melded together into an overwhelming onslaught of visions that threatened to drown me entirely.

I saw my mother, her face creased with love and worry. I saw angels hidden behind the Veil, their actions a mystery. I saw the devastation if Vincent succeeded in enslaving humanity with his fallen angels.

"Help me!" I cried, clutching my head in agony as the images continued to flood my mind.

"Focus, Noa," Vallen urged, his voice firm as he reached for me and took my hands. "You can shield it."

My body shook, my heart raced, and I felt like I was teetering on the brink of madness. As much as I tried to respond, the words remained lodged in my throat. Out of the corner of my eye, Vallen unfurled his wings, a mix of black and white with tips of green casting shadows under the moonlight.

"Stay with me, Noa," I heard him call out to me, then pulled me into his chest. "You're stronger than this!"

"Please," I pleaded, my body trembling under the weight of the disturbing visions flooding my mind. "Make it stop."

In a blur of motion, Vallen wrapped his wings around my trembling form. The strength emanating from him was like a lifeline, keeping me tethered to reality even as my consciousness threatened to shatter beneath the pressure.

Vallen whispered urgently into my ear, his breath hot against my skin. "Breathe, Noa. You can do this."

As Vallen held me in his arms, my body trembled violently, but I focused on his heartbeat. Images grew more intense and overwhelming than the last, pulling at my sanity. But gradually, they began to slow down until they were mere flickers, fading into darkness.

In this darkness, my mind was suddenly filled with boundless space, stretching out in all directions. I could see the interconnectivity of everything in existence, like an intricate web woven by unseen hands. And within this expanse, I could feel a power coursing through me, unfathomable and awe-inspiring. With a single thought, I could manipulate reality itself.

"I...I don't understand," I stammered, awestruck by the knowledge that now coursed through me. "What's happening to me?"

"You are awakening," Vallen murmured, his voice filled with both awe and concern.

"I'm scared," I confessed. My throat constricted in terror. "What if I can't handle it? What if I hurt someone?"

"Hey." Vallen's soothing voice echoed in my mind like a life-line, pulling me back from the edge. "Trust yourself, Noa, and come back to me."

It was difficult to tear my gaze away from the infinite possibilities that had embraced me, but with one last glance, I turned away and followed the sound of Vallen's voice. My eyes fluttered open, but he held me tight, as if afraid that I might slip away from him again. I looked up and saw his intense green eyes, flickering entirely with gold now.

"Do you feel any pain?" he asked, his voice steady.

It was the first time he'd ever asked me a question. I took a deep breath and shook my head, feeling dazed but unharmed. "No, I…I don't think so."

His touch was reassuring as he retracted his wings. "Everything will be all right," he promised, his eyes never leaving mine. "We'll have to start training your human side to block out that angel side sooner rather than later."

I chuckled and raked my hands through my tousled hair. "What do we do now?" I asked.

"Now," he replied, his tone low and intense, "let's take the fight to them for a change. I have a plan, but I need to know, Noa. How far are you willing to go?"

My gaze swept over him as the power surging through my veins urged me forward. I had only one choice left.

"To the death," I told him.

And I meant it.

CHAPTER 36

Once I had painstakingly cleared one of Baz's wooden drawers, I nestled Dust Bunny into her new home. Then I changed into clothes more suited for facing demons and fallen angels. As we all gathered around the campfire waiting for Vallen, Jossy extended his arm toward me, holding a worn leather satchel.

I reached for it tentatively, fingers grazing over the worn leather's rough texture before carefully flipping open the tarnished brass clasp. My hand delved into the bag's depths and brushed against a cold, hard object. Drawing out two gleaming new daggers, their polished surfaces caught the firelight. Unlike the wolf hilts of my other daggers, these bore a single angel wing design and fit into my palm with ease.

A flood of gratitude washed over me; my breath caught as my hand flew to my mouth. I threw my arms around him in a tight hug.

"Thanks, Jossy," I murmured, still clutching one of the new daggers.

Jossy shrugged as if it were no big deal. "We noticed you didn't bring yours back with you," he said, his eyes flicking toward my empty holster.

"I appreciate this." I smiled warmly, feeling the weight of the angel-wing dagger in my hand.

"Maybe you can zap a demon with lightning as you stab it! Fry it right up!" Jossy laughed and wrinkled his nose before heading off to find Nakoma.

"Don't be nervous," I teased before he got too far. "If it weren't for you guys finding me and making me see the truth, we'd all be doomed."

Jossy's grip on my shoulders tightened slightly. "Tell me you're sure about entering this fight, Noa."

"We have the upper hand." I smiled confidently and put my hand on his shoulder in return. "Don't back out on me now, Joss."

"Never," he promised.

As I secured the daggers into a sleeveless leather bodice Ena supplied me with earlier, approaching footsteps broke the momentary silence in camp. We all turned instinctively towards Vallen's looming figure. His presence cast a shadow over us—his beauty was impossible to ignore—as everyone moved toward the edge of camp. Vallen reached out for my hand, and I accepted it willingly.

"It's time to go," he whispered, keeping us a few feet behind everyone as they began their walk. "You know what you need to do."

I nodded and squeezed his hand, then gestured for him to lead the way.

The journey toward Dawson's field was unsettlingly quiet, broken only by the crunch of our footsteps on twigs and leaves. It wasn't until we reached the edge of Dawson's property that Vincent or Maros came into view. My heart pounded against my ribs as I spotted their figures moving around freely.

Maros barked orders to his army, and like clockwork, his soldiers snapped to face us. Their grotesque faces twisted into snarls, accompanied by eerie screeches from above. Vincent quickly noticed the shift and signaled for his troops to merge with them.

I clung tightly to Vallen's hand as Dawson and Nevaeh continued along the perimeter toward their house. They stayed just behind the tree line with two wolves flanking them for protection. Jossy moved like a shadow through the open field, attacking fiercely from every angle to clear a path for Nakoma. Their synergy was breathtaking.

Vallen and I held back, waiting for the right moment as angels and wolves descended onto the field in a chaotic cluster. Ena stepped forward, her presence hidden from view. With a graceful wave of her arms, she summoned tiny twisters out of thin air, whipping them violently toward the demons and leaving them spinning in disorientation.

Maros crept along the back edge of the field, edging closer to Dawson's house. He paused briefly, perhaps sensing my presence but unable to pinpoint me. I couldn't help but wonder what twisted thoughts were churning through his mind.

I turned my attention away from Maros and saw Nakoma grappling with a horde of fallen angels. Their talons slashed at him in mid-air, like a storm of razors slicing through flesh. Ignoring the pain, he readied his bow and rapidly fired arrow after arrow, each shot trailing blurs of silver mist.

None of the demons could match his speed—except one with a thin, skeletal body that slipped past and grazed Nakoma's leg. Blood seeped through his tattered pants, pooling on the ground beneath him.

"Nakoma!" I screamed before quickly covering my mouth.

"Steady, Noa," Vallen remarked calmly.

Jossy expanded his wings and thundered toward Nakoma, his footsteps echoing against the earth. He leapt into flight, feathers cutting through demons like swords until he reached Nakoma. Each swipe thinned their ranks as easily as trimming overgrown hedges.

The scent of blood and sulfur hung heavy in the air, making my stomach churn violently. Bile rose to my throat while my eyes watered from the oppressive stench.

"Go ahead and puke," Vallen advised. "Better now than later."

I swallowed it down, holding back my discomfort, which only served as another source of embarrassment considering Vallen had seen enough of my vulnerability. He needed to see me strong or else our plan would fail because he wouldn't let me do my part.

"Nope. I'm okay," I assured him.

Vallen's eyes darkened, and his grip tightened around my hand. "Well, you're up, Noa."

A sharp pain shot through my fingers as I yanked my hand away. "I need these," I scolded.

"Sorry," he offered. "Are you certain you're ready?" Vallen's eyebrows knitted together, a flicker of guilt crossing his features.

Charging headlong into the chaos with nothing but bare hands and some daggers I still didn't know how to properly use felt like madness, but hesitation wasn't an option.

"I'll see you on the other side, right?" I asked with wide eyes.

Vallen lowered his head, then lifted my chin with his finger and thumb. Looking deep into my eyes, he promised, "I will find you."

I nervously licked my lips, then nodded. "That's all I need to know."

I turned away and walked onto the field where angel bones and demon ashes covered the ground. The battle blurred around me; flashes of demonic wings and gleaming weapons filled my vision while muffled screams blended into an unearthly orchestration. Metallic clangs and sharp thuds of combat mingled with the rough grit underfoot as I searched for my target.

Maros.

A blood-curdling scream shattered the air, sending a jolt of adrenaline through me as I whipped around to find its source. Ena's face drained of color, her arms limp at her sides. I followed her eyes to see Dawson suspended from the grip of a fallen angel, its merciless claws punched clean through his chest. Blood trickled from the corners of Dawson's lips as he stared back at us, his eyes reflecting pure torment as they met ours.

"No!" The word tore from my throat like a jagged blade. I grabbed Ena's shoulders, forcing her to look at me and Vallen. "Not Dawson. Please, not him," I pleaded desperately.

Nakoma and Jossy sprinted towards us, dodging demonic

attacks with fluid precision. Nakoma reached Ena first, clutching her hands tightly to ensure she wasn't hurt.

"Come on, Ena! We need to move!" Nakoma yelled.

They all took off, running around the edge of the clearing. Ena tossed angels and demons out of the way as if they weighed nothing. Nakoma's arrows flew into each demon who dove for Ena; their bodies immediately turned to ash. Jossy hovered behind them, guarding their backs until they reached Dawson.

I stood in the middle of the clearing, paralyzed by fury. My body quivered violently as I saw what happened next. Dawson hung in mid-air like a marionette with cut strings. Higher he rose until, with a dismissive flick, the force holding him let go. He tumbled back to the ground.

I watched in mute horror as he fell, his body striking the ground with a sickening crunch. He lay splayed at an awkward angle, eyes staring sightlessly at the ashen sky, and I knew with horrible certainty that his neck broke.

A red haze clouded my vision. The voice that came from my throat didn't sound like my own, choked with unspeakable grief. All I could focus on was Dawson's broken, dead body and the unholy thing responsible, hovering just out of reach.

In that moment, I didn't care about Maros or Vincent or any locked secrets in my mind anymore. The only thing that mattered was making that fallen angel pay. Even if it killed me, I would send it screaming back to hell, and I would laugh as I watched it burn.

I scarcely made it two steps before a different demon lunged for me, its poisoned claws outstretched. I braced myself for impact, but it never came. A massive shape hurtled over my head, slamming into the demon and bowling it over in a tangle of fur.

I lifted my arms, and with one swift motion, I unleashed an unending round of electricity straight through the demon's body, causing it to explode.

"*Noa!*" Baz's voice cut through the noise, distant and distorted as if he were calling to me from underwater.

I tried to answer him, but my tongue was thick and clumsy in my mouth, now full of demon blood. I blinked and spit the blood from my mouth, and when I looked up, Baz's sapphire eyes were glued to mine.

Sobs overcame me as I laughed, burying myself in his chest. "You're alive!"

"*Takes more than that to get rid of me,*" he said with a grunt.

A heartbeat later, Vallen swooped down from the sky, his massive wings stirring the air around us, causing Baz and me to cough as the sharp smell of sulfur pierced our nostrils.

"*O'Neil told me that Vallen saved my life,*" Baz admitted as he scanned the area for unexpected attacks.

I gestured with a nod at Vallen and smiled. "Baz knows you helped."

"Keep an eye on her then," Vallen told Baz, his voice tinged with urgency.

"Seriously?" I remarked, shaking my head. "It's like that, Vallen?"

"You're the one who has to finish this, Noa. Remember that," Vallen said to me, then turned to face Vincent on the other side of the field.

"I know!" I called after him as my hands found Baz.

I stroked his fur, grateful I had him back with me. It was

almost time for me to do the unthinkable. My hope was the universe wouldn't let me down this time or we were all fucked.

As I whipped my head back around to search for Maros, Vallen had Vincent cornered, and the demons and fallen angels were retreating. Maros had disappeared from view, and I didn't trust that he wasn't waiting for me somewhere.

Baz and I ran up the side of the field closest to Dawson and Nevaeh's now-destroyed home. Nevaeh's face drained of color as she stepped out of the tree line. Her eyes bulged with shock when she saw Dawson's body. Nakoma caught his grandmother, holding Nevaeh up as her legs gave way beneath her.

Nevaeh's wail echoed across the clearing as she cradled Dawson's head in her lap. "Curse you, Vincent, for taking him from me!"

"Stay close to me," I instructed Baz as I looked over at him.

Baz sighed. *"Always."*

Glancing around the field, I asked him, "Where do you think Maros went?"

"No idea," he replied with a low growl, his skeptical gaze not matching my growing alarm. *"Something doesn't feel right, though."*

Vincent's soldiers started to retreat or were gathered up by angels from our side and taken away. The once deafening roars of battle began to quiet as even the Baneful drew back. My attention snapped back to the battlefield when a sudden shout filled the air.

Vincent had next to no time to draw his own sword before they lunged at each other, their blades ringing in a metallic frenzy. Vincent's blade sliced across Vallen's cheek, sending droplets of blood flying. Vallen snarled and retaliated, his sword cutting into Vincent's arm.

Sparks erupted as their weapons clashed again and again. They crashed to the ground in a whirlwind of tangled limbs and feathers, rolling through blood-soaked dirt. Finally, Vallen pinned Vincent beneath him, holding his sword to Vincent's throat.

"It's over, brother," Vallen growled, pressing the sword up into Vincent's jaw.

"You're wrong," Vincent spat back. "I will have, Noa! And if not me, then Maros."

With a burst of strength, Vincent threw Vallen off and lunged at him. But Vallen leaped over Vincent's head, twisted midair, and brought his sword whistling down in a ruthless arc. Vincent let out a shriek of agony as Vallen's blade sliced clean through his wing, severing it in a spray of blood and feathers.

His wing turned to ash in mid-air, and the bones landed in a crumpled heap next to Vincent, who fell to his knees in an excruciating cry. Vallen broke one of the most sacred laws of the angels by taking his brother's wing.

Vincent's voice trembled with agony as he roared at Vallen, "Do the laws of honor mean nothing to you?"

Vallen's eyes flashed with rage. "After keeping me prisoner in a cave and after kidnapping Sasha, you want to talk to me about honor, brother?"

Vallen's sword glinted in the fading light of day, and his grip on it tightened. Vincent knelt before Vallen, wincing as blood seeped from his missing wing.

Vallen towered over him and sneered, "You aren't worthy of honor."

Then, with another strike, Vallen took his brother's other wing, leaving him convulsing in the middle of the field. Vallen lifted his sword and, in one final movement, struck downward, removing Vincent's head. It rolled away from his body and disintegrated. His body immediately followed and I saw Vallen's shoulders slump as he bowed his head.

I took one step forward when a fissure snaked across the field, fracturing the earth open with a deafening roar. My eyes searched for Vallen across the hole, and when he caught sight of me, I ran to him as fast as I could, Baz close behind. Maros emerged from behind the trees, his hulking form silhouetted against the sky. His eyes burned with a sinister glow as he advanced toward us.

I whirled around, and my heart jolted at seeing those crimson orbs searching mine. Then he gestured for his demons to blend into the shadows concealing their true numbers. They watched and waited for his instructions.

"I figured I'd see what you're made of, Noa," he drawled, his breath uneven. "Consider me impressed."

"I'm going to end you!" I promised him as I pulled a dagger from my vest.

"I've already given you plenty of chances, and yet," Maros gave a shoulder lift with raised brows. "Here I am."

Baz snarled, his body coiling and fur bristling, but Maros chuckled. Then, with a quick flick of his wrist, seized my throat. My dagger fell into the earth as he wrenched me up into the air. I scratched at his hand, gasping for air, but his grip was unbreakable.

Black spots danced at the edges of my vision as he pulled me backward, away from Baz, away from Vallen, and away from my hope of salvation. As we reached the edge of the trees, his demons and charred ones gathered close.

Maros smirked, unfazed as he turned me around and dangled me in front of Baz like a chew toy. "Come on, doggy. Let's play."

"You're a coward, Maros!" Vallen's voice rumbled across the field. "Let her go."

Baz lunged forward but halted as Maros tightened his grip on my throat.

"Don't be stupid, pup," Maros sneered. "No one else has to die today. If you're a good doggy, I'll let Noa live."

"Baz, get back," Vallen insisted. "She needs you to live."

Baz released a glass-shattering howl, but did as Vallen asked. I struggled against Maros's hand, unable to breathe, and he pulled me close, bringing my mouth to his ear.

"What's that?" he asked, loud enough for everyone to hear. "Your mom is looking forward to seeing you, and you can't wait to join her?"

Vallen and the others stepped back, their eyes widening with shock. Maros's grip on me loosened slightly, and a malicious grin spread across his face. The other wolves were now gathered and ready to fight again.

"Put her down, Maros," Jossy shouted, his voice low and grave. "Or I swear, I'll rip you apart myself."

Maros's laughter was sharp and mocking. "Oh, I don't think so, little cherub. One more step and I'll snap her pretty little neck."

His iron grip held me as he squeezed the air with his other hand, eyes locked on Ena. She clawed at her throat, gasping. Maros cackled, head tilted back. In that moment, I swung my leg up, ramming into his stomach. He grunted briefly, releasing Ena's neck. In an instant, I hit the ground hard, thrown like a rag doll. Ena coughed into her hand, wiping away tears as I lay on my back in front of her, gulping down air.

"Bastard!" The word barely escaped me as Ena leaned over to help me sit up.

Maros's thin lips curled into a smug grin. "It's possible," he drawled, nonchalance dripping from every word. He laughed as I glared up at him. "Noa," he breathed out. "You're a child only playing at villainy."

"Let's end this now," Vallen snarled as he released his wings and rose into the air.

Maros's head swiveled toward him as Baz stepped forward into a crouch, and the other wolves lined up with him. My eyes grew wide as mine and Ena's bodies trembled. We scurried to our feet and prepared to run, but I felt Maros's hands around my neck again.

"If you value any of your lives, stay still," Maros hissed. He glanced over his shoulder at the lurking darkness, then swiftly yanked me into his grasp once more.

"Fight!" My voice trembled, betraying my attempt at bravery as I called down to my friends.

A cold sweat trickled down my back as I pleaded with my friends. Vallen's eyes flickered with bursts of golden stars as they locked onto mine. His clenched fists trembled slightly, betraying his desire to do more than we both knew he could.

Pulling from the depths of my gut, I nodded and mouthed, "To the death."

Jossy turned to Nakoma. "Get Nevaeh back to camp and stay there."

Nakoma's jaw tightened as his eyes shimmered with unshed

tears that threatened to spill. "I won't leave you, Joss," he whispered, his voice cracking under the weight of his words.

Jossy took Nakoma's face in his hands and pressed their foreheads together. "And I won't lose you. Take care of your leg, and I'll see you soon. Now go."

"It's sweet you think the humans will live through this, little cherub." Maros tilted his chin toward Ena, a cruel glint in his eye. "I know what you did so that girl could practice magic here. She could come in handy for me too."

With a surge of energy, I flung my hands out with all my might and scratched at Maros's face. He recoiled from the shock and rubbed the side of his cheek where a red mark was starting to form. I prayed that would give us the edge we needed, but I didn't know for certain. Baz growled low in his throat, muscles coiled to attack, but Vallen gestured for him to wait.

"You no longer know your place, girl!" Maros's hand shot out; a sharp crack reverberated through my skull as pain exploded in my jaw.

My body went limp like a puppet with cut strings. He fisted my hair and viciously yanked my head back. I hung helpless, feet swinging in empty air, neck arched and throbbing.

"I wanted to kill you." He laughed and pulled me close. "Drain the secrets and let you rot in hell with the rest of your family. But now, now I'll make you watch as I turn your world upside down." Maros's tongue traced the outside of my ear. He bit down hard and growled, "With you at the center, as my bitch."

My neck snapped.

Darkness swallowed me whole, then spat me out into a carnival of dread. Pain speared through me as I landed hard on an unseen surface. The air reeked of decay and stagnant sweat; a vile stench that clawed at my nostrils.

A sharp smack split open my lip once again as I lay there helpless. When I attempted to push myself up onto my knees, I slipped again and slammed my face into the cold ground. The pain and nausea washed over me in waves as I lay there in the dark, unsure of how much time had passed.

Strange noises echoed around me, accompanied by intermittent flashes of light that felt almost taunting. A small, circular, blacked-out window opened and closed repeatedly until its rhythmic clatter annoyed me enough to move. I managed to struggle to my feet, my head spinning with disorientation.

My hands groped through the pitch-black void until they collided with a rough and slimy stone wall. Feeling along its surface, I discovered the window, about the size of a baseball. With trembling fingers, I pushed it open.

"Anyone there?" My voice wavered as I patted around the edges of the hole, flickering lights blocking my vision.

A sudden, unexpected touch grazed my hand, causing a jolt of surprise to shoot up my arm. I yanked my hand back, pulling it so close to my chest that I could feel the thud of my pounding heart against my fingers. An icy shiver ran down my spine as I watched long, bony fingers creep through the small hole in the wall.

Their razor-sharp, black nails gleamed ominously in the dim light, like the claws of some predatory creature reaching out for its prey.

"Noa," a voice crooned from the other side of the barrier, its tone dripping with mischief that made my heart skip a beat. "Hiya, doll!"

A shudder passed over me at the sound of my name spoken in that unmistakable lilt. My pulse quickened to a frenzied pace, and I pressed my back against the wall. Sliding down until I was huddled on the floor, I pulled my knees up to my chest and buried my face in my hands.

When had the last shreds of my sanity begun to fray at the edges, twisting into the abyss of madness?

She couldn't be here. It wasn't possible. Yet the voice was unmistakable - it was her. I dragged my palms down over my face, wiping away the cold sweat that had broken out on my forehead. A soft sniff escaped me as I pushed back the unruly strands of hair that had fallen into my eyes.

As I looked up, the small window in the wall swung open once more, causing me to jump in surprise.

"Uno," I choked out. "Is that you?"

THE END

THANK YOU FOR READING!

Consider leaving a review on Amazon, Goodreads, and Bookbub. Even one can make a difference in supporting an author!

Frosted Torment *is the first installment of an electrifying new-adult urban fantasy trilogy packed with paranormal powers, dark angels, and forbidden romance. From immortal love to elemental magic, this series embodies the best of urban fantasy.*

Book Two of the Marked Mortals Saga releases Fall 2025

ACKNOWLEDGMENTS

About damn time! Oh, the joy, pain, and insanity of writing. The sacrifices, the loneliness, and the late nights into the wee hours of delirium. And I'll do it again. And again, and again, and again.

Whew! Now that that's out of the way, I am going to ramble and spill my guts about all the beings and people to whom I owe my writing life and am forever grateful.

First, thank you, my Jesus! Amen.

Philippians 4:13.

Without God, my life and my writing are not possible, and He is the glory I owe it all to.

Let the blubbering begin.

Thank you to my hubs and my kids! Bryan, you did it all and then some during this project, and there are not enough thank-you's for turning into mine and our family's superhero.

My children and bonus children—all of you, even the oldest stepson who doesn't like me. I say this jokingly, but I never really know. I'm blowing raspberries at you! Youngest stepson, you play it cool and keep it cool always, so stay cool. My favorite oldest daughter and my favorite youngest daughter, every ounce of this is for the both of you. Thank you for inspiring me and making me push myself harder every day. My existence depends on you two. I will continue to write and stick around a little longer, even if it's to haunt you!

My sister, Melanie. I won't make it through this if I write all of the love and thanks for this woman. You're it for me, and you know what I'd do for you! I love you. I love you. I love you.

A thank you to my mother, who supports me from a distance and is still willing to give some shout-outs about my writing even if she doesn't approve of the subject matter. I appreciate you!

To my readers: I never thought in a million years I would want to share my writing with people outside of my family, but I've found some amazing support in the book world. Thank you for taking a chance on me and wanting to play a part in my novel creations.

What I do connects all of you, and you are the reason it gets done.

And one more praise to God above because there is never enough for Him. Thank You for loving me until the end and blessing me with this calling. In Your name, I pray. Amen!

Always and Forever,
    XOXO
    Erin

ABOUT THE AUTHOR

E. L. Valentine is an author of Fantasy Fiction and holds a degree in Psychology from the University of Houston. She lives in Texas with her husband, their youngest child, and fur-babies where she began her career as an English teacher. When she isn't slumped over a desk turning her enthusiastic imagination into stories, she's reading, watching movies, or vacationing anywhere she can sink her toes into the sand.

Contact:
ERIN@ERINVALENTINE.COM
www.erinvalentine.com

tiktok.com/@authorelvalentine
instagram.com/authorelvalentine
facebook.com/AuthorELValentine

www.ingramcontent.com/pod-product-compliance
Lightning Source LLC
Chambersburg PA
CBHW070313310726
48976CB00005B/1696